ROBERT GODDARD's first novel, *Past Caring*, was an instant bestseller. Since then, his books have captivated readers worldwide with their edge-of-the-seat pace and their labyrinthine plotting. He has won awards in the UK, the US and across Europe and been translated into over thirty languages.

'Robert Goddard has been writing imaginative first-class thrillers for nearly thirty years . . . *Panic Room* is an absorbing example of his superior storytelling . . . an excellent read'
The Times

'Is this his best yet? . . . Full of sinister menace and propulsive pace with twisty plotting'
Lee Child

'The world's greatest storyteller . . . this is a tense read full of characteristic Goddard twists'
Guardian

'As always, Goddard can be relied upon to entertain'
Literary Review

'A well-constructed page-turner of a thriller that's very hard to put down'
Choice magazine

READERS ARE SAYING...

'Could not put it down'

'A rollicking good read'

'Head and shoulders above
the best efforts of many
other thriller writers'

'Expect the unexpected'

'A really good read'

'A brilliant fast-paced story with a real
twist at the end, classic Goddard'

'I always eagerly await the next Robert
Goddard and this didn't disappoint'

'A must read'

'Wonderfully tense
and suspenseful'

'Excellent as usual'

'Robert Goddard never fails to deliver'

'I have read all Robert Goddard's
books, this is one of the best'

'Ingeniously plotted'

'More unexpected twists
and turns than a roller
coaster in the dark'

'Ended too soon'

'One of the best books I've ever read'

'Robert Goddard has never written a bad book'

Also by Robert Goddard

Past Caring
In Pale Battalions
Painting the Darkness
Into the Blue
Take No Farewell
Hand in Glove
Closed Circle
Borrowed Time
Out of the Sun
Beyond Recall
Caught in the Light
Set in Stone
Sea Change
Dying to Tell
Days without Number
Play to the End
Sight Unseen
Never Go Back
Name to a Face
Found Wanting
Long Time Coming
Blood Count
Fault Line

The Wide World trilogy
The Ways of the World
The Corners of the Globe
The Ends of the Earth

For more information on Robert Goddard and his books,
see his website at www.robertgoddardbooks.co.uk

ROBERT GODDARD

PANIC ROOM

CORGI BOOKS

TRANSWORLD PUBLISHERS
61–63 Uxbridge Road, London W5 5SA
www.penguin.co.uk

Transworld is part of the Penguin Random House group of companies
whose addresses can be found at global.penguinrandomhouse.com

First published in Great Britain in 2018 by Bantam Press
an imprint of Transworld Publishers
Corgi edition published 2018

A CIP catalogue record for this book
is available from the British Library.

ISBNs
9780552172608 (B format)
9780552175715 (A format)

Typeset in 11/13.5 pt Times NR MT by Jouve (UK), Milton Keynes
Printed and bound in Great Britain by Clays Ltd, Elcograf S.p.A.

Penguin Random House is committed to a sustainable future
for our business, our readers and our planet. This book is made
from Forest Stewardship Council® certified paper.

1 3 5 7 9 10 8 6 4 2

TEN

I FEEL SAFE HERE. THAT'S REALLY WHAT IT COMES DOWN TO. OH, THERE'S the sea as well. I like the ocean in all its moods, from stormy to still: white, grey, turquoise, blue. I can watch the surf crashing on the rocks for hours. On windless mornings, I can hear the skylarks circling above me as I walk down to the beach, my legs brushing through the drifts of wild mustard and cow parsley on the narrow path. And then there are the sunsets, pink and scarlet and gold, out beyond Wolf Rock, over the tilt of the world. Nothing here is like where I came from originally. I don't want to leave, like I did there, all the time. I want to stay. Maybe for ever.

I can't, of course. I don't know how long it'll go on. I try not to wonder. Harkness is in big trouble. He won't have much chance to think about what's going on here. He definitely won't be helicoptering down for a visit any time soon. I've got the place to myself. That's how I like it. Peaceful. Quiet. Alone. I swim. I walk. I run. I clean the place – just in case. I sell my driftwood art. I enjoy feeling safe.

Thanks to Harkness, I've got a lot of luxury to wallow in here. But the biggest luxury of all is the space. Glenys the gardener comes three days a week, Andy the pool man as often as he reckons he needs to. Otherwise, I don't get many visitors. Nor does Harkness, which is a relief. I wondered, when his case hit the news, if the press would come poking around. But they didn't. Maybe they don't know about his Cornish bolthole. Here's hoping they go on not knowing.

It might be best for Harkness as well as me if they did. I have a feeling this place is his biggest secret. And that's saying something. 'Notoriously secretive', they call him. He's not your obvious saviour material. But he's been my saviour. I'm not sure what would've happened to me when Muriel chucked me out if I hadn't been able to come here. Harkness doesn't know that, of course – or anything much about me. I don't suppose he gives me a single thought. Which is probably just as well.

We've got a good thing going, him and me, even if he doesn't realize it.

It's just a pity, one way or another, sooner or later, however hard I pretend otherwise, it's going to end.

❖

Don Challenor had never been one for recriminations, particularly where his own behaviour was concerned. He had inherited more of his father's fecklessness than he would have cared to admit. But the key to living with the consequences was not to acknowledge responsibility for them. Accordingly, he interpreted the circumstances of his departure from Mendez Chinnery as a reflection on their narrow-mindedness rather than his corner-cutting. Estate agency, especially in the overheated central London market, was a dog-eat-dog world. The commission Mendez Chinnery paid him was not exactly over-generous. They should have expected him to take a few liberties and should certainly have been willing to overlook them in view of the amount of business he brought in.

But his boss – young, smug and idle by Don's reckoning – saw things differently. So Don was out, casting around for another berth with age no longer on his side. Only his natural complacency prevented him worrying about what the future held. An opportunity would surely present itself. He had put the word out. He was keeping his ear to the ground.

It was a surprise, nonetheless, when the first contact he had after leaving Mendez Chinnery was not from one of their competitors but from a solicitor several of their clients used. Fran Revell also happened to be Don's ex-wife, which might have caused a less self-confident man to doubt she wanted to do him a favour. But they had communicated cordially enough on business matters since their divorce. And Don for his part remembered their parting as more sorrowful than angry.

The fact that Fran had nominated a nearby coffee shop for their meeting, rather than her office, should perhaps have served as some form of warning. But Don chose to interpret that as her preference for a relaxed and informal environment, which was fine by him. He had even been tempted to suggest putting back their appointment by an hour and meeting in a bar. There were several in the vicinity he could recommend. Wisely, however, he had not pushed his luck. Pushing his luck, after all, was what had wrecked their marriage.

Fran was already there when he arrived, busy on her iPhone between sips of cappuccino. She looked, as ever, some years younger than her age, slim and groomed and glowing. As for her expression when she caught sight of him, well, there was no imagining away the tightness of her smile. But the half-affectionate, half-wary shake of her head suggested his goodwill account had not yet reached its overdraft limit.

'You're looking great, Fran,' he said after an air-kiss greeting.

'Thanks.' She made no comment on his appearance.

'I'll grab a coffee. Then you can tell me all about it.'

'This is just a bit of business, Don.'

'Sure.'

He pondered her remark as he queued for his Americano, but not for long. There was nothing to be gained by trying to guess what Fran was thinking. There never had been.

He went back to her table with his coffee and sat down. The place was crowded with a predictable weekday haul of assorted professionals, killing time between appointments. Glancing around, Don found himself missing the rumbustious characters he had started out his working life with. Everyone now seemed bland by comparison. But the coffee was better. There was certainly no denying that.

'How's the family?' he ventured, smiling across at Fran after trying to drink some of his coffee before realizing it was far too hot.

The 'family' Don referred to comprised the husband and two daughters Fran had acquired since their divorce. 'They're fine,' she said briskly. Perhaps just a little too briskly, Don thought, who secretly hoped to hear one day that his replacement was being ditched in turn.

'So, what can I do for you?'

'You could start by explaining the "ethical differences" Ben said had led to you leaving Mendez Chinnery.'

'I should've got out of there yonks ago. How can I be expected to do my best work when I have to answer to a prat like him?'

Fran closed her eyes for a second. 'Maybe this was a mistake.'

'Look . . . Ben and I had a major falling-out. That's all

there is to it.' Don shrugged. 'I'd probably have resigned anyway. It was time to move on.'

'Where to?'

'Not sure yet.'

'No.' Fran sighed. 'Exactly.'

'Well, if you know of a juicy opening . . .'

'I don't. But, as it happens, I do have an urgent job that needs doing and, since you're available at short notice . . .'

'Good of you to think of me, Fran.'

'Yes. I can't seem to stop myself doing that.' She frowned away the hint of affection. 'Occasionally.'

He grinned. 'So what's the job?'

'I've been handling a divorce for a woman who wants to sell a property ASAP. It's in Cornwall and she's anxious to proceed quickly. I need a valuation, floor plans, photographs, et cetera, to present to suitable agents. We're talking about a price tag of five million or so – the international market.'

'I wouldn't mind having a crack at selling it myself.' Don was hardly exaggerating. A £5 million property could net him more than a hundred thousand. 'I could put several buyers her way.'

'We'll see. For the moment, I just need you to go down there and put the particulars together.'

'She doesn't want this dragged into the divorce settlement. Is that it?'

'She owns the place outright, Don.' Fran looked reprovingly at him. 'And the divorce is done and dusted. She has an unfettered right to sell. I'm simply making the arrangements on her behalf while she spends some time abroad.'

'Of course, of course. I don't know what came over me.'

'Can you do it?'

'Sure. Subject to . . . an agreement over terms.'

'Two thousand. Plus accommodation and travel. On condition I have all the details by the start of next week.'

'That's tight.'

'That's why it's also generous. And I'm guessing you won't find it too difficult to clear your diary.' Fran smiled. 'Do we have a deal?'

'Why not? It'll be a nice run for the car.'

'Don't tell me you still have the MG.'

'She's a classic. Like me.'

Fran did not rise to the remark. She drained her cappuccino, plucked a couple of sheets of paper out of her briefcase and laid them on the table in front of him. 'Sign on the dotted line, please. Both copies. It's our standard contract for freelancers.'

'Do we really need a contract?'

'I'm a lawyer, Don. Remember how much I saved you on our divorce?' Don managed a crumpled smile at what sounded to him like a considerable misrepresentation and cast his eye over the document. Fran thumbed away at her iPhone until he had signed.

'I've just emailed details of the property's location. It's on the Lizard peninsula, near Mullion. Wortalleth West. The client's name is Jackson. Mona Jackson. There was a live-in housekeeper, but she left a couple of months back. Her part-time assistant's been looking after the place since then. There's also a part-time gardener. You might run into them. Otherwise, it's all yours.' She plonked a bunch of keys on the table. Tied to the ring was a label bearing the printed initials FR/MH – some kind of filing reference at Fran's firm. Don pocketed the keys and Fran retrieved her copy of the contract.

'I should be getting back to the office,' she said briskly. 'I think we're done here, aren't we?'

'Yes.' Don nodded compliantly. 'And I can always phone you if something crops up.'

Fran frowned. 'I can't see why it should.'

'No, well . . .' Don shrugged. 'Thanks again, Fran.'

'You're welcome.'

Don stayed on to finish his coffee after Fran left. He paid no attention to a heavily built, bearded man nursing a minute espresso cup in the corner. The man had a vaguely Slavic appearance, though he was reading, or at any rate turning the pages of, an Italian newspaper. He did not seem to pay Don any attention either. But, when Don rose and left, he suddenly found it necessary to rise and leave as well. In a rustle of newspaper-folding and a scraping of chair legs, he was up and on his way.

Which happened to be the same way, though at a discreet distance, as Don was going, west along Piccadilly, towards Green Park station and a Tube ride home.

There was, though Don did not know it yet, something else he had Fran to thank for. He had just become a marked man.

·⁜·

I went down to the cove early this morning to look for driftwood. There wasn't much. The weather hasn't been right. You need storms really. But I'm not complaining. The sea was a millpond, the air pure, the light clear. The tide was on the turn. I took off my shoes and let the water rush in around my feet. The sun was already warm on my back. And there was a fizzing sensation between my toes as the bubbles in the surf started to burst. I looked out at the ocean and saw what I always see, reflected in its shimmering vastness: peace – and freedom.

I was close to the rocks, where the Bonython stream

comes out. The only sound was the sea. There weren't even any gulls screeching. I don't know what made me look up to the top of the cliff. But I knew I'd see something – or someone – if I did.

It was Wynsum Fry, squat and swaddled in a shapeless coat, the sunlight turning her grey mop of hair into a smudge of white. She's got no car, so how did she get there? The first bus out of Helston goes straight to Lizard village. She couldn't have walked all the way from the main road. But there she was. Watching me watching her.

Then she wasn't. I suppose she simply stepped back out of sight. But it was more like she just . . . blinked out. The old bitch has her tricks. If that's all they are. I wish she'd stay away. But she won't.

I hurried back up the beach and walked round the shore road to the lane that heads up towards the top of the cliff. There was no sign of her, of course. I knew there wouldn't be. She moves like a tortoise most of the time. And then, at other times . . .

Maybe it wasn't me she was looking at, but the rock pools she could see from where she was standing. Which one was it her brother drowned in? Could she be sure, all these years later? Maybe the rocks move slowly over time anyway, shifted by storms and tides, and the pools with them, so the actual one isn't there any more. Nothing's really fixed. Nothing's really absolute.

When I got back here, I found a king of spades playing card fixed to the pillar of the entrance gate with a rusty pin. It's her mark. She calls Harkness the King of Spades. But why the card? Why now?

I pulled the pin out and the card fluttered to the ground. I didn't pick it up. I left it lying there, face down. The pattern on the back was some kind of geometrical labyrinth. Did she choose it specially, I wonder?

10

I've just been back down to the gate. The card's gone. I hope she's gone too.

✢

Whatever anyone said – and what they usually said was that his insistence on driving a gas-guzzling relic from another age was both environmentally irresponsible and a transparent as well as ultimately futile attempt to recapture his lost youth – Don had no intention of trading in his 1973 MGB GT V8 for a younger or more economical model. The smell of the leather and the rumble of the engine were as familiar to him now as when he had first travelled in the car as a child, with his father at the wheel. The drive west out of London that morning in early June had, like all his drives, nothing to do with cost or comfort or convenience. It was about cleaving to what he knew and loved.

The M3, A303 and A30 formed his long route to the far south-west. The trees were heavy with summer foliage, the fields richly green in the misty light. From Salisbury Plain onwards, the sky was blue, the day open and dazzling. Through his sunglasses the world appeared golden and inviting. On the open road, reality lost its bite.

At Exeter Services, he stopped for a Coke and a sandwich. He was making good time. He was grateful to Fran, not just for the money he would earn from the trip but for the break from London she had prompted him to take. Leaving the city was like having a weight lifted from his shoulders. He really should have left Mendez Chinnery sooner. Perhaps he could turn himself into a tweed-suited purveyor of farmhouses and cottages in a provincial setting. It was not too late to change. It was *never* too late.

'But don't worry, old girl,' he said, patting the tailgate of the car, which he had raised to create a draught while

11

he was parked. 'I'll never trade you in for one of those.' By 'one of those' Don meant the black, dusty, mirror-windowed off-roader that had pulled in a few bays away. He hated all four-by-fours on principle.

Don pressed on, through the emptiness of mid-Devon, across Bodmin Moor and down the spine of Cornwall towards his destination. He was confident of arriving in time to spend most of the afternoon at the house. He had booked a room at a hotel in Helston. It looked like one night would be enough. The task itself was simple. He had done it a thousand times.

From the outskirts of Helston, he headed true south for the first time, past the long perimeter of RNAS Culdrose and down the road towards Lizard Point. The countryside varied between farmland and moor. The soft and prosperous Home Counties were far behind him.

He turned off the road at the sign for Mullion and drove into the village, following the narrow one-way route round the tight-clustered centre. He found a car park near the church and walked back to the shops to buy a large-scale OS map of the area and the local weekly newspaper. He and the MG naturally had no time for satnavs and he was confident the house would be identifiable on the map. The paper meanwhile would add to what he had already discovered on assorted websites about property prices in the locality, although he anticipated Wortalleth West might be in a price bracket all of its own.

As he exited the shop, another of the four-wheel-drive behemoths he loathed cruised slowly by. It was black, with reflective windows, like the one he had seen at Exeter Services. 'Unsightly bloody monsters,' he muttered to himself as he turned in the direction of the car park.

The map, studied in conjunction with Fran's emailed

directions, put Wortalleth West away to the north of the village, above Poldhu Cove, accessed by a lane off the minor road that led to the cove before curving inland. As for the newspaper, there were a couple of choice properties on the Helford estuary with price tags of two or three million, but nothing approaching the five Fran had spoken of. Wortalleth West would have to be quite something to justify that.

And it was, of course, as soon became apparent. The sea was a mirror of blue beyond the wavering line of hedge and field. Don spotted the turning late and was driving too fast anyway, but he managed it with no more than a touch of fishtail. The entrance to Wortalleth West came up quickly: a white, ranch-style wooden gate, standing open.

The tarmac drive curved between gorse and wind-sculpted Monterey pines, then divided, leading in one direction to a garage big enough to be a house in its own right, with balconied rooms above. There was a lot of white wood and granite beneath deeply eaved slate. Don glimpsed a tennis court in the distance as he took the lower route around a broad shoulder of land on which the main house stood.

More white wood, granite and slate conferred a style that was part Long Island, part Cornish. The building was the shape of a half-hexagon, one side facing the sea directly, the other two sides angled back to form wings enclosing a shrubbery-screened rear garden in which Don saw a flash of water-reflected light that suggested a swimming pool.

He pulled up in front of the house, turned off the car's engine and climbed out, inhaling a lungful of champagne-like air as he took his measure of the place. It stood before him in the brilliance of mid-afternoon, its proportions graceful, its dimensions generous, with a deep, paved verandah, triple gables, wide windows and a low roofline sporting dormers shaped like the backs of dolphins. No expense had been spared. That was immediately obvious. Mrs Jackson – or her ex-husband – had thrown a lot of money at this seaside whim.

Beyond the sloping lawn in front of the house, sea and sky were a realm of blue. In such perfect weather, Wortalleth West presided over something close to splendour.

Silence was part of the splendour. When Don slammed the car door, the sound shifted two fat pigeons from the branches of the nearest pine with heavy wingbeats. He climbed the shallow steps to the verandah, pulling the keys out of his pocket as he went. The entrance was a wide glazed door, with the letters WW painted on the central panel in flowing blue serifs. There were two locks, one Yale, one mortise. But the mortise, as Don soon discovered, was not across, and the alarm Fran had supplied the code for had not been activated either. No electronic beeping greeted him as he let himself in.

The hall was an airy double-height space, with a galleried landing above, reached by twin curving marble staircases. Double doors stood open to right and left. Right led to a dining room, where blinds had been drawn and the light fell softly on a pale-wood table and chairs and a dresser loaded with creamy white plates and bowls. Left led to a drawing room furnished with low-slung sofas and armchairs gathered round a stylized fireplace. There were rugs and pottery in abundance, with framed contemporary seascapes on the walls. Space and light were the dominant themes. The proportions of the rooms and the height of the windows, with transoms above the external doors, ensured plenty of both.

The double doors on the far side of the hall led to a

broad passage running along the rear of the house. Another set of doors gave access to a flagstoned terrace, with a swimming pool at its centre and loungers set up beside it. Beyond lay a neatly shrubbed garden, filled with shimmering blossom.

As Don crossed the passage, he saw movement in the pool and realized, with something of a shock, that he was not alone. Someone was swimming there. He opened the door cautiously and stepped out on to the terrace.

The swimmer had just completed a turn and was moving away. Don replaced his sunglasses as he approached the pool. He looked down. And his eyes widened. The swimmer was a woman, young, lithely built – and naked.

Don watched the refracted shimmer of her body as she sliced through the blue water. When she reached the other end, she paused for breath, then pulled herself up and out of the pool. She tossed her head and swept back her long, dark hair with her hands, casting a scatter of droplets behind her. Then she half turned and moved towards the diving board a few feet away.

And then, from the corner of her eye, she saw him. She stopped and slowly turned to face him. There was no crouching run for a towel, no squeal of outraged modesty. She put her hands on her hips and stared straight at him.

'Who the fuck are you?' she demanded.

❖

I swam a few lengths of the pool because I was angry. Wynsum Fry and her calling card were still bugging me and I wanted to wash away the thoughts of her I'd stupidly let into my head.

I always swim naked when I can. It feels natural. It feels right. I like the water to enfold me completely. It wasn't one of Glenys's days and Andy always rings in advance. I had the place to myself. *Should* have had the place to myself.

15

I sensed something as soon as I climbed out of the pool. But I didn't quite trust the sense. I thought I might still be a bit on edge, because of Fry, though I felt calm. The water had worked its magic. I decided to dive in again. Then as I turned towards the board—

'Who the fuck are you?'

I don't try to hide from him. I stand where I am and let him see I'm not afraid.

He's about fifty, a rumpled, slightly paunchy bloke in a dark suit way too warm for the weather. He's wearing an open-neck blue and white striped shirt. His cufflinks are glistening in the reflected light thrown up from the slopping water in the pool. He has a mop of grey-flecked hair above a square-jawed face. Rugged is what you'd call him, if you wanted to be flattering. Travel-worn, if you didn't. I can't see his eyes. He's wearing aviator-style shades. Is he ogling me? You bet he is.

What is he? Not local, that's for sure. Some underling of Harkness's, maybe. But I don't know. He doesn't look smooth enough for that. Or young enough. Harkness wouldn't send a man like him down here. But someone's sent him. And he's come through the house, so he must have a key.

I'm about to repeat my question when he says, 'I could ask the same of you. But . . . do you want to put something on?' Policeman? Salesman? I don't know. But there's a touch of big city swagger about him. Down from London is my guess. But why? On whose say-so?

'Does nudity disturb you?' I throw back.

'"Disturb" isn't the word I'd use.' He smiles diffidently. He's trying to be friendly without coming over lecherous. I've put him in a tricky position. I take pity. I walk round to the lounger where I left my towel, pick it up and wrap it round me. Then I look at him again. 'So, who are you? And how'd you get in?'

'I'm an estate agent. Don Challenor. From London.'

My stomach lurches. *Estate agent?* That sounds bad.

'I have a set of keys. Supplied by Mrs Jackson's solicitor.'

'Who?'

'Mrs Jackson. The owner of the property.'

He's raving. He has to be. Who's Mrs Jackson? 'I don't know who you're talking about. The owner's name is Harkness.'

'Not according to my information.'

'Well, your information's wrong.'

He frowns at me. 'I don't see how it can be. And you are?'

'The housekeeper.'

'I was told she'd moved out.'

'The previous one did. I took her place. I'm Blake.'

'Well, Miss Blake—'

'Just Blake.'

'OK. Blake.' He nods and walks slowly round the corner of the pool towards me. I'm confused. I don't know if he knows just how confused.

He shows me the keys, as if to prove he's legit. Then he takes a card out of his pocket and offers it to me. I look at it for all of two seconds. *Don Challenor. Residential Associate. Mendez Chinnery. Email. Mobile. Landline. Posh address in London W1.* 'I'm sorry I, er, surprised you,' he says, almost sounding genuine.

'I don't understand. Why are you here?'

'To value the property. With a view to selling.'

'Selling? This place?'

'That's right. As soon as possible, according to my instructions.'

His instructions. From a woman I've never heard of. But somehow I believe him. The bolt was always going to come from the blue. Harkness is in trouble. And this is just one symptom of it. I'm going to be expelled from my sanctuary. I know I am. Unless—

'Sorry if this comes as a shock.'

'You're serious? About this place being sold?'

''Fraid so.'

I decide to play for his sympathy. Actually, it's the only play I have. And I get the feeling he might just be a sucker for it. It's certainly worth a try.

I burst into tears.

⁜

Don's expectations of what he would find at Wortalleth West had been confounded at every turn. Now, Blake, the self-proclaimed stand-in housekeeper, entirely unabashed by parading naked in front of him, had descended into tears. She sat on the lounger, dabbing at her eyes with one end of the towel she was wrapped in. All Don could do was fish a tissue out of his pocket and give it to her.

'Don't upset yourself. Please.'

'I can't help it,' she sobbed. 'You don't understand.'

'You're right there. But look . . . Blake . . . it's not as if this is your home in any real sense, is it?'

'It's the only one I've got.'

'Well, there's not much I can do about that. The house doesn't belong to you, now does it?'

'It doesn't belong to . . . Mrs Whoever . . . either.'

'I'm afraid it does. I'll call the solicitor. Try to sort this out.'

Don took out his phone and selected Fran's office number. Then he noticed what the phone was trying to tell him through the glare. *No signal.*

'Bloody hell. Are we in some kind of dead zone?'

'You have to—' Blake blew her nose in the tissue. 'You have to go to the bottom of the drive to get a signal. There's nothing here.'

'Really?'

'Really. But there's a landline in the kitchen. You could use that.'

'OK. I will. You're . . . all right?'

Blake smiled weakly. 'Sure.'

Don went back into the house and took a left along the wide corridor, guessing the kitchen would be beyond the dining room. It was predictably vast, with multiple sinks, ovens and work surfaces, trailing away past a long breakfast bar to a TV and lounging area. The work surfaces were all gleaming marble, the shelves and cabinets pale wood, the furniture sleek, simple and expensive.

The telephone needed some finding amid all the brushed steel and digital displays. One of the receptionists at Fran's practice took Don's call. In his experience, they all spoke with the same brisk haughtiness. 'Is Mrs Revell expecting your call?' she asked, in a tone that suggested unexpected calls were serious breaches of protocol.

'Tell her it's Don Challenor. And it's urgent. I'm at Wortalleth West.'

'Hold on, please. I'll see if she's available.'

Don bit his tongue and waited. Half a minute or so passed. Then Fran came on the line.

'Don?'

'Yes, Fran. It's me.'

'You're at the house?'

'I am. But I'm not alone.'

'No?'

'You said the housekeeper had left.'

'The live-in one, yes.'

'Well, her successor's also decided to live in. And she's never heard of Mrs Jackson. She claims the owner's name is Harkness.'

The name sounded vaguely familiar to Don as he spoke

it, though he could not say why. He turned away from the wall-mounted phone while he listened to Fran's response and stepped towards the breakfast bar. 'She's confused. Mona Jackson's husband is called Harkness, but she's reverted to her maiden name, although we're still waiting for the decree absolute. More to the point, she *is* the sole owner of the property.'

'They're not actually divorced yet, then?'

'No. But that's a technicality. And, as I say . . .'

There was a copy of the *Financial Times* lying on the bar, near the corner closest to Don. It struck him as an odd choice of reading for Blake. It was folded open at an inner page. A headline caught his eye at once. *Harkness's freedom of movement further restricted as extradition ruling approaches.*

'. . . Now, as to this so-called housekeeper you've encountered, she has no right to reside there. She's nothing more than a part-time cleaner. You'll need to ensure she moves out immediately . . .'

Don stretched out his hand and grabbed the paper. He scanned the first paragraph of the report.

In the latest twist in pharmaceuticals entrepreneur Jack Harkness's battle to escape extradition to the United States, Judge Geoffrey Anders QC yesterday ruled that he could remain free on bail until a full hearing of the case, but only on condition he agreed to be fitted with an electronic ankle tag to monitor his movements. US prosecutors are seeking to try Mr Harkness on multiple counts of fraud, bribery and embezzlement, arising from—

'Don?'

'Sorry?' Don dragged his attention back to the voice in his ear. 'What?'

'Did you hear what I just said?'

'You want me to persuade the cleaner to move out.'

'Not exactly. I said you must insist she moves out. And make sure she goes. As soon as possible.'

'How do I do that? She has nowhere to go to.'

'I doubt that very much. She's taken advantage of the situation. And now she's trying to take advantage of you. You're not to go soft on her.'

Don was losing patience. He had heard of the Harkness case without ever giving it much attention: some high roller caught fiddling the books who was trying to dodge the long sentence that seemed to be the norm in American courts. If he was the owner of Wortalleth West, or even the soon-to-be-ex-husband of the owner, Fran had some explaining to do. 'Mr Harkness, Fran. Would that be Jack Harkness?'

A brief silence. Then: 'Did she tell you that?'

'No. But more to the point, *you* didn't tell me.'

'Because it's irrelevant.'

'He's all over the newspapers, Fran. Fraud is the word. Stolen money. Now—'

'*Allegedly* stolen.'

'This house could be a recoverable asset. You're the lawyer. Shouldn't it be frozen until everything's been sorted?'

'It's not *his* asset. It's my client's. And she's entirely within her rights to sell it. I wouldn't have anything to do with it otherwise. What do you take me for?'

'You should've told me.'

'Why? So we could have had this entirely pointless conversation yesterday? You're being paid well to get a job done, Don. I suggest you get on with it. I don't really know what your problem is anyway. As I recall, Mendez Chinnery didn't dispense with your services because they found your ethics too high-minded for their taste.'

'I don't like being taken for a ride.'

'You're not being. Get rid of the cleaner. Measure up the house. Value it. And get the information to me by Monday. That's all I'm asking you to do in return for your generous fee.'

'Hold on. I—'

'Which I'll up to two thousand five hundred if you solve the cleaner problem.'

'Blake.'

'Sorry?'

'Her name's Blake.'

'Well, thank you. I'll make a note of it. So, do you think you can see Miss Blake on her way?'

'Not sure.' Don was not even sure how hard he would try. He was an estate agent, after all, not a bailiff. 'I'll see what I can do.'

'Good,' said Fran tightly. 'I'll await your report.'

✤

I listened to Don's conversation with the lawyer on the extension in Harkness's study. She sounded like a real bitch to me. There's something between those two beyond business, I reckon, history of some kind. And Don's already misrepresented himself to me. He doesn't work for Mendez Chinnery any more. They fired him. So now he's freelancing for the lawyer. Which means he needs his fee, I guess.

After he puts the phone down in the kitchen, I put the phone down in the study and try to make my brain work. Bitch or not, the lawyer must be telling the truth. Harkness doesn't own this place. His wife does, which is odd, considering I've never seen her down here. Probably some tax dodge. Who knows? Anyway, she wants to sell now he's in trouble and she has her future to worry about. So, a quick sale of Wortalleth West. And for a quick sale you need vacant possession. 'Solve the cleaner problem.' That's what the lawyer said.

And that's when Don told her my name. As if it matters to him. As if he wanted it to matter to her. 'Her name's Blake.' He's already gone a bit of the way to caring what happens to me. Maybe I can take him a bit further.

I could go quietly, I suppose. I could just pack up and clear out. I don't know where I'd go. I can't imagine I'll find anywhere as safe as this.

Or I could try to stay. There'll be some lawyer in Helston willing to argue I have squatter's rights. But that would mean answering a lot of questions about me I don't want anyone even asking. I can't risk that.

So, what to do? Delay's the only hope as far as I can see. Delay until I can think of a plan. And that's where Don comes in.

✣

After Fran had rung off, Don propped himself against the breakfast bar and started reading the rest of the newspaper article.

US prosecutors are seeking to try Mr Harkness on multiple counts of fraud, bribery and embezzlement arising from allegations made against him by Quintagler Industries, Harkness Pharmaceuticals' partner in numerous takeovers and buyouts in the pharmaceuticals field.

Mr Harkness has dismissed the allegations as an attempt by Quintagler to steal his company from under him. The US Department of Justice has stated, however, that they have seen clear prima facie evidence of wrongdoing and are proceeding without regard to Quintagler's commercial interests.

The charges against Mr Harkness have led to big slides

in Harkness Pharmaceuticals' share price, which analysts say would probably have been bigger still but for the continuing and growing popularity of the company's Elixtris range of anti-ageing products. A spokesperson for Harkness Pharmaceuticals said—

'Did you speak to her?'

Don turned to find Blake regarding him gravely from the other side of the bar. She had put on a pair of shorts and a T-shirt. She looked calm now. 'Er, yes,' he said lamely. 'I spoke to her.'

'So?'

'Do you really buy this paper?' He held up the *FT*.

'No. It gets delivered every day by the newsagent in the village. Some special arrangement Harkness has made. Likes to stay in touch when he's down here, I s'pose. Not that he ever is.'

'If you've read this, you'll know why he never is.'

'Yeah. Ankle tag. Not cool. I feel sorry for him.'

'Why? He probably had it coming.'

'Maybe. But he's a free spirit. I feel sorry for him like I feel sorry for a caged tiger in the zoo.'

'How well do you know him?'

'Not very. So, what did the lawyer say?'

'I'm afraid she only confirmed what I told you. Mrs Jackson is the owner. She has every right to sell. And you, unfortunately—'

'What's Mrs Jackson to Harkness?'

'Ex-wife. Well, all but.'

'Right.' Blake nodded and looked serious. 'Got it.'

'Sorry.'

'Me too.' She gazed past Don. 'Looks like I'm out.'

'I'm sure you'll find somewhere else. Move in with your boyfriend maybe.'

24

'There's no boyfriend.' She shook back her drying hair and summoned a smile. 'Well, d'you want me to show you round?'

'I need to take photographs and room-by-room measurements. But . . .' Don smiled too. 'A guided tour to start with would be great.'

The utility room led through to a mud room and cloakroom. From there a rear door gave access to a wisteria-draped colonnade curving away and slightly uphill to the garage block. Back in the utility room, stairs led down into a basement extending about half the width of the house. Here there was a boiler room, climate-controlled wine cellar, home cinema and gleamingly well-equipped gym, with adjoining wet room.

Back upstairs, beyond the kitchen, dining room and hall, the ground floor comprised the expansive drawing room, complete with bar, and a library/study, where Harkness had an enormous desk and all the facilities of a modern office – an office that appeared to have had little actual use, despite the battery of computer ports and swivel-stemmed lights.

The high windows, pale colours and overall spaciousness of the rooms ensured they were filled with light. The sea felt closer than it actually was thanks to maritime-blue fabrics and the scent of the ocean that wafted around the house. Every item of furniture, every detail of decoration, every turn and angle, served the overall design. Wortalleth West was a place of meticulously crafted casualness.

From the hall Don followed Blake up one of the curving staircases to the bedrooms. All had their own bathrooms and were predictably enormous. The most enormous of the lot, the master bedroom, featured an emperor-sized bed on a dais, a lounge area, a dressing room with walk-in closet and a bathroom with two free-standing tubs complete with sea view.

'It's a lot for one person to use as a home from home, isn't it, Don?' Blake asked as they walked into yet another luxuriously appointed but evidently seldom used en suite bathroom.

'He's obviously a wealthy man,' Don replied with a shrug.

'You need a word beyond wealthy to do justice to Jack Harkness. You got any idea just how successful Elixtris is?'

'The anti-ageing wonder treatment? Not really. I've seen it advertised quite a bit.'

'It's, like, everywhere. He must be worth billions.'

'But he still wants more, if you believe the allegations against him.'

'Yeah. If you believe them.'

'Do you?'

'I don't know him well enough to say.'

'But you've been reading about the case?'

'Oh yeah. Thanks to his *FT*s. It's an education, that paper. Deals. Dodges. Boardroom battles. I'd no idea so many rich people skate on such thin ice. I don't really understand it all. It's way over my head.'

Don was far from sure he believed that. But he decided to play along. 'Mine too.'

'Anyway, Harkness is prowling round London with an electronic tag rubbing his ankle, while I'm down here, enjoying his seaside retreat. Look at this.'

Blake walked back into the adjoining bedroom and pressed a button set in the wall between the windows. The blinds filtering the sunlight to a golden haze rose automatically. Outside, the grounds fell away through clumps of gorse and heather and rhododendron towards the sea that lapped in on the creamy sand of the cove. Before them lay the shimmering ocean and the shadow-etched cliffs. The sky held only a few white smoke-puffs of cloud. The rest was intensely blue.

'I don't care about all the stuff that goes on in Harkness's world. This is what matters.'

'It is beautiful.'

'But I have to leave it, right? I bet that lawyer wants you to get me out, like, yesterday. You may as well tell me. How long have I got?'

'It's not up to me, Blake.'

'Maybe I should start packing.'

'D'you really have nowhere to go?'

'Nowhere I want to go.'

'If there's anything I can do to help . . .'

She turned and smiled at him. And it was not a smile Don could easily resist. 'That's kind. Thanks. I'll let you know if there is. Are you staying here tonight?'

'No, no. I've booked a hotel in Helston.'

'You could cancel. As you can see, there's plenty of room. It's a shame not to make use of it. And you won't disturb me. I live over the garage.'

'Tempting, but . . . the lawyer might not approve.'

'Plus you'll get a full English breakfast on expenses, right?'

Don grinned. 'I'd better get on with measuring up. Thanks for the tour.'

'No problem,' Blake said briskly.

Don fetched his camera, Dictaphone and measurer from the car. There was no sign of Blake when he returned to the house. There was an eeriness about it now, in its emptiness and its silence.

Fran had a lot to answer for, in his view. Trying to get him to do her dirty work was shabby to say the least. He was unsure how or if he could persuade Blake to leave, but he was quite sure he did not want to.

Meanwhile, there was work to be done. Dimensions, doorways, fenestrations, baths, showers, sinks, stairs: everything had to be noted. And some tasteful, alluring photographs would have to be taken.

He settled to the task.

It was nearly an hour later, in the dressing room off the master bedroom, that he found it.

✥

I knew Don would have to measure the rooms in the garage block as well as the main house. That's when I planned to tell him there'd been some strange incidents lately – signs of attempted intrusion. I meant to persuade him I was worried and needed his protection. He looked like the kind of guy who'd be happy to discover his inner knight gallant.

I was in the workshop behind the garage, working on my latest driftwood creation, when he showed up. He didn't look quite as I'd expected. Something was troubling him. More, I sensed, than the problem of moving me on.

He's got a bag over his shoulder. He eases it off on to the edge of the bench and looks around. It's cool in the workshop. I like the subdued light and the woody scents in the air. I'm wearing my boiler suit and I've tied my hair back. I think Don has trouble recognizing me for a moment.

Then he looks at what I'm working on and says, 'What is that?'

'It's going to be a three-legged table. I'll probably paint the legs different colours – and leave the top natural. Blue, pink, green. What d'you think?'

'Are you making it to sell?'

'Yeah. There aren't many National Trust shops in Cornwall without a Blake original.'

'They're popular?'

'Well, they sell. Eventually. Listen, Don, I—'

'There's something strange at the house. In the master bedroom. D'you know about it?'

I don't. I wonder what he can possibly be talking about. 'How d'you mean – "strange"?'

'You've never seen it?'

'Never seen what, Don?'

'You really don't know?'

'No. Maybe you should show me.'

'Yeah.' Don nods. 'Maybe I should.'

I step out of the boiler suit, but leave my hair tied back. We walk down the colonnade to the house and along the passage to the hall. We finish up in the study.

'What's that?' Don asks, pointing to the narrower end of the L-shaped room.

'What's what?' I respond, seeing nothing but bookcases.

'Why isn't this room a regular shape? What's in the rectangle that's been taken out of it?'

I shrug. 'Dunno.'

'Nor me. Ducting? Pipework? In a house like this, there's a lot of concealed services, for heating, lighting, plumbing.'

'OK. So that'll be it, then?'

'It was my first thought. But no. That's not it. We're beyond the extent of the basement here. Above us is the bathroom off the master bedroom. Let's go upstairs.'

Upstairs we go, into the master bedroom, then the dressing room between it and the bathroom.

'According to my measurements and the layout diagram I've sketched,' Don explains, 'the closet is above the space

29

missing from the study. Except that it isn't big enough. It doesn't go back far enough to be directly over it. There's another missing space up here. Some sort of . . . void.'

'There is?'

Don pulls the double doors of the closet wide open. The clothes, most of them protected under plastic covers, extend back on their racks as far as the rear wall. There's a walkway in the middle, with a floor-to-ceiling mirror fixed to the wall at the end. I see Don and me reflected in it, standing next to each other.

For some reason, this reminds me of standing next to Dad in the hallway of Gran's house in Sutton Coldfield. She had a tall mirror at the far end. It seems to have stuck as my clearest memory of him. I was a lot shorter than him, of course, whereas I'm about the same height as Don. I was only eight years old then. I think I was happy that day. Anyway, I feel happy remembering it.

'What's behind the mirror, Blake?' Don asks.

I turn and look at him. 'The wall?'

He shakes his head. 'No.'

He walks into the closet, approaches the mirror and pushes his hand against the frame at about waist height.

There's a click. He steps back and the mirror shows itself to be a mirror-fronted door. It swings smoothly open.

Behind it is solid steel.

'I had no idea that was there,' I say, which is true. 'What is it?'

Don taps the steel with his knuckles. 'Thick is what it is. Very thick. Impenetrable, probably. But concealing something. Definitely concealing something.'

'What?'

'Well, I've seen similar arrangements in houses I've sold in London. But on one floor only. If it connects with the void below . . . that'd be unusual.'

'So, what is the arrangement?'

'A panic room would be my guess. You know? Somewhere the householder can retreat to if there's an intruder, with independent lighting and communications. Somewhere they're completely safe. But if I'm right . . .'

'Yeah?' I look at him expectantly.

'Then this is the entrance. A sliding steel door, lockable only from the inside. It should be open, you see. But it isn't, is it? It's shut. Locked shut. From the inside.'

I don't know what to say. I'd decided to invent a threat. Then Don delivers one, right into my hands. But this is real. This isn't invented. This is a locked room, and suddenly I don't have a clue what's going on. Suddenly . . . I don't feel safe any more.

✣

'You mean . . .' Blake stumbled, 'you mean . . . there's someone inside?'

'No, no.' Don gave her what he hoped was a reassuring smile. 'That wouldn't make any sense. Besides, who's been here who could be inside?'

'No one . . . as far as I know.'

'The likeliest explanation is some kind of fault. Either that or someone standing out here leant in and triggered the door to close, then pulled their arm clear before it shut.' Don frowned. 'That wouldn't make any sense either, of course. It'd just ensure the room couldn't be used.'

'This is spooky, Don. I don't like it.'

'It could've happened years ago.'

'Or last week. Or yesterday . . .'

'At the moment it's just a steel door, Blake. Maybe it isn't a panic room at all. Maybe there's just pipework in there.'

'But you don't think so.'

'Only because it looks so similar to installations I've seen in high-end properties in London. Russian oligarchs needing somewhere to hide from Moscow heavies. That sort of thing.'

Don instantly regretted his reference to Russian oligarchs. If Harkness was guilty of his alleged misdeeds, a hiding place from those he had robbed or otherwise defrauded might well be something he felt he needed, even in his Cornish holiday home.

'As I say, the likeliest explanation is a mechanical fault.'

'I guess so.' Blake cast a leery glance at the steel door. 'I just wish I'd never known it was here.'

'Sorry. My fault.'

'Any chance you could change your mind about the hotel, Don? I mean, I could really use some company in the house tonight. Just in case of . . . well, I don't know, but . . .' she sighed. 'This has sort of got to me.'

'Sure. Why not?' Don smiled. 'If it'll stop you worrying.'

'I think it might.'

'OK. That's settled, then.'

Don half wished he had said nothing to Blake about his discovery. He had assumed she would be able to explain it away. Instead, she seemed thoroughly discomposed by it. And who, in truth, could blame her? She did not actually sleep in the house, but the idea that it contained a hidden locked room, contents unknown, was bound to be disturbing.

After telephoning the hotel in Helston to cancel his reservation, Don put another call through to Fran. The haughty receptionist seemed to take pleasure in informing him that Mrs Revell had left for the day. She did not volunteer Mrs Revell's mobile number. Fortunately, however, Don already had it.

Fran answered promptly. Background sounds suggested she was on a train. 'What's going on, Don? I called you for an update before I left the office, but you didn't pick up.'

'There's no mobile signal here, Fran. I'm using the house landline.'

'Have you given the cleaner her marching orders?'

'I can't just order her out. Anyway, I'm not sure she'll want to stay after what we found.'

'*We?*'

'Well, after what *I* found. A locked panic room, I think, off the master bedroom, possibly extending to the ground floor.'

'What's the problem? Some buyers will be attracted by that sort of thing, though why you'd need one down there I can't imagine. And what d'you mean – you *think*? The room either exists or it doesn't.'

'My measurements prove a void of some kind is there. And it's barred by what looks like a sliding steel door. But the door should be open, Fran. The point is it's closed. Locked. If it is a door. From the inside.'

'You mean it's faulty?'

'That's one explanation.'

'What's another? That someone's holed up in there? That's absurd. What does the cleaner say about it?'

'Blake's as baffled as I am. And none too happy.'

'Her happiness or unhappiness is beside the point. What exactly do you expect me to do about this?'

'Well, I thought Mrs Jackson might be able to say whether it really is a panic room, or, if not, what the void contains.'

Fran sighed audibly. 'She won't want to be bothered.'

'She may have to be bothered. Potential buyers will expect accurate information.'

'I agree. Which is what I sent you down there to obtain.'

Don had forgotten just how easily Fran could rile him. He struggled to remain calm. 'You must have some documents relating to the property. Specifications. The original contract to build it. That sort of thing.'

'I have very little beyond my client's proof of title. Her husband owned the property initially. He doesn't seem to have passed anything of that nature over to her when ownership was transferred. And I doubt she'd feel able to ask him about it now.'

'When was ownership transferred?'

'That's none of your concern. You can leave the legalities to me.'

'I'm more than happy to, Fran. But—'

'Maybe there's something in the house that would shed light on the matter. Have a look around. Use your initiative. Is that too much to ask? You are being paid quite well to sort this out.'

'So you keep reminding me.'

'Only because you seem to need reminding. Call me tomorrow when you've resolved the issue. Including the cleaner complication. OK?' When Don was not quick enough for her liking to answer the question, she repeated it more snappily. 'OK?'

'Sure,' said Don glumly.

He was beginning to wish he had turned down Fran's offer of employment. It had sounded like easy money. Now it was proving to be anything but. He recalled one of his father's favourite sayings. *Always look a gift horse in the mouth.* The old man had never followed his own advice, of course. And Don had inherited his chancer's nature. But there were times when caution paid off. The problem, in Don's experience, and his father's, was that you never knew which times those were until it was too late to do anything about it.

The only place in the house where Don thought he might find any information about a panic room was the library-cum-study. But the desk drawers contained nothing more than oddments of stationery. And the filing cabinet beside the desk was locked, with no sign of the key.

He did notice a framed photograph of Wortalleth West hanging on the wall in the alcove behind the desk, however. The house looked brand new, whiter than ever, the gardens around it raw and immature. A tall, leanly built man was standing on the verandah, close to the front door, his face in shadow. He was wearing a pale suit and open-necked shirt. His expression was indecipherable, as were any details of his features. It would have seemed more natural for him to pose at the foot of the steps, in full view. As it was, there was an air of withdrawal about him, perhaps of secrecy.

Don went up to the garage block, which he had yet to measure. Blake was back in the workshop, chiselling and planing her three-legged stool. She looked entirely unworried again, calm and happy. She too, Don realized, was in many ways indecipherable.

'I need to go over these rooms with the measurer,' he explained.

'Go ahead. They're all open. Mine's a bit of a mess. I'd appreciate it if you didn't take any pictures up there.'

'I won't. Do you want to come along and make sure I don't disturb anything?'

'No. It's cool. I trust you.'

'I can't think why.'

She smiled at him. 'Neither can I.'

'There's a framed photograph on the wall in the library. Of the house.'

'Yeah.'

'Is that Harkness on the verandah?'

'S'pose so. It's hard to be sure. But he dresses like that and the height and build are about right. Who else would it be?'

Don shrugged helplessly. 'I don't know.'

'Want to take me somewhere to eat tonight?' Blake asked suddenly.

Don felt ludicrously flattered by the proposal, even though he knew all it probably meant was that she saw him as the source of a free meal. 'I'd be delighted. Where shall we go?'

'There's a nice pub just up the coast. It's your sort of place.'

How she could know what his sort of place was, Don was at a loss to imagine. Perhaps he was more transparent than he supposed. He smiled, as much at himself as at Blake. 'Sounds great.'

✣

I was putting on a front when Don showed up at the workshop a second time. That steel door in the closet – and the panic room he seemed convinced was behind it – were giving me goosebumps whenever I thought about them. Could there actually be someone in there? No. Surely not. But then . . . what's the story? What's going on?

It's like a dream I sometimes have where I swim out to sea from a cove that's pretty much Poldhu. I don't go very far, but when I stop swimming and turn round . . . the coast's gone. Vanished. There's nothing but endless open water. I'm lost. And alone.

I don't like that feeling.

*

After Don goes back to the main house to dump his stuff in the bedroom I made up for him, I go up to my room, to see if anything's been moved, to see if he's the prying type.

There's no sign he's been looking where he shouldn't. And without looking seriously he'll know nothing about me. I don't litter the place with pictures or mementoes. I hold my past inside my head. It's not always easy. But it's safer that way.

A guide to trees and their different wood types; a study of the life cycle of the honey bee; an exhibition catalogue about the paintings of the Cornish abstract artist Peter Lanyon: Don won't have learnt much from the books beside my bed. I wonder if he'll notice the Lanyon Harkness has hanging in the lounge. *Far West*. Oil on canvas, 1964. It's the only thing of his I actually covet. Maybe I can take it with me when I leave and no one will notice. We'll see.

So, Don hasn't disturbed anything, just like he promised. Which— Hold on, though. He's opened the bathroom cabinet. I never leave the hook in that position. Naughty boy, Don. What were you looking for? Prescription tranquillizers? A suicide stock of paracetamol? Whatever, you didn't find anything, did you? I'm clean.

Maybe I should take it as a sign he's genuinely worried about me. I'm not sure how much to tell him. Walking away from all this might be the safest thing to do. But I resent losing the sense of safety I had here only this morning. And right now I don't have anywhere I can walk away *to*.

Also, I have a feeling about Don. When I told him I trusted him, I was as surprised as he was. It's not true. Not yet. But it feels possible. Which isn't a feeling I have about most people – any people, really. I don't understand what it is. I've only known him a few hours. Life's taught me to be suspicious. So why aren't I suspicious of him?

*

We've agreed to leave at seven. I take a shower and put on one of my girlier numbers. I figure it'll make me look in need of protection. It should do the trick with a guy Don's age.

Don looks as if he's taken a shower too. I think I might even be able to catch a drift of aftershave. He's still wearing the suit. He probably didn't bring anything casual with him. I've already seen the car, of course, but he introduces me to it almost formally. 'This is my MG.'

What am I supposed to say? It's cramped, it's old and it's dusty. I ask provocatively, 'What colour is it supposed to be?'

'Harvest Gold,' he replies, beaming proudly.

'How old is it?'

'She's a 1973 model. Which is lucky. They'd phased out chrome bumpers by 1975.'

'You're kidding.'

He catches my smile. 'All right. You've had your fun.'

'I'm guessing this car's almost as old as you are.'

'Yeah. Which means she's just coming into her prime.'

I nod. ''Course she is.'

Before we leave, Don asks if I'm going to set the burglar alarm. I tell him I never use it. It's true. I never do. I've never wanted to – or thought I needed to. I try to explain a little of that to him. It's pretty obvious he doesn't really get it. But he doesn't push it.

I tell him we could easily walk to the Halzephron Inn. It's only a few miles along the coast path and it's a fine evening, the sun still strong, the sea sparkling like a beaded mirror. He prefers to drive, even though it's a long way round by the main road. He probably wants to show off the car. 'She', as he calls it.

It certainly goes fast. I ask him if he feels guilty about damaging the planet by driving around in such an environmentally unfriendly machine. He replies he's loyal and so is the car.

I really don't know whether that's good news or bad. Maybe he's an anachronism driving an anachronism.

We get to the Halzephron around half seven. There are quite a lot of people there, some of them sitting outside. I don't recognize anyone, though.

It's a cosy place, low-ceilinged and traditional. On stormy nights, with the sea booming a couple of fields away, it can feel like being below deck on some old galleon. But the weather's calm and the light's mellow. Everything seems tranquil. I tell Don I'm glad we came out. And I am. I start to relax properly for the first time since Don showed me the door to the panic room – if that's what it is.

I have a G&T. Don drinks beer. He declares the Doom Bar excellent. He orders fish and chips. I order soup and salad.

He talks a lot. Well, he's a salesman, so I suppose that shouldn't come as a surprise. He asks me a few questions he maybe hopes will encourage me to talk about myself. But I'm not going to be drawn and it's easy to make him believe I'm genuinely interested in hearing all about him instead.

Don Challenor. Born 29 April 1967. He mentions the date as part of a story about being conceived the night England won the World Cup. I try to break it to him that I'm even less interested in football than vintage sports cars. 1967 is ancient history. Quite a lot of what Don says about himself comes from a place that feels remote to me.

His father was a salesman too: brushes door to door, then venetian blinds, then . . . I stop listening as he goes on. There's something about a gambling problem, father's, not his. Then there's Don the up-and-coming estate agent. 'The Englishman's home is his cash cow,' he announces as he starts his third pint.

I ask if he has a family. Not really, he replies. There was a marriage. Then there was a divorce. No children. Don claims relations with his ex-wife are good. He lets her name slip a couple of times. Fran. That's the lawyer, then. Fran Revell. I knew they had history.

There's a brother, but he lives in Australia, with a wife and children and Don's mother. Father's long dead. Which leaves Don pretty much alone in the world. Divorced, childless, parentless – and unemployed, I happen to know. He doesn't mention that, of course. He doesn't want to admit things aren't exactly hunky-dory in his world. I don't blame him. I wouldn't want to admit that either.

Maybe the beer and talking about himself make him soulful. That could be why he insists on following his last pint with a double Scotch, which puts him way over the drink-drive limit. When we leave, he can't even cross the car park in a straight line.

I tell him I'm not going back in the car with him. It's still not quite dark. I'll walk home. I suggest he comes with me and picks his car up in the morning. He bristles. I'm making a fuss about nothing. I point out I'm not making any kind of fuss. I'm just telling him what I'm going to do – and what I'm not going to do.

Hitting his head on the door frame as he climbs into the car seems to clear this thought. I hear myself suggesting a compromise. We drive to the far end of the lane, the car park at Church Cove. That's only half a mile from Poldhu. We leave 'the old girl', as Don is now addressing her – *it*, I mean – there and walk the rest of the way. In a tone suggesting it's a vast and magnanimous concession, Don agrees.

'I'm glad we decided to do this,' Don announces, slurring his Cs and Ss, as, an hour or so later, we walk down the lane towards Poldhu Cove. The night is sweet and still and sound-less. You'd think it was completely dark if you weren't out in it. The banks of thrift and valerian have been drained of their colour, but they're still visible. I don't want to leave this place. I really don't. And I hope I don't have to. 'I can see why you like it here,' Don adds.

We're nearly home. Except it isn't home of course. I'm not allowed one of those here – or anywhere else.

✣

Don knew Blake was right about not driving all the way back to Wortalleth West via the main road. He was not sure why he had drunk so much. Maybe, as he recalled later, it was because Blake had somehow persuaded him to sketch out the less than glorious passage of his life to date. Or maybe it was actually because he was nervous about sleeping at the house, a few bedrooms away from the locked panic room. He believed his own explanation, that it was faulty. But beliefs, in his experience, could be hard to hold on to in the middle of the night.

The walk from Church Cove cleared his head a little and the serene beauty of the clifftop stretch had a soothing effect on him. By the time they reached Wortalleth West, he felt confident there really was nothing to worry about.

He would not have stayed that way had he realized their approach up the drive prompted a signal, in the form of a briefly flashing light on a belt-worn pager, to a heavily built, bearded man dressed in black who was at that moment searching the pockets of the jackets hanging in the closet of the dressing room off the master bedroom.

With a barely audible sigh of irritation, he switched off the flashing light and made his way, at a swift, soft-footed pace, out of the room in the direction of the stairs, a faint reflection of his moving form dwindling in the mirror on the end wall of the closet as he went.

As Don and Blake neared the front door of the house,

the black-clad man let himself out through a rear door on to the patio around the swimming pool. He steered a deft path between the poolside loungers and headed off swiftly into the garden. A shape in motion. A sliver of black joining a slab of darkness. He was gone.

NINE

DON SLEEPS DEEPLY, IF NOT SOUNDLY. BUT WORTALLETH WEST, in all its automated intricacy, functions as it was designed to, by night as well as by day. The panic room is an enclosed space, nested within the house, walled in steel, equipped with cameras, enabling an occupant to observe every other room while safe themselves from observation. The door cannot be opened, except from inside – if, and only if, there is someone inside who wishes to open it. Otherwise, it will remain sealed. The security it confers on what exists within it is absolute. It is the perfect hiding place, concealing the very nature of what it conceals.

Until, or unless, the door opens.

Don slept deeply, if not soundly. When he woke, the grey light of an early summer dawn already filled the room. His throat was dry and there was the insistent throb of a low-grade headache. It was a familiar sensation. Fran had once described him as a man who learnt just enough from his mistakes to go on repeating them.

He got up and went to the bathroom. Then he threw on the towelling robe supplied for his use and descended to the kitchen. Solitude in such a large house carried with it an inescapable eeriness, but he was relieved there was no tangible cause for concern. He reminded himself of his own explanation for the closed door in the bedroom closet: a technical fault – nothing more. He downed a tumblerful of water and made himself some coffee. This necessitated grinding beans of unknown age and fiddling with a high-tech espresso machine.

The sun was already shining palely through the dawn mist that had billowed up from the sea. Hoping fresh air might add to the reviving effects of the coffee, he ventured out on to the verandah.

The sea was calm, the sky a blue-tinged grey. The house was still and silent, so silent the lap of the surf on the beach down in the cove sounded far closer, as if Don was standing within a few yards of it.

He absorbed the cleanness of the air along with the aroma of the coffee as he stood there, marvelling at how newly minted the world seemed in such a place.

A sound suddenly penetrated the gentle swash of the surf. The telephone in the kitchen had started to ring. At first, Don thought he had misheard, that maybe it was a telephone ringing in some neighbouring property, even though there were none within earshot. Only when the ringing continued and he realized where it was coming from did he turn and head back into the house.

It had stopped by the time he reached the kitchen. He cursed the caller for interrupting his brief idyll on the verandah and wondered if they would leave a message.

Then the telephone began ringing again. Don snatched it from its cradle with irritable haste.

'Hello?'

'Don Challenor?' Don did not recognize the voice – male, American, slightly husky. But he was immediately

46

puzzled that anyone other than Fran and her secretarial staff knew he was there.

'Who's this?'

'The name's French. I'd like to talk to you.'

'You are talking to me.'

'Face to face.'

'Why?'

'I'll explain when we meet.'

Don's puzzlement was rapidly turning to anxiety. Who in hell was this man? 'Look, Mr French, I—'

'I'm up at Church Cove, where you left your car last night. You'll want to come fetch it, I guess. I'll wait for you. I'll give you an hour. It's no hardship. It's beautiful here. OK?'

'Well, I—'

'Don't stand me up, Don. That'd be a big mistake. Believe me.'

Don did not like being told what to do or what not to do, especially not early in the morning by someone he had never met. He dressed and set off at once, in a mood of simmering anger, most of it directed at Fran for putting him in this situation.

It was only after the stiff ascent from Poldhu Cove to the clifftop, with a headache pounding away ever more aggressively behind his eyes, that Don considered a worrying point. French had telephoned directly after Don had walked out on to the verandah, as if he knew then he would be able to speak to him, as if he was actually watching for Don to show himself.

To his left, the sea stretched placidly to the horizon. The rising sun cast long shadows of him over the pink banks of thrift as he went. But his pace was slowing. Just what did French want with him? What exactly had he been sucked into?

47

He descended to Church Cove, where, at beach level, the tide appeared to have marooned the strange little church Blake had told him the previous evening was called St Wingwall's or some such – his recollection was hazy on the point. Ahead, beyond a farmyard, at the end of the lane they had driven down from the Halzephron, was the car park where he had left the MG. And there she was, waiting patiently for him.

But she was not alone. A black, four-wheel-drive giant had pulled in next to her. 'Might've known,' he breathlessly grumbled. No good could come of consorting with 4WD drivers, in his opinion. But it did not appear he had much choice in the matter.

As he entered the car park, stepping gingerly over the cattle grid, the driver of the 4WD cast him a leery glance. The man was bearded and slab-faced, with something in his eyes that was deeply worrying. He looked at Don as a bear might look at a fish flapping on a riverbank.

Then the passenger door of the car opened and another man climbed out. He was an altogether slighter figure, dressed in sports coat, jeans and workman's boots, though the windcheater looked expensively soft and the boots had very obviously never been near a serious place of work. His face was narrow, his eyes small and close-set, his hair thin and straw-coloured.

'Hi, Don,' he said, extending a hand. 'I'm Amos French.'

Don had no wish to shake the man's hand, but found himself doing so. Being addressed by his Christian name was in no way reassuring. 'Morning,' he said guardedly.

'And a grand one it is.' French took a deep breath. 'The air's a deal sweeter here.'

'Sweeter than where?'

French smiled. He had the dazzling white teeth of most Americans, which did nothing to make him look less predatory. 'We drove down from London yesterday. Like you.'

A memory stirred. 'Did I see your car at Exeter Services?'

'Maybe.'

'You followed me.'

'Don't take it personally. We followed Mrs Revell. Then we followed you.'

'Have you been watching the house?'

'Harkness's place, you mean? Wortalleth West?'

'The owner's name isn't Harkness.'

'No? Well, Harkness is a slippery one where legal title's concerned. But he's the owner, according to my informants.'

'They're mistaken.'

French crooked his neck and looked at Don sideways. 'You're some kinda realtor, right?'

'I'm an estate agent. Here to value the house prior to sale by the rightful owner. I've had no dealings with anyone called Harkness.'

'But you must've heard of Jack Harkness. Pharmaceuticals billionaire. Elixtris. You'll have seen the ads. And the news coverage of his extradition case.' French's head swivelled back upright. 'Whose name has he put on the deeds, Don?'

'That's none of your business.'

'Oh, but it is. My business is finding out where Harkness has hidden the money he stole from my employers. And this very stylish bolthole I didn't previously know he possessed could help me do that.'

'You work for Quintagler Industries?'

'You see? You *do* know about Harkness, Don. You may as well drop the pretence. To answer your question, I don't work for Quintagler. Not directly, anyhow. And you, of course, don't work for Mendez Chinnery, do you?

Your LinkedIn profile needs updating about your sudden departure to become . . . what shall we call it? Freelance?'

'What do you want with me?'

'I want us to help each other.' French leant back against the wing of the MG. 'I need information. You need money, I'd hazard a guess. Unemployment at your time of life can be an uncomfortable experience. Whatever Mrs Revell's paying you I'll more than double for anything you can dig up about where Harkness has squirrelled away the money.'

'Assuming he really has squirrelled it away.'

'Yeah. Assuming that. But, believe me, my employers wouldn't have hired me if they weren't seriously out of pocket. I don't come cheap.'

'What about your friend?' Don nodded towards the sullenly staring driver of the 4WD.

'Zlenko? Oh, he's on my payroll. There are some things I don't do personally. Negotiation's my forte. Whereas Zlenko . . . isn't a negotiator.'

'I'll bet.'

'Who owns the house – legally?'

'That's confidential information.'

'Confidential. But not hard to come by. Or to guess at. The soon-to-be-ex-wife, maybe?'

'All right. Yes. Mona Jackson.'

'Ah. She's already dropped his name, has she? I suppose it's not an asset any more.'

'It's her house. She wants to sell it. There's nothing more I can tell you.'

'That's entirely possible. We went through the place last night. While you were out boozing with the girl.'

'*What?*'

'Didn't you notice?'

The answer to that was no. Don had noticed nothing

50

amiss. Although it was also true he had not been in much of a state to.

'You weren't meant to, of course. We take pride in our work, Zlenko and me. Anyhow, I may as well tell you we drew a blank. Nothing. Zilch. Not a damn thing. Majorly disappointing, I have to say. Which I suppose is why we're having this conversation, you and me.'

'If you found nothing, what makes you think I can do any better?'

'Incentivization. An important consideration in my line of work. You see, if you can't help us, or won't, we'll have to look elsewhere. The girl will inevitably enter the frame.'

'Leave her out of this. She's just a housekeeper. Not even that. A cleaner.'

'Maybe. Maybe not. Either way, you seem to be on good terms with her. Also, according to Zlenko, with Mrs Revell. I'd have to waste time on introductions. Whereas you can tap both of them on my behalf. But if you're not willing to . . . I'll have to deal with them directly. That's something you might want to avoid, if you have their best interests at heart.'

'The girl knows nothing.' Don was surprised to find himself trying so hard to protect Blake. 'And Mrs Revell is Mona Jackson's lawyer, not Harkness's.'

'Whether Blake's as ignorant as you say remains to be seen.' French smiled thinly. 'I do know her name, Don. Now, Frances Revell. Fran, as you call her. You and she were an item once, right?'

Don sighed. 'Sort of.'

'Excellent. That gives you something to work with. Thing is, we have reason to believe her loyalties may be divided. Mona's lawyer or not, she's also met Harkness a couple of times recently, in circumstances you could call covert if you were of a suspicious frame of mind.'

'*What?*'

'Let me lay this on the line for you, Don. I'll pay handsomely for information pointing me towards where he's stashed the cash. Exactly how handsomely will depend on the value and accuracy of the information. How, where or from whom you get it is your affair, although I'll expect to be kept apprised of progress. As a bonus, Blake and Fran will hear nothing from me. I'm giving you the opportunity to earn some money – maybe a lot of money – by charming or wheedling out of them – or otherwise learning – what I need to know. It's a time-limited opportunity, naturally. I can spare you a week. I have other leads to follow up in the interim, but if, after that week, you've got nothing for me, well, then I'll have to try a more forceful approach, if you catch my drift.'

Don caught it. And catching it left him confronting a problem he had little hope of solving. This was where accepting a favour from his ex-wife had led. He should have known better.

'So,' said French, 'are we in business?'

❖

I'm on my way back up the beach from the tideline – nothing worth collecting – when I hear the MG growling down the lane. I hear it, in fact, well before I see it, but I guess at once it's Don. He's come back from Church Cove, the long way round by road, through Gunwalloe and Cury. He must've got up much earlier than I expected.

He sees me as he takes the bend just before the bridge over the stream. I wave from the path between the dunes. He waves back and signals he'll pull into the car park on the other side of the lane.

He stops the car, gets out and walks across to join me. He

looks rough, unshaven and probably hungover. But he manages a smile.

'How you doing this morning, Don?' I ask brightly. I feel fine – just as long as I don't think about the future, even in the short term. Or the panic room, of course. I can tell myself a hundred times there can't be anyone inside. But still I know there might be, even so. There might be – and, at any moment, they could come out.

'Fair to middling.'

'What are your plans?'

'Strictly speaking, I should ask what yours are.'

'You'd better tell me. I mean, how long can I persuade you to persuade Fran to let me stay here?'

'Fran? Did I mention her name?'

'You did.'

Don rubs his brow and eyes. 'You got any paracetamol back at the house?'

I suspect he technically knows the answer to that question. But maybe he's forgotten. 'No. I'm not that into pharmaceuticals.'

Don smiles ruefully. 'If everyone was like you, Harkness would be penniless.'

I shrug. 'I guess so.'

'Can we sit down?'

There are several picnic tables set out for use by customers of the beach café, which is still several hours away from opening. We walk over and sit down at one.

Don squints towards the sea. 'Time was this would have been the perfect moment for a cigarette,' he muses.

'But you've given up?'

'Feels like it gave me up.' He rasps his hand round his chin. 'Still, you've got to know when to quit something.'

'Are we still talking about smoking?'

'No.' He looks directly at me. 'You should leave Wortalleth West, Blake. As soon as you can.'

'Why the rush? No madman with an axe came out of the panic room during the night, did he?' I'm trying to make light of the threat the panic room poses. I want Don to make light of it too.

He grins. 'Not that I recall.'

'I've got workshop space and a nice flat. It's a lot to walk out on.'

'Still, you should. Not just to help me sell the house. For your own safety.'

'You think it's not safe?' Why might he think that? Has something happened he's not telling me about?

'Well, it might not be. I mean, all this money Harkness is supposed to have stolen. People could come looking . . . for what they can get.'

'But Wortalleth West isn't his, is it?'

'They wouldn't necessarily care about that.'

'What sort of people are you talking about?'

'I don't know.' Don spreads his hands, but somehow I don't buy his ignorance. Somehow, I get the feeling he does know. 'I just don't think you should stick around to find out.'

'I've nowhere to go.'

'Where were you living before?'

'Helston. I was live-in housekeeper to a guy called Glasson. Retired accountant. In poor health.'

'Why'd you leave?'

'His daughter took against me.' I'm not in a hurry to tell Don why she took against me, though I expect him to ask.

And he does. 'What was the problem?'

'Personality clash.' And then some. What really bugged Muriel, as far as I could tell, was that I cared more about her family than she did.

'She lives with her father?'

54

'No. Bristol. She doesn't come down much. Well, she didn't while I was there. Even so, she didn't like the idea of help living in. Not when that help was me, anyway.'

'How did her father feel about you leaving?'

'He didn't want me to go.'

'And when was this?'

'Oh, round the turn of the year. She came down for Christmas. Didn't like how I was doing things.'

'But Glasson – the man you actually worked for – did?'

'Yeah. He and I got on just fine.'

'Maybe you could go back there.'

'Doubt it.'

'What if I put in a word?'

He's offering to act as a go-between. I'm surprised. I mean, I know he wants to help me. But this is going the extra mile and then some. Ordinarily, I'd tell him to stop interfering. But maybe interfering is just what I need him to do at the moment. 'You'd speak to Andrew – Mr Glasson – about re-hiring me?'

'Why not? It's worth a try, isn't it? If he liked having you there, he probably misses you. If I explain you'll soon be homeless, well, he might volunteer to take you in and to hell with what his daughter thinks. Then he'll get his favourite housekeeper back and you'd have somewhere to live. Would that be so bad?'

'No. I liked it there. But . . .' Why is Don so anxious to move me out? To earn his fee from Fran, obviously. But there seems to be more to it. 'Nothing did happen in the night, did it?' I wouldn't have slept well so close to the panic room, that's for sure.

'Of course not.' He smiles innocently. 'I slept like a baby. Well, a baby whose milk had been spiked, anyway.'

'So, where'd you get this idea about debt collectors coming to call?'

'I just think you can't be too careful, Blake. Harkness is obviously mixed up in some murky business. Best to detach yourself from him completely.'

'Plus getting rid of me makes Fran happy.'

'I'm thinking of you, not her.' Strangely, I believe him. He is thinking of me. Which isn't necessarily reassuring. 'What have you got to lose by letting me try to persuade Glasson to take you in?'

I shrug. 'Nothing, I s'pose.' I've had no contact with Andrew since I left his house on New Year's Eve. That's more than five months ago. He won't be expecting to hear from me again. I don't believe he's got the nerve to defy Muriel. If I'm right, Don will just be wasting his time. But maybe it's easier to let him do that than try to stop him. And Don wasting his time gains time for me. 'I thought you'd be heading back to London today.'

'Let's see how it goes.'

'All right, Don.' I still wish I'd been able to help Andrew more than I did. I'm not going to tell Don about that, though. I just wonder if Andrew will. 'Let's do that.'

✠

The Glasson house was a sizeable art deco villa on the main road into Helston. Don approached the front door unsure about what he might gain from the visit. It was quite possible Glasson was content with the housekeeping arrangements his daughter had made for him since Blake's departure. Fran was certain to have envisaged a more direct approach to the problem Blake represented than trying to find her a job elsewhere.

But the problem now went beyond her living at Wortalleth West. His encounter with French had left Don genuinely worried for her. He had checked the house for signs of intrusion and had found almost none. He might have been able to persuade himself French had lied about searching it but for the fact that the filing cabinet in the study was unlocked now, where before it had definitely been locked. The ability of French and his silent henchman, Zlenko, to come and go without leaving any other trace of their presence only increased the threat they posed.

Don felt protective towards Blake. The best thing he could do for her was to find somewhere else for her to live. And fast. That would also keep Fran happy and secure payment of his fee. Blake would be out of French's orbit. Without knowing she had ever been in it. Don could head back to London, deliver the property particulars and drop out of the picture. He meant to warn Fran to do the same herself, though he doubted she would take his advice.

There was an intercom by the doorbell of the house. When Don pressed the bell nothing happened for quite a while. He was about to press it again when the intercom crackled into life.

'Yes?' came a reedy voice.

'Mr Glasson?'

'Yes. What . . . can I do for you?'

'I wonder if I could have a word with you, Mr Glasson. My name's Challenor. Don Challenor. I'm here on behalf of your former employee, Blake.'

'Blake?'

'Yes. You remember her, I'm sure.'

'What do you . . .' The voice tailed away, then resumed. 'What is it . . . you want?'

'A chat, that's all. To see if you can help Blake in any way.'

There was a lengthy pause, during which Don thought he could hear laboured breathing. Then: 'Come round the back.'

Don set off, following a path that led, via a gate in a wooden fence, to an overgrown rear garden. Turning the corner of the house, he came to a conservatory.

Several of the windows were open. At one of them, leaning heavily against the sill, stood a thin, balding, hollow-cheeked man Don would have put in his seventies. He was wearing baggy beige trousers, a grey cardigan and a checked shirt, the collar of which looked far too big for his wizened neck. His face was gaunt and pale, his eyes rheumy and magnified by large-lensed glasses. There was a dusting of white stubble on his chin. Round his neck, on separate cords, hung a nebulizer and a mobile phone.

'Good morning,' said Don as he approached the window.

'Who did you say you were?' Glasson asked breathlessly.

'Don Challenor.' Don held out his hand, but Glasson made no effort to reach through the window and shake it.

'How do you know Blake?'

'Bit of a long story. Mind if I come in?'

Glasson's eyes flickered anxiously, though whether Don was the cause of his anxiety was unclear. 'I'd like to know . . . what you are to Blake, Mr Challenor.'

'Nothing, really. I'm an estate agent.' Don flourished his Mendez Chinnery card and offered it to Glasson, who took it warily. 'We're selling the house she currently lives in, which means she'll soon be homeless. She told me she used to work for you on a live-in basis. I just wondered . . . if there was any chance . . .'

'I could take in . . . your sitting tenant?'

'I'm concerned for her welfare. I thought you might be too.'

'Blake's a good girl,' Glasson said, nodding weakly. 'I'd like to help her.'

'There you are, then.'

'But I can't.'

'Are you sure about that?'

'Where is she . . . now?'

'A house near Mullion. I'm acting on behalf of the absentee owner.'

'She used to do some cleaning . . . at Wortalleth West.'

'That's the place.'

'She shouldn't be there.'

'No?'

'Will you be seeing her . . . when you leave here?'

'Yes. I'm going straight back there.'

Glasson gave another few weary nods. 'That's good,' he said, for no obvious reason. 'All right. Come in. It's open.' He flapped his hand towards the door into the conservatory.

A wall of heat struck Don as he entered. Numerous large-fronded plants in giant pots added a heaviness to the air. Glasson half fell into a cushioned wicker chair. The exertion left him needing several sucks on his nebulizer before he could manage to invite Don to sit down.

Glasson appeared marginally revived by the nebulizer. 'Do you normally . . . go to this trouble . . . for a sitting tenant, Mr Challenor?' he asked.

'No. Blake's a bit of a special case.'

'Yes,' Glasson acknowledged. 'She is.'

'She told me you didn't want to lose her services.'

'No. But my daughter . . .' Glasson frowned. 'Has Blake told you Muriel . . . insisted she leave?'

'Well, she said she and . . . Muriel . . . didn't get on.'

'"Didn't get on"? No. They certainly didn't. But . . .' Glasson's focus shifted to Don from somewhere past his left shoulder. 'I can't take her back, Mr Challenor, much . . . much as I'd like to. Muriel simply . . .'

'Does she have to know? I mean, how often does she

59

come to see you? Even a temporary arrangement would be better for Blake than nothing.'

'She could have come herself.'

Don smiled. 'I think she's reluctant to ask for help.'

Now Glasson also smiled, apparently at some irony he detected in what Don had said. 'More likely, Mr Challenor, she fears I've reflected on letting her put me in touch with . . . the Fry woman . . . and that I've concluded I'm better off without her.'

'The Fry woman?'

'Hasn't Blake told you about . . . Wynsum Fry?'

'No. Who's she?'

'A local . . . fortune-teller. A witch, maybe?' Glasson shook his head, as if in disbelief. 'You don't imagine . . . such people exist . . . in the twenty-first century . . . until you learn they do.'

'Blake put you in touch with a fortune-teller?'

'She really hasn't told you?'

'Hasn't told me what?'

'I'm surprised . . . she let you come here without . . .' Glasson never finished the sentence. He frowned thoughtfully, then said, 'Maybe she thought . . . I wouldn't mention it. And maybe I wouldn't have, but for . . .' He stared into the middle distance again.

'What are you trying to say, Mr Glasson?' Don prompted.

Glasson smiled wanly. He pointed to a small silver-framed photograph standing on the glass-topped wicker table between them. 'That picture's faded rather . . . in the sun . . . but I like to have it out here . . . to look at when I want.'

Don sensed he was being invited to look at the picture as well. It showed two fair-haired girls in their early teens, similar enough in appearance to be sisters. They were smiling toothily at the camera. One was slightly taller and older-looking. The younger-looking one was more obviously attractive, with high-set cheekbones and large, immersive eyes.

'Muriel's on the left,' said Glasson. 'That's Jane . . . on the right.'

'Did Jane have an opinion about Blake working for you?'

'No one's seen Jane . . . no one I know of, anyway . . . for the past twenty-two years, Mr Challenor. She disappeared in June 1996.'

'God. I'm sorry to hear that. When you say disappeared . . .'

'Vanished, if you prefer.' Glasson pursed his lips pensively. 'Without a trace.'

'How? I mean, under what circumstances?'

'She'd finished her second year at Cambridge. She and a friend . . . took the train down to London together at the end of term. They parted at King's Cross station. Jane said she was taking . . . the Tube to Paddington to catch the train to Cornwall. I drove up to Camborne to meet her . . . but she wasn't on board. As far as we knew . . . she was never on board. At the time, I thought it was just a misunderstanding, that she'd be . . . on a later train. But she wasn't. I still thought we'd find her. And later I thought at least we'd learn at some point what had become of her.' Glasson shook his head dismally. 'It killed her mother . . . the not knowing. Not officially, of course. But it did.'

'What has this to do with Blake . . . and Wynsum Fry?'

'We talked about Jane quite a lot . . . Blake and I. She was very . . . sympathetic. One day . . . one day she suggested I consult a . . . a seer, let's call her . . . to see if she could tell me at least . . . if Jane was still alive. I thought about it for quite a while. Then I said . . . yes. Yes. I wanted certainty. I didn't know if this woman . . . could give it to me. In fact, I assumed . . . I assumed I'd realize she was a charlatan as soon as I met her. But . . .'

'You didn't?'

'She has a way with her. A routine, probably. A bag of tricks. Somehow . . . she makes you believe her.'

'And what did she tell you?'

'She had me shuffle a pack of cards. Ordinary playing cards, not Tarot. Then I had to cut the pack and deal out twelve cards, face down. She turned them over . . . in some sequence I can't quite . . . Anyway, the remarkable thing was . . . they were all red, hearts or diamonds, bar one. That was good . . . she said. Red was life. It meant . . . Jane was alive.'

'You were convinced by that?'

'At the time . . .' Glasson grimaced. 'At the time . . . I allowed myself to be convinced. It's difficult not to clutch at straws in such circumstances . . . believe me.'

'I do.'

'I told Muriel. That was my mistake. She was furious. I'm not sure why. I think she'd convinced herself Jane was dead . . . and didn't welcome any suggestions to the contrary. To do her justice, I think she was also afraid Fry . . . meant to exploit me in some way. Which is quite possible, of course. She came down here . . . and read me the riot act. No further contact with Fry . . . and Blake to be given her marching orders.' He sighed. 'Muriel's all I have left, Mr Challenor. I complied. I did what I had to do . . . to appease her. Naturally, Blake was upset. But she understood. I have a rota of young women who come in to help me now. Muriel organized it. They're very pleasant. Very . . . efficient.'

'But they're not Blake.'

'Indeed they're not.' Glasson's expression suggested he

genuinely missed her companionship. 'Alas, I can't take her back, even so.'

'Perhaps just for a few weeks?'

'What purpose would that serve?'

'In an emergency, I meant.'

Glasson frowned in puzzlement. 'What form of emergency?'

Don did not know how to answer. He spread his hands helplessly. 'I'm not sure. But . . . she may need your help . . . in unforeseeable circumstances.'

'Well, I'll . . . do what I can.' Glasson was still clearly puzzled. 'But—'

'Thanks for being so frank with me, Mr Glasson.' Don made to rise. He reckoned it was best to leave before his host could withdraw the offer of assistance Don had wheedled out of him. 'I won't take up any more of your time.'

'Wait a moment . . . if you will.' Glasson signalled feebly for Don to sit back down. 'There's something I want you to tell Blake. Something . . . I think will interest her. Concerning . . . Jane.'

'Oh yes?'

'Tell her to look up Holly Walsh on Facebook. Holly M. C. Walsh.'

'Who's she?'

'Blake will know. If she wants to . . . she'll explain. I've probably . . . said enough.'

'Well, I'll certainly tell her.' Don stood up again. 'Your daughter's disappearance must have been hard for you to bear, Mr Glasson.'

'You have children?'

'No.'

Glasson nodded grimly. 'Harder than you can possibly imagine.'

'Have you any idea at all what happened?'

'None whatever. To this day.'

'Well, I'm sorry. Truly.' As Don moved to the door, a question occurred to him. He looked back at Glasson. 'The cards were all red suits bar one, you said.'

'That's right.'

'What was the odd one out?'

Something close to a smile twitched at the corners of Glasson's mouth as he replied. 'The king of spades.'

⁕

I really rate Glenys. She always works hard, despite the fact no one's monitoring her, least of all Harkness. He pays her – and me via her – on the first of every month. Ironic, considering he apparently doesn't actually own the place any more – or come down to get the benefit of the garden. But payment's payment.

She's thin and sinewy, with a weather-tanned face and a dazzling smile you don't see very often. She cuts her own hair and I only ever see her in jeans and a woolly in winter and T-shirt and denim shorts in summer. She's no glamour queen. But she's genuine.

I go out to her in the garden as soon as she arrives. Don's already left on his mission to Helston, so there's nothing to tell her anything unusual's going on. But I want to break the news to her before there's any chance of her finding out some other way.

She takes it as I expected, deadpan, philosophically. 'Sorry for you, Blake,' she says. 'Where'll you go?'

I shrug. 'Dunno.'

'Selling this place'll take months, anyhow. Long as Harkness keeps paying, I'll keep tending the plants. And you'll have plenty of time to look around for somewhere else to live.'

'They want me gone right away.'

'Yeah? Well, wanting's not the same as having.'

'I'm not going to get into a fight with the wife's lawyer.'

'Don't suppose you are.' She's picked up the fact that I'm running away from something. She's never said so, of course. That's not her way. 'If it comes to it, I can put you up for a while.'

It's a generous offer, delivered in typical throwaway Glenys fashion, while she's digging out a weed. She lives in St Keverne. I've never been to her home. Somehow, I suspect it's tiny. And she's used to solitude. I get that. She wouldn't want me there. But she'd make it work. 'Thanks, Glenys,' I say, making eye contact to let her know I really do appreciate it. 'I'll sort something out.'

'Just in case you don't . . .'

'You're an angel.'

'In heavy disguise if I am.' She looks up at the sound of a car engine. A vehicle's coming up the drive. 'Who's this, then?'

It's far too soon for Don to be back. And I already know the sound of his MG. It's not a car at all, in fact, but a white van with a company name and a Plymouth phone number on the side.

'Expecting someone?' asks Glenys.

'No. I'll see what they want.'

I nod and walk round to the front of the house, where the van's pulled up. Some young guy in working trousers and shirt with a company logo gets out as I approach. I register the words *Home Security Electronics* on the door behind him as he smiles cautiously at me. He's got a shaven head and several tattoos, but cornflower-blue eyes and, as it turns out, an oddly gentle voice. 'Mr Challenor about?' he asks.

'No. What can I do for you?'

'Dale. Home Security Electronics.' He waggles some photo-ID at me. 'Here about a problem with a panic room. So, are you, like . . . the lady of the house?'

He grins as he says it, acknowledging how absurd it sounds. 'I live here, yeah.'

'And Mr Challenor?'

'He doesn't live here.'

Dale scratches the stubble on his head. 'OK. Look, my boss had a call from some lawyer in London, like, big emergency, y'know? That's why I'm here. There's a panic room in the house, right?'

'Maybe.'

'Well, either there is or there isn't.'

'It's not as simple as that.'

More scratching. 'I've come all the way from Plymouth. D'you want me to take a look at . . . whatever the problem is . . . or not?'

I let him suffer a bit longer. Then I say, 'S'pose you may as well.'

I show him the steel wall in the master dressing-room closet, though getting that far involves him gawping around a lot and murmuring 'Jesus, what a place' several times. I explain Don's calculation that there's a two-floor void we can only assume is a panic room or some other secure storage space. Dale presses his hand against various parts of the steel, taps nearby walls and fires up his laptop. He goes up into the attic, which involves folding down a ladder from inside the access hatch. I follow him out of curiosity – I've never been up there before – but there's nothing to see except rafters, felt and insulation. Dale prowls around with some kind of meter, then retreats.

'This is weird,' he says when we're both back down. We descend to the study, where he does some more wall-tapping. Then he asks if there's a basement. I take him down there. He goes into the gym. Yet more wall-tapping and fiddling with his laptop. We go upstairs again, then down to the hall, where he squints at the meter's readings (without explaining what they're readings *of*), scratches his head and announces, 'This is *seriously* weird.'

'What d'you mean?' I ask.

'D'you know if there's actually a panic room or not?'

'No. I didn't notice anything until Don – Mr Challenor – pointed it out to me.'

'See, the steel barrier could be a sliding door, closed and locked from the inside. Then there'd be a two-floor chamber inside. But I can't track any electrics or air supply. There should be ducted cables and pipes independent from the rest of the system. Plus a separate phone line. If they're there, they're well shielded, that's all I can say.'

'Don reckons the door must be faulty. Or someone triggered it to close and lock before jumping out.'

'There should be a fail-safe so you can't do that. And a fault should work the same way, so the room's non-functional but accessible.' That doesn't sound good. That actually sounds like it's conceivable there really is someone in there. 'When was the house built?'

'Late nineties, I think.'

'Who was the builder?'

'Dunno.'

Dale does some more frowning – and tapping at the laptop, cradled in his serpent-tattooed arms. 'I can't seem to log on to our back-catalogue site.'

'You won't get a signal here.'

'Great.' He closes the laptop with a peevish clunk. 'Look, you want the bottom line?'

'Sure. I'll pass on what you say to Don.'

'OK. I'll report back to my boss. If that is a panic room, my first thought would be someone's shut themselves inside. But that's crazy, right? I mean, you'd know if they had.'

''Course.' A shiver runs through me despite the absurdity of the idea. 'That *is* crazy.'

'See, there'll be a separate phone line, so they could call for help if somehow they were trapped. That's if they couldn't, well, just open the door and walk out. I mean, there'll be cameras too, giving them a view of selected rooms. So there'd be no reason ... But there's no one in there, right?'

'Definitely not.' And it is definite, in the sane world I want to believe I live in. 100 per cent. Or maybe just 99. Which leaves a 1 per cent chance someone could be watching us at this very moment from inside.

'Otherwise it's some kind of fault that doesn't make any sense.'

'How would you deal with that?'

'Christ knows.' Dale puffs out his cheeks. I think he's thinking. 'If you could find the dedicated power supply, you could cut it. But there'll be battery back-up. That could have capacity for, like, months. So ...'

'If that is a door, Dale, how d'you open it?' It's time, I feel, to put the question.

'Don't see as you could ... without drilling through. And if it is a panic room, the steel'll likely be a hundred and fifty mil. That's a big job. You'd need some serious kit.' He rolls his eyes.

'Any other suggestions?'

Dale ponders, then slowly shakes his head. 'No. I, er ...' He looks at me apologetically. ''Fraid not.'

No suggestions. After Dale's gone, I go back and look at the steel wall behind the wardrobe mirror. I think about the cameras he said would feed images to anyone inside of various rooms in the house – maybe of me, standing there, staring helplessly at some hidden lens.

For me, there can't be a much worse feeling than being watched. Spied on. My every move secretly monitored. It makes me shudder. In fact, it'll scare the shit out of me if I let it. There's that moment when the hairs go up on the back of your neck because you think there's someone behind you. Then you turn and it's OK. There's no one there. But what if there *is* someone there? What if I turn round and someone's come out of the panic room and is just standing there, behind me? What then? The torture is not knowing if or when something's going to happen.

It can't be true, I tell myself. There can't really be anyone inside. Can there?

When I leave, I don't turn my back until I'm out of the room. I want to run. But I don't. I won't let the house do that to me. I walk. With my heart beating like a tom-tom.

⁘

Don sat in the MG, just round the corner from Andrew Glasson's house. His phone worked perfectly in Helston and there, on the screen in front of him, were blogs from Holly Walsh to her Facebook followers.

She suffered from multiple sclerosis. She lived somewhere in Hampshire. She described herself as a forty-something. There were references to a *'loving partner'* called Anna. The subject of the blogs was her battle against the disease, greatly aided, apparently, by a new experimental drug she had dubbed *'the Wonderpill'*. It was astronomically expensive and she could only afford it thanks to the generosity of an anonymous benefactor she often mentioned. *'Huge gratitude, as ever, to my secret saviour, whoever you are. I don't know why you've done this for me, but thank you from the bottom of my heart. The symptoms are under control. I've got my life back. That's down to you and no one else!'*

Don could see nothing in the blogs to explain why Glasson had drawn his attention to Holly Walsh. He would have to ask Blake and see if it made any sense to her.

Before going back to Wortalleth West to report the limited success of his pleadings with Glasson, however, he had more business to attend to in Helston. He drove into the centre and parked, then set off on foot.

His destination was an estate agent's listed in his copy of the *West Briton*: Pawley & Co, Coinagehall Street, Helston, established 1933. They sounded like the kind of people who would know as much as there was to know about Lizard property. And Don needed a friendly chat, agent to agent.

The town was busier with traffic than people, the buildings grey monuments to a past age, cast in a gaunt, unforgiving light by the strident sunlight. Pawley & Co's offices were just beyond the Methodist chapel. Don turned on the charm with the easily charmable receptionist and was rewarded with the promise of a few minutes of 'young Mr Pawley's' time when he returned from a valuation in Porthleven, ETA 2.30.

'Right, then,' said Don brightly. 'I'll call back after lunch.'

A few doors further down the street, Don came to the Blue Anchor, a thatch-roofed, stone-floored tavern that looked centuries old. It offered, according to a sign, Spingo ales brewed on the premises. In need of a hair-of-the-dog pint (or two) to see off the last of the hangover, Don hesitated for all of about two seconds before going in.

Dale tried to phone his boss in Plymouth from the driveway of Wortalleth West, but the lack of a signal frustrated him. Eventually, he gave up and drove into Mullion, where he pulled into the car park opposite the church and tried again.

He paid no attention to the dusty black 4WD that pulled into a nearby bay, just as he had given no thought to its reflection in his rear-view mirror as he drove into the village.

French and Zlenko climbed out of the 4WD and approached Dale's van with no sign of haste. But what happened next unfolded, from Dale's point of view, with bewildering speed. French pressed a button on the jammer in his pocket, cutting off the phone call. Zlenko opened the driver's door and pulled the key out of the ignition as French opened the passenger door and hopped in beside Dale.

'Hi,' he said. 'Got time for a little *conversazione*?'

Dale's mouth opened. But no words emerged.

French smiled. 'I'll take that as a yes.'

Don retreated to the empty rear bar of the Blue Anchor, where he tried not to hurry his pint of IPA while contemplating the period bric-a-brac and the wisdom of ordering a pasty, the only food that appeared to be on offer.

Thoughts of food were banished, however, by an overheard remark from the front bar. 'What'll you have, Wynsum?'

Wynsum was an unusual name. Don doubted there were two of them in town. He craned up from his seat to see what she looked like.

Wynsum Fry, for Don did not doubt it was her, was a short, barrel-shaped, red-faced woman with close-cropped grey hair. She had small, darting eyes, an oddly childlike button nose and a thin-lipped, crooked mouth. She was not smiling as she paid for her half of still cider. Nor looking at the barman as she handed him the money. Her eyes met Don's directly. And in that instant he profoundly wished they had not.

A few moments later, Fry walked into the rear bar. Beneath a loose, shapeless brown coat, she was wearing a red sweater and calf-length grey skirt. Her legs were bare, displaying unsightly varicose veins and mottled skin. On her feet she wore grubby grey trainers. All in all, she should have looked merely old and shabby, but Don was uncomfortably aware of a cold, piercing light gleaming in her blue-green eyes.

'Do I know 'ee?' she asked.

'I don't think so,' Don replied, smiling uneasily.

'You looked at me as if you knowed me.'

'Sorry. A mistake.' Yes, he thought. It was definitely a mistake.

'Wynsum Fry.' She plonked her cider down on the table he was sitting at and offered him her hand, on which the joints stood proud.

A moment passed. Her hand remained extended. Eventually, feeling shamed into it, Don reached out and shook it. Fry's other hand closed over his as he did so. The sensation was oddly and disturbingly intimate.

'Sure you don't know me?'

'I really—'

'Only I'm not a good person to lie to.' She smiled. 'Not good by a long stretch.' Then, at last, she released Don's hand.

'I'm quite sure we've never met.'

'Ah, well, meetin' and knowin' are two different things.' She sat down opposite him and took a gulp of cider. 'What's your name, then?'

'Does it matter?'

'Might do.'

72

'More likely not. I'm just passing through.'

'You'm not from these parts. I can see that. Down from Lon'on, is it?'

'Er, yes.'

'What line o' business? No, don't tell me. I'll guess.' She gazed at him with theatrical thoughtfulness. ''State agent.'

She was playing a game and enjoying it. Don knew that. The problem, short of standing up and walking out, was how to avoid being drawn into playing it as well. 'You must've seen me come out of Pawley's offices.'

'Oh, you bin in there. That settles it, then. Question is, what's a Lon'on 'state agent doin' down 'ere? Not many 'ouses in 'Elston likely to interest your clients. We'm all poor as church mice, Mr, er . . . What'd you say your name was?'

'I didn't.'

'Secret, is it?'

'No.'

'You'll feel better when you tell me.'

Don greatly doubted that. But further refusal only seemed likely to provoke the woman. 'Challenor,' he said neutrally.

'There. Not so 'ard, was it?' Her yellow-toothed smile was not a cheering sight. 'You'll be down 'bout some big, posh place. Out at the coast, like as not. Want me to guess which one?'

'Not particularly.' Don knew she would anyway. And he felt he also knew she would guess correctly.

'Wortalleth West.'

'Well, I can't confirm that . . . Miss Fry. Client confidentiality. I'm sure you understand.'

'Oh, I understands right 'nough. You'm not to worry on that score, Mr Challenor.' She took another swallow of cider. 'Like our ale, do 'ee?'

73

'It's very good.' He drank some.

'When'd you come down 'ere, then?'

'Yesterday.' Suddenly it felt to Don as if he had arrived much longer ago.

'Seems much longer ago, I bet.'

He drank some more beer. 'No. It seems just as long as it is.'

She cocked her head as she looked at him. 'Not gone 'cording to plan, 'as it? Like you've stepped into clear water and invisible tendrils 'ave wrapped theirselves round your feet.'

'I don't know what you're talking about.' But he did, of course. He knew exactly.

'I could 'elp 'ee.'

'I doubt it.'

'Everyone doubts. Till they see what I do.'

'And what precisely is that?' He tried to stare her down, in which he soon realized he could not hope to succeed.

From an inside pocket of her coat she took a pack of cards, held together with a pair of rubber bands, one black, one red. She snapped the bands off, looped them round her wrist and laid the pack on the table. 'I'll scry the cards for 'ee. Shuffle, split and deal out twelve. People pay me to do this. I'll give it 'ee for free.'

'No thanks.'

'You'm turning me down?' She manufactured an expression of childlike disappointment.

'Sorry. I don't believe in this kind of . . .'

'Mumbo-jumbo?'

'If you like.'

'Cartomancy. That's the dictionary def'nition.'

'I still don't believe in it.'

'Sure?'

'Yes.' He engaged her eye to eye. 'I'm sure.'

She smiled at him and closed her thumb and forefinger round the pack of cards. 'Last chance.'

'I'll pass, thanks.'

'Your loss.'

'I'll risk it.'

'Please yourself.' She picked up the cards, adroitly wound the rubber bands round them and slipped the pack back in her pocket.

'I must be going.' Don drained his glass and rose from his chair. There could be no question of ordering a pasty now. All he wanted was to be out of the pub and away from Wynsum Fry.

She gazed intently up at him. 'You go careful, Mr Challenor. I reckon you need to.'

Don left telling himself not to be taken in by anything the old witch had said. But her parting words stayed with him as he reached the brightness of the street. And the sunlight did not dispel them.

✤

I couldn't settle to anything after Dale left. I kept thinking about the panic room. I kept wondering what I might be in the middle of. Wortalleth West seems a different place now: watchful, secretive, ominous. Like something's just waiting to happen – something bad. Maybe I really should leave. I promised myself I'd never run from anything again when I left Birmingham. I don't like running. But . . .

When Glenys says she's off, I ask if she's going via Helston. I claim I need a few things from Sainsbury's. She says she's going home, but doesn't mind a detour to drop me off. I can take the bus back.

It's an excuse, of course. The panic room has spooked me. I just want to be away from the house for a while. I think

Glenys senses that, though she says nothing. She doesn't ask anything about Dale's visit and I don't tell her anything either. She's shrewd enough to know I'll talk if I want to and not if I don't. I can imagine confiding in her about a lot of things when I'm ready. And I may be readier sooner than I thought.

I climb into her pick-up and off we go, the quick way to the main road, through Mullion. She smokes one of her roll-ups. It smells more of nettles than tobacco. She doesn't talk. But the silence between us is almost comforting.

We meet the tail end of some crawling traffic near the winding stretch through Bonython Plantation. At the second bend, we see the reason. A van's gone off into the hedge. It's up at an angle in a deep ditch by an overgrown wall. There's a police car there, blocking our side of the road.

Glenys pitches her dog-end out of the window and breaks her silence. 'Looks like someone was going too fast,' she says with a sigh. 'Hold on, though.'

We both see it at the same time. The name and telephone number on the side of the van. It's the one Dale was driving.

Impulsively, I get out. Glenys doesn't have to slow. We're stopped dead now. I jog down to the police car. There are two policemen, one directing the traffic, the other peering at the van and talking into his radio.

The front of the van's a serious mess, with crumpled metalwork and a smashed windscreen. Broken glass crunches under my feet as I approach.

The policeman looks round at me and breaks off from his radio conversation. 'Watch out, my luvver,' he says. 'You shouldn't be here.'

'Sorry,' I say, treating him to my most winning smile. 'It's just . . . I think I might know the driver. His name's Dale.'

'Could be. In no state to identify himself, I'm afraid, when the ambulance took him away.' The policeman grimaces. He

76

regrets what he's just said. 'It might not be as bad as it looked,' he goes on, doing his best to sugar the pill. 'You'll need to speak to the hospital. They've taken him to Treliske.'

'Right. OK. How did it . . . I mean . . .'

'Looks like he was just going way too fast.' He shakes his head. 'God knows why.'

✛

Don's nerves settled slowly while he sat in the MG in the town centre car park in Helston, munching a supermarket sandwich and sipping a Coke. He was unsure why he had managed the encounter with Wynsum Fry so badly. Meeting her had to have been a coincidence, but he was unable to convince himself of that and could not deny she had got under his skin with considerable ease.

By the time he had finished the sandwich and crushed the empty Coke tin, his watch told him he should set off for his appointment with Pawley. 'Pull yourself together, man,' he said to himself as he climbed out of the car.

'Young' Mr Pawley, a spruce, sandy-haired fellow no more than a few years younger than Don, greeted him with surprising warmth and led him to his inner office, where a large Ordnance Survey map of the Lizard peninsula hung behind a desk, with pins stuck in it which Don took to represent properties Pawley's were marketing.

'Lovely day,' remarked Pawley, after Don had accepted an offer of coffee. 'How can I help?'

'I'm down here to value a house near Mullion,' Don explained, with an attempt at casualness. 'I'm working freelance at the moment and it's possible the agent the vendor appoints will want a co-agency arrangement with someone local.'

'You couldn't do better than us. What is the property?'

'Wortalleth West. Overlooking Poldhu Cove.'

'I know it. Extraordinary place. I should imagine London – even international – interest is quite likely.'

'I agree. But we shouldn't neglect the Cornish angle either.'

'And you thought of us. I'm flattered.'

The coffee arrived. The first few sips coursed revivingly through Don's system. 'D'you know when Wortalleth West was built, Mr Pawley?'

'Turn of the millennium, as I recall. And, please, it's Robin.'

'Who was the builder?'

Pawley furrowed his brow. 'Not local. An up-country firm. From London, probably.' He snapped his fingers. 'No. That's right. There was comment on it at the time. Well, complaints really. They didn't hire any local tradesmen. And the firm wasn't even British.'

'Not British?'

'German, I think. Well, you can imagine the resentment that caused. But . . . why d'you ask?'

'I'm having difficulty drawing up a complete specification. There are one or two . . . structural ambiguities.'

'Oh yes?' Pawley's curiosity was clearly aroused. 'That sounds intriguing.'

'Look, Robin, I'd be very grateful for any advice you can give me at this stage. How could I find out the original construction details?' They held the key to the mystery, Don felt sure. He could not persuade himself to leave the matter alone. If Fran wanted the job done, he would do it – his way.

'The council, perhaps. They must've been supplied with them as part of the planning application. But that's nearly twenty years ago, so whether they're still on file . . .' Pawley leant back in his chair, with his hands behind his head. 'One thing. The vendor. Would he be Jack Harkness? Only—'

'No, no. His wife – soon to be ex-wife – owns the property outright.'

'Does she indeed? That's interesting.'

'She's free to sell. And wants to do so as soon as possible.'

'In that case, do these . . . structural ambiguities . . . really matter? Any buyer would have the place surveyed. And if they didn't . . . *caveat emptor.*'

'I like to be thorough.'

'Admirable, I'm sure.' Pawley looked at Don as if it was also not entirely credible. Thoroughness was probably not something he associated with London agents. 'I'd be happy to delve into the particulars if we became contractually involved.'

'I'd hoped you'd say that. But I'm not sure I can just let the situation hang until you're officially on board.'

'Understood. I wouldn't encourage you to try your luck with the Planning Department on a Friday afternoon, though. I suppose . . .' Pawley stroked his chin thoughtfully. Don could see the co-agency potential of a multi-million-pound property gleaming in his eyes. 'I have a few contacts there. If you leave it with me, I'll see what I can find out. Not likely to have anything for you before early next week, I'm afraid, but . . .'

Don smiled gratefully. 'Anything you can dig up would be much appreciated.'

'Of course.' Further thoughtful chin-stroking suggested Pawley might yet have more to reveal. Don waited patiently. Then it came. 'The planning officer who'd have signed off on a project of that scale would have been Maurice Dyer. It's a pity he's retired. Otherwise . . .'

'But he lives locally?'

'No. Spain, I believe. And it's a long time ago, anyway. Fifteen years or more. Pleasant fellow, Maurice. Very accommodating. Someone told me he'd come into money. He certainly didn't wait to reach pension age.' Pawley smiled ruefully. 'Not like the rest of us will have to, eh?'

'No.' Don smiled back at him. So, Maurice Dyer, prematurely retired local government officer, had swanned off to Spain with money in his pocket. An inheritance – or a pay-off for a blind eye turned? Don knew which he would have laid his own money on. 'Not like the rest of us at all,' he concluded with a sigh.

Don checked his phone while walking back to the car park. A message had come in while he was talking to Pawley. It was from Fran.

'A progress report would be nice, Don. Are we still on track for Monday delivery of photos and particulars? You should've had a visit from a company that's the nearest I could find to a local expert on panic rooms. Home Security Electronics of Plymouth. And I need assurances that the cleaner's moving out. Bring me up to speed, please.'

Don was about to call Fran back, but something stopped him. There was nothing about the situation he was in that he liked. He suspected Harkness had gone to some lengths to conceal the design details for Wortalleth West. French and Zlenko posed a real threat. And he was still disquieted by his encounter with Wynsum Fry.

As he drove out of the car park and headed for the main road, a tempting thought came into his mind. Why not just drive straight back to London and do his best to forget everything that had happened? He could compile an illustrated report on the house over the weekend, deliver it to Fran on Monday, claim his two and a half thousand pounds and wash his hands of the whole thing.

He reached the traffic lights at the junction with the main road and joined the lane to turn left, towards Redruth, the A30 – and London. He thought of Blake and how vulnerable she was, how unaware of the danger she might be in. He thought, fleetingly, of the whole passage of his life to that point. He was not to blame. He was not responsible. He was not involved.

The lights turned green. He moved forward, then suddenly switched indicators and swerved into the lane for turning right, towards Culdrose and the Lizard, towards Wortalleth West – and Blake. An aggrieved driver blared his horn and Don raised an apologetic hand. Soon, he was on the main road, heading south.

❖

I tell Glenys about Don's discovery of the panic room – and what Dale said about it – as we drive away from the scene of the crash towards Helston. The idea that she doesn't need to know what's going on seems stupid now, somehow. I know an accident's an accident and I shouldn't make too much of it, but it's only added to the doubts nagging away at me. Twenty-four hours ago, life was simple. Now I feel like I've walked into a quagmire and I can't find a way out.

Glenys doesn't say anything for quite a while after I finish. She lights another of her roll-ups and scans the road ahead as if she's concentrating on the traffic, which has actually thinned a lot since we cleared the spot where Dale went into the hedge. I don't try to prompt her to speak. I know better than that. She isn't someone you can hurry.

As we approach the roundabout near Culdrose, she says, through a cloud of cigarette smoke, 'You should clear out of Wortalleth West, Blake. You truly should.'

'It's not that bad, is it?'

'Might be. Why wait to find out? Harkness is finished.

81

I read those *F* bloody *T*s when you chuck 'em out. The wolves are circling.'

'You've never mentioned his problems before.'

'Why should I? Thought they weren't *my* problems – or yours. But a sealed panic room? And this "accident"? You have to read the weather, Blake. A storm's brewing.'

'Are you saying you don't think Dale's crash was really an accident?'

'What *is* an accident? Things converge. Sometimes you shouldn't be there when they do. I'm just the gardener. I come and go. You live there. But I don't think you should any more. I can put you up while you decide what's best.'

Maybe she's right. It all means something. And what it means isn't good. 'I'll think about it, I promise.'

'Don't think too long. It's not just about Harkness's creditors anyway, is it?'

'Isn't it?'

'I've seen Wynsum Fry hanging round.' Glenys shoots me a glance. 'You don't want to have anything to do with her.'

'You're right. I don't want to. But it's not exactly up to me, is it?'

'My dad lived as a tramp for a good many years before Mum took him in.'

'Really?' She's never talked about her parents before – or herself, come to that.

'One thing he told me. "You've got to know when to move on, girl. You've got to know when to take to the road." It's that time for you, Blake.'

'You reckon?'

We're on the roundabout at the edge of Helston as I ask the question. Suddenly, before Glenys can say anything else, I see Don in the MG coming in the opposite direction.

'That's Don's car. Go round twice, can you?'

Glenys signals right and steers slowly past Don as he

waits to join the roundabout. I lower the window and wave and shout his name.

He sees me and raises a hand. Then we're past him. But he gets the message. He falls in behind us as we leave the roundabout second time round and head along the bypass towards Sainsbury's.

'This bloke's an estate agent, right?' Glenys checks. 'Working for Harkness?'

'Working for *Mrs* Harkness.'

'Same difference.'

'He's not a bad guy.'

'Sure 'bout that?'

'I feel sure.'

'How long have you known him?'

'About twenty-four hours.'

Glenys says nothing to that.

'I'll be careful. Don't worry.'

'Oh, I won't. But that's only because I'm not the worrying kind.'

We pull into Sainsbury's car park. Don follows us in.

'You won't forget what I said, will you?' says Glenys.

'No. I won't.'

She swings into one of the bays and stops. As I open the door, she looks at me. 'I'll come tomorrow.'

'Saturday isn't one of your days.'

'I'll come anyway. Just to check how you are.'

'I'll be fine.' I hop out and smile back at her. 'Thanks, Glenys.'

'What for?'

'Caring, I s'pose.'

'Yeah, well . . .' She almost smiles herself. But in the end she doesn't. 'There's no charge for that.'

*

Don did not recognize the battered pick-up truck or its driver. She cast him an unsmiling, scrutinizing glance as she reversed out of the parking bay and pulled away.

He wound down the window as Blake approached. Hazy cloud had obscured the sun and suddenly the summer's day had cooled and lost its edge. Blake was wearing jeans and a denim shirt, open over a white vest. Her hair was tied back and her eyes were shielded by circular sunglasses.

'Hi, Don,' she said brightly. 'Can you give me a lift back when I've done some shopping?'

'Sure. I'll even carry the basket for you.' He got out of the car and they walked towards the supermarket. 'Who was that woman?'

'Glenys Probert. Harkness's gardener. She comes in three days a week.'

'The gardener. Of course. I suppose that explains why she looked at me as if I was a slug she'd found in a flower bed.'

'She's all right when you get to know her.'

'Pity I won't have the chance.'

'Get anywhere with Andrew?'

'You can stay with him if you need to. He certainly doesn't think you should stay on at Wortalleth West.'

'No one does. Glenys has offered to put me up as well.'

'There you are, then.'

They reached the supermarket. Blake took off her sunglasses, grabbed a basket from the stack and handed it to Don. 'Want me to cook something tonight?'

'You should really spend the time packing.'

'Should I?'

'Like everyone says, it's time to go.'

'How about spag bol?'

'What?'

'Spaghetti Bolognese. To eat.'

Don shrugged helplessly. 'OK.'

'Follow me, then.'

They set off round the aisles. At first, Don followed Blake in silence. Then, as they headed towards chilled meat, he said, 'Glasson told me about his missing daughter.'

'Did he?'

'And Wynsum Fry.'

'I should never have introduced him to her.'

'I met her myself earlier.'

Blake pulled up and stared at him. 'You met Fry?'

'By chance. In a pub.'

Blake went on staring at him. 'You think it was by chance?'

'What else?'

She let out a slow breath. 'There's something I have to tell you.'

'Snap.'

She glanced around, then said, 'We shouldn't talk about this here. Wait till we're in the car.'

Don glanced around too. The only people he saw were shoppers wandering the aisles with trolleys and baskets. Nobody was watching them. Nobody was listening. 'OK,' he said appeasingly. 'Let's get on with this.'

Within a quarter of an hour, they were in the MG, heading south. Don started relating what had happened during his visit to Glasson, but was diverted by Blake, who wanted more urgently to hear about his encounter with Wynsum Fry. He was surprised, when he came to talk of it, by how patchy his recollection of their conversation was. All he could clearly remember was the strange, watery menace in her eyes and the sense of undesired intimacy that had seeped into their exchanges.

'You shouldn't have spoken to her,' said Blake in an ominously subdued tone.

'*She* spoke to *me*.'

'You should've avoided her altogether.'

'How exactly could I have avoided a chance meeting?'

Blake sighed heavily. 'You don't meet Wynsum Fry by chance.'

'What's that supposed to mean?'

'She's a witch, Don. Don't you get it?'

'You don't really believe she's an actual witch, do you? Spells, broomsticks, cauldrons – all that crap?'

'It doesn't matter what I believe. Or what you believe. Things happen. When they do, you know what it is.'

'And what it is is witchcraft, right?'

'It doesn't matter what you call it either. Wynsum Fry is bad news.'

'I wouldn't argue with that. But what's her interest in Wortalleth West?'

'Listen, Don, this doesn't have anything to do with Harkness's money problems or his wife's decision to sell the house. It can't have.'

'But what is "this"?'

Blake glanced out of the window at the passing grounds of the Air Station, where all was neat and trimmed and signposted. But there were other worlds, where routes were harder to find. 'Fry's brother drowned in a rock pool at Poldhu Cove when he was twelve. It's a long, long time ago. Fry's never believed it was an accident. I don't know why, but she thinks Harkness killed him.'

'*Harkness?*'

'He grew up round here. His father was a fisherman.'

'Jack Harkness's father was a *fisherman*?'

'Yes, he was. And in 1970, when Jory Fry drowned, aged twelve, Harkness was a fourteen-year-old schoolboy living in Mullion.' Blake shrugged. 'Well, that's the story. And Glenys says it's true. But as for killing Jory . . .'

'I don't suppose Wynsum Fry has any evidence against Harkness.'

'She doesn't need any. In her own mind, she's certain.'

'What about a motive?'

'Dunno. I've never actually discussed it with her. But she hates Harkness. That's for certain. She calls him the King of Spades.'

'The King of Spades? Hold on. Glasson said that was the only black card to come out of the deck when Fry went through her fortune-telling routine for him.'

'He told you that as well, did he?'

'Why did you introduce him to her?'

'I thought it might help. I was wrong.'

'How did you come across her?'

'A woman I used to clean for mentioned going to her. I expected she'd be some harmless old biddy who told you what you wanted to hear. I expected her to . . . I dunno. She wasn't what I expected, anyway. That's the point. Not remotely. She's a long way from harmless.'

'Come on. The woman doesn't have supernatural powers. Some sleight of hand with playing cards? You don't want to set any store by that. It's just tricks.'

'Just tricks,' Blake echoed solemnly.

'It's true.' But was it? Don was less confident than he sounded. Sooner or later, he would have to pass on Glasson's message about Holly Walsh. But he felt more and more reluctant to do so. Seeking to defer the moment as long as possible, he said, 'What was it you had to tell me, Blake?'

'Oh yeah, right. A guy called Dale came to the house after you left. Seems Fran contacted some firm in Plymouth that knows a bit about panic rooms and they sent him down to take a look.'

87

'What did he say?'

'Nothing much. He couldn't make any sense of it. A lot of head-scratching. Then he left. He didn't get far, though.'

'What d'you mean?'

'Wait a few minutes and you'll see. Don't take the Cury turn. Stay on this road and we'll go through Mullion.'

Don did not try to push the point. They drove on for a mile or so in silence. Then, rounding a bend, they caught up with the tail end of a slow-moving line of traffic. It moved in fits and starts before reaching a stretch of road that dipped and wound through a patch of woodland.

A van had crashed into the ditch on one of the bends and was now being winched on to a lorry. Blake pointed across to it. 'That's Dale's van. See the company name on the side and the Plymouth phone number?'

'What the hell happened?'

'He went off the road on his way back from Wortalleth West. I got out when we were held up earlier and spoke to a cop. Dale's in Treliske Hospital with serious injuries.'

'Christ.'

'Makes you think, doesn't it?'

'Think what? He was probably just careless.'

'Maybe.'

'It was an accident, Blake. They happen.'

'Yeah. Like chance meetings.'

Don mulled that over for a moment, then said, 'We're going to Poldhu. I want to see these rock pools.'

The tide was on the turn, trickling in over the wrinkled sand. The sun winked and gleamed at them through barred clouds moving in formation on the western horizon. Blake jumped over a curve of the Bonython stream that cut across the beach. Don tried to follow her and ended up with a shoeful of water.

She pointed to the shelf of rocks beneath the cliff bordering the northern side of the cove. 'There are always pools there at low tide,' she explained. 'It's in one of those Jory Fry drowned.'

'Let's take a look.' Don scrambled up on to the nearest rock. There were several pools within sight, glinting in the sunlight. None looked deep enough to drown in. 'D'you know how it happened?'

Looking round, Don saw Blake was no longer below him, but standing on the narrow peak of a nearby rock, balancing perfectly. 'According to Glenys, they thought at the time he must've slipped and knocked his head, finished up face down in the pool and drowned while he was unconscious.'

Don glanced around. 'Well, I suppose he must.'

'But did he really slip? Or was he pushed and held down in the water?'

'By a boy only a couple of years older than him? I don't buy that. And why would the other boy do it anyway?'

'Harkness, you mean?'

'Was Harkness seen nearby?'

'Not sure. It's like nearly half a century ago, Don. Glenys is too young to actually remember. It's all . . .' She shrugged. 'It's all legend and guesswork.'

'How old would Wynsum Fry have been then?'

'Late teens, maybe.'

Don squinted towards the sea. 'So, she remembers. Even if nobody else does.'

'Yeah. She remembers.'

Don turned, intending to clamber back down to the beach. Deciding he would only look a fool if he jumped and fell over, and with a wet foot to remind him he had displayed precious little agility so far, he stooped and steadied himself with his right hand. Then, just as he put some weight on it, his wrist gave way and he descended in a sudden, ungainly slither.

'Careful,' said Blake, hopping down coolly beside him. 'Want some help?'

'I'm fine,' Don snapped. He struggled to his feet. 'I obviously need more practice on beaches.'

'Obviously.'

He shook his hand. 'Seem to have strained something.'

'Always a risk at your age, I s'pose.'

'Shut up.'

She grinned at him. Eventually, he grinned too.

'There was something you were going to tell me,' she said. 'Remember?'

'Oh yeah.' The moment could be delayed no longer. 'Glasson asked me to pass on a message.' He paused.

'Better pass it on, then.' She looked at him promptingly.

'Right. Well, he referred me to a woman on Facebook. She's suffering from MS but has got a lot better after taking some fantastically expensive wonder drug, paid for by an anonymous benefactor. He said you'd be interested.'

'Why?'

'I got the impression he thought you'd understand the significance of it when you knew her name.'

'Which is?'

'Holly Walsh. Mean anything to you?'

But the question was redundant even as Don asked it. It was quite obvious from Blake's expression that the name meant something to her. She stared at him for a moment, then said simply, 'Wow.'

❖

Holly Walsh: the name of the friend who travelled down to London from Cambridge with Jane Glasson the day she disappeared. She's basically the last person who ever saw her. That's her 'significance', to use Don's word.

I tell him what I know about her, which isn't a lot. According to Andrew, she was Jane's best friend at boarding school and then Cambridge. After Jane vanished, she met him and his wife several times. She did what she could to help, but it wasn't much. Jane going missing was a total surprise to Holly and her other friends.

It doesn't take a genius to work out the likeliest explanation. Somewhere between King's Cross and Paddington that summer's day in 1996 she got picked up by a man – the wrong kind of man – and ended up—

I never told Andrew I thought she was probably dead. I let him believe he might find her one day. Belief's good for you. Hope's healthy. Well, it's sure healthier than the alternative. I guess that's why I put him in touch with Wynsum Fry.

And now? Now I know what he's thinking. Who could Holly Walsh's anonymous benefactor be? Who else could it be, in fact, but . . . Jane?

'You don't believe that, do you?' Don asks as we walk slowly back up the beach. 'I mean, there's absolutely no reason to think this proves anything one way or the other about Jane Glasson.'

'No,' I respond. ''Course it doesn't. But that won't stop Andrew wondering, will it?' It doesn't stop me wondering either. Fry says Jane's alive. And her best friend has a fairy godmother who pays her medical bills. 'I bet the only reason he hasn't contacted Holly is he's frightened what Muriel would say if she found out. Maybe that's really why he wanted you to tell me.'

'What d'you mean?'

'Maybe he wants *me* to contact Holly.'

'You shouldn't get involved, Blake, you really shouldn't.'

'OK.' But I *am* involved. Have been ever since Andrew first told me about Jane. You can regret doing things. But you can regret not doing things as well. I totally know that feeling. I glance round at Don, to see how he reacts to what I say next. 'But you could contact her.'

He shakes his head. 'No way.'

'Not your concern, I s'pose.'

'Nor yours.'

'Bound to be, if I go back there.'

'Then don't.' Don pulls up. He flexes his strained wrist and kicks irritably at the sand. He's just warned me off the exact course of action he was recommending only this morning. 'Can't you go back to your family – wherever they are?'

'No, Don. I can't.' I make it clear by the look I give him that I'm saying no more on that subject.

He sighs. 'I'll take you to London if you like. You can stay at my flat till you get yourself sorted.'

'I don't like cities. But thanks for the offer.'

'You have to leave here, Blake.' He really does look as if he means it.

'Yeah. So everybody says.'

'Because it's true.'

I gaze up towards Wortalleth West. You can see the cove clearly from the verandah when you're up there, but from down here the house is weirdly kind of sheltered from view. 'I'll think about it,' I say, as if it's a grand concession. 'Honest, I will.'

Everything's quiet at the house. Everything looks exactly the same as it always does. But it doesn't feel the same. Don goes up to his room while I take the food into the kitchen. I've already decided to call Treliske Hospital and ask how Dale is. But, as I walk towards the phone, it rings.

I pick it up. 'Hello?'

'Is that Blake?' The voice is male, American, flat and slightly husky.

'Who's this?'

'French. Don knows who I am.'

'Well, d'you—'

'Tell him this from me, Blake. We know about the panic room. We spoke with Dale. You met him earlier, didn't you? Nice kid. Not accustomed to being questioned the way I question people, though. Shook him up a mite. Anyhow, now we know the room's there . . . we want to know what's in it. And we expect Don to find out for us. Got that?'

'I—'

The line's dead. French has hung up.

Don walks into the room and looks across at me. He frowns. He can probably read the alarm in my eyes. 'I heard the phone,' he says. 'What's wrong?'

'Who's French, Don?'

'Ah.' His expression tightens. 'Well . . .'

'Seems he knows about the panic room. Squeezed the details out of Dale, so he said. Is he the kind of man who could do that?'

Don nods miserably. 'Yeah. He is.'

'And he knows you?'

'We met. This morning. At Church Cove.'

'You didn't tell me anything about that.'

'I, er . . . didn't want to worry you.'

'No? Well, I'm worried now.'

'Sorry. I should have . . .' His voice tails away. He walks slowly round to where I'm standing and looks directly at me. 'Sorry.' And to be fair to him, he looks it.

EIGHT

DON SLEPT POORLY. THE HOUSE HAD MINOR TICKS AND CREAKS, as was only to be expected, but every one of them made him believe for a second that something had stirred in the master bedroom. His strained wrist felt more painful every time he woke and his brain exhausted itself thinking of ways to extricate Blake – and him – from the coils of intrigue surrounding Jack Harkness.

Eventually, just as dawn was breaking, he fell into a sudden, deep slumber. It was as if a tired man walking for miles had stepped into an uncovered well. He went down a long way.

When he surfaced, the morning was well advanced. He was aware he had dreamt of his father, which was unusual. They had been walking somewhere in the countryside, the North Downs maybe. Don was a child. Patch was with them. He had arrived as a puppy when Don was five. Patch was fully grown in the dream, though. He ran away into a wood and Don went after him. But look as long and hard as he liked, he could not find him.

As soon as the dream had faded and Don made to get out of bed, he realized his wrist was much worse. He could hardly bend it without wincing. Moving the fingers on that hand hurt like hell as well. He stumbled into the bathroom and confronted a far from refreshed face in the mirror. The wrist was so painful he had to wash and shave one-handed. He managed to cut himself twice in the process.

He found himself going into the master bedroom to check nothing had changed in the dressing-room closet – nothing had – before he went down to the kitchen. There he tried to coax the espresso machine into life. The *Financial Times* had already arrived – the fat weekend edition. Don turned the pages with his left hand, looking for a mention of Harkness, while the machine warmed up. There was none, which was either good news or bad, though he could not decide which.

A deal of steaming and gurgling announced the delivery of a cup of coffee. Don tried instinctively to pick it up with his right hand, only to spill most of it. 'Bloody hell,' he grumbled.

Suddenly, he was transported in time and space to the fetid, meanly furnished flat in Honor Oak where his father had died. Don had been summoned there one summer's day in 1995 by a neighbour, complaining about a plague of flies and a bad smell. Don had a spare key. He knew what he was going to find before he went in, though he prayed he was wrong. The old man had been going downhill for quite a while. The failed business ventures, the cheap supermarket vodka and the creeping certainty that his luck would never turn again had left him with no way out. Yes, Don knew what he was going to find.

Except that he did not know. The physical reality of a lonely death, undiscovered for many days, was something he was unprepared for. The wreckage of his father's body was a terrible sight, decomposing, rotting, almost melting, crawling with maggots. And then there was the smell – the clinging stench of decay – that invaded Don's nostrils. Flies buzzed round his head as he stared down in horror and revulsion at all that remained of the once handsome, debonair, man-about-town Rex Challenor.

Don was a phlegmatic manager of his own memories. He was not often caught out by them. But he was caught out by them now.

'Are you all right?'

Don turned to find Blake gazing at him from the doorway with a concerned expression on her face. There was freshness and energy in her eyes. She had obviously had a much better night than he had, despite all he had told her about French and the sinister Zlenko.

'You don't look so great, Don,' she said, which he suspected was a considerable understatement.

'I cut myself shaving.' He held up his right hand. 'Can't seem to use this at all.'

She walked over and peered at his wrist. 'It isn't swollen.'

'You don't miss much, do you?'

She frowned at him. 'What's in that cup?'

'It *was* coffee. But, er . . . I spilt it.'

'I'll make you some more.'

'Thanks.'

She went over to the machine and set it brewing again. Don slumped down at the table. He could not shake off the memory of his father. A foul smell seemed to waft briefly past him and he suddenly felt so sick he rushed back to the sink, where just as suddenly the sensation faded. His wrist throbbed.

'You didn't stay up drinking, did you, Don?' Blake asked.

'No.' He shambled back to the table. 'This is no hangover.'

'It's something, though.'

The machine delivered a second cup of coffee. Blake plonked it in front of Don and sat down opposite him.

'When I came in, you looked . . .' She shrugged. 'I dunno. You looked . . . wounded.'

'That'll be the wrist.'

'Wounded inside, I mean.'

He summoned some kind of smile. 'A few gloomy thoughts, that's all.'

'Are you going to be able to drive with your wrist like that?'

The question had not yet occurred to Don. As he considered it and tried painfully to straighten his fingers, he realized driving – certainly all the way back to London – would be next to impossible. 'Could be tricky,' he said drily.

She looked at him thoughtfully. 'When did it start playing up?'

'I jarred it somehow climbing up on those rocks in the cove. No . . . hold on.' Don turned the point over in his mind. 'Actually, it was sore before then. I noticed it . . . when we drove into Mullion.'

'On the way back from Helston, then?'

'I guess so.'

'Interesting.'

'That's not what I'd call it.'

'I think I know what the trouble is.'

'OK, Nurse, what is it?'

She shook her head. 'You wouldn't believe me if I told you.'

'Try me. I'm desperate.'

'Really?'

'Yeah. Really. Like you said, I can't drive one-handed. And I need to get myself – and you – a long way away from here. Today, preferably.'

'I'm not sure that'll be possible, Don.'

'You know about French and his Russian chum now, Blake. It's important we put some distance between you and this house.'

'You reckon running away from a guy like French will work?'

Don sighed. 'Have you got a better suggestion?'

'Not sure about better. But there's a woman we should talk to, here in Mullion, before we do anything else.'

'Who is she? And why haven't you mentioned her before?'

'Maris Hemsley. And I didn't think of her. Till this happened.' Blake nodded towards Don's wrist.

He made a face. 'I don't need the services of a local quack.'

'That's all right, then.' She smiled. ''Cos you're not going to get 'em.'

⁙

I met Maris because she bought a three-legged table I'd made and commissioned me to make a couple of chairs. I seriously liked it when she used that word. 'Commissioned'. It sounded professional, like I was doing something properly commercial. Plus selling the table so soon after it went on display in the gallery at Trelowarren meant they were keen to stock more of my stuff. She was a stroke of good luck just when I needed it, right after I'd had to move out of Andrew's place.

I knew Maris was some kind of historian. You could tell that from the books on her shelves. Retired from Exeter University, so she told me. Historian *and* anthropologist, she emphasized to explain why a lot of the books were about folklore and pagan religions. I guess that's why I asked her if she knew anything about Wynsum Fry. I could tell at once the name hit a nerve. She kind of froze.

101

She got me to tell her everything that had happened between me and Fry and Andrew before she told me her own story. She'd bought her cottage as a weekend place originally, back in the late 1970s, somewhere to come down to from Exeter.

Right from the start, apparently, she began hearing stories about local people, farming folk mostly, going to a white witch – seer, fortune-teller, whatever – to predict the future and help solve their problems. Illnesses. Miscarriages. Money troubles. Sickness in a herd. Blight on a crop. They didn't go to their doctor, their accountant or their vet. They went to Calensa Fry.

Calensa was Wynsum's grandmother. She raised her and Jory after their mother deserted them. Maris was fascinated by how her brand of witchcraft could survive in the twentieth century. She thought it could be the basis for a book: a proper academic study of the subject.

According to the people Maris talked to, Calensa Fry was a de-witcher on top of everything else: someone you went to if you thought you were bewitched; someone who could lift the spell that had been cast on you by another witch. It sounded crazy when Maris first told me about it. I couldn't get my head round the idea that people actually believed in that kind of crap. But I'd seen Andrew with Wynsum Fry and I knew if people wanted to believe something badly enough . . . they did.

Maris cooked up a story that she was bewitched: experiencing a series of inexplicable accidents. She persuaded a local farmer's wife to introduce her to Calensa Fry. They met. Calensa quizzed her about enemies. She did some card-reading. That was all Maris could remember about the session, though she was sure there'd been more to it. When she went to see Calensa again, she took a tape recorder, hidden in her handbag. As before, she came away unable to remember much. And when she played back the tape, there was nothing on it, just white noise.

Then things turned seriously weird. Accidents started happening – the kind she'd made up as her cover story for seeing Calensa. The brakes on her car failed. A heavy book fell off a high shelf, knocking her clean out. She slipped over walking on the harbour wall at Mullion Cove and fell in the sea. An angler dived in and pulled her out.

Maris was frightened stiff by the end of all that. She reckoned Calensa had rumbled her as a fake client and put a real spell on her as a punishment. She burnt the tapes, even though they were blank. She sent Calensa a letter confessing she'd been looking for material for a book but was now dropping the idea.

The accidents stopped. Dead. Calensa was satisfied, I guess. Ironically, she contacted Maris then, offering to help her with her research – for a fee. She'd made her point. And Maris had taken it.

I tell Don all this, but he doesn't seem to see the connection with him, though it's obvious to me. I don't push it. I'll let Maris make it plain to him. I phone her and ask if I can bring a friend to meet her. She knows me. She agrees straight away. 'Come for coffee.' I think she already senses it isn't a social call.

Don makes a bit of a fuss. He's all for taking himself – and me – away from Wortalleth West right away. The fact he can't drive is a problem he's reluctant to face up to. When he does, he suggests I drive. I guess that shows just how worried he is. I nix the idea, by saying I can't drive. Not strictly true, but never mind. He runs out of objections to walking into Mullion for coffee with Maris. We set off, along the coast path round Angrouse Cliff.

*

The weather's clear and warm again. It's unusual for it to be stuck like this. No wind. No rain. Just the blue sky, a faint breeze and skylarks singing. Not Lizard weather at all. The cliffs are brilliant with thrift and campion and tormentil. Gwennap Head lies like a giant basking whale on the other side of Mount's Bay. I can't quite convince myself, in all this peace and beauty, that we're in any kind of actual danger.

I start trying to reason my way – *our* way – out of it. 'French gave you a week, didn't he, Don? So time's on our side.'

'I wouldn't say he was necessarily a man of his word,' Don pants in reply. 'He didn't know about the panic room when I spoke to him.'

'But he's looking for money, isn't he? Money Harkness has supposedly stolen. That'll be the smart white-collar kind of theft. Figures on spreadsheets. Megabucks in tax-haven bank accounts.'

'Sounds about right.'

'So, he doesn't need a panic room at Wortalleth West to store it in, does he? It's not like he's got a load of gold bars to stash away. Cornwall isn't a tax haven.'

'You're right,' Don admits. 'But I didn't tell French about the panic room when I could have. He had to hear about it from Dale. So, he'll be even more suspicious of me than he was. And you heard him. He wants to know what's in the room.'

'Why doesn't he just blow it open?'

'I don't know. Maybe he can't risk drawing attention to himself – and who he's working for. He also said there were other leads he had to follow up. Maybe he's left the area.'

'I'd like to believe that.'

'Me too. But I still think the best thing we can do is get the hell out.'

Don's probably right. I know that. But I've had practice in getting the hell out of somewhere. That's how I finished up here, on the very edge of England. If you always give in to fear, when do you stop being frightened?

I realize in that instant, as I gaze out across the blue water, into the nothingness of the ocean, that I hate French as well as fear him. I hate him *because* I fear him.

❖

Maris Hemsley was a tall, thin, erect woman of seventy or so, with grey hair, keen eyes and a fine-boned face. She had a brisk, efficient air to her, talking quickly and moving fast as if needing to cram as much thought and activity into her day as possible.

Her cottage was small and whitewashed, set back from the cliff above Polurrian Cove, screened by bushy growths of gorse and broom. She shared it with an enthusiastically friendly Sealyham terrier and a vast hoard of books. Don did not really understand why Blake had taken him to meet Maris, but he assumed he would find out soon enough.

Blake went into the kitchen to help, leaving Don slumped in an armchair in the airy, light-filled lounge with Dandy the terrier. He stared vacantly at the phalanx of books with titles like *Religion and the Decline of Magic* and *The Symbology of Early Modern Spiritism*. For someone who had supposedly had her fingers burnt in a long-ago encounter with Wynsum Fry's grandmother, Maris Hemsley appeared reluctant to give up her interest in the subject of magic and superstition.

She and Blake were soon back, with a pot of coffee and a plate of biscuits. Maris managed a light but expert interrogation of Don while pouring the coffee. What did he do for a living? What had brought him to Mullion? He did not resist. With Blake's eyes resting on him, he felt almost obliged to be candid.

'I gather you've met Wynsum Fry,' Maris said once she had gleaned as much as she wanted to about him.

'Yeah. And you're the expert on the Frys, according to Blake.'

'As much of an expert as you can be, I suppose.' She eyed Don with an analytical sharpness. 'You met Wynsum yesterday?'

'Yeah. In Helston.'

'She did a card-reading for you?'

'No. I turned her down.'

'How did she react to that?'

'Like I was a disappointment to her.'

'Oh, you would have been. Anyone associated with Wortalleth West – and therefore Harkness – is of great interest to her. She'd have hoped to draw something out of you.'

'Because she's convinced Harkness murdered her brother?'

Maris nodded. 'Exactly.'

'I made it clear I didn't believe in the occult.'

'That won't have pleased her.'

'His right wrist is giving him grief,' Blake put in. 'Since an hour or so after meeting Fry.'

'Hang on,' said Don. 'That's got—'

'Did she touch you?' Maris cut in.

'Sorry?'

'Did Wynsum Fry touch you?'

'Er, yeah. We, er, shook hands.'

'Show me how.' Maris extended her right hand.

Don sat forward and extended his own right hand to meet hers. Maris took it lightly.

'Like this?' she queried.

'No. Er, she put her other hand on top of mine as well.'

Maris rested her left hand on top of Don's right. 'Like *this*?'

'Yeah.' A small amount of pressure made him suck in his breath.

'Does that hurt?'

'Yeah.' Don held himself stiffly. 'Quite a bit.'

'Sorry.' Maris let go. 'Can you move your fingers?'

'Not much.'

'So, it'll be difficult to drive, I imagine.'

Don glanced sharply at Blake. 'Difficult's putting it mildly.'

'Meaning you can't very easily leave Mullion.'

'What are you getting at?'

'Isn't it obvious? Wynsum Fry has done this to you, Don. There's not a doubt of it in my mind. It's her way – and she does have her ways – of ensuring she keeps you where she wants you.'

'Come off it. I strained my wrist. It's as simple as that.'

'And he's having gloomy thoughts,' Blake pointed out.

'Who doesn't, from time to time?'

Maris smiled at Don sympathetically. 'So, what were these gloomy thoughts about?'

He sighed. 'My father . . . and how he died.'

'Not well, I assume.'

'Alcoholic poisoning, if you really want to know. He wasn't found . . . for several days.'

'And when he was found, it was by you?'

'Yeah.' Don grimaced. 'I've never felt the same about bluebottles since.'

'Christ,' said Blake softly. 'Sorry, Don.'

'Do you often think about how you found him?'

'Hardly ever.'

'Till now.'

'Wynsum Fry's doing, you're going to say?'

107

Maris nodded solemnly. 'I am.'

'I'm not swallowing that,' Don protested. 'She has no power over me. Bloody hell, I could catch a train back to London any time I like, couldn't I? Then I wouldn't be where you think she wants me.'

'No. You wouldn't. And your wrist would probably feel better. That's certainly what happened to me whenever I went back to Exeter after a tussle with her grandmother. No accidents. No fear. No anxiety. My susceptibility felt stupid when I was a hundred miles away. But as soon as I returned . . .'

'It all came on again?'

'It did. To the rational mind – and I do have a rational mind – it seemed absurd. But there's no gainsaying what we experience. When I confessed to Calensa Fry that I'd tried to deceive her, I was suddenly no longer accident-prone. I don't believe that was a coincidence. Wynsum has come to resemble her grandmother more and more. Calensa was in her sixties when I first met her and she lived well into her nineties. She never lost her ability to intimidate me. It offended me, how easily she could do it.'

'Did you take her up on the offer of help with your research?'

'Rather against my better judgement, I did. I soon came to regret it. Not because I had any more bad experiences. Quite the reverse. Calensa claimed at first that she had no supernatural powers and merely practised a little psychological manipulation in order to sustain her reputation and hence her business. She said anything that happened to people was actually self-induced – nothing to do with her at all. I suppose she was double-bluffing me, daring me to write it all off as nonsense while I had good cause to know it wasn't. And then, after several fruitless meetings, she gave me to understand there were some juicy trade secrets she could reveal if she chose to but there was something I'd have to do for her in return.'

'What?'

'She wanted me to accuse Jack Harkness – in print – of responsibility for her grandson's death. I couldn't have done that even if I'd wanted to, of course. There was no way I could shoehorn a wild theory about Jory Fry's drowning into an academic study of witchcraft. But Calensa Fry was unworldly in that sense. She thought I was a writer and she wanted her conviction that Harkness had murdered Jory written about.' Maris shook her head as the memories stirred within her. 'There was some kind of feud between the Harknesses and the Frys going back generations. Calensa told me they were on different sides in the Cornish rising of 1648.'

'*1648!*' spluttered Don.

'Yes, I know. But the Frys don't count time the way you and I do. For them, it doesn't so much heal as congeal. They were tenants of Tredarvas Farm. It's a ruin now. I went there whenever I met Calensa. She never came to me. We sat in the kitchen. Always the kitchen. I never saw further into the house. Calensa had married a cousin – another Fry – but he was dead by then. They'd abandoned the land, but stayed on in the house for a while. It was there Calensa declared her certainty to me that Jack Harkness had murdered Jory. Held him face down in the rock pool where he was found till he'd drowned. That's what she claimed. On Saturday the first of August, 1970. It's not hard for me to remember the date. She mentioned it often enough. Jory Fry drowned early that morning, the first of August. Lammas, which apparently was significant, though I never understood why.'

'Did she have any evidence to implicate Harkness?'

'None. Except that Wynsum, who was sent to look for

Jory when he didn't show up for breakfast, saw Harkness cycling away up the hill towards Mullion as she approached the cove. Which was enough for both of them.'

'Where did the Harknesses live?'

'A cottage down at Mullion Cove. That's where Jack's father kept his crabber.'

'And Jack was how old at the time?'

'Fourteen,' said Blake quietly.

'So he could just have been out for a bike ride like any other fourteen-year-old boy.'

Maris nodded. 'Quite.'

'This is all bullshit then. And absolutely bloody nothing to do with me.'

'Ah, but I'm afraid it is.' Maris looked genuinely regretful. 'I imagine Wynsum sees you as someone with access to Harkness. And therefore as someone she can use to punish him for what she believes he did.'

Don groaned. 'Has she ever said *why* Harkness might have wanted to do such a thing?'

'To kill off the male line of the Frys.' Maris shrugged. 'I'm sorry. I know it's preposterous. But she's convinced. Like her grandmother before her. And she doesn't think Harkness's sins ended with murdering her brother.'

'No? What other—' Don's phone began to ring. ''Scuse me a second.' He fished it out of his pocket. It was Robin Pawley. Don wondered at once if he had news of the Wortalleth West planning application. 'Sorry. I'd better take this.' He scrambled up. 'It won't take long.'

Don headed to the front door, which stood open to a cooling breeze.

'I didn't expect to hear from you so soon, Robin.'

'Don't suppose you did. But I happened to bump into John Troke on my way to work this morning. The very man in the Planning Department I was intending to contact on

110

Monday. He gave me some rather interesting information I thought I should share with you.'

'Right.'

'Well, the whole thing's a little . . . delicate, actually. It'd be better if we could discuss it face to face.'

'OK. But—'

'I'm stuck in the office until lunchtime, but maybe I could drive down to Wortalleth West afterwards. I'd like to have a look at the place anyway, considering we're likely to be taking it on.'

Don had been careful to make no promises and strongly suspected Fran would veto Pawley's involvement anyway. He also suspected the supposed delicacy of the situation was just a pretext for nosing around the house. But he could hardly point any of this out. 'All right. If you're happy to come down.'

'No problem. I should be with you by two o'clock.'

'OK.'

'One thing, though. Have you run into a chap called Mike Coleman?'

'Who?'

'That sounds like a no.'

'It is. Who is he?'

'I'll explain when we meet. What John Troke told me was, er . . . puzzling, shall we say?'

'D'you want to explain what you mean by that?'

Pawley paused lengthily for thought, then said, 'No. It'll have to wait. I'll see you at two.' And then he was gone.

Don had missed a call from Fran earlier, while he was in the Wortalleth West dead zone. Deciding to let her stew a while longer, he turned and headed back into the cottage.

*

Maris looks at me sharply as Don hurries from the room. She's got a good heart, but her brain's so keen she can sometimes be just too perceptive. I don't like feeling people can see inside my head. But with Maris I have to put up with it. It's in her nature.

'So, Blake,' she says, pitching her voice low, 'Harkness wants to sell Wortalleth West.'

'His wife wants to. Technically, she owns it, according to Don.'

'It's unsettling for you, of course. But you could see the sale as a chance to untangle yourself from Harkness and the Frys.'

'Not to mention the Glassons, right?'

'If you prefer, I won't tell Don what I was about to.'

'No. You should finish now you've started.'

'You've only known him a couple of days, Blake.'

'It feels longer.'

'Something's going on, isn't it? Something beyond Wynsum Fry and all this ancient history.'

'Things have turned kind of weird.'

'Just weird? Or dangerous?'

There she goes again. There's no fooling her. There never has been. 'Here's Don,' I murmur.

He shambles back in. 'Sorry,' he says with a shamefaced smile. He sits down. 'Where were we?'

I decide to take the lead, to show Maris I really don't want her to hold back. 'Maris was just going to tell you Calensa and Wynsum Fry also believe Harkness had a hand in Jane Glasson's disappearance.'

'*What?*'

'It's true,' says Maris. And then she describes an encounter with Calensa Fry six months after Jane Glasson vanished in June 1996. Calensa and Wynsum had left Tredarvas by then and were living in a bungalow near Helston football ground.

'I'd come down for Christmas and I stopped at Sainsbury's

to stock up with food. Calensa was the last person I expected to meet there. She didn't seem in the least surprised when we almost literally bumped into each other. It would be easy to believe she'd planned it. Ninety or not, she was still as spry as ever. And as sharp-witted. She asked if I'd bought the *West Briton*. Said there was a letter in it from Andrew Glasson – "that Glasson party" as she called him – appealing for information about his daughter. Not the first such letter, she said. "Shall us tell 'im or will you?" she asked. I told her I didn't know what she meant. So she leant close to me and said, "'Arkness took 'er. You knows that, don't 'ee?" I assured her I didn't. Wynsum hove into view at that point, pushing a trolley. Calensa told her I didn't believe her and Wynsum said, "People never believe truth till they'm forced to." Then they beetled off together.'

'This was just another fantasy of the Frys', right?' says Don.

'I assumed so. I still do. After all, Harkness had only the most tenuous connection with the Glassons.'

'How tenuous?'

'Well, there was a café in Mullion called Sea Breeze. It closed about five years ago. I saw Harkness there quite a few times back in the nineties. He was always very distinctive, in his linen suits, reading the *Financial Times*. As it happens, Jane Glasson worked there as a waitress during school holidays before she went to Cambridge. I recognized her when her photograph was in the *West Briton* at the time of her disappearance. I remember being served by her. She was friendly with the customers. Charming, in fact. So, I suppose it stands to reason she must have spoken to Harkness.'

'Along with scores of other people stopping by for coffee.'

'Quite true. It's hardly significant in and of itself.' No. But it's haunted me ever since Maris first mentioned it: the idea of a connection between Jane and Harkness, the vanished girl and the man of mystery.

'It's kind of you to have told me all this, Maris,' says Don, though he doesn't look specially grateful. 'I'm not sure there's anything I can do about the Frys, though, or their crazy theories. I don't believe Wynsum Fry's cast some kind of spell on me. I don't believe in spells. It's as simple as that.'

Don stands up. Looks like he's planning to leave. Looks like he's settled on leaving, in fact, as his best defence against having to accept Wynsum Fry might actually be a witch. Then he grimaces. Something's wrong. He draws a deep breath. He's definitely gone pale. 'Excuse me,' he says and hurries out, heading for the front garden.

Maris looks meaningfully at me. 'I'm afraid poor Don's in denial, Blake,' she says, with a sorrowful shake of the head.

'Shouldn't think he's ever experienced anything like this before.'

'I know the feeling. I remember it well.'

'What should I try and persuade him to do?'

'Leave. Or give Wynsum some evidence to use against Harkness. Those are the only choices before him. Unless . . .'

'Yeah?'

'He follows the advice I was given.'

I look hard at her. When she first told me what the advice was, I thought it sounded like a step through a doorway better left closed. And apparently she'd thought the same. 'You didn't follow it, Maris.'

'I made my peace with Calensa, after a fashion. So, I didn't have to consider . . . extreme measures. I hope Don doesn't have to either.'

'Yeah.' I look her in the eye. 'So do I.'

I catch up with Don out front. He's looking less pale. Dandy's followed me out and is gazing curiously at him. I don't ask if he had to leave the house because he felt sick. It's pretty obvious. He looks angry and ashamed all at the same time.

'I don't need all this,' he complains. 'I'm just an estate agent, for God's sake.'

'Sorry,' I say. There doesn't seem to be anything else I *can* say.

'Witchcraft doesn't exist. Not in England in the twenty-first century. And even if it does . . .'

'You're not susceptible to it, right?'

He nods glumly, totally unconvinced by his own argument. 'Right.'

'OK. What now, then?'

'What now' turns out to be a drink, which Don reckons he badly needs. He makes it into Mullion and we go to the Old Inn, near the church. We sit outside, me with a half of fizzy cider, him with a pint, which he gets down pretty much before he sits down, then goes for a refill, muttering that he obviously doesn't have to worry about drinking and driving now.

When he comes back, I ask if he's decided to stay for another night at least. He says he hasn't decided anything. Then he tells me what the phone call at Maris's was about.

'When I've heard what Pawley's got to say, I might be able to fathom out what to do.'

'How's the wrist now?'

'Great. So long as I don't try to use it.'

I think about admitting I could drive the MG for him. And I think about sharing with him the dewitcher's advice to Maris. But I don't do either. Maybe Pawley's got the answer to the panic-room mystery. Then again, maybe not. Until we know, nothing's clear. It probably won't be even when we do.

Don's phone rings. He looks at it, but he doesn't take the call. He lets it go to voicemail.

'Who was that?' I ask.

He sighs. 'Fran.'

'Keeping her in the dark?'

'It's only what she did to me. I'll speak to her when I'm good and ready.'

'What you said to Maris about catching the train back to London. You could do that, y'know. Any time you like.'

'Would you come with me if I did?'

I wait a beat before I answer. 'No.'

He puffs out his cheeks and looks despairingly at me. 'Leaving is the smartest move, Blake.'

'I've never been smart.'

'I don't believe that.'

'All right. Here's me trying to be smart. You can't prove or disprove Harkness murdered Jory Fry. Not after nearly fifty years. Agreed?'

He frowns, wondering where I'm going with this. 'Agreed.'

'But if you could prove Jane Glasson was alive and well and Harkness had nothing to do with her disappearance, that'd mean the Frys were wrong about something, wouldn't it?'

'I . . . suppose so.'

'This is what I'm thinking, Don. Follow Maris's example. Go and see Wynsum Fry. Tell her you're looking for Jane and that, if you can find her, hey, who knows what she might reveal about Harkness? She should be all for it, shouldn't she? If Maris's example is anything to go by, your wrist'll suddenly be OK.'

'But . . . I'd have to mean it. I'd have to go ahead and look for Jane.'

'You could make a start. We could track down Holly Walsh. See what she has to say about her mystery benefactor.'

'*We?*'

'I'll help you.'

'I thought you wanted to stay here.'

'I don't want to run, Don. This wouldn't be running. Important difference.' And it would mean trying to find Jane. Trying to put one family at least back together.

Don flexes his right hand, wincing as he does it. 'My wrist isn't going to get better just because I go and grovel to Wynsum Fry.'

'Sure about that, are you?' I look him in the eye. 'There's one way to prove it, isn't there?'

Time. I think of it – its untouchability, its elasticity – as Don sits there, reluctantly composing an email to Holly Walsh. The sunlight moves a marbled shadow of Don's half-empty beer glass across my hand. I've seen a photo of the Old Inn, dating from early last century. There are no trees around it. You can see clear beyond it to the masts of the Marconi radio station up on the headland above Poldhu Cove. The pub windows are open. It looks like summer. There's a bicycle propped against the wall. It's the same place. But the masts have gone. The trees have grown. The owner of the bicycle is dead. Like we'll all be. One day.

Don shows me the message. *We're friends of Andrew Glasson. We're trying to find out what happened to Jane. We think you may be able to help. Can you contact us?*

'Send?' he asks.

I nod. 'Send.'

⁜

Don was preoccupied by the weirdness of Wortalleth West: an emptiness that was somehow solid, a hollowness that was somehow filled. He did not know if Blake imagined how they looked on the camera screens Dale had told her would have been installed in the panic room. He hoped she did not. Because he had. And his skin crawled every time he thought of it.

Blake took herself off to her workshop, saying there were things she needed to catch up on. It seemed more likely to Don she wanted to avoid meeting Robin Pawley, though quite why he could not decide. Maybe she had no wish to advertise their . . . what was it exactly? Friendship? He had no children and Blake had made it clear her father played no part in her life. It was strange to feel faintly responsible for her, as Don did, despite telling himself he did not need to. Strange – but somehow good.

Pawley arrived bang on time, in a practical estate agent's Ford. He seemed delighted to set foot inside the house, exhibiting an almost childish pleasure in seeing the internal layout and design. This, Don supposed, was how someone with a genuine vocation for the business behaved. It made him feel old and cynical.

Enthusiastic though he was, Pawley did not appear to notice anything odd about the dimensions of the rooms. Neither had Don, of course, until he got busy with his measurer. And he had no intention of letting Pawley do any actual measuring. As for the structural ambiguity he had mentioned, he spoke vaguely of a concern about the foundations and how they related to the basement. Not surprisingly in the circumstances, Pawley seemed to think he was worrying about nothing.

The room-by-room tour ended in the kitchen. Don did not press Pawley for details of his encounter with Troke of Planning until they had sat down at the kitchen table and Pawley's observations on the house – 'extraordinary', 'stylish', 'very special' – had begun to subside.

'So what did you learn from your Planning contact, Robin?' Don asked in a casual tone.

'I was just coming to that, naturally.' Pawley beamed at him. 'Just wanted to be sure you appreciate how keen I am to be involved in marketing this property.'

'Oh, I appreciate it, I really do.' Don beamed back. 'And I'll be recommending it.'

'Excellent. I'm sure we can work well together.'

'Me too. So . . .'

'Ah yes. John Troke. Well, I had to wheedle it out of him, actually. And he told me in confidence. So you will keep what I tell you under your hat, won't you?'

'It'll be strictly between us, Robin.'

'Good. Well, it's all more than a little odd. When I asked him about the original planning application for this place, he said I was the second person to have asked him recently.'

'Someone else has been digging around?'

'Yes. And as a result, John was able to tell me what he'd already discovered in response to the first enquiry. The Wortalleth West file isn't in the system.'

'What d'you mean?'

'It's missing. No trace at all.'

'*Really?*'

'Clerical error, I suppose. Who knows?'

'Who indeed?' Don did not for a moment believe the loss of the file was a bureaucratic blunder. He was not sure Pawley believed it either. As to the first person who had asked after it . . . 'I assume this Mike Coleman is the other interested party?'

'Correct.'

'You know him?'

'Met him a couple of times at business gatherings. A bit larger than life, if you know what I mean. He runs Sympergy, a renewables outfit. They supply wind turbines and solar panels, that kind of thing.'

'Why should he want to know about this house?'

'I really can't imagine. You could ask him. Sympergy's offices are in Helston. Water-ma-Trout Industrial Estate. And he lives on the Lizard.'

'Whereabouts?'

'Not sure. But he gave John Troke his card.' Pawley laid the card on the table and slid it across to Don. 'Apparently, Coleman was a serious pain.'

'Thanks a lot.' Don glanced down at it. Sympergy's mission statement was *Harness the power of nature with Devon and Cornwall's leading wind and solar energy experts.* Address, telephone, email, website: the usual particulars. On the back were two handwritten phone numbers, one landline, one mobile. 'Maybe I'll give him a call.'

Don saw Pawley on his way with repeated thanks and assurances that his involvement in the marketing of Wortalleth West was more or less in the bag. As soon as his car had rumbled off down the drive, Don headed for the phone.

There was no answer on the landline. Don decided to try the mobile number before leaving a message.

'Yeah?' came the gruff response through a lot of crackle.

'Mike Coleman?'

'That's me. What can I do for you?'

'My name's Challenor. Don Challenor. I hear you're interested in, well, the construction of Wortalleth West.'

'Construction's an interesting choice of word, Don. What's your interest? *Fuck me.*' The sudden change of tone and a blare of horns revealed Coleman was on the road, though quite possibly with his mind elsewhere. 'Sorry, Don. Fucking tourists, hey?'

'Er, yeah. Look, er, I was wondering—'

'What's Wortalleth West to you, Don?'

'I, er, represent the owner.'

'You do? Harkness the pharma king?'

'He's not the owner.'

'He isn't? Weirder and weirder.'

'Can I ask why you wanted to see the building plans?'

'Who said I did, Don?'

'The Planning Department.'

'So much for fucking confidentiality, hey?'

'Why did you want to see them?' Don pressed.

'They're public documents. I don't have to give a reason. Just a pity the planners didn't take better care of them is all I can say.'

'Maybe we've got off on the wrong foot, Mr Coleman.'

'You can call me Mike, Don. Everyone does.'

'OK, Mike. Look, I'm not complaining about your request to see the plans. I just want to know what you were hoping to find out.'

'Are you some sort of lawyer, Don?'

'Absolutely not.'

'How come you represent the owner, then?'

'I'm trying to sell the house for her.'

'*Her?*'

'Mona Jackson.'

'*Who?*'

Don sighed. Prevarication seemed pointless. 'Mona Harkness.'

'Ah. So that's how the wind's blowing, is it? And you're . . . an estate agent?'

'Yes.'

'Which company?'

'You won't have heard of us. I'm down from London.'

'But phoning on a local landline, I see.'

'I'm at the house.'

'Wortalleth West? Are you really? Well, why don't I drop by on my way home? Maybe we can help each other out.'

'That'd be—'

'See you soon.'

⊹

121

Don comes into the workshop to tell me Pawley's gone but this guy Coleman's arriving before long. I stop fiddling with the blade setting on my plane – I've not been able to settle to anything serious – and listen to Don's account of his phone conversation with Coleman, who sounds like a total dick-head. I suddenly feel I need some air. Don can deal with Coleman. I suggest taking his phone with me to see if Holly Walsh has responded to his email. He hesitates, then remembers he trusts me, so hands it over.

'Don't worry, Don,' I tell him as I wander out. 'I promise not to scroll through every one of your messages for the past year.'

I take my bike, aiming for the track from Angrouse Farm up on to the headland. I'll get a signal somewhere along there. Just after I ride out into the road, though, I hear a car roaring up from the cove. I look round and see it turn into the lane leading to Wortalleth West. It's a big red Mercedes convertible, with the roof down and music booming out. I see the driver and figure he must be Mike Coleman: ruddy-faced, lots of sun-bleached blond hair, a face like it's been moulded from Plasticine. That's when I realize. I've seen him before. At Wortalleth West.

It was the last time I saw Harkness. He's never turned up while I've been living in the house, though we've spoken a couple of times on the phone. Back last October, while Vera was still working for Harkness and I was helping out part-time, I heard him and Coleman arguing in the study, though I didn't know who Coleman was then. I didn't even catch his name. I didn't know what they were arguing about either. Coleman did a lot of shouting, a lot of fucking this and fucking that. Harkness didn't raise his voice much. He kept his cool, like he always does. I heard something smash just before Coleman stormed out. I remember what he bellowed back at Harkness over his shoulder. 'It'd be really nice if just for once I could get a straight fucking answer.'

He was angry. He was like *very* angry. But when he noticed me he still spared a moment to look me up and down, getting to my face last of all. Oh, and he gave me what he obviously thought was a seductive smile. A lech, then, with a short temper. Yuck.

I went into the study to see if Harkness needed anything. He was sitting calmly behind his desk. There was a broken glass on the floor and a pool of what smelt like whisky. I asked him if he wanted me to clear it up.

The faraway expression he had on his face is how I always think of him. Grey hair, handsome features, velvety brown eyes, sixty plus but looking good on it. Poised. In control. Yeah. That's Harkness. Never surprised. Never wrong-footed.

'I'm going to have a swim later,' he said, smiling at me. 'You can do it then.'

I prop my bike against the five-bar gate near Seven Pines bungalow. In the middle of the field is one of the old platforms for the Marconi masts. I feel relieved I'm not at Wortalleth West while Coleman's there. It'll be interesting to hear what Don makes of him.

I perch on the top bar of the gate near the post and check Don's phone. It takes a moment to get its act together. Then there's incoming traffic.

A text from Fran. *Update me now please I don't expect to have to ask again.* Ouch. She doesn't sound happy.

There's an email too. From Holly Walsh. *Dear Mr Challenor, Ms Blake.* Very formal. But prompt. And polite. *I have always been willing to do everything I can to help Jane's family learn the truth. I am not sure there is much I can contribute all these years after the event, but please feel free to contact me.* She gives her phone number. No brush-off, then. No resistance. She's open to an approach.

I think about Andrew as I bike it back. He should've done this, whatever Muriel said. He shouldn't have given up. Well, maybe we can do it for him.

I don't go straight back to the house. I want to give sleazy Coleman plenty of time to clear off. So, I drop down to Poldhu Cove and sit on the sand among the marram grass and the sea beet and let the breeze carry the cleansing scent of the ocean over me. There are children on the beach, laughing and screaming playfully, families relaxing in the sun, couples strolling, dogs scurrying. Everything's ordinary, everything's tranquil. I can almost believe it's going to be all right.

✤

The burly, smirking bloke with too much beach-blond hair who emerged from the gleaming red Merc confirmed Don's worst suspicions of Mike Coleman before he even said a word. He had also pulled up too close to the MG for Don's peace of mind.

An agonizingly powerful handshake followed, then the salesman's patter about Sympergy Ltd. 'We're basically the face of renewables in the south-west, Don. The friendly face, as you can tell. Solar and wind farms, mostly. Plus initiatives in wave and tidal energy. It's the way, the way ahead, trust me. We're turning the future into the present.'

Pioneering or not, Coleman struck Don as a classic product of the barrow-boy tradition. Pile 'em high and sell 'em cheap, whether they were solar panels or Gucci rip-offs. It took quite an effort to keep smiling and make appropriately impressed remarks about his business model. Don was surprised by his own resilience.

124

'So,' Coleman went on as they walked into the house, 'you've got the job of shifting this place to top up Mona Harkness's alimony, have you, Don?'

'You could say that,' Don replied, taking care to drain the irritation he felt out of his voice.

'Shouldn't be too difficult. It's a fucking amazing property. I'd be happy to have it as a seaside getaway.' Coleman gazed up at the galleried landing.

'You've been here before?'

'Oh yeah. A few times.'

'On business?'

'Well . . .' Coleman smiled at Don. 'Harkness and I have never exactly been buddies.'

'I'm basing myself in the kitchen. Shall we?' Don led the way.

'Great. Any chance of a coffee? I'm seriously low on caffeine.'

'No problem.' Soon there were two double espressos between them as they stood by the breakfast bar.

'Top of the range kit, I see.' Coleman gestured towards the machine with his cup. 'Only the best for Harkness.'

'So, Mike,' Don began, 'your interest in the original plans for—'

'The transfer to Mrs H is some kind of tax dodge, presumably,' Coleman blithely butted in.

'I don't know.' Don gave him a measured look. 'It's really none of my concern.' *Or yours*, he could have added.

'S'pose not. But Harkness is slippery as a fucking eel, isn't he? His business partners are just beginning to find that out.'

'I've never met the man.'

'That probably explains why you've still got a shirt on your back.' Coleman laughed. He appeared to have a high opinion of his sense of humour.

Don smiled warily. 'You said on the phone we might be able to help each other out. What did you mean?'

'Well, I have a lot of connections, Don. A lot of *affluent* connections. Harkness isn't the only rich bastard who likes to spend time down here. I've had dealings with quite a few of them. I could introduce you to the ones who might be interested in swapping their marginally less stylish homes from home for this place.'

'I guess that could be useful.' Don guessed no such thing, but he judged it best to draw Coleman out.

'Now, you're probably wondering what I want in return for a bespoke referral service. Cooperation, Don. That's what I need. See, a few years ago, when as far as I know Harkness was still the legal owner of Wortalleth West, he hired Sympergy to set up a big solar array in a field he'd rented just half a mile or so inland from here, providing him with an exclusive power supply. It was supplemented by photovoltaic film installed on the south-facing walls of the house and garage block.'

'What film?' asked Don, suddenly curious. 'I didn't notice any.'

'Good.' Coleman grinned. 'It's intended to be inconspicuous. Ground-breaking stuff, actually. Transparent and less than a millimetre thick. Based on oligomer cells rather than silicon. We've always been ahead of the competition, as Harkness obviously appreciated. Still, I couldn't help wondering why he needed so much electricity, especially when he also bought through us a radical new design of flow battery. It was the same story as it was for the PV film. We were the sole UK source, so he had no choice about buying the battery from us. Big beast it was too. Shedloads of kilowatt hours. And pricey with it. But perfect back-up for when the sun don't shine, which is all too fucking often in my experience. Flow batteries have it over lithium ion because—' Coleman broke off and squinted at Don. 'Am I losing you, Don?'

'Battery technology's not exactly my field, Mike.'

'Understood. I'll just give you the bottom line, then. Harkness tied up an independent power supply for this property that's totally fucking excessive. I was happy to oblige, naturally, but it doesn't make a scrap of sense. For instance, where *is* the flow battery? It was a full rack of modules, about the height of this room. Where did he put it?'

'I don't know.' That was not exactly true. An obvious answer had already occurred to Don. But he had no intention of telling Coleman about the panic room. 'And to be honest—'

'You don't care, right? But maybe you should. See, I was hoping for a bit of publicity out of the deal. *Pharmaceuticals billionaire sees benefits of renewables and calls in the best in the business.* You get the drift? But I couldn't get Harkness to play ball. I hadn't dealt with him direct on the contractual front. The arrangements had been made by this guy Schmitz at Harkness HQ in Switzerland. Then Schmitz suddenly becomes uncontactable and Harkness's HR outfit tell me they've never heard of him. I'd only ever communicated with him by email and when I checked the paperwork I discovered the bills hadn't been paid by Harkness Pharmaceuticals. It had all been done through some Swiss shell company. Anyhow, the money for maintenance of the system kept on coming, so you could ask what the fuck was I complaining about. Then Harkness gets arrested and accused of bribery, embezzlement and Christ knows what and I can't help wondering if Herr Schmitz and a deniable little off-the-books operation isn't part of something bigger. See what I mean?'

'It certainly sounds odd.'

'What I'm suggesting, Don . . .' Coleman leant closer and lowered his voice, though since they were alone in the house the precaution seemed unnecessary. 'Is you and me take a good look round this house, find where the battery is and what it's powering, then consider whether we couldn't do well for ourselves by selling the information to these Quintagler people in the States. I don't know what Harkness has been up to here. It's all deeply weird. I reckon he arranged for the original plans of the house to go missing to stop the likes of me finding out what it is. But if we can figure it out, Don, you and me . . .' He rubbed his hands together. 'Then I reckon there's money to be made. A lot of money. For both of us.'

'You'll have to count me out, Mike.' Don tried to pitch his voice somewhere between reluctance and regret. 'I can't imagine Mrs Harkness – or her lawyer – approving of anything like that.'

'They don't need to know anything about it.'

'It would simply be unethical.'

'For fuck's sake, man, you're not a priest in holy orders.' Coleman looked incredulous that Don had said no to his proposition. 'You're an estate agent!'

'I wouldn't be happy about acting against her best interests.'

'She might actually approve of blackening Harkness's name. Think about it.'

'Or she might not. I'm pretty sure she wouldn't approve of us nosing around here without her knowledge or consent.'

'OK.' Coleman flung up his hands. His eyes widened in disbelief. 'Have it your way. I get the message. You don't want anything to do with it.'

'I'm afraid not. Sorry, but there it is.'

'Well, I may as well take a look around on my own account while I'm here.' Coleman drained his espresso, then headed for the door. 'There's a basement, right? I'll start with that.'

For a moment, Don was too surprised to react. Then he hurried after Coleman. 'Hold on.' When Coleman did not oblige, Don laid a restraining hand on his shoulder. 'I said hold on.'

'I heard you.' Coleman turned and glared. 'Thing is, Don, I don't plan on passing up this opportunity to find out what Harkness has been using Sympergy technology for. Could be a secret self-contained accounting system for his nefarious deals. That'd definitely be a tradable asset. Which might also get me some of the publicity the elusive Herr Schmitz originally implied would be mine for the asking. So, unless you intend to try and stop me – which I really wouldn't recommend – I suggest you just let me get on with it.' He switched his glare to a superior smile. 'OK?'

Don never got the chance to respond, because at that moment Glenys Probert walked into the doorway behind Coleman. She was in her gardening kit and was carrying a hoe, which the steely expression on her face suggested she was capable of using for more than weeding if she had to.

'Don?' she said, with an upward tilt of her eyebrows. The use of his Christian name seemed calculated to imply an acquaintance between them that did not in reality exist.

'Hello, Glenys,' said Don, playing along.

'Who the fuck are you?' demanded Coleman. She was blocking his way, so he could hardly ignore her.

'I'm on the staff here, Mr Coleman. Comings and goings aren't usually anything to do with me, but they can be if they need to be.'

The implication of Glenys's words was clear. And it looked to Don as if she would be willing to back them up. It must have looked the same to Coleman, because much of his bluster suddenly left him. 'Dunno what you're talking about. I was just having a chat with Don here.'

'I reckon we've said all we needed to say, haven't we, Mike?' Don suggested in a tone of sweet reason.

Coleman's lip curled. He was not ready to take both of them on. 'S'pose so,' he conceded. 'For the moment.'

'I'll see you out, then.'

Glenys stepped aside and Coleman set off at a moody plod towards the front door, with Don in close attendance. Nothing was said as they crossed the hall, though Coleman shot several suspicious glances around him, as if he might spot what he was looking for at every step.

At the door, he stopped and treated Don to a hostile stare. 'You're making a big mistake,' he said sullenly.

'Is that so?' Don leant past him and opened the door. 'Well, thanks for dropping by.'

Don waited until Coleman's Mercedes had roared off down the drive before he returned to the kitchen. Glenys, however, was nowhere to be seen. Exiting through the rear door, he spotted her up by her pick-up, in front of the garage block. He waved to her as he approached, but if she acknowledged the wave at all it was with the faintest of nods.

She was smoking a roll-up and drinking tea from a plastic Thermos mug. 'He's gone, then,' she said matter-of-factly.

'You seemed to know him.'

'Better than I know you. Seen him here a couple of times. And I've seen him drunk in St Keverne on Ox Roast Day. Likes the sound of his own voice does that one. And getting his own way.'

'Thanks for, er . . .'

'No need to thank me. I was looking out for Blake. Told her I'd call in today and see she was all right. Thought she might be in the house. Recognized Coleman's car. Decided to take a look.'

'Glad you did.'

'He's a bully. I know how to handle bullies.'

'So I saw.'

'Where's Blake?'

'She'll be back soon. She's fine.'

'She should leave here.'

'So I keep telling her.'

'She likes you.' Glenys ran her eye over Don as if he was a shrub that did not suit the local soil. 'And she trusts you.'

'Really?'

'Right to, is she?'

'I hope so.'

Glenys nodded. 'So do I.'

'What can you tell me about Harkness, Glenys?'

'He pays me regular as clockwork. Must make me more or less unique, from what I read about him.'

'A man of secrets?'

'Of a good many, I dare say.'

'D'you think he killed Jory Fry?'

'No sense asking me. No sense *you* asking at all. I garden. You sell houses. Stick to what you know, Don, that's my advice. As for Harkness . . .' She drew thoughtfully on her roll-up and narrowed her gaze. 'You've never met him and you probably know him as well as those who reckon they're close friends of his. He's not someone who *can* be known.' She nodded in evident satisfaction with her analysis of Harkness's character. 'That's his real secret.'

✤

131

When I get back to Wortalleth West, I find Glenys strimming a lawn edge while Don stares at a wall – literally. Glenys doesn't break off, just gives me a nod that tells me she's satisfied I'm all right. As for Don, I have to pat him on the shoulder to get his attention above the roar of the strimmer.

'If it had just been painted, I'd have guessed you were watching it dry,' I say as he whirls round.

'Have you ever looked at this?' he responds, gesturing with his working thumb.

'At the wall?'

'No. At the photovoltaic film on it.'

'The what?'

'See?' Don takes my hand and guides my fingers over the surface. It's smooth and, I realize, plastic: a clear layer of the stuff over the white render beneath.

'I wouldn't have noticed that. What is it?'

The roar of the strimmer dies as I'm speaking, so I end up sounding as if I'm shouting. Don smiles. 'It works like a solar panel. Harkness bought the system from Coleman's company, along with a massive back-up battery. He seems to need a lot of electricity. Coleman wanted to know where the battery is.'

'But Don sent him packing,' says Glenys, walking up behind me.

'Actually, Glenys sent him packing,' Don says shame-facedly.

I turn and look at Glenys. Her expression gives nothing away. 'I know how to deal with his type,' she says.

'Any news?' Don asks.

I tell him Holly Walsh is willing to see us. I don't tell him I've already arranged for her to see us. That can wait a little.

'I'll be off now,' says Glenys. I get the strange feeling she knows I've spoken to Holly and said Don and I will go and see her – knows and is pleased. It'll get me away from

132

Wortalleth West, of course – at least for a while. 'Give me a call if you're going anywhere, won't you?' She looks slyly at me. 'Just so I know I don't have to worry about what's happening here.'

We go into the house and I make tea. I ask Don how he's feeling. He says the nausea seems to have stopped and his wrist doesn't ache so badly, though that could be due to the paracetamols he's been packing down. I show him Holly Walsh's email and he fills me in on Coleman. He doesn't say what I know he must be thinking. The battery's in the panic room. All this electricity is to power something in there. Maybe Coleman's on the right track, even though he doesn't know where it leads. Or maybe not. You don't need much power to maintain secret financial records, do you? The way I see it, the power's got to be for something else, something bigger. I reckon that's how Don sees it too, though he doesn't straight out say as much.

We take the tea out to the table by the swimming pool. The sunshine is warm and mellow. It's time to tell him. I can't put it off any longer. 'I phoned Holly Walsh, Don. I spoke to her. And I made a date for us to go and see her. Tomorrow.'

He's surprised, to put it mildly. That wasn't part of the deal as he remembers it. And he's right. But when I read Holly's email again, sitting down at the cove, I suddenly thought: why wait? All this agonizing about whether to stay or leave. All this fretting about the panic room. Not to mention Wynsum fucking Fry. I'm not good at waiting things out. Never have been. Let's get on with it. If I can find out what really happened to Jane Glasson – whether or not Harkness is involved – it'd count for something. And maybe go a little way to making up for something else. So, I called Holly. Like I go on to tell Don, she sounded nice. Kind. Concerned. Still very concerned, in fact, about her long-missing friend. I explained my connection to the Glasson family and why Andrew felt he couldn't contact her. I didn't say exactly what we want to ask her about, but she guessed anyway. 'I know what you're wondering,' she said. 'I've wondered too.' There was a silence her end then. I didn't rush her. I let her get her head round whatever it was that made her hesitate. I wasn't sure she was alone. I couldn't quite read her by her voice. Then she said, 'I don't think I can talk about this now.' I said I understood, though I didn't really. How about if we visited her? I said Don was a friend who also knew the Glassons, which is kind of true. I said we wouldn't put any pressure on her. I did a better job than Don would have if he'd called her, that's for sure. I can see that thought forming reluctantly in his mind as he listens to me.

'So,' he says when he's calmed down, 'you talked her round.'

'I did.'

'I suppose I should say, "Well done."'

'You should.'

'When's she expecting us?'

'When we get there.'

'And where's "there"?'

'Brockenhurst. New Forest.'

'That's a lot further than I can drive as things are.' He raises his right hand. 'Have you forgotten this?'

'No. Which is why we should call on Wynsum Fry this evening.'

Don groans. 'Christ, no.'

'You agreed earlier.'

He rolls his eyes. 'I gave in earlier, you mean.'

'If you don't believe she has special powers, talking to her can't do any harm, can it?'

He's got no answer to that. Except the wrist. 'She lives in Helston, right? I'm not sure I can get even that far.'

'No probs. I can drive us.'

Don frowns. 'I thought you said you couldn't drive.'

'Did I?'

He nods. 'Yes. You did.'

'I meant I *haven't* driven. Much. Lately. But . . . yeah, I can drive.' I remember the practice runs out along the Redditch road with Terry, the only one of Mum's boyfriends I liked, which is probably why he didn't last long. The countryside was pretty scrabby, but it was for sure better than the inside of our house. 'You'll have a car of your own one day,' Terry used to say. He never was any good at prediction. It was probably lucky for him Mum chucked him out. But not for me. Because that's when—

'How's your little finger feel, Blake?' Don asks.

'My little finger?' He's lost me. 'Fine. Why?'

'It should feel quite tight. With me wrapped round it.'

'Come on, Don. You know this makes sense.' I force a smile out of him.

'You leaving here makes sense. What we'll learn from Holly Walsh and what good it'll do I don't know. But OK. We'll go and see her. As for Wynsum Fry . . .' He shrugs. 'Have it your way.'

'Great.'

'The New Forest's more than a day trip, though. Whoever's driving.'

'I guess we'll have to stay over somewhere.'

'And then?'

'Dunno. Depends, doesn't it?'

He drinks his tea and looks at me over the rim of the mug. I can see what he's thinking. Once he's got me away from Wortalleth West, it's job done. He won't be bringing me back. He won't be coming back himself either. Not if he can help it. This'll be out for both of us.

It might be true. I'm not sure, though. It doesn't feel like out to me. It feels like further in.

Don sets his mug down on the table. He's about to say

something. But a sound from the open doorway leading back towards the kitchen stops him. It's the telephone.

⁘

'Aren't you going to answer it, Don?' Blake asked, looking across the table at him.

'You could answer it,' Don retorted. 'You move faster than I do.'

Blake shuddered. 'I don't want to end up talking to French again.'

'Let whoever it is leave a message, then.'

'That phone doesn't take messages.'

The ringing continued. The caller was not giving up in a hurry. Eventually and reluctantly, Don stood up and marched into the house.

He reached the kitchen. The telephone was still ringing. He waited another moment, hoping it would stop. But it did not. He grabbed the receiver.

'Hello?'

'Don.' It was Fran. Don winced.

'Hi, Fran. I've been meaning to get back to you.'

'Have you really?'

'Yes. I've just been, er . . . rather busy.'

'So have I.' Fran's voice had an extra ratchet of tightness to it that Don recognized as not boding well. 'Mr Matheson of Home Security Electronics has been on to me. The technician he sent to look at the panic room ended up in hospital. He's trying to blame me. Apparently, the technician claims he was harassed by two men after leaving Wortalleth West.'

'That could be true.'

'What the hell's going on, Don? Why are you still there? Why haven't you responded to my calls?'

'I've been busy trying to deal with a . . . volatile situation.'

'What's that supposed to mean?'

'You should've warned me this wasn't a straightforward job, Fran. From what I hear, you're closer to Harkness than his soon-to-be-ex-wife's solicitor's got any right to be.'

'I beg your pardon?'

'You've been seen with him.'

'Says who?'

Don was about to reply when doubt suddenly sprang into his mind. Was this phone line secure? Was anything secure? 'I can't get into that now,' he said hurriedly. 'The point is you've put me in the middle of a serious mess. I'm not sure you understand just how serious either.'

'Have you got rid of the cleaner yet?'

'Never mind about Blake. She's an innocent bystander.'

'She's a problem you're supposed to have solved. And where are we with this panic-room nonsense?'

'It's not nonsense.'

'Am I going to have your report on Monday morning?'

Since Don had not done any work on the report since measuring the rooms and taking a few photographs, the honest answer to Fran's question was no. He plumped for something more evasive. 'There could be some slippage on that.'

'Slippage? You're not being paid for slippage. The job I asked you to do is remarkably simple. Why haven't you done it?'

'There's nothing simple about it, Fran, as I suspect you know.'

'I certainly don't.'

'You have to—'

'No,' Fran cut in, her tone ominously clipped. 'I don't *have* to anything. I gave you this job as a favour, Don.'

'Some favour.'

'Obviously, I should've known better. Very well. You're

no longer acting for my client in this matter. Is that clearly understood?'

'Hold on. I—'

'I'll email you confirmation of the cancellation of your engagement.'

'But—'

But nothing. Fran had rung off.

Don slammed the phone back down and mentally waved goodbye to two and a half thousand pounds – and maybe a lot more. 'Shit,' he murmured to himself.

Then the telephone rang again. Don smiled. Fran must have regretted giving him the boot. He snatched the receiver from the hook.

'Hi, Fran.'

'It's not Fran, Don,' said Amos French in his flat, frayed-around-the-edges voice.

Don groaned silently. 'What do you want?'

'Progress. Got any to report?'

'No,' Don replied dolefully, his capacity for prevarication drained.

'What's the news on the panic room?'

'There isn't any. It may not even be a panic room. If it is, it's got no bearing on what you're after.'

'That so?'

'Money stolen by the likes of Harkness ends up in tax-haven bank accounts. Grand Cayman. Panama. Liechtenstein. That kind of place. There aren't going to be ziggurats of cash stashed in a hidey-hole in the man's Cornish holiday home.'

'Ziggurats? Kinda high-flown imagery for you, Don.'

'I can't help you. I explained that when we met.'

'Do I strike you as the sort of guy who relies on folk to *volunteer* their help?'

Don drew in a deep breath and let it out slowly. 'I

haven't got the information you want and I can't see any way of getting it. You should be looking elsewhere.'

'I don't necessarily disagree with you there. In fact, I *am* looking elsewhere. If I find what I need, I'll likely cut you out of the loop, which means you'll miss out on a big pay day. But, hey, it's not as if you need the money, is it? Or have I got that wrong?'

'I'll survive, thanks,' Don said leadenly.

'Don't be too sure. Survival isn't some kind of default position. You've got to work at it. How much does Blake know, Don? That's what you oughta ask yourself. D'you want to find out? Or d'you want me to? If I draw a blank with these other leads and have to circle back to Wortalleth West, she and I will have to have a talk. Which is an experience you might want to spare her.'

'She can't help you any more than I can.'

'Wish I could take your word for that. As it is . . .' Silence echoed down the line. Then French said, almost in an undertone, 'I'll catch you later.' And he was gone.

Don walked slowly back out to the poolside table, where Blake was waiting. He slumped down in the chair. 'Fran,' he said glumly. 'And French.'

'What did they say?' Blake asked, anxiety skittering in her gaze.

'Fran sacked me. French threatened me.' Don rubbed his eyes. This made nothing clearer, except his certainty on one point. 'I need to get out of here. So do you. So I guess . . .'

'Yeah?'

'I guess you'd better drive me into Helston.'

The drive featured a lot of gear-crunching, with Don switching between exasperated mutterings to Blake and abject apologies to the MG, something Blake made it clear she found annoying.

The trauma of the journey had at least the advantage of taking Don's mind off what awaited him at the end of it. They reached Helston as the long June evening was fading towards dusk. The narrow streets in the area where Wynsum Fry lived, a jumble of council houses and flats, were strangely quiet considering the fine weather. Her bungalow, small and roofed in what looked like corrugated asbestos, was wedged between a block of maisonettes and a church hall, accessible by a path that zigzagged between them.

Blake found a place to pull in by a line of tumbledown garages. She said she would wait there.

Don approached the bungalow apprehensively, his doubts about the wisdom of the visit dragging at his feet. It was a short walk, but plenty long enough for him to imagine all manner of disasters. His bluster on the subject of the occult did not quite match his beliefs. Something buried deep within him suggested there was more to witchcraft than charlatanry. And he doubted he was equipped to tell the difference.

The question of whether Wynsum Fry was at home was at least swiftly answered. The half-glazed front door opened as Don approached and there she was, regarding him beadily from the threshold.

'Well, well, well,' she said, smiling thinly. 'Mr Challenor come a-callin' on a summer's evening.' Summer's evening or not, though, she was wearing a long cardigan over the same skirt and sweater Don had seen her in at the Blue Anchor. She seemed to carry her own winter around with her.

'I think we might have got off on the wrong foot yesterday,' Don said hesitantly.

'If us did, 'twas by your choice.'

'Well, I'm sorry about that.'

She nodded. 'Reckon you might be.'

'I was wondering . . . if we could, er, have a chat.'

''Bout what?'

'Jack Harkness.'

She looked at Don for a long, silent moment. Then she said, 'We can talk about 'im if you wants. But I'll give 'ee no second chance of card-reading 'less you pays me good money.'

'That's all right. I didn't, cr . . .'

'Come to 'ave your future told?'

'No. I didn't.'

'First wise thing I've 'eard come out of your mouth, Mr Challenor.'

'Really?'

'See, some futures are better *not* told. Reckon yours might be one of 'em.'

Don summoned a defiant smile. 'That's comforting.'

'Not meant to be.' She stared him down. 'So, what you got to say 'bout Jack 'Arkness?'

'Can I, er, come in?'

'Reckon not. Seein' as you'm an unbeliever.'

'Well, I . . .'

'You can sit yourself there.'

Her nod directed Don's attention to a steel and plastic camp-chair set up by the front step, which until then he had not noticed. 'OK,' he said, sitting down somewhat awkwardly.

He turned away from Fry briefly while moving to occupy the chair. When he turned back towards her, he saw she had unfolded a matching chair and sat down herself.

'Glad you wants to speak to me, Mr Challenor, when you didn't afore,' she said.

'I've made a few, er, thought-provoking discoveries.'

''Ave 'ee now?'

'About Jack Harkness.'

'Go on, then.' She engaged Don eye to eye. 'Say your piece.'

⁑

I leave the MG and walk away from her. God, Don's got me at it now. I mean I walk away from *it*. I can see the chimney of the bungalow over the curved roof of the church hall. Smoke's curling up from it. Somehow, I'm not surprised Fry's lit a fire in June.

I step in round the wall surrounding the church hall. From there, I can just get a view of the corner of the bungalow without showing myself. By the front door there's a chair, facing away from me. Fry's sitting in it, looking at Don, I guess, though I can't see him. She made me sit outside when I called to ask if she'd do a reading for Andrew. I don't know what you have to do to get invited in. I was sure Don wouldn't qualify, though. In fact, I was counting on it.

Maris never named the other dewitcher she went to after she ran into so much trouble with Calensa Fry. She told me she was dead now anyway. The woman knew Fry well, though. They'd crossed swords before.

The other dewitcher's advice was weird but pretty specific. She said it was sure to work and Maris believed her, though she never needed to try it.

Don's visit to Fry gives me a chance to do that, though. He has no idea what I've got in mind. I might not be able to pull it off. Whether I can or not, I have to be back at the car before he finishes with her.

Sometimes you've got to take a risk. And this is one of those times. I'm quick and quiet when I need to be. I climb and scurry well. I could be a great burglar.

Here goes.

⁑

Don gave it his best shot. His cover story, as he set it out under Wynsum Fry's beady gaze, was as close to the truth as he could contrive. Visiting Andrew Glasson to see if Blake could move back in with him after leaving Wortalleth West, Don had heard the sad tale of Glasson's missing daughter. Considering what Blake had told him about Fry's dead brother, he had started to wonder if there was anything he could do to establish what part Jack Harkness had played in those events.

'Why should you care?' Fry challenged him, which brought Don to the crux of the matter. They both knew why he might care, but Don did not propose to admit she had any power over him. Instead, he recycled Mike Coleman's self-serving motivation for digging up dirt on Harkness.

'Between you and me, Miss Fry,' he said, 'I'm hoping the American company that's after Harkness will pay handsomely for information that'll land him in even bigger trouble than charges of bribery and embezzlement.'

'You'm in this for what you can get, then?'

'That's one way of putting it. But I'm going after the truth. Isn't that what you want uncovered?'

'I already knows the truth.'

'You knowing doesn't harm Harkness. But if the world knows . . .'

'The King of Spades'll lose his crown.' Fry gave Don a long, hard look. 'What makes you reckon you can take it off 'im?'

'I have a lead to follow.'

She frowned curiously. 'What might that be, now?'

'It concerns a schoolfriend of Jane Glasson's. I think she might know where Jane is. If she does . . .'

Fry sat forward in her chair. 'Why you'm telling me this, Mr Challenor?'

143

'Since you're Jory's sister, I suppose I hoped . . . you'd give me your blessing.'

'Is that so?'

'If I do make any money out of it, it'd only be fair, as Jory's closest surviving relative, for you to get a share.'

'Oh, it comes down to money, do it?' Her expression darkened. 'You reckon I can be bought, do 'ee?'

'No, I don't. But I don't see why you should miss out either. Money makes the world go round, whether we like it or not.'

'The world you lives in right enough.'

'I just wanted you to know what I had in mind. So that we . . . understand one another.'

'I understands you, Mr Challenor, you can be sure. You'm a sheet o' clear glass to me. But I'll not worrit over your reasons if you can bring 'Arkness down. I'll give my blessing to that any day o' the week.'

'Well, I'm . . . glad to hear it.'

'Take my 'and. I'll know you'm in earnest then.'

She extended her right hand, the palm open. Don was back where he had started with her, in the rear bar of the Blue Anchor. There was no dodging a commitment of some kind. It was required of him.

Bracing himself against the pain it was likely to cause, he half rose from the chair and stretched forward to shake her hand. The contact was light – and painless. She smiled at him and closed her left hand over his right. His wrist felt oddly warm, but nothing more than that.

'A promise lightly given is a 'eavy thing to break,' she said so quietly it seemed to Don he had merely imagined her speaking.

Suddenly, a wave of nausea swept over him. He pulled his hand away and leant over, grasping his knees.

'What's the matter, Mr Challenor?'

'I don't . . . feel well.'

'There's a bathroom down the passage.'

Raising his head, Don saw her pointing into the house. He nodded his thanks and stumbled past her. The passage was narrow and dark. Only one of the three doors off it stood open. Through it Don glimpsed a wash hand basin and the rim of a roll-top bath. He blundered towards it.

As he pushed the bathroom door fully open and entered, a frosted-glass window ahead of him clunked shut, the loose stay rattling against the frame. He felt too sick to make anything of it. The loo was to his right, an old-fashioned wooden-seated WC with the cistern at ceiling height. He flung up the lid and instantly vomited, copiously, into the pan.

A minute or so slowly passed as he recovered himself. He flushed the loo a couple of times and rinsed his mouth out with water from the basin, then douched his face and looked in the circular mirror above it. His reflection was so blurred he started back in surprise. There was nothing wrong with his eyesight. At least, there *had* been nothing wrong with it. The rest of the room was in clear focus. He looked in the mirror again. His reflection was pin-sharp now. He shook his head in bafflement.

When he went back out into the passage, Wynsum Fry was waiting for him, standing in the doorway straight ahead. He could not see the expression on her face, cast in shadow as it was by the evening light behind her.

'Better now, Mr Challenor?' she asked as he walked towards her.

'Yes thanks. I'm, er . . . sorry about that.'

'No need. Purgation is good for the soul.'

Don looked at her as he reached the front door. Her gaze

was feline, observant, superior. He could find nothing to say.

'Look in the mirror, did 'ee, Mr Challenor?'

He nodded.

'There's a flaw in the glass. An aberration, they calls it. You can't always trust it.' She smiled faintly. 'But, then, there's not much you can.'

He wanted to be away from her, but somehow he could not bring himself to squeeze between her and the camp-chair.

'I'll be 'earin' from 'ee. Do I 'ave that right?'

Again he nodded.

She took a step back. 'Then good evenin', Mr Challenor. You go careful now.'

Blake was waiting for him in the MG. He clambered into the passenger seat with a sigh.

'How'd it go?' she asked, looking round at him.

'Not sure.'

'How's the wrist?'

He had forgotten the pain in his wrist. Flexing the joint, he realized it no longer hurt. 'Bugger me,' he murmured.

'Miracle cure?'

'Apparently.'

'We got what we came for, then.'

'I guess so.'

'And there's nothing to hold us back?'

'No.' He shook his head and glanced over his shoulder in the direction of the bungalow. 'Nothing at all.'

SEVEN

THE LIGHTS ARE OFF IN THE ROOM BEHIND THE MIRROR, BUT there is light nonetheless: stand-by amber on off-line computers shrouded in darkness, red on wall-mounted digital clocks recording the time in seven different time zones: London, Frankfurt, Moscow, Beijing, Tokyo, Los Angeles, New York; grey and white on a bank of flickering video screens.

The pictures on the screens are fed by cameras concealed around the house, in light fittings and cornices and intrusion sensors. On one, hidden within the master-bedroom closet, Don Challenor looms into view. He approaches the mirror and stands close to it for a minute or more, then retreats, reappearing on a second screen in the bedroom itself shortly afterwards. A third screen shows Blake, standing by the hob in the kitchen, stirring porridge, a fourth Don again, on the landing.

Elsewhere there are views of rooms in which nothing moves: empty chairs and tables, vacant lengths of hallway, a gym filled with equipment, a wine cellar racked high with bottles.

Everything is videoed, everything recorded: minutes, hours, days, weeks of the comings and goings and all the much longer absences of Wortalleth West. Everything is seen. Nothing is missed.

Except what happens inside this room, the invisible centre of the house, the secret heart of what Jack Harkness has built. Here, unobserved and unsuspected, the provisions he has made bide their measured time and await their moment.

Don slept dreamlessly. He woke feeling calm and refreshed. It was how his Australian sister-in-law had assured him he would feel if he ever adopted her favourite detox diet of lettuce smoothies. He had no wish to credit his clear-headedness to Wynsum Fry, but the fact remained his wrist was completely free of pain.

By the time he had showered and shaved, Blake had come down to the house from the garage block. She shouted up an offer of porridge, which he accepted after fruitlessly requesting bacon and eggs.

He went into the master bedroom before going downstairs. The mirror at the back of the closet threw back his reflection with disarming clarity. If there was an aberration here, it was behind the glass, not within it.

Don pressed the frame of the mirror where he had before and it swung open, revealing the steel door behind. He rested his fingers lightly on the door's smooth surface and was almost certain he could detect a faint vibration from within, a thrill of contained energy. He pressed his ear to the steel, but heard nothing. There was, he assured himself, nothing to hear. And yet . . .

He clicked his tongue in irritation at his own lack of certainty, swung the mirror back into place, then turned and walked away.

Three hundred miles away, in the flower garden in the south-eastern corner of Hyde Park, Fran Revell sat down on a bench and spread out the *Sunday Times* on her lap. She was casually dressed, in cool summer trousers and light top. She was wearing sunglasses and a baseball cap pulled low over her eyes. Altogether, someone who knew her could easily have walked by without recognizing or even noticing her, which was in fact her intention.

She took sips from a takeaway coffee as she pretended to read the newspaper and did not look up when a man walked into the flower garden carrying a newspaper of his own and sat down on the bench next to hers.

He was tall and lean, dressed in tracksuit and trainers, though he did not appear to have been running. His thick grey hair and weathered features suggested he was in his fifties or sixties and he could easily have passed for an American with his orthodontically perfect bright white teeth. There was a quizzical, faintly amused tilt to his mouth and eyebrows, but a seriousness, a sense of purpose, in his gaze.

He laid the paper beside him on the bench and stretched down to adjust the left leg of his tracksuit, which had snagged on something fitted to his ankle. Then he sat back, took a deep appreciative breath of the clear summer air and glanced across at Fran.

'When you get to the business section,' he said in a voice so accentless judging where he came from would have been difficult in the extreme, 'don't read the piece about me. It's bollocks.'

'Thanks for the warning,' said Fran, who did not return his glance.

'How's my divorce going?'

'Smoothly.'

'Good. I only want the best for Mona.'

'Of course you do.'

'You say that as if you doubt it.'

151

'Is there a panic room at Wortalleth West, Jack?'

'You surely didn't want to meet me just to ask that.'

'I had to sack the agent I sent down there. Since I'm going to have to sort this out personally now, I'd like to know what I'm walking into.'

'A highly desirable property on the Cornish coast, generously made over by me to Mona. That's what you're walking into.'

'Is there a panic room in the house?'

Jack Harkness pondered the question for a moment, then said, 'No. There isn't.'

'Don insists there's some kind of void adjacent to the master bedroom.'

'He's an architect, is he?'

'No, but he's accurate enough.'

'I see. Well . . .'

'I sent in someone from a Plymouth company, with panic-room experience. They seem to think there's something there.'

'I didn't say there wasn't. I just wouldn't call it a panic room.'

'What is it, then?'

'Why don't we say it's what Don suggested – a void? Maybe I allowed for a panic room, but never went ahead with installing one. That sounds plausible, doesn't it? After all, why would I want a panic room down in Cornwall?'

Fran set down her coffee and pushed her sunglasses up on her nose. Something in the action suggested she was not as calm as she appeared to be. 'I wish I'd never agreed to any of this.'

'To be fair, you had no choice but to agree.'

'Peter's a good man.'

'Maybe. But he does have his fallibilities. And, while you're married to him, they're your fallibilities as well.'

'Why don't you tell me what this is all about?'

'Because you don't need to know. Just do what Mona wants. Sell Wortalleth West and deposit the proceeds in whichever of her accounts she nominates.'

'For a man accused of embezzlement, you seem strangely indifferent to money.'

Harkness smiled. 'I'm generous to a fault.'

'The panic-room engineer ended up in hospital, you know.'

'I thought you said that was a road accident.'

'Yes. But according to his boss he crashed because he was upset after being grilled about Wortalleth West by a couple of heavies.'

'Heavies? Aren't you being rather melodramatic?'

'I don't know, Jack.' Now she looked at him. 'Am I?'

'Just get on with the sale.'

'All right.' Fran sighed. 'I'll go down there tonight on the sleeper and start things moving.'

'Excellent.' He paused, then added, 'You will take care, won't you?'

⁘

Now Don's wrist is OK, he insists on doing all the driving. It's obviously a relief to him he doesn't have to trust me with the MG. He even says it's a relief to *her*. Apparently he can tell by how smoothly she – *it* – is running. I let this go over my head and focus instead on where we're going – and why.

It turns out to be a five-hour-plus drive to Brockenhurst. Even with her master at the wheel, the MG can't beat the traffic. Don's bumper-hugging and lane-dodging doesn't make any difference, though occasionally – just occasionally – he manages a throaty burst of acceleration that pins me back in my seat.

He starts asking too many questions. It's light conversation

153

to him, I s'pose. But I'm not going to tell him anything about myself I don't want him to know and, for the time being, decent guy though he basically is, what I want him to know about the early life of Blake is as close to zero as I can get.

Don isn't hard to deflect. He has a lot of estate agency anecdotes he can work his way through. And he's the butt of a few of them, which is nice. Don is way short of perfect, but at least he knows it. And he doesn't try to hide it.

We stop for lunch at a pub near Honiton. While we sit out in the garden, soaking up the sun and in Don's case the local beer, I ask him what he thinks we're going to learn from Holly Walsh. He says he doesn't know, but I get the message just by the way he says it. He wants us to learn nothing. He wants it to be a dead end. So we can just give up. Bad luck, Don, I don't say. It's not going to be a dead end. I've got a feeling about Holly Walsh. There's a secret she wants to share. All we have to do is help her share it.

Don gets a couple of emails from Fran – working on a Sunday, she must be a woman under pressure – while we're at the pub. One's termination of his contract. The other's a request for information. That sets him fuming.

Eventually, he fires back a reply to Fran, giving her Pawley's name as an agent who'll arrange a quick sale of Wortalleth West. Then we get back on the road.

I've never been to the New Forest before. The roads are busy, with cars towing caravans and horseboxes. It's a warm, sunny Sunday afternoon. There are picnickers and hikers out and about. The woods are thick and full-leafed, the stretches of heathland purple with drifts of heather. There are ponies, too, and wandering cattle. Everything looks softer and sleeker here. We're a long way from Cornwall.

*

I suppose I thought Holly Walsh's home was going to be a chocolate-box cottage: thatched roof, creaky wooden gate, hollyhocks round the front door. In fact, Furzelands turns out to be a modern bungalow in a cul-de-sac of other modern bungalows on the outskirts of Brockenhurst. There's a big garden, though, and lots of flowers. Somebody works hard to keep the place up.

We're expected. A woman who moves far too lithely to have MS comes out to meet us as Don unwinds himself from the car. She's slim and brisk, wearing a neat skirt and top. She has bobbed fair hair and a face that could be pretty but for a tight little mouth that gives her a kind of perma-pout.

There's a round of smiles, introductions and handshakes. She's Anna Marchant, Holly's partner – and carer, I guess. She says a lot of friendly, welcoming things that Don seems to swallow, but there's a brittleness about her. Maybe she's worried we'll upset Holly or stir up trouble. I don't live with an MS sufferer, so what do I know? I decide to give her the benefit of the doubt.

She takes us round the back of the house, trilling about how nice it's warm enough for tea in the garden. Everything's trimmed and prinked and colourful. Glenys wouldn't like it. 'You've got to give plants a bit of freedom,' I can hear her saying. 'Otherwise they go stir-crazy.'

Holly Walsh is waiting for us on the patio, sitting in one of four chairs drawn up round a table. The furniture's trad wrought iron. There's a big parasol, sheltering Holly from the sun. She doesn't get up. She's sitting on two cushions and there's a crutch propped against her chair. She's thin and pale, dark-haired, with a heart-shaped face and big engaging eyes. There's a tinge of pink in her cheeks, though, and her smile is the kind it's hard to fake. She looks fragile rather than frail. But spirited.

More introductions. Anna goes to make tea. They've

already had some. There's cake as well. Don wolfs down a slice so greedily you wouldn't believe he's had roast lamb and apple crumble for lunch.

While Anna's away, Holly tells us what a wonder the woman is. I get the feeling they haven't been together that long, though Holly doesn't say exactly *how* long. But she talks about Anna and Ditrimantelline – the wonder drug that got her out of a wheelchair – as if they arrived in her life kind of around the same time.

I ask if I can use the loo. I need a pee, but it's also an excuse to see inside the house before we get caught up discussing what's brought us here. Holly gives me directions and off I go, while Don agonizes over whether to have a second slice of cake. I bet I'll see it on his plate when I get back.

Inside, everything's spick and span – like a bit too spick and span. Wonder woman's probably a whizz at housekeeping as well as gardening. It's all a bit clinical, uncluttered, controlled. I meet Anna coming out of the kitchen with the tea-tray as I head for the bathroom and catch her frown. We're some kind of threat to her. You can see it in her eyes.

The knitted cover over the lid of the loo's a bit of a surprise. Likewise the yellow rubber duck eyeing me from the side of the bath. There are wall-mounted grab-handles to help Holly move herself around and an electric toothbrush she probably uses. I take a look in the cabinet above the basin. Elixtris face cream and body scrub. Do they both use Elixtris, I wonder? There are lots of pills as well, including several cartons of Ditrimantelline. Ten-milligram tablets to be taken daily. *Warning: do not drive, operate machinery or drink alcohol while using this medicine.* Then there's *Made in Switzerland* and the manufacturer's name: *Harkness Pharmaceuticals.*

156

I look at the carton and wonder how much it's worth. Harkness is everywhere. You just can't get away from him.

⁜

Don was beginning to think the second slice of cake was a mistake. He had wanted to please Holly by accepting it. Her frailty and her captivating, wide-eyed gaze were hard to resist. The return of Anna, with more tea, and Blake shortly afterwards supplied cover for him to push his plate to one side.

There was further superficial chit-chat while Anna poured tea, then she – rather than Holly – asked exactly how Don and Blake had come to know the Glasson family. Blake answered, with a substantially accurate account of her own involvement. Don's she glossed over. He said he was 'just trying to help', which Holly seemed to have no difficulty accepting. As for Anna, she subtly pressed Don to say what he did for a living. He told her readily enough, without mentioning the sale of Wortalleth West.

'I feel terribly sorry for Mr Glasson,' said Holly. 'Jane's disappearance must eat away at him, especially since his wife died. I stayed with the family several times during school holidays and university vacations. Lovely people.'

'Muriel doesn't sound so lovely,' remarked Anna.

'No. Well, having a younger sister as beautiful and intelligent as Jane can't have been easy.'

'You and Jane were close friends, then?' Don asked, before wondering if the question came across as crass. Perhaps they were more than friends.

If so, Holly took the issue in her stride. 'She was the best,' she said. 'So alive. So . . . inspiring.'

'Maybe she's still the best,' said Blake softly.

'Maybe,' Holly acknowledged. 'I don't think the opinion of this fortune-teller Mr Glasson went to is significant

157

one way or the other, though. Put simply, I can't believe Jane would put her parents – or me – through the agony of not knowing what happened to her. What would be the point? Why would she do such a thing?'

'Nothing occurred on the day she disappeared that made you think later she was planning something?' Don asked.

'No, nothing at all. Everything was completely normal. We had coffee at King's Cross before we went our separate ways on the Underground. We chatted about this and that. Jane had just ditched some soppy young man from King's who thought he was her boyfriend. I teased her about that. But teasing Jane wasn't really possible. She soared above most things. We agreed I'd go down to Cornwall at the beginning of September, after we'd both earnt some spending money. It never occurred to me – never would have in a million years – that I was never going to see her again. And now . . .'

Holly looked for a moment as if she was about to cry. Anna moved consolingly towards her, but Holly waved her away and summoned a smile.

'Sorry. Anyway, that's twenty-two years ago. In the end, you just have to accept . . . Well, you just have to accept. I don't know what happened to her and I almost certainly never will, which is probably for the best, because, whatever it was, it can't have been anything good.' She swallowed hard. 'We lost her. It's as bleak and as simple as that.'

'Surely,' ventured Blake, 'the anonymous offer of funding for your supply of Ditrimantelline . . . must've made you think.'

'Some people prefer to do good without personal recognition,' Anna jumped in. She was keen – maybe keener than Holly – to block the suggestion that Jane might be responsible.

'Of course it made me think,' said Holly. 'But to believe Jane is the source of the money would require me to believe she deliberately and calculatingly abandoned her family and friends twenty-two years ago. That makes no sense to me. Not a scrap.'

'Where does the, er, money actually come from?' Don asked hesitantly.

'Credit Suisse, London. An account in the name of Nightingale. They won't reveal whether that's a personal or company name.'

'So, you have asked?'

'Naturally,' said Anna, her tone sharpened by otherwise well-disguised irritation.

'How did your benefactor first contact you?' Don pressed on.

'An email. From someone called Luscinia. Or more likely not called Luscinia, since that's Latin for nightingale. She said she worked in pharmaceuticals and was appalled by how expensive some of the most effective drugs had become. She'd read my blogs about living with MS and wanted to help by supplying Ditrimantelline. It had to be done anonymously or she'd get into trouble. Well, I'd heard about how successful Ditrimantelline had been in the States. I wasn't likely to say no. It was an answer to a prayer. If you'd met me eighteen months ago, you'd be amazed by the difference.'

'It's true,' said Anna. 'The treatment's been transformative.'

'Who makes the drug?' asked Blake.

'Harkness Pharmaceuticals,' Holly replied. And Don was instantly alert.

'So,' Blake went on, 'd'you think Luscinia works for them?'

'Not necessarily,' Anna cut in. 'It's quite possible she

works for an independent lab that supplies Harkness with the drug. A manufacturer's label on a box doesn't prove they actually produce the contents.'

'Does it matter?' Holly asked, frowning slightly.

'It might,' said Blake. 'After all, Jane did know Jack Harkness, didn't she?'

'Did she?' Holly's frown deepened.

'He was born in Mullion. That's only about six miles from Helston.'

'Even so . . .'

'And she had a holiday job at a café in Mullion where Harkness was a customer.'

'Well, she never mentioned him to me,' said Holly. 'Of course, he wasn't so famous back then, but still I don't recall her saying anything about him. Besides, a less likely recruit to the pharmaceuticals industry than Jane is hard to imagine.'

'Why's that?' asked Don.

'For a start, she was a biologist rather than a chemist. But the real objection would be the strong principles she held. Jane was horrified by the harm being done to the environment. She was worried about global warming while most people of our age, including me, were hopelessly blasé on the subject. I remember her giving me a lecture about what a let-down the Rio Earth Summit had been. We were in the sixth form. 1992, it would have been. Then, during our gap year, we travelled together to Thailand, Indonesia and Australia. I was all for spending as much time on the beach as possible. She was more concerned about the shrinkage of the rain forest and the degradation of coral reefs. Later, at Cambridge, I remember her railing against the use of chemical fertilizers and pesticides. She believed the human race was upsetting the balance of the ecosystem without understanding how interdependent all life forms are.' Holly shook her head as she drew on her memories. 'I hear her voice whenever I see a dead bee. And I see a lot of dead bees these days.'

'She must've been great to have as a friend,' said Blake.

'Oh yes, she was.' Holly sighed. 'Have you ever seen a photograph of her?'

'Andrew Glasson showed me a snap of Jane and her sister when they were in their early teens,' said Don.

'You should see a later picture.' Holly looked across at Anna. 'Can you get the one from my bedroom, Anna?'

'Certainly.' Anna sprang up and headed into the house.

'Did Jane ever travel to Switzerland?' Blake enquired gently.

'I don't think so. Although . . .'

'Yeah?'

'Well, she went to Italy with the soppy boy from King's during the Easter vacation the year she disappeared. They went by train, so I suppose they might've gone by way of Switzerland. But . . . why do you ask?'

'Harkness Pharmaceuticals' HQ is in Switzerland. And Credit Suisse is a Swiss bank, right?'

'Luscinia isn't Jane,' Holly said emphatically. 'I'm certain of that.'

'We're simply doing everything we can for Jane's father, Holly,' Don cut in to soften the exchanges. 'Asking every question that can be asked.'

'Of course,' said Holly, signalling with a nod that she understood.

Anna reappeared then with a framed photograph she handed to Don.

'We hired a punt on Jane's twenty-first birthday,' said Holly. 'I took that picture somewhere along the Backs.'

The Jane Glasson Don saw in the photograph was eight or nine years older than the one he had seen in the photograph in Helston. She also looked older than twenty-one, more mature somehow, though unquestionably very attractive, in the full bloom of early womanhood. She was wearing a cheesecloth blouse and jeans. Her hair was slightly darker than it had been in her teens. And her eyes had acquired a cast of mysteriousness, of unknowability it seemed to Don. He passed the picture on to Blake.

'She's beautiful,' Blake said at once.

'She was, wasn't she?' mused Holly.

'Sorry,' said Blake, though exactly what she was sorry for remained unclear to Don.

Holly, on the other hand, seemed to grasp her meaning quite distinctly. She looked directly at Blake and said, 'Thank you.'

'The soppy boy from King's,' said Blake softly. 'D'you remember his name?'

'Gareth something. Beyond that . . . I don't know. I never actually met him.'

'Not even after Jane's disappearance? It must've been a shock to all her friends at Cambridge.'

'I never went back to Cambridge,' Holly replied, her voice heavy now with sadness. 'I had a breakdown. There were physical symptoms as well. The start of all this.' She raised her hands in an expressive gesture. 'I sometimes wonder whether I'd have contracted MS if Jane hadn't vanished, though my doctors say there's no reason to think that. It's just . . . bad luck.' She sighed. 'All of it's bad luck really. Nothing more. Nothing less.'

✣

There aren't many more questions we can ask. Holly just goes on insisting Luscinia isn't – can't be – Jane. Whether she's as sure as she says she is I don't know. She and Anna keep glancing at one another. What the glances mean I can't tell. They both bottle up their emotions.

They're on safer ground – or think they are – talking about how they met. Anna rented a house nearby when she moved to the area to open a recruitment agency in Lyndhurst. That's just over a year ago. They act like they've been together a long time, but they haven't really. I suppose you'd call that instant compatibility, if you weren't kind of suspicious of Anna's whole loving support act, like I am.

I want to ask Holly exactly when she first heard from Luscinia. I'm still trying to work the question into the conversation when she successfully pours herself some tea and supplies the answer herself. 'The winter before last I couldn't have done that. It was the worst I've ever felt. Then Luscinia's email landed in my inbox. What a New Year's gift it turned out to be. I've been improving ever since I started taking Ditrimantelline.'

So, here's the sequence. Luscinia makes contact, early last year. Then Anna breezes into town in the spring. And Holly's got a new lease of life.

She doesn't get up when we leave, though. I guess we've exhausted her. Anna walks us out to the car. Don thanks her for the tea as we go and blathers on about how delicious the cake was. Anna gives him one of her smiles, which are beginning to remind me of a crack in a sheet of ice when you drop a rock on it.

Don's relieved. I can tell. He wanted this to be a dead end and he thinks it is. But I don't reckon it is. And it looks like Anna can tell I don't.

'Are you going back to Cornwall tonight?' she asks as we reach the pavement.

'No,' Don replies. 'We're—'

'There are more leads to follow up,' I cut in. 'We haven't

163

given up on Jane.' I look at Anna as I say that. I don't want her to think we can be brushed off so easily. I can sense Don frowning at me as I speak. What leads? he's wondering.

'What will you tell Mr Glasson?' Anna asks. She shakes back the curls of her bob from her jaw and gazes at me intently. I've got her attention, that's for sure.

'That we're going to have to try other ways to find out if Jane is the source of the drug.'

'You heard Holly. You know she's certain it has nothing to do with Jane.'

Don's eyes are fixed on me. At least he's had the sense to shut up. 'We're not certain,' I say in my best friendly but firm tone.

Anna gives me a long look. She's weighing her options. I let her weigh them. Then she says quietly, 'There's a little more I can tell you that'll remove all doubt in the matter.'

'There is?' Don asks in surprise.

'Can you meet me an hour from now?'

I nod. 'Sure.'

'Lyndhurst. There's a parking area on the eastern edge of the town. You take the Beaulieu turning off the Southampton road, then turn left straight after the cattle grid.'

I nod again. 'We'll be there.'

She watches us drive away. As we take the bend in the road, she turns and goes back indoors. I watch her in the wing mirror, walking briskly, hurrying, if you like.

Don must've been watching her too, in the rear-view mirror. He lets out a breath and says, 'What was that all about?'

'Secrets, Don. Our anal friend Anna is carrying a lot of them.'

'You still think Lucinda might be Jane Glasson?' He turns out of the cul-de-sac and heads back the way we came, towards the town centre.

'Luscinia,' I correct him. 'Latin for nightingale.'

'Manebo, manebis, manebit,' he recites. 'Manebimus, manebitis, manebunt.'

'Come again?'

'It's Latin. I learnt it at school. Can't remember what the hell it means, though.'

'Thanks, Don. That's really helpful.'

'Everything Holly said seemed genuine to me.'

'What about everything Anna said?'

He doesn't answer at once. A gear change up and gear change down later, he says, 'Not sure.'

'Well, maybe we will be sure. An hour from now.'

❖

The parking area was nearly full. The stretch of heathland it faced was a popular spot for strollers and dog-walkers late on a sunny Sunday afternoon.

Don and Blake had arrived early for their appointment with Anna Marchant. But she was not late either. Blake pointed to a mint-green Fiat that had turned in and was moving slowly towards them. The bob-haired driver was Anna, her eyes obscured by sunglasses. 'Here we go,' said Blake.

At that moment, Don's phone burbled. 'Not Fran again,' he complained as he pulled it out and squinted at the screen. 'No,' he said, sounding surprised. 'Not Fran.'

'Whoever it is'll have to wait,' said Blake.

'It's Holly Walsh.'

'What?'

Anna pulled in close to the MG and stopped.

'You'll have to speak to Holly later,' Blake whispered to Don. 'Turn the phone off.'

'Right.' Don switched the phone to silent and buried it in his pocket.

Anna got out of the Fiat and walked towards them. She had added a boxy little jacket to her teatime outfit, making her look more like the businesswoman she evidently was. The sunglasses stayed on. And she did not return Don's smile of greeting.

'Hello, Anna,' he said in a tone designed to sound friendly but which somehow failed to pull off the trick.

'Does Holly know you're meeting us?' Blake asked with instant candour.

Anna pursed her lips in what might have been irritation. With her sunglasses on, her expression was hard to interpret. 'I'm sure you realize I prefer not to worry Holly with this.'

'We're not trying to put you on the spot,' said Don.

'But I find myself there, nonetheless. Shall we walk a little?'

They headed away from the parking area across an undulating stretch of heath and rough grass. To Don, it seemed the afternoon retreated around them, the colour and noise of their surroundings fading as they went.

'You must understand,' said Anna in a clipped, uncompromising tone, 'that Holly's health and peace of mind are my primary concerns.'

'Of course,' said Don. Unlike Blake, who had already made plain her distrust of Anna, he hoped the woman would convince both of them she was holding nothing back.

'Holly would never admit this,' she continued, 'but secretly she'd like to believe Luscinia is Jane. She doesn't want to have to accept that her friend's almost certainly dead. I suspect you know as well as I do that's much the likeliest explanation for Jane's disappearance.' She gave a decisive toss of her head, as if relieved to have come out and said it. 'I hope you agree it's best to speak frankly.'

'You're probably right,' said Don, aware of Blake glancing at him as he did so.

'The wish to sustain the possibility of Jane's survival explains in part Holly's reluctance to press the question of Luscinia's identity. Feeling no such qualms myself, and worrying that Holly was coming to rely so much on the generosity of an anonymous stranger, I emailed Luscinia, pleading with her to tell me at least a little about herself.'

'Did she respond?' asked Blake.

'Eventually, after I'd sent her two or three messages. She said she'd be willing to meet me, though I'd have to go to Chicago. As it happened, there was a conference coming up in Philadelphia that I was due to attend, so I added on a day and fitted in a flight to Chicago while I was there.'

'Convenient,' said Blake, her scepticism evident without being blatant.

'It certainly enabled me to arrange a meeting without Holly becoming aware of the fact. I hope I can rely on you to say nothing to her about it now.'

'You'd deny it anyway, right?'

Don winced. Blake was definitely not holding back.

Anna took the challenge in her stride, however. 'I'd have to deny it, in Holly's best interests. A positive outlook is almost as important to her welfare as the Ditrimantelline regime.'

'You're saying you met Luscinia?' Don cut in. He did not see how Blake's sniping was likely to help.

'Yes,' said Anna. 'In a coffee shop at O'Hare Airport. She's not Jane Glasson. She's an Asian American in her mid-thirties. She inherited a fortune from her father and uses some of it for altruistic purposes. She didn't wish to say much about her present circumstances beyond that, but I gathered her husband might not approve if he discovered what she was doing, despite being wealthy in his own right. She only agreed to meet me because she feared otherwise I'd go on digging until I inadvertently brought her activities to his attention. Holly's not her only beneficiary. She explained that one of her brothers had died when he was a child for lack of proper medical treatment. Her parents had divorced by then. Her mother was virtually penniless and couldn't afford the drugs the boy needed. That's why now she does her best, when she can, to help people in such situations.'

'D'you know her name?' asked Blake.

'I glimpsed it on her credit card when she paid for the coffee. Later, I Googled her husband. And her father. Which was illuminating. But I've no intention of enabling you to do the same. She deserves her privacy. Her generosity to Holly – and to others – entitles her to that.' Anna pulled up and turned to face Don and Blake. 'I didn't intend to tell you any of this, for obvious reasons. But I can't allow you to put Holly's health at risk by continuing to poke and pry.'

'We're just looking for the truth about Jane,' Don said emolliently.

'That's not poking,' said Blake, looking straight at Anna. 'Or prying.'

'Well,' said Anna, 'one truth about Jane is that she isn't Luscinia.'

'We understand,' said Don.

'You accept what I've told you?'

'Naturally we do.'

'I'd like to hear *you* say it.' Anna nodded to Blake.

Blake shrugged. 'Sure. I get it, Anna. You checked Luscinia out. She absolutely isn't Jane. We have to look for her somewhere else.'

'Do you have somewhere else to look?'

'That's like Luscinia's real name, Anna. We don't need to know it. And you don't need to know what we're going to do next.'

'No.' Anna smiled tightly. 'Well, good luck, anyway. You'll contact us if you do turn anything up, I hope.'

'For sure.'

'Yes,' said Don, still playing the peacemaker. 'Of course we will. Thanks for being so . . . open with us.'

'Open with us?' Blake muttered a few minutes later, back in the MG, as they watched Anna drive away. 'Did we just talk to two different people, Don?'

'I didn't see any sense in antagonizing her.'

'But you didn't believe her, did you? I mean, you can't have.'

'Could she really have made all that up?'

'It's called a cover story.'

'Cover for what?'

'Phone Holly back. Maybe she can tell us.'

'I can't let Holly know we've met Anna. We gave our word.'

'Technically, we didn't. But just phone her, Don, OK?'

'OK.'

The mint-green Fiat had turned out on to the main road by now and was heading back into Lyndhurst. As soon as it had passed out of their sight, Don reached for his phone.

To his considerable relief, Holly answered straight away. 'Hi, Holly,' he said cheerily. 'Don Challenor here. You rang me earlier.'

'I'm so glad you've called back, Don.' And she did sound glad. 'Anna's had to go out and I didn't, well . . . Sorry. It's just that Anna probably wouldn't think it wise to tell you this. She'd see it as putting my Ditrimantelline supply at risk unnecessarily.'

169

'Well, er . . . you shouldn't do that, of course.'

'No. But since you contacted me I've been thinking about Jane's father. We should do everything we can for the poor man, shouldn't we?'

'Absolutely. And that's what we are doing. But—'

'It probably has no connection with Jane anyway. Really I don't know what it amounts to. But maybe you and Blake can find out.'

'We can try, certainly.'

'A man got in touch a couple of weeks ago and subsequently came to see us. Somehow he knew I was receiving money from the Nightingale account at Credit Suisse. He wanted to know why. Anna was all for telling him to mind his own business, but I saw no harm in disclosing what the money was for. He said nothing about Jane, though. As far as I could judge, he didn't know anything about her. She wasn't why he was interested.'

'Why was he, then?'

'He's a private investigator, working for some of Harkness's creditors. He wouldn't confirm it, but I'm worried Luscinia may be a Harkness employee who's diverted company funds to pay for my medication. If so, those payments could be stopped at any moment, though he assured me nothing's likely to happen until Harkness's case has gone through the American courts, which, assuming he's actually extradited, could take years.'

'That may be true, but I appreciate why you're anxious about it, Holly. Thanks for telling me.'

'I think this investigator may know who Luscinia is, Don. If you can persuade him to tell you – or at least tell you enough to prove she isn't Jane – you'll have accomplished something on Mr Glasson's behalf.'

'Yes. We will.'

'You'll let me know what comes of it, won't you?'

'Of course.'

'Just me, Don, OK? I'd like to keep Anna out of this. Her concern for me sometimes . . . well, distorts her judgement.'

'Understood.'

'I'll give you the investigator's contact details. I'd, er, prefer not to text them to you.'

Don wondered why, but did not pursue the point. He grabbed the newspaper he had brought from Wortalleth West, fished a pen out of his pocket and wedged the phone under his ear. 'OK. Fire away.'

⁂

'I'm just trying to be logical.' I was always saying that to Mum. I was wasting my time. You can't reason with her. She doesn't really understand what reason is. It's like that part of her brain is missing. Since I ran away from all the madness she calls normal life – the rows, the drinking, the total fucking chaos of everything – I've realized there are loads of people like Mum in this world, more than there are like me. It doesn't matter to them if you can prove you're right and they're wrong. They'll never accept it. It's not their fault. They don't understand. They just don't get it.

Luckily, Don isn't one of those. He does get it. We sit in the MG looking out at the people wandering across the green, rolling stretch of heath ahead of us. There are fewer of them than when we arrived. It's getting late for afternoon strolls, though the sun's still high in the sky.

I look down at the folded *FT* Don's shoved in the tray between the gearstick and the dashboard. There's a name written on it – Perkins – and a phone number. That's all. But it says a lot.

I didn't believe anything Anna told us. Don's finally admitted he's having a hard time believing any of it himself.

171

Some rich Asian American in Chicago – nowhere local, of course – who prefers to remain anonymous is just too good to be true, specially with that neat little touch about seeing the woman's name on her credit card but feeling unable to reveal it because her privacy has to be respected. I mean, please!

My theory about Anna's a bit strong for Don to swallow straight off, but I can see him turning it over in his mind. He knows it makes more sense than anything else. Moving close to Holly and making friends with her wasn't some happy accident. Anna was *sent*. She was instructed to stop Holly – or anyone else, like us – probing the mystery of the Nightingale money. That's why she invented the woman in Chicago. To stop us before we make too many waves.

That's a complicated set-up, of course. And expensive. I shouldn't think Anna comes cheap. Who has the resources to do it? Well, it's got to be Jack Harkness, hasn't it? There's no one else in the frame. But why? What's the point? What's he got to hide?

The money's the puzzle. If Harkness has found out someone in his empire is helping Holly, using Harkness company money, why not just put a stop to it? Why go to the bother and expense of sending Anna to cover things up?

We've got to talk to this Perkins guy. It's totally obvious. Don knows that. He doesn't want to admit it, because he keeps hoping we'll hit a wall. But we won't. That's what *I* know. Jane's out there somewhere. Carrying Harkness's big secret as well as hers. We can't stop now.

'Are you going to phone him, Don?' I ask. 'Or d'you want me to do it?'

'I'll phone him.'

'Luscinia links to Harkness. So does Anna. And Harkness links to Jane. You're not going to deny it, are you?'

'No.' Don sighs. 'It's just . . .'

'Just what?'

'Last Sunday I had a late lunch at the pub and watched a DVD in the evening. Denzel Washington on a runaway train. Great stuff.'

'So?'

Another sigh. 'I think I'd like my simple, boring life back.'

'Are you phoning Perkins or not?'

'You're a heartless young woman, Blake. Has anyone ever told you that?'

'Oh yeah. Many times.'

'I'm not surprised.' Don gives a resigned growl and pulls out his phone. 'He won't answer, y'know. It's Sunday. He's probably gone to the pub too.'

'You could be right.'

'I haven't been right about much so far, though, have I?'

'You said it.'

Don harrumphs and makes the call. And I can tell from the look on his face, even before he speaks, that he's wrong again.

'Mr Perkins? . . . My name's Challenor. Don Challenor. Holly Walsh gave me your number . . . Well, I'm hoping we can help each other concerning . . . Yes. The Nightingale account . . . I'd rather not get into that over the phone . . . We have some information I think you'd find useful and . . . We is me and a friend, Blake. She and I, well, we're looking into something that, er, may connect with your investigations . . . I'm not asking for anything beyond an exchange of information . . . Mutually beneficial. Exactly . . . No. As I say, I think this is something we have to discuss face to face . . . We were with Holly earlier this afternoon . . . Yes. Still in the New Forest. Lyndhurst, at present . . . I see . . . OK . . . Yes, let's say there, then . . . An hour? Yes, we should be able to manage that . . . a seventies MG . . . OK . . . OK. 'Bye.'

Don ends the call and sighs heavily. 'You get your wish.

We're meeting Perkins at Fleet Services on the M3 in an hour's time.'

I smile at him. 'See? That wasn't so difficult, was it?'

I don't get a direct response. He just starts the car and pulls away.

❖

Keith Perkins had sounded gruff and guarded to Don, but also curious. He had said he was travelling to London and suggested the service area rendezvous to suit both parties.

The motorway was busy and it took slightly more than the allotted hour to reach Fleet. But Perkins had waited for them. In the farthest corner of the car park, a man was sitting in the raised tailgate of a dark green Volvo estate, smoking a cigarette and watching them carefully as they approached.

He was lean and heavy-browed, with close-cropped grey hair. His clothes were superstore casuals. His face was lined and weary. He looked like a thousand other middle-aged men worn down by the compromises and disappointments of life. He did not acknowledge them as they drove towards him and pulled into the vacant bay next to his car. But it was Perkins. The Volvo was just where he had said it would be.

'He looks a real barrel of laughs,' Blake murmured.

'Snooping for a living probably doesn't make for a sparkling personality.'

'Unlike selling overpriced houses?'

Don summoned a grin. 'Exactly.'

They climbed out and walked round to the back of the Volvo. Perkins looked at them, but did not speak.

'Mr Perkins?' Don ventured.

Perkins nodded. 'Mr Challenor? And Miss Blake?'

'You can drop the "miss",' said Blake.

'Will do.' The accent was flat, faintly estuarine, the tone neutral and non-committal.

'Good of you to meet us,' said Don, striving for a touch of amiability.

'Got to check everything out in my line of work.'

'I suppose so.'

'We're not here to waste your time,' said Blake pointedly. Don sensed she was not warming to Mr Perkins.

'I won't waste yours, then. What've you got for me?'

'You're interested in the Nightingale account,' said Don. 'So are we.'

'Why? Does Harkness owe you money?'

'Not exactly.'

'We're interested in the holder of the account,' said Blake.

'D'you know who that is?' Perkins asked.

'Do you?'

Perkins took a last drag from his cigarette and flicked it away. Then he gave both of them a long, hard look. 'Are we in "I'll show you mine if you'll show me yours" territory here?'

'Maybe.'

A people carrier with a large family aboard pulled in a few bays away. Children and a dog burst energetically out of it. Perkins regarded them with a jaundiced eye. 'Let's get in the car.'

He stood up and closed the tailgate, then plodded round and got into the driving seat. Blake headed for the rear bench-seat, signalling for Don to sit next to Perkins.

As they settled in their places, Perkins adjusted the mirror so he could see Blake. She had had to push an anorak, a laptop and a bulging briefcase to one side to make room for herself, while Don found his feet obstructed by several empty takeaway coffee cups and a burger carton.

'What did Miss Walsh tell you about me?' Perkins asked.

'That you've been hired by some of Harkness's creditors to look for their money,' said Don.

'Yeah. That covers it. I've nothing to do with Quintagler. A lawyer representing smaller fry – sub-contractors and such – has called me in. Now, what's your interest?'

'Luscinia,' Blake said simply.

'I can't discuss the details of my enquiries with you, young lady.' *Young lady* did not strike Don as a profitable way for Perkins to address Blake; he foresaw trouble ahead. 'If you've got something to tell me and it turns out to be helpful, I might be able to recommend an ex gratia payment. That's it.'

'We're not looking to make money out of what we know, Mr Perkins,' Don said levelly.

'You're not?'

'Do you know who Luscinia is?'

'Whatever I dig up I pass on to my clients in confidence.'

'Is that a yes or a no?'

'It's neither. There are people paying me to supply hard-to-get information. They wouldn't react kindly if they found out I was giving it away for free to strangers. I mean, what exactly is your stake in this?'

'We know who Luscinia is,' said Blake suddenly. It was a big claim, one Don knew they could not back up. But Perkins had annoyed her. And that had made her impatient.

'If that's true,' said Perkins, 'what d'you need from me?'

'The link to Harkness.'

'Why does it matter to you?'

'It just does.'

'We don't seem to be getting anywhere,' Don cut in. 'Maybe we should lay it on the line for you.' He had Perkins' attention now – and Blake's. 'I expect you know

Amos French.' Don thought he detected a tensing of Perkins' jaw muscles at the mention of French's name. 'He's offered to pay us – handsomely – for what we know. We haven't taken him up on it because he can't give us what we think you may be able to give us. The connection between Luscinia and Harkness. But if we can't get anywhere with you, well, we may decide to cash in. So, are you in a position to trade – or not?'

Perkins took his time about answering. He lit a cigarette and lowered his window to disperse the smoke, letting in a gale of shrieking and barking from the nearby stretch of grass, where the children and dog were cavorting. 'I'd need to check with my partner,' he said at last.

'No point if you're against it,' said Blake.

'I'm not,' Perkins replied, holding Blake's gaze in the mirror.

'Are we in business?' Don asked. They had the advantage now. It was time to press it home.

'Yeah. There won't be a problem. But . . . I'll have to run it past her.'

Her was a surprise. Was there a Mrs Perkins? All the signs were surely against it. 'How long will that take?'

'Come to my office tomorrow morning. Let's say ten o'clock. We'll both be there. Over the tanning salon at the top of Stockwell Road, opposite the Tube station. That suit you?'

'We'll be there,' said Don.

'You can count on it,' Blake added for emphasis.

'Yeah.' Perkins looked at her in the mirror again. 'I'm sure I can.'

✢

We're getting somewhere, like really somewhere. That's what I tell Don as we head on up the motorway. He can't

177

exactly deny it, but still it's obvious he'd prefer to have hit a brick wall with Holly – or with Perkins. This isn't working out like he imagined. We're on the trail. I don't know where it leads. But we're on it. And that feels good.

We're going to stay at Don's place overnight. That was an easy decision – nothing else makes sense – but it's just a bit worrying as well. Don's home may show me more of him than I've seen so far. And it may not be good.

Then there's the whole thing of London, the great grey, gobbling metropolis. I went there, of course, when I made a break for it from Birmingham. Cliché, right? Poor little runaway girl heads for the bright lights and big chances of the capital. Well, we all know how that ends. And it could've gone that way for me. Not sure where I found the nerve – the honesty with myself – to pull back and take a different road. The road west.

Don's place is in Islington. Good area, he tells me, though nowhere here looks that good to me. He lives in a tall yellow-brick house, part of a terrace, Georgian, according to Don, as if that's supposed to impress me. It's divided into flats. His is on the first floor. 'The best floor.' Naturally.

Big relief. The flat's not bad. Spacious, tidy and comfortable. Not a whole load of personality, apart from a huge bookcase full of paperbacks and a stack of CDs and DVDs by the hi-fi. No framed photographs. No art. Not much in the way of knick-knackery. But that's OK. Clean and simple is fine by me.

'Bet you thought it'd be like the inside of Perkins' Volvo,' says Don.

'You're getting perceptive, Don,' I lob back at him. 'Must be my influence.'

I follow him into the kitchen and suggest a multi-coloured stool made by a struggling young Cornwall-based artist could really lift the room. He says I can give him one for

Christmas and I think for a moment about how strange and remote and yet cheering the idea is that we'll actually still know each other six months from now.

Don says he can cook risotto after he's been out to the local Tesco Express. Meanwhile, I can take a shower. But the shower has to wait while the water heats up, so we have a drink: Don a bottle of beer, me a G&T seeing as there's actually a lemon in his fridge.

'When all this is over, Blake,' he says, slumped on the sofa next to me in the lounge, 'I could try and get you a job with an estate agent. Nothing special. Glorified tea-girl at first. But it might lead on to better things.'

'You're kidding me, right?'

'No.' He looks offended. 'If you dressed the part and, well, moderated some of your attitudes, you could probably make a go of it. And then . . .'

'I could turn into a version of everybody else.'

'I'm only trying to be helpful. Some people would jump at the chance.'

'I'm not some people.'

He grimaced. 'I've noticed that.'

I suddenly see myself from his point of view and realize I'm being really ungrateful. I can't help it. But I can sugar the pill. I turn round to face him. 'It's kind of you, Don. I appreciate it. I do, honestly. But I can't be . . .'

'Fenced in?'

'Definitely not.' I smile. 'Big mistake even to try.'

'Not one I'll repeat.'

'Good. Because we have much more important things to worry about than my career prospects.'

He sets down his glass and looks at me seriously. 'It's not too late to bail out of this, Blake. We don't have to keep our appointment with Perkins tomorrow. We don't have to go on asking questions.'

'Why would we stop?'

'Because stopping might be the safest option.'

'Fuck that.'

He smiles wearily at me. 'Right. Of course.'

'I mean, you can stop. But I won't.'

'No.' He picks up his glass again and swallows some beer. 'You won't, will you?'

❖

When Don returned to his flat from Tesco Express, shopping bag in hand, he noticed the bathroom door was half open, with steam billowing out. Blake moved briefly into blurry view. Somehow he was not surprised to see her naked again. He was almost growing accustomed to it.

'That *is* you, Don, isn't it?' she called from out of sight.

'It's me.'

'I'll be out soon.'

'Got something against closed doors, Blake?'

She leant round the edge of the door, wet hair plastered to her head, shoulder beaded with water, and blinked at him. 'Hasn't everyone?'

Later, while Don rustled up a risotto in the kitchen of his Islington flat, Fran Revell packed a case for her trip to Cornwall at her house in Belsize Park.

The atmosphere between her and Peter had been tense over the weekend and the girls had been no help at all, engaging in a contest to determine who could be the more difficult daughter of the two.

They, of course, did not know about their father's gambling addiction – conquered now, he claimed, though Fran was not sure – and Peter did not know the full extent of what she had been obliged to do to repay Harkness

180

for bailing them out. As far as he was aware, the trip to Cornwall was a simple and straightforward assignment.

The truth, which worried Fran whenever she considered it, was that she had no clue as to what Harkness's long-term intentions were. Nothing she had done for him so far had been to Mona's disadvantage, rather the reverse. But Harkness was a man in deep legal trouble. He surely had to have some plan to extricate himself. How Fran might be implicated in that worried her deeply.

Go to Cornwall. Expedite the sale of Wortalleth West. And ask no questions. That was what Harkness required her to do. And she was bound to do it. But it would not end there. She knew that. She was a pawn in a game Harkness was playing for very high stakes. And she had no idea what the rules of the game were.

She closed the case and pulled it off the bed. A glance at the clock told her what she already knew. It would soon be time to leave.

At Wortalleth West, nothing moves. The house is silent and empty. The video screens in the room behind the mirror show only stillness. The hidden cameras record only absence. The digital clocks mark the passing of every second, in London, Frankfurt, Moscow, Beijing, Tokyo, Los Angeles, New York. The counting goes on. The waiting continues.

But it will not continue for ever.

SIX

THE WEATHER CHANGED OVERNIGHT. LOW CLOUD HUNG OVER London and there were drifts of rain in the fitful breeze. Don and Blake took the Tube to Stockwell as the morning rush began to abate. The contrast with the start of a day on the Lizard could hardly have been greater: the close horizons, the stale air, the litter blown on a tunnelled wind, the mournful saxophone of a distant busker, the hurrying, self-absorbed travellers, heads down, eyes averted.

'This is the city full of golden opportunities, right, Don?' murmured Blake as they were jostled first by those leaving the train at King's Cross and then by those boarding it.

'People your age are supposed to enjoy the buzz,' Don retorted.

'What I enjoy most is being free.'

'It's fair to say, Blake, I don't think I've ever met anyone freer.'

'Wow.' She grinned. 'That's one of the nicest things anyone's ever said to me.'

The sun was still shining in Cornwall. Fran had left the sleeper at Truro and picked up a pre-booked hire car. She had had a surprisingly restful night, lulled by the motion of the train, and felt more optimistic than she had before leaving London. She was on the road to Helston now, hoping to find Robin Pawley in his office at the start of the working week. She had emailed him the previous evening and anticipated he would be keen to take over where Don had left off. Maybe this was all going to be easier than she had feared. Maybe there really would be no problems.

The Stockwell Tanning Studio had not yet opened for business. A door leading to the floors above had two bell-pushes fitted next to it, one labelled *Perkins Associates*, which Don prodded at. He strained to hear the buzz of the lock-release over the roar of the traffic on Clapham Road, but failed. Only at the third attempt did he manage to time a shove at the door correctly.

'Impressive entrance,' Blake muttered as they went in.

'I'd have asked you to do it,' Don rejoined, 'but I know you've got a thing about closed doors.'

'Just get up the stairs without falling over, will you?'

'I'll do my best.'

Up they went.

⁂

Up we go. Don's switched to a different suit since we got to London, but basically he still looks standard-issue white-collar male. I've gone for tight jeans and my favourite black leather bomber jacket. The way it creaks slightly when I move sounds way more expensive than it was. I want to come across as sharp and savvy. Something in scruff-bag Perkins' eyes when he looked at me in the mirror in his scruff-bag car told me he'll secretly enjoy being given the runaround by the likes of me.

I can't predict what Perkins' partner will make of me,

though, or me of her. As it turns out, she's a curvaceous black woman, probably in her forties, with big watchful eyes and a soft voice. Clarice Dow's the friendly but cautious type. She isn't giving anything away. Better be sure we don't either.

My guess is Clarice's partnership with Perkins is business and that's it. He's no catch and he's looking gruesomer than ever today. They've got the blinds down this grey old morning and light the place like the electricity bill's a big concern. There are more PCs and laptops than two people can reasonably need, with lots of cables snaking off to extra hard drives.

'Are you worried about surveillance?' Don asks, gesturing at the blinds.

'I would be if we didn't take precautions,' says Perkins.

'You're on Mendez Chinnery estate agency's website, Mr Challenor,' says Clarice. 'But when I called them this morning, they said you'd left the company.'

'You've been checking up on me?'

'That's what we do,' says Perkins. 'Check up on people.'

'Nothing on you, though, honey.' Clarice smiles at me almost maternally. 'But then one name doesn't give us much to go on.'

'Good.'

'How'd you two hook up?'

'Don hired me for S&M sex.' I enjoy watching her trying not to look startled. 'But we agreed I was better suited to an admin role.'

'Are we going to talk seriously?' growls Perkins. I get the feeling he'd register a zero on the sense of humour scale.

'Of course,' says Don the genial negotiator.

'You don't know who Luscinia is.' I'm looking at Clarice as I speak. I'd rather deal with her than Perkins. 'Right?'

'At this time,' she admits, 'we don't.'

'But you want to find out?'

'The operator of the Nightingale account is a person of interest to us.'

'Why?'

'He or she ties together a whole web of suspect dealings.'

'How exactly?'

'If you know who Luscinia is, tell us and we'll let you in on what we've uncovered so far.'

'About Harkness?'

'He's not someone you should necessarily be asking after.' Clarice seems genuinely concerned about me. 'Keith says you've been in contact with Amos French.'

'We have,' says Don.

She goes on looking at me. 'Just so you know, we're investigators pure and simple. We dig up whatever we legally can. We might cut a few corners, but we're basically respectable. French, on the other hand, is from a whole other area of the business. You shouldn't get involved with him. You really shouldn't.'

'Look, this is what I suggest,' says Don. 'We tell you as much as we know about the person we think Luscinia is without actually identifying her. Then you give us what you've got on Harkness. And we give you her name.'

'We'll give you an *outline* of what we've got on Harkness,' says Perkins.

'We'll answer your questions about him,' says Clarice more reasonably. 'Isn't that what you want?'

'Yeah,' I say to her. 'It is.'

Perkins slumps down in a swivel chair and creaks round in it to look at us. 'So?' He spreads his hands impatiently.

Don starts. I've got to give it to him. He knows how to make half a story sound like most of it. 'Luscinia' met Harkness in Cornwall in the early nineties and disappeared while she was at university in 1996. She'd be forty-three now. This doesn't seem to ring any bells with Perkins and Clarice. I guess they've been concentrating on his recent financial ducking and diving. Don reveals 'Luscinia' was a schoolfriend of Holly Walsh and volunteers that we think she's been using the Nightingale account to pay for Holly's Ditrimantelline treatment.

'Let me get this straight.' Clarice frowns. 'You're saying Luscinia was close to Harkness in some way you don't properly understand. And probably still is.'

'If she's operating the Nightingale account using Harkness money,' says Don, 'I guess she must be.'

'So why the disappearance? Why the secrecy?'

'Perhaps she knew her parents wouldn't approve of her going off with an older man.'

'Leaving them to spend the rest of their lives wondering what had happened to her is kind of an extreme solution, wouldn't you say?'

'Then maybe she didn't just disappear,' I suggest. It'll be the first time I've voiced this idea. But it's got to be said. 'Maybe Harkness is paying Holly to ease his conscience.'

'His conscience about what?'

'About whatever he did to her friend in 1996.'

Clarice turns to Perkins. 'Do we know of any forty-three-year-old native English speakers in Harkness's orbit who this woman could be, Keith?'

Perkins thinks for a moment. 'Harkness Pharmaceuticals employs thousands of people. We don't have biographical data on more than a handful. There are no obvious candidates popping into my head. But between the London, New York and Tokyo offices on top of HQ, the production hub and research satellite in Switzerland, there must be any number of forty-something English-speaking women on their books.'

'Harkness is on the hook for fraud,' Clarice reasons.

'You're hinting at something violent in his past, honey, have I got that right?' She looks at me, inviting a response.

'I was just floating a possibility,' I say.

'One hell of a possibility. Sounds like you may know more about Harkness's past than we do.'

'How much attention have you given the Cornish angle?' Don asks.

'Not a lot,' admits Perkins. 'It doesn't figure on the financial radar.'

'Are you planning to suggest Harkness may have murdered this girl?' Clarice faces me with the question.

I shrug. 'It'd explain why no one's seen her for the past twenty-two years.'

'Anything you know of in his past that could suggest he's the murderous type?'

I glance at Don, who warns me off the subject of the Frys with the faintest shake of the head. I don't know whether Clarice or Perkins has spotted it. I decide to bring down the shutter. 'Maybe we've said enough.'

'Just tell us how you've both got involved in this,' says Perkins. He looks across the dimly lit room at me. 'Without smart-arsing about.'

'I met Blake when I went down to Cornwall to value Harkness's house near Mullion for a quick sale,' Don responds. 'Technically, it belongs to Mona Harkness, so its disposal is part of their divorce settlement.'

'And you, young lady?' Perkins is still looking at me.

'I know the family. Her mother died without knowing what happened to her daughter. I don't want her father to die without knowing either.'

'That's big of you.'

I shrug. 'Not everybody has to be paid to do something.'

'So, neither of you stand to make a penny out of this?'

190

'Not unless you force us to do a deal with French instead,' says Don.

'Massively unwise,' says Clarice. 'He has a bad reputation. And his Russian sidekick, Zlenko, has an even worse one. Have you met him?'

'Yes,' Don replies. 'I didn't take to either of them.'

Perkins frowns at him. 'But you don't rule out getting into bed with them.'

'We'll push this forward any way we can,' I say, making sure I sound clear and uncompromising. 'If you want to know who Luscinia is, now's the time to give us what you have on Harkness.'

'Straightforward answers to straightforward questions is what I proposed,' says Clarice. 'And, as I recall, you accepted.' I can't deny that. And I don't try. 'So . . .' She smiles. 'Shoot.'

※

'We seem to know more than you do about Harkness's early life in Cornwall,' said Don, measuring his words carefully. 'But you clearly know more than us about everything else, especially his business career. Why don't you start talking us through that?'

Perkins breathed out noisily through his mouth. 'I'll let Clarice fill you in. She's the expert on dates and details.'

'OK,' said Clarice brightly. 'John William Harkness, known as Jack. Born February twenty-ninth 1956. A Leap Day baby. Educated Truro School and St John's College, Cambridge. Scholarships to both. Bright boy. First-class degree in Archaeology and Anthropology. What are you going to do with that? Teach? Excavate Roman ruins? Not Harkness. He travels. We're not sure where or how widely, but between 1978 and 1981 he's basically off the grid. Then he pops up in Switzerland as personal assistant to Lenore Furgler, who's recently inherited from her father control of Furgler Gesellschaft, a medium-sized pharmaceuticals company based in Basel. Somehow, in the course of the eighties, he gets himself a seat on the Furgler board with responsibility for company strategy. Lenore obviously trusts him, though the rest of the family doesn't. Lenore's widowed with three sons, all just waiting for the day they take the reins and send Harkness packing.

'That day never comes. Harkness marries Mona Jackson, daughter of Fred Jackson the multi-millionaire builder, who's retired by then to Monte Carlo. There are no children, though in a later magazine interview Mona talks about the tragedy of miscarriage. They divide their time between Basel, London and Monte. And Cornwall too, I guess. By 1995, with Lenore ailing, you'd think Harkness must be wondering what the future holds. Well, the answer's not long in coming. Suddenly, Lenore sells the company. To Harkness. The price isn't exactly premium, but isn't a total joke either. As to where Harkness got the money, no one knows for sure. There are rumours he's borrowed it from a Russian oligarch, Vladimir Drishkov, supremo of a corruptly acquired mining corporation. Drishkov gets himself shot dead by unidentified assassins a few months later, so who knows? The result's clear even if nothing else is. Harkness is in charge. Of what's now called Harkness Pharmaceuticals.

'The new company grows fast. Harkness opens a dedicated research lab in Locarno, where a pharmacological wunderkind called Filippo Crosetti starts developing a succession of beauty treatment products that turns Harkness into a player on the world stage. This culminates in Elixtris, the revolutionary anti-ageing cream. Its release in 2009 means the downturn doesn't really touch him. He sets up a partnership with Quintagler Industries, the US conglomerate, to fund buy-outs that see off a clutch of middle-ranking competitors in North America, Europe and Asia. He's one of the big boys now. Thanks principally to Elixtris, Harkness Pharmaceuticals is a money-making monster. It hardly seems possible that anything can go wrong.'

She paused, as if for effect, and Don said, 'But it does.'

'Oh yeah. This past year, the problems have just piled up for Harkness. Quintagler have basically accused him of stealing vast sums of money from their joint venture operations. Meanwhile, the US authorities are pursuing him over allegations that there's been widespread bribery of doctors to prescribe Harkness's medical products. It looks like there's a serious case to answer. He could be facing decades behind bars – and quite a few years just awaiting trial.'

'If the company's what you called it – a money-making monster,' put in Blake, 'why would he need to steal from his partners or resort to bribery?'

'Good question, young lady,' said Perkins. 'He's rich as Croesus. Why put himself the wrong side of the law to make himself richer still?'

'Is the young lady going to get an answer to her good question?' Blake asked acidly.

'I'll do my best.' Perkins was clearly immune to sarcasm. 'There are basically three possibilities. One, he's pathologically greedy. He just can't help himself. I don't buy that. He's too subtle, too calculating. Always has been. It wasn't chance that took him into Swiss pharmaceuticals. Swiss in particular, I mean. That choice guaranteed he'd be able to keep much more of what he took out of the company than if he'd gone into business in the UK, or elsewhere in Europe. Around the time Elixtris was released, he transferred the company's HQ from Basel, where production's still centred, to Zug, by far the lowest-taxed canton in Switzerland. And most of his personal salary gets channelled through Liechtenstein, an easy day trip by fast car from Zug. So, he's made himself pretty much tax-proof, despite owning a big house here in London, an apartment in New York overlooking Central Park and a mansion in Newport, Rhode Island. The guy's got it all sewn up.

'But now the stitches have started to come loose. Which brings us to possibility number two. The rumours about Drishkov are true. Harkness borrowed his Furgler stake money from the Russians. But he can't simply repay the money to whoever took over Drishkov's empire. The new man in charge realized it was more lucrative to blackmail Harkness for ongoing hush money. And the bill's just kept on going up and up as Harkness has prospered, to the extent that he's had to steal from Quintagler to cover it.'

'Got any evidence for that?' asked Don.

'Not really. But then Russian gangsters don't exactly file regular tax returns. The only real pointer in that direction is your friend Zlenko. He's generally believed to have been employed by Drishkov as a bodyguard, but somehow he survived when his boss was gunned down, perhaps because he'd sold him out. If that's true, French may be acting for Harkness's Russian blackmailer – dodgy company to keep, even by French's standards.'

Don gave Blake a worried look, but she ignored him, simply asking, 'What's the third possibility?'

'Ah. The billion-dollar question.' Perkins smirked, as if quietly pleased by his expositional technique. 'Well, let's get into the mechanics of what he's been accused of doing for a moment. Clarice?'

'Quintagler allege Harkness diverted the funds over a period of several years to subsidiaries of shell companies ultimately owned by Harkness himself. Those companies are also the alleged source of the bribes allegedly paid to doctors. That's a lot of allegedlies, I know, but it's what the case against Harkness amounts to. Anyhow, the bribes are only a fraction of what was supposedly taken. So, where's the rest? What has Harkness done with it? We just don't know. The shell companies are all based in tax havens with limited accounting and disclosure requirements. They won't be in a hurry to volunteer any details. The Nightingale account's a one-off. It was opened in London and it's basically only peanuts anyway. For the rest, we're in the dark.'

'I keep asking myself,' said Perkins, 'what's he done with the money? We're talking billions according to Quintagler. If Harkness really has taken it, what's he bought with it? What's he used it for?'

'Is that possibility number three?' asked Blake. 'That he's funded something big, something huge, that no one knows about?'

'Pretty much,' said Perkins. 'But you wouldn't have thought whatever that might be was easy to miss. Yet there's no sign of Harkness being involved in anything on the side, big or small, and this'd have to be enormous. It's like the money's . . . disappeared.'

'It can't have.'

'Obviously not.'

'But you're saying it has?' put in Don.

'As far as we can establish.'

'So, you can't tell us what he's up to?'

'Fraid not.' Perkins smiled. 'If we could, we'd have told our clients already.'

'You said you planned to push this forward any way you could.' Clarice was looking at Blake again as she spoke. 'Did you mean that?'

Blake nodded. 'Yeah. Absolutely.'

'Anything you learn, honey, you should bring to us. We'll broker it for you fairly.'

'We certainly will,' said Perkins. 'Meanwhile . . . I think it's time you gave us Luscinia's real name, don't you?'

While Don answered Perkins' question, Fran sat in Robin Pawley's office in Helston, doing her best to explain why Don was no longer playing any part in the sale of Wortalleth West. 'I had cause to question his commitment, Robin, so, to ensure my client's best interests are protected, I've had to dispense with his services.'

It was already clear from Pawley's keen, obliging expression that he was willing, if not eager, to take Don's place. 'Perhaps what you need,' he suggested, 'is a local agent with an established reputation both for regional and wider promotion of high-end properties who can devote the necessary resources to manage the whole procedure as closely as its . . . more sensitive aspects . . . require.'

Cutting through Pawley's self-serving verbiage, this sounded to Fran like exactly what she needed. But she needed one other element which she hoped he could supply: speed. 'This has to be handled diligently but also expeditiously, Robin. My client wishes to proceed as quickly as possible. I need hardly add that your fee would reflect the tightness of the schedule.'

'Completely understood, Fran,' said Pawley. 'You can be assured I'd give this project my personal and concentrated attention.'

'Excellent. So, assuming we can agree terms, how soon could you put the property on the market?'

'If I survey and photograph the house today, I could, er . . .' Pawley considered the point while Fran eyed him interrogatively. 'Well, if I pull out all the stops . . .'

196

'I rather hope you will, Robin, given the level of the fee I can offer.'

'Well, then, I could probably have it listed online with a full illustrated description tomorrow. A printed brochure would take a few more days, but—'

'I'll require the widest possible coverage.'

'There's a London agent I work with who has a large international as well as metropolitan clientele. I can get them on board more or less straight away. As to the survey . . .' Pawley cast an eye over the diary lying open on the desk before him, then flipped it shut. 'Why don't we drive down there now?'

Perkins greeted the naming of Jane Glasson as if it was rather less than he had expected in return for all he and Clarice had disclosed. He made it clear he thought it highly unlikely Harkness had anything to do with Jane's disappearance and even unlikelier she was playing any part in his present existence.

Clarice too was sceptical, though less obviously dismissive. 'I don't see there's anything we can do to chase down a link like that. Jane would have to be a Harkness Pharmaceuticals insider to channel Nightingale account money to Holly Walsh, and to check that notion we'd need much fuller access to the company's personnel records than we've any way of getting. Sorry to say, this could well be a non starter.'

'Haven't you got any moles inside the company?' Blake asked.

'You talk as if we're resourced like MI5,' said Perkins with a toss of the head. 'Jane Glasson *could* be Luscinia. Harkness *could* be paying Holly Walsh conscience money because he was responsible for Jane's disappearance. It's all supposition and it's basically ancient history anyway.'

'I guess we were hoping her name would ring a bell with us,' said Clarice.

Don looked at her. 'And it doesn't?'

'Not a tinkle.'

'We'll bear it in mind, of course,' said Perkins, smiling tightly. 'Just in case.'

'What'll you do now?' asked Clarice. She turned to Blake. 'Any other ideas?'

Blake shook her head. 'I'm all out of them.' She stood up abruptly. 'Let's go, Don.'

The assurances Don exchanged with Perkins before leaving that each would be in touch with the other if they learnt anything new about Jane Glasson lacked conviction. Don had the distinct impression as he and Blake descended the stairs that there would be no return visit.

Blake's view of the matter was uncharacteristically terse. She sounded simmeringly angry as she objected to going back into the Tube station after they had crossed the road. 'I need to walk,' she said. 'Which way is the river?'

Whether she was angry with him or Perkins, or Harkness, or the situation in general, Don could not tell. 'That way,' he said, pointing up South Lambeth Road. And she was off at a fast stride.

'What's the matter?' he panted as he caught up with her.

'As soon as they got Jane's name they were finished with us, weren't they?' she snapped.

'You heard Clarice. They were hoping her name would mean something to them. And it didn't.'

'Didn't it? How do we know that?'

'Well, they . . .'

'Said so? Right? *They said so.*'

'You don't believe them?'

'Do you?'

198

Don was having difficulty keeping up with Blake now, short of breaking into a jog. Pedestrians coming in the opposite direction were moving out of her way. 'They also gave us a lot of information, Blake. Let's not forget that.'

'You could probably have got most of it off Wikipedia. I've read that stuff about Harkness outsmarting Lenore Furgler's sons in the *Financial* fucking *Times*.'

'You can't look Zlenko up on Wikipedia.'

'That was to frighten us off. Don't you get it, Don? They don't take us seriously. They throw us a bone. Then they kick us out.'

'You marched us out, Blake, actually.'

'Yeah. Just before you told Clarice what our other ideas are.'

'And what are they?'

'Dunno. Haven't thought of any yet. Have you?'

'No.'

'There you are then. It's better to leave them thinking we may still know something.'

'But we don't, do we? You've got to face it, Blake. If Jane Glasson's still alive, there's nothing more we can do to find her. And it looks like there's nothing Perkins can do either.'

'We'll see about that.'

'OK, but—'

'Just leave it for now, Don, will you?' Blake made a warding-off gesture with her hand as she pounded along the pavement.

Don fell silent and let her keep several paces ahead. It was clear she did not react well to being told there was nothing to be done.

'Welcome to the real world, Blake,' he murmured. But she did not hear him above the noise of the traffic.

*

By the time they reached Vauxhall Bridge, she appeared to have come to terms with the setback. She stopped halfway across the bridge and gazed downriver towards Big Ben and the Houses of Parliament, fingering her breeze-blown hair out of her eyes as she squinted into the distance. Then she said, 'Fancy a coffee?'

Fran had followed Pawley's car down the Lizard road and out through Mullion to where Wortalleth West basked in cloud-dappled sunshine above Poldhu Cove.

The house was more striking than she had anticipated. It seemed a perfect match to its surroundings. She had a brief, tantalizing vision of what it would be like to idle the days away in such a setting, with the deep blue sea to swim in and the mind-cleansing freshness of the air to savour.

Pawley was already in conversation with a lean, tanned woman in a T-shirt and shorts when Fran finished taking her first appreciative look at the house. She joined them by a flower bed the woman had been weeding.

'Glenys works part-time as a gardener,' said Pawley. 'I've just been explaining why we're here.'

'I work direct for Harkness,' Glenys said, running her eye over Fran. 'I'll stop any time he tells me to.'

'Where's the housekeeper?' Fran asked, more bluntly than she intended.

'Gone away,' Glenys replied, no less bluntly.

'But coming back?'

'Couldn't say.'

'You met Mr Challenor?'

'I did.'

'I should make it clear he's no longer acting for my client.'

'That's none of my concern.'

'No. Of course not.'

'Shall we go in?' Pawley asked.

'Yes,' said Fran with some relief. 'Let's.'

The interior of the house was cool, stylish, light-filled and spacious. Pawley gushed for a while about its design features, then set to work with his camera and measurer. Fran followed him through a few rooms, marvelling at how Harkness had been willing to hand such a wonderful seaside retreat over to Mona without so much as a quibble and wondering, as she often did about his actions, what his true motive was. Eventually, she left Pawley to it and settled in the drawing room, where she checked messages on her phone and drafted a few emails.

That did not take long and she soon found herself assessing the situation she was in. She knew the only way she could tolerate the position Peter had put her in was not to think about it too much. Unfortunately, both her personality and her profession inclined her to think too much about virtually everything. It required the summoning of all her willpower to persuade herself that what Harkness had sent her there to do was essentially uncomplicated. Pawley was a competent man. There was no reason to anticipate any problem.

She sighed and looked at her appointments for the week ahead. She had planned to take the sleeper back that night, but she knew she had to make sure the house was on the market before leaving. Chivvy Pawley however much she liked, that could not be accomplished before tomorrow. After her slip-up with Don, she could not afford to make any mistakes. To satisfy Harkness, this had to be done correctly. And she had to satisfy Harkness. An overnight stay was therefore unavoidable. She would ask Pawley to recommend a hotel when he came back.

As for the panic room, *if* Pawley noticed the discrepancy in dimensions Don had reported, she would tell him to ignore it and press on with putting sales particulars together. She did not anticipate any resistance. She was paying Pawley enough to ensure his compliance. And Pawley, unlike Don, was the sort to do as he was told.

At least the housekeeper had gone. There was that to be grateful for. Whether Don had arranged her departure Fran did not know, but it was a blessing nonetheless. And the gardener was clearly not going to cause any difficulty.

Perhaps thought was profitable after all, Fran concluded. It had taken her to a position in which her task did not seem so very onerous. And maybe, after she had done Harkness this service, he would trouble her no more. Sitting in the pastel tranquillity of that room, gazing at a strangely soothing painting that hung on the wall – an abstract of blue and green shapes that somehow contrived to convey mobility – she felt for once it was easy to believe in such an outcome. And the feeling made her happy.

Don sat in a coffee shop off Vauxhall Bridge Road, sipping his Americano and waiting for Blake to say something. After several futile attempts to start a conversation himself, he had decided it was best to let her set the pace.

His view, which he knew it would be disastrous to express, was that they had come to the end of what they could hope to accomplish. Perkins had greater resources than they did. If he turned up anything on Jane, he would tell them. There was no sense getting in his way. It was time to move on.

'You reckon we're going nowhere, don't you, Don?' Blake asked suddenly, as if reading his mind.

'Well . . . I think we've done everything we can.'

'Could be.' She drank some coffee.

'There are a lot of people working on this, Blake. Lawyers. Police. Private investigators. If Harkness is hiding some dark secret about Jane Glasson, they'll turn it up eventually.'

'So, you reckon we should basically just leave them to it?'

'Maybe.'

'While you fix me up with a job?'

'I'd be happy to try.'

She drained her coffee, then looked across the table at him intently. 'Giving up is totally not what I want to do, Don.'

'I know.'

'Give me the rest of the day, will you? I need to be alone. I'm not used to being with someone from breakfast to supper. I need to walk. I need to think. I'll see you back at your flat this evening.'

He shrugged, knowing better than to argue. 'All right.'

'And don't worry about me. Please. I don't like people worrying about me.'

A few minutes later, Don was alone with the dregs of his coffee. Where Blake meant to go he did not know. He was not sure she knew either. He was not even sure she would show up at his flat that evening. There was a chance, he sensed, that she would choose to drop out of his life, to take some course that did not involve him. But there was nothing he could do about it, saddened though he was by the thought. She was a free spirit. In the end, he had to let her decide.

⁜

I walk the city. I don't know what I'm looking for or what I'll find. It's big and bright and full of strangers. Lots of Japanese tourists are taking selfies on sticks in St James's Park. I feel like the pelicans look: out of place, out of patience.

What am I supposed to do? In Cornwall I had a life. I knew what I was doing. It couldn't go on. I understand that now. When Don walked into Wortalleth West, it was over. But it was always going to end. I should've made a plan. I should've worked out where I was going to go next.

Maybe I shouldn't have tried to track down the truth about Jane. I never knew her. She should be nothing to me. But somehow she matters. I looked at her photograph every day while I was living in Andrew's house. He talked about her a lot – her energy, her passion, her fears about the environment. I tried to imagine what had happened to her. I saw her ghost in her father's face. I saw another ghost as well, of someone I might've been able to save but didn't. I guess I really want to know if Harkness is responsible for Jane's disappearance – and, if he is . . .

I could go back to Cornwall. Glenys is happy to take me in. I could try to stick with it there. Or I could take up Don's offer. See if he can find me a job. In London? In an office? Nine to five? Who am I kidding? That'll never work.

But then . . . what's the alternative?

I go for a ride on a tourist bus. The sun's out now. We see the sights. There's a commentary as well, but I don't really listen to it. I don't really see the sights either. I sit on the open-top deck, while the traffic growls and the crowds swirl below me. I'm in limbo. I don't know what to do or where to go.

I get off the bus in Piccadilly, near the Ritz. It's late afternoon now. Green Park's heavy with heat. I sit on a bench and eat a salad wrap. I feel angry with myself, angry with my lack of decisiveness.

I go back to Piccadilly and into a branch of Boots to buy some tissues. The thick city air has blocked my sinuses.

While I'm there I see a display of Elixtris on the shelf. I look at the slick packaging and the enticing claims. *The most effective anti-ageing treatment of them all. Recapture that youthful glow.* A woman buys a jar while I'm standing there.

'Does it work?' I ask her.

'Yes,' she replies, beaming enthusiastically at me like some convert to a religious cult. Her skin glows, as promised. 'It really, really does.'

'Kind of transformative?' I borrow the word Anna used to describe the effect of Ditrimantelline on Holly.

It hits the mark. 'Exactly. That's exactly right.'

Harkness is a mystery. I walk up Bond Street, looking in the shop windows at all the things he could buy without blinking. The watches. The jewels. The thousand-pound suits. He's the last man who needs to steal from anyone. Why has he done whatever he's done to get him into so much trouble? I don't understand. It makes no sense. There has to be more to it. There has to be a reason.

Then a thought comes into my head.

Why don't I just ask him? I can do that. Unlike the woman at Boots or all the millions of other Elixtris buyers, I can talk to Jack Harkness.

I've got his phone number. I've also got his London address. I never asked Perkins for it and neither did Don. He wouldn't think confronting Harkness was a good idea anyway. But a confrontation isn't exactly what I'll be going for. And I didn't need to get the address from Perkins because I've written it on letters for Harkness that were delivered to Wortalleth West from time to time. Vera used to forward them on to him in London and I did the same. There weren't many. Fewer and fewer lately. But enough.

53 Belgrave Square.

*

Size and . . . grandeur. Those are the words. The only words you need. The square is vast, surrounded by huge wedding-cake white blocks with pillars and parapets and high windows and steepling chimneys. You could fit ten families into any one of them. But at number 53 there's just Jack Harkness.

I walk round the square. The garden in the centre is railinged off, locked and private. Lots of the houses are embassies: Syria, Austria, Germany, Spain, Turkey, Argentina. Their flags are flying, claiming their territory. There's a policeman on patrol outside the Turkish Embassy. He looks bored. Nothing's happening. The square's silent and empty.

Number 53. No flag. No brass plate. Just a pillared porch, wide steps and a big wooden door with a polished handle and a dolphin knocker. I look up at the house, at the windows reflecting the cloud-barred sky. I wonder what sort of life Harkness leads behind the glass, closed off from the world. I stand there, looking and wondering.

Then one of the windows on the second floor slides up, the wood squealing on the sash. A man leans out and gazes down at me. Harkness.

'Blake?' he calls. 'Is that really you?'

I smile up at him. I feel nervous, uncertain what to say. In the end, some words come. 'Yeah. It's really me.'

'What are you doing here?'

'I had to leave Wortalleth West.'

He frowns. 'I suppose you did. You should have phoned me.'

'I kind of prefer face to face.'

He smiles. 'Me too. Do you want to come in?'

'If it's, er . . .'

'I'll open the door. Just push it.' Then he's gone. Just like that.

As I walk towards the door, I hear an electronic buzz from inside. I grasp the handle and push, as instructed. The door opens.

I let it swing shut behind me as I step inside. There's a clunk. The buzzing stops. There's a few seconds of silence. I'm in a big, empty, high-ceilinged hallway. The walls are panelled, with gold-leaf edgings. There's a huge chandelier above me. Ahead is a wide, curving staircase, with marble treads. There's no furniture, though. As I glance through some open double doors into a large front-facing room to my left, I can't see any in there either.

Footsteps on the stairs, descending. I move forward and see Harkness's shadow on the wall, a shimmer of grey against a pale wash of light. Then he appears, smiling, with his arms held apart, as if welcoming me to the house is a genuine pleasure. He's wearing loafers, jeans and a loose sweater. He looks relaxed, at ease with himself and the world in general. He doesn't look like a man facing extradition to the US and the inside of a jail for the rest of his life.

'Come up,' he says. 'I do most of my living on the second floor.'

I start up the stairs and he turns and goes back up ahead of me. We reach the first floor. There's an enormous triple-windowed drawing room ahead of me, overlooking the square. This does contain some furniture, but it's all dust-sheeted. There are no pictures on the walls, no signs of use. Everything's cream and white, washed in evening light.

'Is there anyone else here?' I ask.

'Juanita. In the basement. She cooks and cleans. And leads her life. We respect each other's privacy. Her nephew's here quite often as well. Otherwise . . . I'm on my own.'

'Has it always been so . . . empty?'

'Most of the contents belonged to Mona. She's removed quite a lot. Doesn't want her possessions to go down with the ship, I guess.' He smiles. 'I'm sorry I didn't warn you Wortalleth West was to be sold. I didn't want to disrupt your life there any sooner than was necessary. But I should've remembered Mona isn't one to let the grass grow.'

'You don't owe me anything.' Not even the truth, really, about the money, about him and Jane. But maybe I can get it anyway. 'You've had a lot on your mind according to those newspapers of yours I read.'

'Ah, Ray Hocking still delivering the *FT*, is he? Excellent. Do you know I was at primary school with Ray? You could rely on him even then.'

'I don't know what to call you,' I say, realizing suddenly that I don't. '"Mr Harkness" doesn't seem right any more.'

'Jack's fine.'

'Not sure I can get used to that.'

'Try.'

I shrug. 'OK . . . Jack.'

'Why did you come to London, Blake?'

'Didn't feel comfortable at Wortalleth West any more. A few things happened. I reckoned it was time to leave.'

'But London?'

I shrug again, keeping it all as casual as I can. 'Someone offered me a lift. Seemed like a good idea.'

'I'm not sure it was.'

'Neither am I.'

'Come upstairs. I can fix us a drink.'

We go up the next flight of stairs. The second floor is different. The rooms are slightly smaller and lower-ceilinged. They're furnished too, one as a lounge, a second as a study, a third as a bedroom.

There's a refrigerated wine rack in the lounge. Harkness pulls out a bottle of white and pours a couple of glasses. They're not small. 'This is very expensive,' he says. 'New Zealand Sauvignon. Tiny grower. Great flavour. Cheers.'

I drink some. I don't go much on wine. But I can taste this is good.

I glance round. On one of the walls there's a big framed photograph of the Earth seen from outer space: an almost complete circle of brilliant blue and pure white, floating in a sea of black. As I look at it, I see my reflection in the glass, overlaid on the photograph of Earth with Harkness standing beside me.

'Taken from *Apollo Eight*, in December 1968,' he says quietly, almost in a whisper. 'It blew my mind when I saw it the first time. I was twelve years old, home for the Christmas holiday. I'd never seen anything so perfect or so beautiful – or so fragile. That was when I realized just how vulnerable we all are, just what a delicate thread all life hangs by. It was as if the Earth was one of the baubles on the Christmas tree in our sitting room. You could pull it off the branch and smash it under your foot in a second. Or you could just watch it hang there.'

I look at him. 'That's quite something for a twelve-year-old to think.'

He nods. 'I suppose it was.' And then he smiles and swallows some wine. 'Why did you come to see me, Blake?'

This is the moment. I can back out, give some excuse. Maybe even ask for a handout. That'd make sense to him. Or I can do what I came to do.

'If you want help finding—'

'No. That's not it, Jack. That's not why I came.'

'Why, then?'

'Questions. I basically can't get them out of my head.'

'Questions for me?'

'Yeah.'

He spreads his hands. He goes on smiling, like he's the most open and accessible guy on the planet. 'Ask away.'

'OK.' I take a sip of wine. Then: 'Did you really do what you're accused of – steal all that money from your partners?'

The smile doesn't falter. He doesn't look annoyed or evasive.

He looks as if he's happy for me to ask . . . whatever the fuck I like. 'You can't steal what already belongs to you, Blake.'

'Is that argument playing well with the court?'

He chuckles. 'Not at all. Nor with my lawyer. He despairs of me. He thinks there's no way I'm going to be able to avoid extradition.'

'You don't seem worried.' And he doesn't. I just can't read him.

'It's one of my characteristics that used to drive Mona to distraction. Nothing worries me.' Can that really be true? *Nothing?*

'I'm sorry about your marriage.'

'Thanks. It's kind of you to say that.' He wanders across to an armchair and sits down. As he crosses his legs, I see the electronic tag he's wearing on his left ankle. He waves an inviting hand towards the sofa opposite. 'What else do you want to ask me?'

I don't sit down. I prop myself on the arm of the sofa. 'Is there a panic room at Wortalleth West?'

'What makes you think there might be?'

'The guy Mona's lawyer sent to survey the house found a void of some kind behind the master-bedroom closet, extending downstairs.'

'Did he now?'

'So . . . what is it?'

'There's no panic room in the house, Blake. You have my word. I let you live there because I trusted you to leave every-thing of mine well alone. And you have, haven't you?'

'Yeah.' I look him in the eye. I don't want him to think I've been poking and prying. And there's just the hint of a threat in his voice. *You better not have.* 'Absolutely.'

'Good. Enough said, then. Any other questions?'

He's not going to be pushed. That's clear. He's not going

to be riled either. That's also clear. 'There have been some strange characters hanging around.'

'Besides the guy Mona's lawyer sent down?'

'I didn't mean him.'

'Who, then?'

'An American called French. With some Russian sidekick. Zlenko.'

'I don't know them.' He's got to be lying about that, specially if Zlenko worked for Drishkov, like Perkins says he did. But I can't mention Drishkov without revealing I've been doing some serious checking up on Harkness, so I bite my tongue. 'I'm afraid Quintagler have set quite a few unsavoury types on my tail. I'm sorry if you ran into a couple of them. No wonder you decided to leave. Probably wise in the circumstances.'

'Then there's that renewables salesman, Coleman.'

Harkness sighs. 'A major pain. Sorry again.'

'And Wynsum Fry.'

'Ah. The witch. I'd almost be disappointed if you didn't mention her.'

'She thinks you murdered her brother.'

He laughs. 'I know. Absurd, isn't it? What possible reason could I have had to kill Jory Fry?'

'I don't know.'

'There you are, then.' But there could be a reason. I get that if nothing else. He *could* have had a reason.

'I lived at Andrew Glasson's house in Helston before I moved into Wortalleth West. You know that, of course.'

'Yes. Which brings us, I suppose, to the witch's even more absurd belief that I had a hand in the disappearance of Glasson's daughter.'

'You didn't though, did you?'

'What do you think?' The question is a dare as well as a challenge.

211

'You did know her, right?'

'Slightly. She worked as a waitress at a café in Mullion. It closed before you came to the area.'

'That was it? You didn't know her otherwise?'

He smiles. 'She was twenty years younger than me, Blake. What are you suggesting?'

Yeah. What *am* I suggesting? 'Apparently, Jane had strong environmentalist principles.'

He nods. 'She did. She told me about them a few times.' While serving him coffee at Sea Breeze? There's the hint of a contradiction here, but he doesn't seem to care. I can't make out whether he wants to brush me off or draw me in. 'She didn't approve of the pharmaceuticals business, to put it mildly.'

'So, there's no way she could've worked for you, is there?'

He chuckles, amused by the idea, apparently. 'We wouldn't appear to have much in common.' There's the ambiguity again. He hasn't given me a flat-out denial.

'No. You wouldn't.'

'Appearances can be deceptive, of course. But can you imagine any way in which they could be as deceptive as that?'

I shake my head. 'Not really.' And I can't. But I can't get rid of the idea that there might be.

'Is there something bothering you that you haven't mentioned yet, Blake? Only I don't want us to miss the best of the light.' He glances over his shoulder towards the window.

'The light?'

'It's gorgeous just now. The first softening at the onset of evening. Come up on to the roof with me. The city looks beautiful from up there.' He jumps up and refills his wine glass. He pours more wine into my glass as well. 'We can take our drinks. And this.' He grabs his phone from the low table in front of the sofa and sets off.

212

I follow. I'm not sure I should. The roof sounds kind of worrying. I don't feel frightened or even threatened by Harkness. But I wonder if actually I should. There's just so much about the guy I don't understand. He doesn't seem to do anger. He hasn't tried to patronize or intimidate me. He's treated me almost like his equal. Maybe *that's* what should worry me.

We go up two more flights of stairs, the second flight much narrower than the others. We're in the attic now. The rooms are bare, though there's a stack of cardboard boxes in one. Beyond the stack, beneath a dormer window, a stepladder's standing ready. Harkness climbs up on it, opens the window and steps out into the gully behind the low parapet at the front of the house.

'Are you coming?' he calls back.

I climb out after him. He offers me a hand, but I don't take it. He smiles and sits down sideways on the parapet, one knee raised. Sunlight gleams in his glass.

'Great, isn't it?'

The light's got a golden, fuzzy tinge to it. The garden in the centre of the square is half in shadow. The lowering sun has bathed the whole city to the east in a sort of soft mellowness. There are all the buildings I can't name and just a few I can. There are all the thousands and thousands of rooftops and the millions and millions of people beneath them.

But not a single one of those people is in sight. Except Jack Harkness. We're utterly alone. He sips his wine as the feathery breeze stirs his hair. He squints into the distance. Then he looks up at me, where I stand, trying not to notice the long sheer drop beyond the parapet to the basement area five floors below.

'How's the funky furniture business going?' he asks.

I'm surprised. I wouldn't have expected him to know what I do to earn some bread. 'How'd you hear about that?'

213

'The Web.'

'I'm not on it.'

'Yes you are. You just don't know it. Everyone is. We can't move in this world without leaving a trace. Unless we're very very careful. And you haven't been quite careful enough.'

It's the first hint of something faintly menacing. He's still smiling, still amiable. But there's a shadow stretching towards me that distorts and lengthens his posture into something almost predatory.

'I assume you don't have any savings,' he says quietly.

'I don't even have a bank account to put my savings in – if I had any, which I don't.'

'That can easily be remedied. You haven't put down many roots, have you, Blake?'

'No, Jack,' I say, trying to keep a grip on where we're going. 'I haven't.'

'I'm not going to ask why. I'm not going to ask anything at all about your past.'

'OK.' I get the disturbing idea he doesn't have to ask – that he already knows.

'I like you. As a matter of fact, I admire you. But poverty's no fun, Blake. Even at your age.'

'I get by.'

'You should do more than that. Grasp the opportunity you've been given. Travel. See the world. Taste its pleasures – while they're still there to be tasted.'

'Are they going somewhere?'

'We're wrecking the planet, Blake. Haven't you heard? We're in a new geological era: the Anthropocene. Man is shaping the future. And it's not a future you'll want to live in. Heat. Drought. Famine. Thirst. War. Conflict. And extinction for thousands, maybe millions of other species. Deforestation. Desertification. Hell and damnation. Here's to us. All of us.'

He takes a swig of wine. 'What I'm saying is: enjoy yourself while you can.'

It should seem strange to hear a pharmaceuticals billionaire talking this way after all the chemicals his company has shoved into the biosphere over the last twenty years. But somehow it doesn't. 'Where's the opportunity you reckon I should grasp?' I ask.

'Oh, her name's Ingrid Denner. My fellow Board members at Harkness Pharmaceuticals have hired a New York crisis management firm she works for to limit the damage caused to the company by my difficulties with the US Justice authorities. The decision was taken in my absence. A waste of money in my opinion, but hey ho. Anyway, Ingrid's over here handling the London end of the operation. Staying at the Dorchester, which doesn't come cheap, of course. Now, one of her roles is to stop people passing embarrassing or compromising information to the press. Her usual method is a substantial cash payment in return for a signed non-disclosure agreement.'

'What's this got to do with me?'

'Maybe you've come across some revealing documents while you've been living at Wortalleth West. I'll tell her it's all too likely.' He flourishes his phone. 'She won't want to take any risks. It can be a nice pay day for you, Blake.' He grins. 'I wouldn't settle for anything less than fifty thousand if I were you.' His grin broadens. 'You can do a lot of globetrotting with that.'

He's joking. He's got to be. But, looking at him, I don't think he is. 'You're serious, aren't you?'

'Absolutely.' He waggles the phone. 'Want me to make the call?'

'No. Of course not.'

'Come on. Why miss out? I can make this happen. I really can.'

'Are you trying to bribe me?'

'No.' He smiles at me like he's exasperated. 'I'm trying to do you a favour. Quite a big favour, actually. But I've always been generous. And whatever Quintagler or my fellow directors say, it's my money, so why shouldn't I spend it how I like?'

'If I took it, they'd think I really did know something.'

'Not at all. Ingrid operates on a precautionary basis. And the Board's given her carte blanche. As long as you keep out of their hair, they won't be interested. Besides, with that sort of capital to play with, you can go wherever the mood takes you. You can . . . disappear.'

I catch his eye. 'Like Jane Glasson?'

He sets the phone down on the parapet and looks at me with an expression I can truly only describe as protective. 'The offer's open, Blake. Go and see Ingrid. Or don't. It's your call. She'll contact me if you do and I'll tell her she'd be wise to offer you a substantial settlement. That's all there is to it. No strings. No traps. No treacherous small print. This is something that seems too good to be true, but really is true.' He smiles. 'And as for disappearing, I didn't mean literally.'

'How could you?' I meet his gaze and engage with it. 'No one – like – literally disappears, do they?'

He smiles. 'No. They don't.'

'Why would you want to make me rich, Jack?'

The smile broadens. 'Fifty thousand isn't rich, Blake.'

'It is for me.'

'Good. Then take it. Or hold out for more. If that's how you decide to play it. Either way, use it. Have fun. On me.'

'You really mean it, don't you?'

He nods, holding the smile. 'I don't know why you even need to think about it.'

'I always look before I leap.'

'Good policy. But don't look too long.' He glances away,

216

across the square. 'There's a lot of world out there for you to explore. You should get started. Take the money . . . and run with it.'

When I walk away from the house, Harkness is still perched up on the parapet, wine glass in hand, surveying the world from his roof. I can't see the expression on his face, of course, but I bet he's smiling. He does a lot of that, even though most people would say the guy has nothing to smile about.

I don't get him. I just don't understand him at all. But he doesn't mean me to. He's got some kind of secret agenda. You get the feeling everything's turning out just like he's planned.

I'm not in his way. I'm not a problem. Unless I want to be.

Not turning myself into one has become a much more attractive option, of course, thanks to him offering to arrange for Ingrid Denner to buy me off. He says it'd be easy and I believe him.

Money's money. I can put myself a long way away from everything with fifty thousand quid. It's tempting – just like he knew it would be. But the problem is . . . what is he trying to stop me doing? And does this mean I'm closer to the truth than he wants me to be?

I walk round the Wellington Arch and the war memorials at Hyde Park Corner, wondering what I should do. Don wants me to give up looking for the truth. Harkness is happy to reward me for giving up. All I have to do is talk my way into a pay-out from Ingrid the crisis management consultant and then . . . I'm free to go anywhere and do anything.

The Dorchester Hotel is just a short walk away up Park Lane. I can't ignore Harkness's offer. I can't pretend he didn't make it. Or that I didn't like the look of the future he dangled in front of me.

Seeing Ingrid Denner isn't the same as taking the deal. I can get the measure of her without committing myself. I can listen to what she has to say and tell her I'll think about it. Discussion isn't decision. And who knows what I'll learn from her?

I've got to give it a go. In the end, it's obvious. There's no other choice that makes any sense.

I walk into the foyer of the Dorchester trying to look like grand hotels are my natural turf. There's a lot of gleaming marble, a lot of high fashion, a lot of uniformed deference.

I tell the guy behind the desk I've come to see Ingrid Denner. He's very polite and as helpful as he can be. But Ms Denner, he says, is out. She's left instructions, however, that if anything urgent crops up, he can call her on her mobile. Is this urgent? You bet.

He's standing with the phone to his ear, waiting for Ingrid to answer, when someone pops up beside me and says, 'Excuse me. I couldn't help overhearing. You're here to see Ingrid Denner?'

He's a medium-height, medium-build guy in a suit like a hundred others I've already seen today. The suit's grey and his skin matches, like he puts in a lot more time in an office than out in the sun. He's wearing a tie, but the knot's loose. He's bald, with what hair he's got left shaven. He looks about forty-five. There are lines round his eyes and mouth. The eyes are a nice dark brown, ever so slightly enlarged by his rimless specs. I get a feeling of sadness – and wariness. He's spoken to me, but he's not sure he should've.

'Thing is,' he goes on, licking his lips nervously, 'so am I. I wondered—'

'Ah, Ms Denner,' says the guy behind the desk. 'Anton here, from the Dorchester.'

'Can we talk?' asks the Suit.

'There's a young lady who wishes to see you on a matter

that's evidently quite pressing. Her name? Excuse me.' Anton looks at me enquiringly.

'Tell her Harkness sent me to see her,' I say, dodging the question.

'Is that true?' asks the Suit.

'What's it to you?' I fire back.

'Jack Harkness seems to have a lot of secrets. Are you one of them?'

'Are *you*?'

'Ms Denner would still like to know your name, Miss . . . ?' Anton puts in after conferring with Ingrid.

'*My* name's Gareth Lawler,' says the Suit. He's sensed my reluctance to identify myself. But what he can't have sensed is the difference this name is going to make to me.

'*Gareth* Lawler?'

'Yeah.'

'Miss?' Anton says with a touch of impatience.

'Where were you twenty-two years ago, Gareth?' I ask, already sure I know the answer.

'Why d'you—'

'Just tell me.'

The forcefulness of my interruption makes him take a step back and blink at me. 'OK. I was a student. King's College, Cambridge.'

'You're right. We should talk.' I look round at Anton. 'Sorry. Tell Ms Denner something's come up. I'll get back to her.'

We stand out the front of the hotel, where the taxis pick up and drop off and the doorman hovers. Gareth looks a bit better in the open air, less grey, less woebegone. He's still nervous, though. He keeps glancing round, as if he's afraid someone's spying on him.

'You were Jane Glasson's boyfriend at Cambridge, weren't you?' I ask.

He shakes his head in mystification. 'How the fuck d'you know that?'

'What d'you want with Ingrid Denner?'

Gareth runs his hand over his shaven head. 'Were you actually alive twenty-two years ago?'

'Yeah. The last summer before primary school. Definitely alive.'

'Who are you?'

'Blake.'

'That's it? Just . . . Blake?'

'That's my name.'

'What's your connection with Jane?'

'Why don't we go and get a drink somewhere?' I don't want to lose Gareth now I've found him. I can't risk frightening him off. Maybe a drink will help.

'Well . . .'

'You said you wanted to talk.'

He takes a deep breath. Then: 'OK. There's a pub up the road. Let's go there.'

We set off. There's a church up ahead, with a clock showing the time. It's nearly eight. Don will be wondering where I am. Gareth lights a cigarette and offers me one. I don't take it. 'No one seems to smoke actual cigarettes any more,' he says as he coughs out a lungful of smoke. 'I gave up myself, until . . .' His voice tails off.

'Until?'

'I need to know who you are, Blake, before we . . .'

'Andrew Glasson's ex-housekeeper.'

'You worked for Jane's father?'

'Ever met him?'

'Er, yeah. He came up to Cambridge with Jane's mother after she . . .'

'Disappeared?'

'Did Harkness really send you to see Ingrid Denner?'

'I've been working as his housekeeper too. In Cornwall.'

'So, what's your . . .'

'Buy me a drink and we can tell each other all about it.' I smile encouragingly at him. I need to get inside his head. I need to find out what he knows. But he has to want to tell me. And I have to make him want to tell me.

'OK,' he says, though he's still hesitant. 'OK.'

The pub's on a corner, with chairs and tables arranged out front. I sit down at one while Gareth goes in to get the drinks. I'm on sparkling water. I can't guess what he'll be on. The answer turns out to be lager. But there's a whiff of the hard stuff as well. I reckon he's downed a Scotch at the bar.

He sits down awkwardly, lowering his shoulder-bag to the ground. He buys some time by slurping his lager and lighting another cigarette. He still doesn't know how much – or how little – to tell me.

I try to help him out. 'Jane's mother died a few years ago, Gareth,' I say, calmingly, soothingly. 'And her father's in poor health. I'm fond of him. I don't want him to die as well without knowing the truth.'

Gareth gives me a wintry little smile. Life's not worked out how he hoped, to judge by the dullness in his eyes. Divorce, maybe. A weekend daddy. Career stalled. Prospects flaky. And part of him blames Jane's disappearance for a lot of that. 'If I knew the truth,' he says in an undertone, 'I'd tell the old man what it is. But I don't.'

'You know something, though.'

'So do you. My name for a start. I'd be surprised if Glasson remembers it. We only met briefly, in Jane's room at Newnham. He and his wife weren't taking a lot in at the time. They were too upset. There was nothing I could tell them anyway. So, how'd you find out about me?'

221

'Holly Walsh.'

'The best friend. Of course. She always wanted to be more than just a friend to Jane.'

'She's not well. Multiple sclerosis.'

'Christ. Sorry . . . to hear that.'

'She's better than she was, apparently, thanks to a revolutionary new drug.'

'Oh yeah?'

'Fantastically expensive. Holly couldn't afford to pay for it . . . without an anonymous benefactor.'

Gareth leans across the table towards me. 'Anonymous?'

'It made me think. Who'd want to help Holly without revealing their identity?'

'Which company makes the fantastically expensive drug?'

It should sound like an odd question. But it doesn't. And we both know why. 'Harkness Pharmaceuticals.'

Gareth nods thoughtfully. He's putting two and two together. 'How'd you come to work for Andrew Glasson *and* Jack Harkness?'

'I worked for several other people in the area as well.'

'OK. But why'd you leave those two jobs?'

'Jane's sister took against me. As for Harkness, he's selling the Cornwall house. Or his wife is. She owns it. Either way, I'm out.'

'And you've decided to chase after Jane instead?'

'Is she alive, Gareth?'

'How should I know?'

'Dunno. But I get the feeling you do.'

He looks at me for a long time. Then: 'I don't know if I can trust you.'

'I guess you don't.' Why should he? I don't trust him either. I hold his gaze. 'But I guess you'll have to.' I want him to understand he has to take a chance with me. Otherwise, we're out of business.

'What did you want with Ingrid Denner?'

'What did *you* want with her?'

'All right.' He's got it. He's going to take the chance. He pushes his fingers underneath his glasses to rub his eyes, then has to adjust them on his nose. 'All right. I'll tell you what there is. A couple of months ago, at Paddington station, I, er . . . saw her.'

'You saw Jane?'

'Yes.' He means it. He means he knows for a fact she's alive. 'I suppose I've always looked for her, subconsciously, over the years, always hoped I'll see her again. That she'll re-enter my life. She's not an easy person to forget, though there was a time when I thought I would forget her. But it didn't work out. A lot of things didn't work out. You're too young to understand how that happens, how this thing called middle age closes on you like a vice that traps you tight and . . . keeps on squeezing.' He smiles awkwardly. 'Sorry. Too much self-pity there. Way too much.'

'What happened at Paddington, Gareth?'

'Oh, I was waiting for a train to Cardiff. A business trip. I was sitting in one of the seats out on the concourse, under the departures board. There was this woman sitting in the row in front of me, working on an iPad. It was a wet day. She was wearing a shiny black raincoat and a Hermès scarf. There was a small wheelie suitcase next to her, with a bag looped over the handle. She had fair hair, with some darker tones, shaped to her neck. I don't know what it was exactly. The neck, maybe. You know how you see someone from behind and they look like someone you know, but when they turn round you realize you don't know them after all – not in the slightest?'

I nod. 'Yeah.'

'Well, that's what I thought was going to happen when I stood up and walked round the end of the row to get a look at her face. I thought there was no way it could actually, really, truly be her – Jane.'

'But it was?'

Gareth wipes his hand across his mouth. He's still caught between belief and disbelief. But he knows what – who – he saw. 'I knew it was her as soon as I looked her in the face. She was older, of course, but basically exactly the same. She certainly hadn't altered as much as I have. She was . . . my beautiful Jane.'

'You spoke to her?'

'Yes. But she saw me looking at her before I had a chance to say anything. She recognized me. I'm sure of it. There was a split second in which her eyes met mine. And in that split second I knew what was going to happen. I saw it in her gaze. She was going to deny she was Jane. I just . . . knew it.'

'And she did?'

'I walked along the row to her. She didn't get up. She closed down the iPad and frowned up at me, as if wondering what I wanted. It was an act, but it was a good one. It would've convinced me if I was a bystander. I said her name. I said, "It's me. Gareth." I said her name again. It didn't make any impression. "I'm sorry," she said. And it was her voice. It was Jane's voice. "I'm afraid you're making a mistake. I don't know you." "Come on," I said. "Don't try to blank me. For God's sake, Jane." She stood up, gathering her things. "I'm really sorry," she said. "But I'm not who you think I am. We've never met before. And I have to go now." She started to walk away. I stepped into her path. "What happened to you?" I asked. "What the hell's going on?" "I don't know what you're talking about," she replied. "Would you mind getting out of my way?"'

Gareth pauses. He takes a drag on his cigarette and a swig of lager. He swirls the rest of the lager in his glass and stares into it for a moment. Then he goes on. 'She stepped round me and headed off across the concourse towards the platforms. I went after her, calling her name as I went. Then some bloke who'd overheard us – big, looked like a soldier – got out of his seat and intercepted me. "The lady doesn't know you, pal. Why don't you leave her alone?" He wasn't the kind of bloke you said no to, so I walked away towards the shops. But I watched Jane over my shoulder. She went on to the Heathrow Express platform. I waited until the army type had lost interest and sat down again, then went after her.

'The train was due to leave in a few minutes. That didn't matter to me. I wasn't thinking about my trip to Cardiff any more. Jane was all I was thinking about. Where she'd been for the past twenty-two years. Why she was pretending not to know me. And yeah, I have to admit, whether it was possible I really was mistaken and it wasn't actually her.

'I got on and started walking through the carriages, looking for her. I'd gone through three or four without spotting her when the beeper went and the doors closed just prior to departure. I stayed on. It seemed the only thing to do. She had to be on the train. But I still couldn't see her. Then we started moving. And that's when I saw her.'

'She was still on the platform, right?' It's a guess. But it feels like how it must have ended.

Gareth nods miserably. 'Yeah. She was walking back towards the concourse. Maybe she'd got on the train, then got off just before it left. Maybe she'd never got on at all. I don't know. She was looking straight ahead. She never once glanced towards the train. I banged on the door, but she just went on walking and the train accelerated. And she was gone.'

'You think she lured you on to the train?'

He nods again. 'Yeah. That's what I think. I had to go all the way to Heathrow once the train had started. I waited out there for the next train from Paddington, thinking she might be on it. But she wasn't. In the end, I went back to Paddington, but there was nothing I could do to find her by then. I only had one chance. And I blew it.'

'Sounds like she'd have managed to give you the slip whatever you did.'

'Probably. At least the trick she pulled convinced me it was her. Otherwise I might've come to doubt it.'

'It was definitely her?'

'I go over what happened in my head several times a day. I've told a couple of friends about it and they think I'm nuts. But I'm a hundred per cent certain it was her. Jane's alive.' He lets out a slow breath. 'But she doesn't want anyone to know it.' Then he spreads his hands. 'Christ knows why.'

'I can't tell her father she's alive without proof, Gareth.'

'Good luck with finding that. I haven't got any to give you.'

'What took you to Ingrid Denner?'

'The only clue I had to follow. I racked my brains after I got back to Paddington and remembered I'd seen a company logo on the screen Jane was working on before she knew I was there. I recognized it, but I wasn't sure from where. It drove me crazy, until eventually I saw it on a TV news report of Jack Harkness's extradition hearing. The logo belonged to Harkness Pharmaceuticals.'

Harkness Pharmaceuticals. Here we go again. There *is* something between Jane and Harkness. 'And you knew Jane had lived close to Harkness in Cornwall?'

'No. She never mentioned it that I can recall. As far as the pharmaceuticals industry was concerned she was certainly no fan. She always maintained it was wrecking the environment. Jane was very eco-conscious, worried about global warming even before it was fashionable.'

'That's what Holly said. Which means the idea she wound up working for Harkness is crazy, right?'

'Right. Except, judging by a glimpse of her iPad, that's what I'd have said the woman I saw at Paddington was: a Harkness employee. Maybe she really was heading for Heathrow, to catch a flight back to Harkness HQ in Switzerland.'

'Did Jane ever go to Switzerland that you know of? Like, before she disappeared, I mean.'

Gareth frowns. 'I've thought about that. Jane and I went to Italy that Easter. Rome, Florence, Venice. We had such a great time. They were probably the happiest few weeks of my life. We travelled by train. On the way back, she said she had to stop in Switzerland to visit a friend from school. She'd never mentioned this friend before. She'd never mentioned we wouldn't be going the whole way home together either. I was in the middle of suggesting we stop in Paris for a couple of days – I basically didn't want the trip to end – when she broke the news, making it very clear I wasn't included in the diversion. She could be like that sometimes. Hard just when you expected her to be soft. And the other way round. Anyhow, she got off the train in Lausanne and I carried on without her. So, yeah, she went to Switzerland, just a couple of months before she disappeared. Harkness Pharmaceuticals were still headquartered in Basel then. And what's Basel from Lausanne? A couple of hours by train. I didn't make the connection at the time, but since I saw her at Paddington, well . . . I've wondered about that. I've wondered a lot.'

'Holly said you broke up with Jane after that trip.'

Gareth winces. 'She ditched me halfway through the following term. We didn't have a row or anything. It was weird. She just announced we were finished, in a note she left in my college pigeonhole. No reason. Just, it's over. I tried to talk to her, but she wasn't having any. I don't know why I bothered. You could never talk her out of anything once she'd made her mind up. Then . . . she disappeared.' He takes a thoughtful last drag on his cigarette, stubs it out and lights another.

'Since I learnt she was alive, since I realized she must have staged her disappearance, I've wondered if breaking up with me was a way of letting me down lightly. It didn't work. But . . . maybe she thought it was the kindest way to do it.'

'Why do it at all, Gareth? Why disappear like that?'

'That's what I keep asking myself. What the hell's it all about?'

'You think Ingrid Denner can tell you?'

'I contacted Harkness Pharmaceuticals to see if Jane really was working for them, or if somebody who *might* be her was working for them – I never expected she'd be using her real name. It was hard to get their attention in the middle of Harkness's legal problems. I had to make a serious nuisance of myself. Then, out of the blue, I get a call from Ingrid Denner. She wants to meet me. So, we get together for coffee. She's friendly but . . . edgy, if you know what I mean. No, Jane Glasson doesn't work for the company. Nor does anyone who arguably could be Jane with a fake identity. Absolutely not. Rigorous background checks on all staff rule the possibility out conclusively. But, purely as a gesture of goodwill and considering the genuineness of my concern, is there perhaps something they can do for me, some way they can help me focus on other matters? Yeah. That's actually how she put it. It seemed to me she was trying to buy my silence.'

'She does that quite a lot, according to Harkness. He recommended I take her up on it.'

'Well, you could do worse, I suppose, if money's what you're after.'

I look him in the eye. 'It isn't.'

He nods, accepting the assurance. 'OK.'

'You turned Ingrid down?'

'Yeah. Of course I did. Although she reacted as if there'd never been anything to turn down in the first place. A pleasure talking to you, sorry, I can't help, we *won't* be expecting to hear from you again, so goodbye and kiss my arse. Ass, I should say. She's *very* American.'

'What were you planning to do at the Dorchester?'

'What were *you* planning to do, if a pay-off wasn't your motive for going to see Ingrid?'

I drink some of my water and look at him openly. I have to tell him something. But it's not going to be much. 'I'm not sure. See what I could get out of her, I s'pose.'

'About Jane?'

'Amongst other things.'

'Oh?' He raises his eyebrows. 'There are other things, are there?'

I'm not ready to tell Gareth any more. Right now he doesn't need to know the Nightingale account connects Jane to Harkness Pharmaceuticals even without his glimpse of their logo on her iPad. Assuming it really was her. Which is what I absolutely am assuming. Gareth wouldn't have done as much as he has without being certain the woman at Paddington was Jane, living and breathing. That's why he can't stop now. That's why I can't stop either. Fifty thousand pounds to walk away? Sorry, Jack. I don't think so. 'Listen, Gareth. I'll help you if you'll help me. We're both after the same thing. The truth about Jane.'

'Yeah.' He looks searchingly at me through a cloud of cigarette smoke. 'I guess we are.'

'But how do we get it?'

'There may be a way.' He nods thoughtfully. 'And maybe you can help me pull it off.'

⁜

Don had filled the rest of his day with mindless but essential chores. He tried not to wonder when – or even if – Blake would return to the flat. She was not his responsibility, nor was he hers. She could do as she pleased and probably would. And he would have no grounds for complaint.

Evening set in and there was still no sign of Blake. Exasperated with his own anxiety about her, Don left a Post-it note stuck to the front door and adjourned to his local for a calming pint or three.

An hour or so later, Blake arrived to interrupt Don's aimless football chat with another bar-propper. She was not alone.

Gareth Lawler was a surprise package, dull dog though he seemed to Don. He had some kind of proposal to make which Blake had already agreed to. But she wanted Don on board as well. The details, however, needed to be discussed in the privacy of his flat. Gareth looked around the bar twitchily, as if it was a nest of spies. Don polished off his pint and they headed back to the flat.

More surprises followed: Blake's account of her visit to Harkness's house; his suggestion that Ingrid Denner would be willing to buy her off; Blake's encounter with Gareth at the Dorchester; Gareth's claim to have seen Jane Glasson at Paddington station. There was a lot to take in.

What seemed clear, as Don felt forced to admit, was that Jane really was alive and somehow mixed up with Harkness Pharmaceuticals. The question was what they could or should do about it. All the other questions Don had – notably whether more had transpired from Blake's meeting with Harkness than she was willing to admit in Gareth's presence – were going to have to wait.

Gareth looked to Don like a man who was ever so slightly out of his depth – and the strain of standing on tiptoe to keep his head above water was beginning to get to him. He asked to use the bathroom before unveiling his plan.

'You know friend Gareth is bottling up a lot of stress,

230

don't you?' Don whispered while he was absent. 'Reminds me of someone I used to work with. Got a lot of good sales. But it took too much out of him.'

'How did that end?'

'Tilbury Marshes. He was washed up there after abandoning his car on the QE2 Bridge at Dartford and jumping off.'

'I'm like so glad you told me that. Gareth's our big chance and you know it.'

'Or we're his.'

'Same difference.'

'We'll see about that.'

'Don't fuck this up, Don. Please.'

'All right, all right. I won't.'

Gareth was notably calmer when he returned from the bathroom. He spoke more slowly and blinked less. Don harboured the suspicion he had taken something while he was away.

Gareth opened up his bag and took out a small black tile about a centimetre square which he laid on the coffee-table. 'This,' he announced, 'is what they call a sapper. It's magnetic. All you have to do is attach it to Ingrid Denner's laptop. It won't be obvious against the black of the case. As soon as she logs on, I can remotely access all her files, including whatever she has on Jane.'

'Assuming she has anything.'

'There'll be something,' said Blake, glancing sharply at Don.

'She knew I was barking up the right tree,' said Gareth, sounding confident on the point. 'That's why she made the offer she did. But I turned her down, so she'll be suspicious of me.' He looked at Blake. 'She won't be suspicious of you.'

'It'll still involve quite a bit of sleight of hand,' Don objected. 'And a lot of luck. What if la Denner doesn't bring her laptop along when Blake meets her – or keeps it buried in her bag the whole time?'

'I'm betting she's never parted from it,' said Gareth.

'You're *betting*? That's it?'

'She'll have it with her, Don,' said Blake. 'She's bound to. As for me planting the sapper on it, that's where you come in.'

'It is?'

'You'll be close by. If it looks like we need to seriously divert her attention for me to get at the laptop, you'll have to do the diverting.'

'Any ideas how?'

'Not yet. We don't know where I'll be meeting her. But we'll come up with something.'

'Even if we do, she's sure to notice the sapper sooner or later.'

'I'll only need a few seconds,' said Gareth.

'But she's bound to suspect you're behind it.'

'It won't matter by then. We'll have what we need. Call her now.' Gareth was clearly eager to get on with it. 'Let's see if she bites.'

'I need to use your phone, Don,' said Blake. He handed it over. 'Harkness didn't give me Ingrid's number. But we can get hold of her at the Dorchester.'

'I've got her number,' said Gareth.

'But *I* haven't.'

'That's a good point,' said Don, treating Gareth to a superior grin.

⁂

Ingrid Denner has returned to the Dorchester. The hotel puts me through to her room. I imagine a glammed-up ball-breaker

232

in some over-the-top suite. The voice kind of fits. Very American, as Gareth said.

'You called by earlier, evidently,' said Ingrid in a slightly echoey voice. 'Who was the guy you went off with?'

'He said his name was Lawler. But I didn't go off with him. I just sensed it would be best to speak to you without him hanging around.' Gareth looks anxious at the turn the conversation's already taken. Don doesn't look exactly optimistic either. But I know how to play this.

'Did he say what he wanted with me?'

'No. And I didn't ask. I concentrated on shaking him off.'

'Good girl.' It sounds like she believes me. But I guess that's part of her job. 'Harkness has spoken to me about you.'

'Has he?' He didn't say he would. But maybe he wanted to find out if I'd contacted Ingrid after all. Or maybe he was just trying to help me. I have no idea what his real motives are.

'I dunno exactly what you hope to get out of this, Blake.'

'A fresh start, I guess.'

'Well, there probably is something I can do for you. But don't get your hopes up unrealistically.'

'I won't.'

'I can meet you tomorrow morning. Early.'

'OK.'

'There's a café in North Audley Street called Le Truc Vert. I'll see you at one of the pavement tables at nine o'clock.'

'I'll be there.'

'You better be. I won't wait.'

⁜

Don could not deny Blake had managed her telephone conversation with Ingrid Denner artfully. Nor, having promised to, could he refuse to play his part in the stunt she planned to pull the following morning. Blake did not tell him what exactly she had in mind until Gareth had left.

233

They had Gareth's phone number, but, as Don reflected, they knew precious little else about his current existence. He lived in Clapham, though they did not have his address. He worked in the oil industry, though for which company was unclear. What he had done with his life since Jane Glasson's disappearance was also a blank, though his obsession with Jane suggested it had not featured much in the way of stable relationships.

The only comfort was that Gareth knew as little about them. This, however, did not reassure Don. 'Has it occurred to you, Blake,' he said, as he poured himself a large Scotch, 'that if we get what Gareth wants, he could just take off with the information and freeze us out?'

'There's no reason why he should. And we're not going to get the information any other way. Besides, you'll be there to stop him doing that.'

'I will?'

'D'you know this place where I'm meeting Ingrid?'

Don pulled a battered *A–Z* out of the bookcase and thumbed it open at the large-scale page covering Mayfair. Blake pressed the book flat on the coffee-table and peered intently at it. 'Grosvenor Square can't be more than five minutes from any café in North Audley Street,' she announced after a minute or so. 'Gareth said he'll be waiting there to download whatever we get from Ingrid's laptop. So, you can join him as soon as I've clamped the sapper on.'

'After staging this diversion you're planning?'

'If I can't get to the laptop without it, yeah. Give me fifteen minutes with her. Then walk by on the other side of the road. If I've got my teacup in my hand, you're needed. If it's in the saucer, you're not.'

'And what is the diversion?'

'You're holding it.'

Don looked at his glass. 'Whisky?'

Blake smirked at him. 'You'll make a great early morning drunk.'

It was only later, after Don had rustled up sandwiches – bacon for himself, cheese and tomato for her – that she revealed any more about her encounter with Harkness. Gareth, she said, was an open book compared with the founder and president of Harkness Pharmaceuticals.

'I just don't understand him, Don. I don't get where he's coming from. He's got to have a hidden agenda. He's too clever to let all this shit just happen to him unless it suits his purpose. But what *is* his purpose?'

'Maybe Jane knows.'

'Maybe.' Blake munched thoughtfully on her sandwich. 'Which is one more reason to find her.'

'The pay-off from Ingrid Harkness has lined up for you . . .'

She frowned at him suspiciously. 'What about it?'

'You could do worse than take it. Tell Gareth you messed up with the sapper then start thinking how best to spend the money.'

She looked not so much annoyed as disappointed. 'You know I'm not going to do that.'

'I suppose I do.'

'Just like you know you're not going to let me down tomorrow.'

Don sighed. 'I suppose not.'

As he lay in bed that night, tired but finding sleep elusive, Don asked himself why he was still helping Blake in her pursuit of the truth. The answer was more about him than her. His brief taste that day of life before Blake had made him realize just how empty it was. He had urged caution and compromise. But Blake was having none of that. Her determination was contagious. And if she was set on taking risks, he could not allow her to take them alone.

Some roads insisted on being followed. And this was one of them. Where it would take him he could not imagine. But he knew now, for all his protestations, that he was going to find out.

FIVE

FRAN LEANT OUT OF THE WINDOW OF HER ROOM AT THE Polurrian Bay Hotel and breathed in deeply. The air was cleansingly pure, borne in on a sea-scented breeze. For the first time, she was actually glad she had been obliged to come to Cornwall.

Robin Pawley had shown himself to be compliant and efficient. He had noticed the same spatial discrepancy in the layout of the master bedroom and the library-cum-study as Don had, but had not made the slightest fuss when told to disregard it. He clearly knew which side his bread was buttered. He was also no slouch when it came to earning his commission. Draft particulars for the sale of Wortalleth West would be available for Fran's inspection and approval later that morning. There seemed no reason why she should not be able to catch a late afternoon train back to London.

The gloriousness of the vista had lulled her into a self-indulgent mood. She would have a leisurely breakfast before checking out and proceeding to Helston for her appointment with Pawley. She might even suggest lunch with him to mark the satisfactory conclusion of her visit. Harkness would pay, after all, one way or another.

*

In Grosvenor Square, Gareth Lawler sat on a bench near the Roosevelt Memorial, fiddling with his iPhone. A laptop also lay open in front of him. Office workers hurried past on their various routes across the square, paying Lawler no heed. He was dressed casually, in trainers, jeans and a hoodie, with a white Nike baseball cap pulled low over his eyes. Viewing him from twenty yards or so away, it struck Don that the guy could melt into the crowd more or less at will, dressed as he was. He was the epitome of anonymity.

Lawler glanced towards Don and they acknowledged each other's presence with the faintest of nods. Then Lawler switched his apparent attention back to his phone and Don pressed on across the square.

He planned to approach Le Truc Vert along the opposite side of North Audley Street, arriving on cue at a quarter past nine. By then he would have taken a swig from the plastic bottle in his pocket, containing not sparkling water, as per the label, but Bell's whisky, rolling it around his mouth to ensure it would be evident on his breath. A suit way overdue for donation to Oxfam, a frayed shirt, an unshaven chin and uncombed hair already made him look like a middle-aged dropout from the rat race. Breakfast-time whisky was sure to complete the effect.

For the rest, it was all down to Blake. She was making the running. And he would have to do his best to keep up with her.

❖

Ingrid said she wouldn't wait, but it's me doing the waiting as nine o'clock comes and goes. Le Truc Vert is a popular happy-feeling café on the corner of a side-street. I've ordered green tea and French toast with bananas and maple syrup. Seeing it on the menu made me feel hungry. And I guess Ingrid's paying.

Ingrid arrives just after the waiter brings me my tea. She's smaller than I expected, stylishly dressed in a pale grey trouser suit. Her face is way too immaculate, like her volumized blonde-tinted hair. She's probably ten years older than she looks. I can't see much of her eyes behind extra-dark sunglasses. Her smile is wide and dazzling, but there's no smile in her clipped, twangy voice.

'Blake?' she says, sitting down opposite me. She's carrying an expensive tooled-leather briefcase, which she dumps on another chair. I'm guessing that's where the laptop is, along with quite a lot else. 'Hi,' she goes on. 'I'm Ingrid.'

'Hi.'

'You having breakfast?' She nods to the knife and fork I've been given.

'French toast.'

'Nice.' She leans back and waves through the open door of the café, making a cup-holding-and-drinking gesture. 'I've gotten to be quite a regular here since being posted to London,' she explains. 'They know it's just strong black coffee for me every time.'

'Harkness keeping you busy?' I ask in a casual tone.

'You mean the corporation or the man himself?' She gives me more of her girl-of-the-world smile.

'Both, I guess.'

'Well, I'm busy, for sure, so let's get into it, shall we? I understand you've been working for Harkness as some kind of live-in housekeeper down at his place in Cornwall.'

'Yeah.' I grin, shaping my persona to fit what she'll expect of me. 'Harkness seemed to think you needed to consider my . . . situation.'

'And that's what we're doing. Mind if I take a few notes?' She unclasps the briefcase, prises it open and pulls out her phone. She doesn't close the case. I can see the laptop inside. I could lean over the table and touch it. I have the sapper in the

241

coin-pocket of my jeans. This is going to work. I'm sure of it.

'First name?' Ingrid opens, her eyes trained on the phone.

'Just Blake.'

'Date of birth?'

'My own business.'

Sunlight gleams on Ingrid's teeth as she smiles at me. 'Are you gonna say that to every question I ask?'

'Probably.'

'Then we're—'

The waiter appears with her coffee and my French toast. She says nothing while he sets them down. I thank him as he leaves. Ingrid takes a sip of coffee. I pour the maple syrup over my French toast and cut it into bite-sized portions.

'That looks good,' she says.

'Want some?'

'No thanks. Bad for the figure. Not something you need to worry about, though.'

'D'you use Elixtris, Ingrid?'

The question surprises her. I can see that from the tilt of her head. 'Yes. Why?'

'Just curious.'

'I *will* need a few particulars if I'm to do anything for you, Blake.'

'Why? Either I represent some kind of minor risk Harkness Pharmaceuticals needs to insure themselves against or I don't.' I swallow a scrumptious mouthful of French toast and prong another.

'You don't believe in the soft sell, do you?'

'Do *you*?' Down goes the second forkful.

'It kinda depends . . . on the context.'

I pick up my teacup and take a sip. I glance up the street. There's no sign of Don. I put the cup back in the saucer. 'I've got no intention of telling anyone – press, creditors, investigators – about anything I've seen at Wortalleth West.'

'That's good to hear.'

'But is it good *enough*?'

'From the point of view of Harkness Pharmaceuticals, probably not.' She purses her lips. She's choosing her words *very* carefully. 'My brief is to supply them with certainty regarding the potential dissemination of negative, unhelpful or misleading information regarding the company's founder and his current legal difficulties.'

'And certainty has a price?'

'Everything has a price, Blake. You'll realize that as you grow older.'

There's Don. I can see him now, appearing and disappearing between parked cars on the other side of the road. Even at this range, he looks like shit. I pick up my cup and take a sip. This time, I don't put it down.

'I'm willing to put together a confidentiality agreement, which you'll have to sign at the offices of the company's lawyers here in London.'

'OK.'

'There'll be a one-off payment to reflect the company's appreciation of your willingness to enter into such an undertaking.'

'One-off? Right.' I'm stalling now, playing for time. 'And, er, like, er, how much would that be?'

'Piece of advice, Blake. Don't be over-eager in negotiations like this.'

I'm still holding the cup. Don's nearly opposite us. He sees me watching him. He grimaces slightly as he realizes he's going to have to go through with the plan. He starts across the road, then stops for traffic.

'I'll email you a full proposal based on what you've so far told me.'

'How soon?'

'Tomorrow?'

'OK. But forget the email. Do me a letter. I'll collect it from your hotel.'

'I'll need an address for you.'

'I'm kind of between addresses at the moment.'

'The lawyers won't let you get away with this mystery-girl routine, Blake, believe me.'

The traffic clears. Don hurries across the road towards us.

'I'll give them whatever details they want once I know the deal's good enough.'

'Oh, it'll be good enough.'

'No problem, then.'

Here comes Don. I signal to him with a glance that the laptop's in the briefcase. She doesn't see Don or hear him. *He's behind you.*

Then he isn't. 'You ladies . . . spare any dosh?' he slurs, half falling on to the table.

'Oh my God,' cries Ingrid, seriously shocked. The smell of whisky is obvious. I just hope Don hasn't drunk as much as he smells like he has.

'Careful,' I say, sweet saint that I'm not.

'No need to—' Don begins, then he artfully loses his balance and topples sideways, knocking over the spare chair and sending the open briefcase thumping to the ground.

Ingrid jumps up and tries to push Don away. The laptop's slid out of the case, along with a slew of files and other paperwork. I'm out of my seat and round the table after the laptop while Don grasps Ingrid's arm and mumbles something about meaning no harm.

'Get your hands off me,' Ingrid shouts.

'Sorry, I—'

The waiter's out now, to see what the trouble is. Don stands up unsteadily. He raises his hands like he's surrendering to the cops.

'No harm done,' he gets out. 'Just a . . . misunderstanding.'

I bend down and grab the laptop. The sapper's in the palm of my hand. I slap it on to the machine, black on black, as I move to gather up the scattered files and papers. Ingrid's still vocalizing her outrage. 'Call the police,' she demands. 'This guy's totally out of it.'

The waiter doesn't look desperately keen on that idea. Nor does Don. 'Can't, er, apologize enough,' he says in a clearer voice. 'Inexcusable. 'Fraid I've, er, disgraced myself. Best thing I can do is, er, get out of your way.'

He's off then, heading towards Grosvenor Square with a bit of a stagger that doesn't look quite real to me but convinces Ingrid. 'Horrifying,' she declares. 'You'd think this was Soho at midnight.'

'Not cool.' I hoist her briefcase up on to my chair while cradling the laptop, etcetera. 'I picked everything up before he could trample all over it.'

'Oh my God.' Ingrid only now registers what has happened to her possessions. She glances around to see if I've missed anything. Then she holds the briefcase open while I lower the stuff back in. 'Thank you, Blake,' she says.

'You're welcome.'

She's about to close the case when a thought strikes her. She pulls out the laptop, sits back down and opens it up. The sapper's out of sight on the underside. 'Better check this is still working. If that guy's broken the goddam thing . . .'

I sit slowly down. The waiter's gone back into the café, relieved everything's blown over. I look over my shoulder and see Don in the distance, walking fast. Then I hear a little ping that announces Ingrid's laptop is up and running.

'Great,' she declares. 'It seems fine.'

'Pleased to hear it,' I say. And I totally am.

⬍

Don popped a peppermint into his mouth as he headed across Grosvenor Square towards the Roosevelt Memorial. He did not want anyone else, notably the police, taking him for someone who had breakfasted on Scotch.

There was Lawler, just where he had been all the time. He was stooped over his laptop, frowning in concentration and shading the screen with one hand while he tapped at the keyboard with the other.

Don sat down on the bench beside him. 'It went like a dream,' he announced, irked by Lawler's apparent indifference.

'So I see,' said Lawler. 'Ingrid's already gone online. And I've already accessed one of her files. It's entitled Jane Glasson question mark. I'm downloading it now.'

'Will she know you're doing that?'

'No reason why she should. Sooner or later, she'll notice the physical presence of the sapper. Until then, we've got the run of her files.'

'What's in Jane Glasson question mark?'

'Just looking.' Silence followed, while Lawler scrolled through the contents of the file. Peering over his shoulder Don saw copies of emails and pages of text. Then Lawler said, 'There's a lot here,' which appeared to Don to be an understatement.

'Well, we'll need to study it all, however much there is.'

'Agreed.' Lawler looked round at Don. 'I suggest we do that somewhere else. Ingrid's only a few minutes up the road. I'd prefer to be well out of her reach. I'll send the file on to you, OK?'

'OK, but—'

Lawler tapped a key. 'There it goes. It'll be on your phone as an email attachment in a few seconds.'

Don pulled out his phone to check. Something substantial was in the process of being downloaded.

'You can read it all on your desktop at home. Why don't I come round later and we can talk through our options?'

'All right.' Don felt he had no alternative but to agree. Lawler's suggestion seemed sensible enough. There was a tiny ping from his phone. He opened the email and there was the promised attachment: *Jane Glasson?* He opened that too. The first item was a report composed by Ingrid about Lawler's claim to have seen a Harkness Pharmaceuticals employee at Paddington station on 10 April that year whom he identified as missing person Jane Glasson.

'Got it?' asked Lawler.

'Yeah, I—'

'I'll call round at two. That'll give us a few hours to digest it all. I'll make myself scarce now.' With that he closed his laptop and stood up.

'Hold on,' said Don. 'Blake will want to—'

'Tell her she did an awesome job. I'll see you both later.'

Then he was off, at an anxious half-jog. And all Don could do was watch him go.

✣

Ingrid orders a second coffee after Don the drunk's disappeared. Then she lights a cigarette. It comes from the pack of Camel Lights that spilt out of her briefcase. She slides the laptop back into the case without noticing the sapper. I barely spot it myself. She'll notice it at some point, of course. And she'll realize either Don or I must've put it there. But that's just the way it has to be. She won't know where to find me. And she won't be expecting to need to. She thinks I'll grab the bribe she's going to offer me with both hands.

'Mind if I ask you a personal question, Blake?' says Ingrid after a pull on her cigarette. 'About Jack Harkness.'

'You can ask.'

'What's your impression of him? What kind of a man d'you think he is?'

'I was just his temporary stand-in housekeeper, Ingrid. How should I know?'

'You're a perceptive young woman. We both know that. You've lived in his house. You've seen and heard things.'

'Yeah. Things you want me to guarantee I'll never talk about.'

'You can talk about them to me.'

'No, Ingrid.' I smile. And she smiles. But she realizes she's not going to get anything out of me. 'I can't.'

'Good girl. That's exactly what I was hoping you'd say.'

She doesn't fool me. She'd have taken whatever I gave her. She's just covering her tracks now. Her second coffee appears then. But I'm going to leave her to drink it alone. 'OK,' I say. 'So, I'll call at your hotel mid-morning tomorrow and—'

'We'd better say noon. The proposal will be waiting for you then.'

'Great. Then I'll look at it . . . and get back to you.'

'You'll like what you see, Blake. Trust me. Especially the number with the zeros after it.'

'I'm sure I will.' I stand up and take a five-pound note out of the pocket of my jeans. She waves it away.

'Don't worry,' she says. 'I'll cover this.'

'OK. Thanks. It was, er, nice to meet you, Ingrid.'

'You too, Blake.' She looks up at me through her sunglasses. 'That temporary stand-in housekeeper's job is going to turn out to be the best-paid job you've ever had. Maybe ever will have.'

I smile non-committally. And all I say is, ''Bye for now.'

I leave Ingrid sipping her coffee and head for Oxford Street. I'm due to rendezvous with Don and Gareth in the shopping mall above Bond Street Tube station. I walk fast, eager to hear what's happened. I glance back at the next corner and I can see Ingrid still sitting at our table. In the chair next to her, inside her briefcase, the sapper is clamped to her laptop, doing its tricksy little job. 'Not bad, Blake,' I murmur to myself. 'Not fucking bad.'

Just as well I've stopped congratulating myself by the time I reach Bond Street Tube. Don's waiting for me by the Pret sandwich counter. But there's no sign of Gareth.

'Don't worry,' says Don, who still smells strongly of whisky. 'I've got what Gareth was looking for on my phone.'

'But where's Gareth?'

'Gone to study the contents of this.' He shows me the screen on his phone. There's a file symbol at the bottom with *Jane Glasson?* printed under it. 'I suggest we do the same. He's coming round to the flat this afternoon.'

'It worked, then.'

Don grins. 'Like a dream.'

'Have you seen what's in the file?'

'Just a glimpse. But it looks like everything Ingrid knows on the subject. Come on. Let's go.'

⁜

With time to spare before her appointment with Robin Pawley, Fran decided on little more than a whim to call in again at Wortalleth West. She would be able to gain a clearer impression of the house on her own and she would probably never have another chance to wander round it.

There was no sign of the gardener, for which she was grateful. But a car was parked in front of the house that certainly did not belong to Pawley: a red Mercedes convertible. The driver was nowhere to be seen.

Fran hardly knew what to make of the car's presence. It

was faintly disturbing. She listened for a moment, but could hear no sounds of movement, just the cooing of pigeons in the pine trees behind the house and the susurration of the surf down in the cove. She marched up to the front door and let herself in.

The mortise, she noticed at once, was not across. She was more than faintly disturbed now.

She stood in the hall, listening intently. But there was nothing to hear. She considered turning round and going straight back to the car. The stillness and emptiness of such a large building was eerily unsettling.

Then she heard footsteps on the landing and a figure appeared above her: a big, broad-shouldered man in a pale suit and striped shirt, with a mass of blond hair and a ruddy face. He was built like an out-of-condition rugby player and was smiling down at her with the sort of condescending amiability he probably thought won women over.

'Hi,' he said, starting down the stairs. 'Are you Fran Revell?'

'Yes,' Fran replied cautiously.

'Mike Coleman, Sympergy Renewables. Robin said I might bump into you here.'

'He did?' Well, maybe he had. But, if so, he had not bothered to tell her.

Coleman reached the hall with a heavy-footed thud. His smile broadened still further as he extended his hand. 'A pleasure to meet you, Fran.'

Fran smiled weakly and shook his chubby-fingered hand. 'How did you get in here, Mr Coleman?'

'Mike, please.'

'OK. Mike. So . . .'

'I've had a key for quite a while. Jack wanted me to be able to deal with any glitches in his very particular domestic renewables system as and when they occurred.' *Jack?* Coleman seemed to think familiarity would trump any amount of implausibility. And right now Fran found the idea of Harkness giving this man a key very implausible. 'Not that there have been many glitches, thanks to our policy of only using components that have been rigorously tried and tested. That's the secret of success in this game.' He flourished a card and slipped it into her hand.

She glanced down at it. *Mike Coleman, Sympergy Renewables Ltd.* Address, phone numbers, email and website addresses were followed by what she took to be the company's mission statement. *Harness the power of nature with Devon and Cornwall's leading wind and solar energy experts.*

'Jack made a far-sighted commitment to our systems for battery-boosted independent energy sources,' Coleman went on, sounding battery-boosted himself. 'I've always believed in giving him my personal attention whenever required.'

'And it's required now, is it?'

'Well, with the house going on the market, it's a good idea to check everything over. The previous agent, Don Challenor, seemed keen when I suggested it.' Coleman's perma-grin was becoming wearing. 'I was happy to oblige. As always.'

'So, what are you actually doing this morning?'

'Like I say. Checking everything over.'

'Found any problems?'

'No. None at all. But what can I tell you? Our workmanship is second to none.'

'So—'

The sound of something falling – heavy but fragmentary – carried at that moment from the upper floor. Coleman did not react, although, to Fran's eyes, it seemed he was going to great lengths not to.

'What was that?'

'What was what?'

'That noise.'

'I, er, didn't actually hear anything.' The grin was congealing now into some kind of grimace.

'It was quite distinct.'

There was another noise somewhere above them, then a heavy clunk.

'Did you hear that?'

'Some timer kicking in, probably. There's a whole underfloor heating system with pipework that expands and contracts.'

'What exactly were you doing upstairs?'

'I thought I—'

'Never mind. I'll see for myself.'

Fran made for the stairs and Coleman followed. She had only climbed a few steps when she felt his hand on her elbow. 'There's really no need to go up there.'

She stopped and looked round at him. 'Would you mind?' she said sharply.

He pulled his hand away. He was no longer smiling. 'My advice, Fran, my *sincere* advice, is don't go up there.'

'Why not?'

'It's, er . . . in your best interests.'

'*What?*'

Before he could shape a reply, Fran whirled round and marched briskly up the curving stairs to the landing. From there she headed to the master bedroom, which she strongly sensed was where the noises had emanated from.

The bedroom itself was quiet and empty. Nothing looked out of place. Fran's pace slowed as she listened intently.

No more sounds reached her. She glanced round, wondering if Coleman had followed her. But he had not.

She walked slowly through the dressing room, where the closet doors were firmly closed, into the bathroom. Her reflection met her in one of the full-length mirrors. Nothing else moved as her footsteps echoed on the tiled floor. She stepped up on to the low plinth that supported the two free-standing bath tubs in front of the windows, from where there was an expansive view of the sea and clifftops. Silence deepened around her as she gazed out at the vista.

Then, as she turned, she saw it. A large, jagged patch of plaster was missing from the wall backing on to the dressing-room closet. Fragments of plaster of varying sizes were lying on the floor. Beside them, propped against the wall, was a sledgehammer. And where the plaster had been removed there was a gleaming surface of solid steel, in which the light from the windows caught the outline of several dents.

Fran guessed at once that she was looking at the wall of the panic room. Someone – Coleman, presumably – had made a clumsy attempt to smash through it.

She suddenly wanted to be out of the house, away from Coleman and whatever he was trying to accomplish. She stepped from the plinth and headed towards the door.

But, as she did so, two men walked in from the dressing room. One was a big, bearded bear of a guy, dark-haired and Slavic-featured, with cold, predatory eyes, dressed in black. The other, smaller and slimmer, wore a denim shirt and jeans. He was narrow-faced, with close-set eyes and thinning fair hair. Fran guessed at once they were the pair who had frightened the panic-room engineer she had sent in. And she was frightened now too.

She could not leave the room unless they stepped aside, filling the doorway as they did. And they showed no sign of stepping aside.

'Who are you?' she asked, trying to sound brusque and unaffected, but to her own ear failing.

'I'm Amos French,' the man in denim replied, smiling coolly at her. He sounded American – and very sure of himself. He jerked his thumb towards the other guy. 'This is my associate, Gennady Zlenko.'

'What are you doing here?'

'Looking for the money your boss Harkness stole, on behalf of some of those he stole it from.'

'He's not my boss.'

'We think he is, Fran.' He marked the first use of her name with a widening smile. 'Matter of fact, we *know* he is.'

'You're mistaken.'

'No. The only mistake was made by you coming here this morning.'

'Are you responsible for the damage to that wall?'

'Yeah. And I reckon we may be responsible for a helluva lot more damage before we're done. Unless you tell us how to open up this . . . can of secrets . . . Harkness built his house around.'

'I've no idea what you're talking about.'

'I hope you're lying, Fran. For your sake.'

'I'm leaving now. I must ask you to do the same.'

'No one's leaving just yet.'

'I most certainly am.'

She moved towards them. They did not give way. Zlenko planted himself directly in her path and gazed down at her with an indifference that clearly did not preclude violence. She began to tremble with fear. Her heart was pounding. Her palms were clammy.

254

'Get out of my way,' she said, forcing the words from her mouth.

'I'm really sorry, Fran,' said French. 'You're not going anywhere until we've finished with you. And I doubt that'll be any time soon. See, I have to make the best use I can of the means at my disposal and right now . . . that's you.'

The *Jane Glasson?* file held more than Don had anticipated. He and Blake sat in front of his desktop computer in Islington, scrolling slowly through the contents. Blake read quicker than Don, which led to sighs and tongue-clicks of irritation from her while she waited for him to catch up. He kept his hand on the mouse and her hand off it.

Ingrid had certainly not ignored Gareth's claim that Jane was alive and well and working in some capacity for Harkness Pharmaceuticals. There was a lengthy series of emails between her and the company's HR department, which elicited several ever longer and fuller lists of current and former employees.

Later, as the dates on the communications edged closer to the present, Ingrid became more focused and demanding in her requirements. An increasingly tetchy deputy head of HR eventually admitted that, though no one of Jane's age and nationality had worked for any part of the business during the twenty-two years since Jane's disappearance, there was a whole cohort of staff not previously mentioned – notionally self-employed consultants, advisers and bought-in specialists – about whom no information had yet been supplied to Ingrid.

A vast slew of data was then extracted from HR records at Ingrid's insistence. Refined down, it yielded no one who had been attached to the company since 1996 on such a basis. Generally, contracts were of short duration, with only a few extending beyond two years.

And only one extending beyond five.

Retained specialist contractor number 55 was a forty-six-year-old woman of British nationality attached to the staff of chief researcher Filippo Crosetti. HR stated they were unable to divulge any personal information about her because Crosetti insisted on absolute confidentiality where his personally recruited specialists were concerned. He supervised their work from the company's research facility in Locarno and was solely responsible for them.

Ingrid was not about to take no for an answer, however. At any rate, not yet. She had a meeting scheduled with Crosetti at Harkness Pharmaceuticals' head office in Zug on 14 June to discuss a separate issue she referred to as *the contra-indications position statement*. She proposed to press him on the matter of retained specialist contractor 55 at that time.

'June fourteenth is two days from now, Don,' said Blake as soon as he reached that point in the file.

'I know that,' he responded, a touch irritably.

'Gareth may already have learnt what "contra-indications position" means.'

'Then I suppose he'll tell us when he gets here.' Don glanced at the time on the screen. *14.13.* Gareth was late.

'He'll reckon contractor fifty-five is Jane.'

'She might be. She might not be.'

'Female. British. Three years older than Jane. Supposedly. It's got to be.'

'There's no—'

Don was cut short by the burbling of his phone. Blake grabbed it before he could and glanced at the caller's number. 'Gareth,' she said, her eyes narrowing suspiciously as she handed the phone over.

'Gareth?' said Don.

'Yeah. Sorry, but I'm not coming.' Don caught a drift of railway station PA in the background as Gareth spoke. 'You probably know why if you've got as far through the material as you should've by now. I've got to be where that meeting's being held. I'm leaving straight away.'

'You mean you're—'

'Best not be too specific on the phone, Don. You obviously get my drift. I've also looked at the other file you'll have seen mentioned. There's a lot going on beneath the surface. We can talk about it when you join me over there.'

'You expect us—'

'I don't *expect* you to do anything. It's your choice. But if you're serious about achieving what you said you wanted, you'll be on your way soon enough. Call me when you know what time you'll be arriving.'

'Hold on. I—'

But Gareth was gone. Don set the phone down and grimaced at Blake. 'He's plainly convinced contractor fifty-five is Jane. And he knows what these contra-indications are, apparently. He must've got into that file as well. But he's saying nothing until we meet. I think he's at Paddington, about to take a train to Heathrow. Destination Zürich, I guess. Then Zug, in time for Ingrid's powwow with Crosetti the day after tomorrow. He wants us to follow.'

''Course he does. And we—' Blake's face fell. 'Oh shit.'

'We don't have to follow him,' Don said, hoping Blake had suddenly questioned the wisdom of what they were doing. '*You* don't have to go anywhere.'

'That's not the problem, Don.' She shook her head, closed her eyes and smiled with little apparent pleasure. 'Shit, shit, shit.'

'Blake?' He touched her shoulder.

She opened her eyes. 'We have to go to Switzerland. This is our chance of finding Jane. She's the key to everything. And I don't trust Gareth not to fuck it up.'

'I'm not sure that's—'

'*We have to go.*'

'Well, I—'

'How long would it take to drive to Birmingham and back?'

'Er, four or five hours, I suppose. Depending on the traffic. Why?'

'Because you need a passport to fly to Zürich, right?' She laughed bitterly. 'And my passport's in Birmingham.'

❖

Most of Mum's boyfriends were shits, but Lee was pure evil. The way he got his hooks into Daisy was just horrible. I tried to save her. But I suppose I didn't try hard enough. She never listened to me. I was just her too-young-to-understand kid sister. But I understood all right. I saw what Lee – and the drugs he was pushing her way – were doing to her. And then, the night it all ended, I saw where it had been leading.

Maybe Mum did too. But she didn't do anything to stop it – just drank more so she'd care less. She was always good at that. I try to remember Daisy alive and laughing and vital. And I try to use that memory to keep that other memory – of Daisy dead at twenty-two – buried deep. But it doesn't always work.

Gran died only a month or so after Daisy. She was sick by then, but Daisy dying was what really broke her. It nearly broke me too. But Gran always said I was the strong one of the family and it turned out she was right. Lee was afraid I was planning to tell the cops about his drug-dealing. I knew from the way he looked at me he wasn't going to risk that happening. He was out of it a lot of the time, but he wasn't too far gone to understand I was a problem. Because he knew, with Daisy gone, he couldn't control me. Mum did whatever he wanted. Not me, though.

Why didn't I go to the cops, then? I could have got Lee in big trouble. But the other low-lifes he was mixed up with would have come after me then. And none of it would have brought Daisy back.

I'd got the passport a year before, using Gran's address. Mum never knew about it and I'd reckoned I needed to keep it that way, so I hid it under the floorboards in my bedroom. I'd been thinking of getting out for quite a while. Ever since Lee came on the scene, really. Mum was always useless. But he turned her into something worse, which I'd never have thought possible until it happened. It was the look in Lee's eyes that morning that decided it for me, though. I realized time was running out. Fast.

It was a Saturday. I went into the city centre with some friends from college. I made an excuse for not going back with them. I just know going home was a big mistake – maybe a fatal one. I couldn't do it. I just couldn't. It stopped being a moment. It became *the* moment. I bought a ticket to London and got on the next train to Euston. It was raining. Night was falling. I was on my own. I'd never felt more certain I was doing the right thing.

But I didn't need my passport to go to London. And I haven't needed it since. I need it now, though. I need it badly.

Don's not wildly keen to fly to Zürich chasing after someone he's never met, but he knows he won't talk me out of it. He's not wildly keen to drive me to Birmingham to hunt down my passport either. He'd be even less keen if I told him about Daisy and the kind of men Mum gets in with, so naturally I don't tell him. All I say is that I left in a hurry after falling out with Mum and forgot to take my passport with me. He knows I'll go anyway, of course, and he suspects – rightly – that it'll be much easier to pull off if he goes with me. He's made a big mistake. Which I gently point out to him. He's let himself care about me.

'I don't need protecting, Don,' I tell him, which I realize might not be one hundred per cent true.

Don obviously reckons the percentage is much lower. 'Yes you do,' he insists.

'I could use your help. I'll admit that.'

'That's big of you.'

'Are you going to help me?'

'What makes you so sure your passport will be where you left it?'

'I hid it under the floorboards in my bedroom. Only I know where. No one will have found it. They won't have been looking. And Mum can barely find her own mouth with a glass most days.'

'Have you really had no contact with her since you left?'

'You bet I haven't.'

'How long ago is that?'

'Seven years.'

'For God's sake, Blake, she could've moved in all that time.'

'No chance. It's a council house. She's still there. I know she is. And I still have a key to the front door.'

'So, you're just going to let yourself in, prise up a floorboard, retrieve your passport and slip out again?'

'If we get there at nine, she'll be in the Highwayman.' The sour, threatening atmosphere of that shit-hole pub invades my memory as I say its name. I can hear Mum's laugh – the tinny, shrieking laugh she saved up for her drinking buddies there – and I shudder as I remember the sound. 'She never misses. No reason why she should ever know I've been in the house.'

'Simple as that?'

'Yeah. Why not?' Plenty of reasons, actually. More than Don knows. But I reckon Lee is almost certainly not one of them. Dead. In prison. Moved on. Seven years is long enough to have flushed him out of Mum's life.

Don looks seriously at me. 'Because it's never simple, Blake.'

'There's no choice.' I lay it on the line for him. 'I'm going after Jane. I'm not going to let whatever the truth is get away from me. To do that, I have to get my passport. I don't want to go back there, Don. It's the last place I want to go. But I have to. Don't you see that?'

Don nods. 'I see it.' He sighs. 'Who are you really doing this for, Blake? Don't say Andrew Glasson, because I won't believe you. And don't say Jane Glasson either. If she's living in Switzerland under a false name, working for Harkness Pharmaceuticals, it's because she wants to.'

'It's about more than Jane.'

'What, then?'

'Not sure.' It's true. I'm not. Turning the Glassons back into a family can't turn my family into any less of a disaster zone. But I let Lee destroy Daisy and then I ran away. I'm not going to run away from this. There's something big behind the game Harkness is playing. He wants me to take the money from Ingrid and go round the world. Why? What's he afraid I'll find out if I don't? That's the question I'm really set on answering. 'I can't let this go now, Don. I've come too far to turn back. All I need to know is: are you going to come with me?'

But I know already. I can see it in his face.

⁘

They left as the rush hour was fizzling out. The early evening was grey, with drifts of drizzle, the light flat. There were questions – lots of them – Don wanted to ask

Blake about her family. But he knew her well enough by now not to ask them. She had been a fugitive for seven years. And now they were going to the very place she had fled from. Every time he glanced at her, he saw the tension in her jaw. And every time she glanced at him, he sensed she was grateful to him – but would never say so.

They drove into the outer suburbs of Birmingham from the south. Blake's plan was that Don would confirm her mother was drinking the evening away in the Highwayman before Blake went to the house. This required her to describe her mother, which she did with obvious reluctance – and even more obvious distaste.

'Squat, barrel-chested, with dyed blonde hair. Normally wears a hoodie, leggings and trainers. Too old for the style and looks it. Chews gum even when she's drinking. Red-faced and fish-eyed.' Blake shuddered. 'That's the photofit of the woman who always claimed I was her daughter.'

Don could think of little to say in response to that. In the end, all he came up with was, 'Sorry.'

'Not your fault, Don. You can't choose your parents, right?'

'Your father—'

'Died when I was nine years old. Hit and run on his way home from work on his bike. In case you're wondering, I totally adored him.'

'You've not had a lot of luck, have you?'

'Life sucks, Don. No one ever tell you that?'

The Highwayman was a faded Tudor-style roadhouse, sporting posters advertising Sunday barbecues and forthcoming Sky Sports spectaculars. There were tables outside on the wide pavement, facing a busy junction, where the smokers were sitting. They looked a forbidding bunch of beer-bellied men and woebegone women. A couple of large dogs were snarling at each other by one table, barely restrained by their owners. Even viewed from a side-street on the far side of the junction, where Don had parked, the place looked a long way from enticing.

The part he had to play in Blake's plan required him to go in and order a drink while checking for the presence of her mother, so there was nothing to be gained by quibbling about the clientele. Blake's face was obscured by a large tweed cap Don had dug out of a cupboard, which for some reason made her look ridiculously young. She was sitting as low in her seat as she could and was very obviously ill at ease.

'As soon as you're sure she's there, come out and signal to me. I'll walk to the house from here.'

'Where is the house, exactly?'

'The next street over. There's an alley I can cut through by the next lamppost but one.'

'OK. All set, then?'

'*I* am.'

Don sighed. 'Me too.'

He climbed out of the car and made a slow approach to the Highwayman, dutifully waiting for the green man before crossing the junction. He was anonymously dressed in jeans and fleece, but somehow did not feel anonymous. The difference between him and the men sitting outside the pub was a gulf between two tribes. They registered that with the merest glance in his direction.

Inside was no better: crowded, hot and noisy. The pub was a barn of a place, with a U-shaped bar in the centre. A giant-screen television was playing highlights of a football match. Don drifted watchfully through the cluster of drinkers, some sitting, some standing, until he found himself eye to eye with one of the barmen. He ordered a pint and did a lot of looking around while it dribbled unappealingly out of a gigantic pump.

Suddenly, he saw her: the woman Blake had described so memorably. The brittle, dyed blonde hair, the clothes, the face, the gum-chewing between slurps of what he guessed was Bacardi and Coke: it had to be her. He would have put her age at fifty, but suspected she was actually younger. She was with four other women of similar age and appearance. They were doing a lot of cackling and coughing. Whether they were actually enjoying themselves was hard to tell. Don felt the weight of their desperation beneath the heavy make-up and the hard voices.

He should have looked away as soon as he had satisfied himself the woman was Blake's mother. As it was, he let his gaze linger a moment too long. She caught his eye. And smiled at him.

He turned away instantly, downed some of his beer and plotted a course to the door. Before he could leave the bar, however, she was standing next to him, hoodie open over a low-necked T-shirt, breasts very nearly spilling out of it. A heart with an arrow through it, distorted by the bulge of her flesh, was tattooed low on one of her breasts, nearly buried in the faintly crinkled cleavage.

''Ullo, darlin',' she said. 'Come lookin' for fun, 'ave you?'

Don was briefly lost for words. Identifying Blake's mother was one thing, flirting with her, or she with him, was quite another. 'I, er . . .'

'You're not from round 'ere, are you?'

'Er, no.'

'I'm Bren. Wot's your name?'

'Don.' He cursed himself for not making something up.

'Pleased to meet you, Don.' She rattled the ice cubes in her glass, which he noticed then was nearly empty. 'You look like the kind o' guy who'd buy a girl a drink if she needed one. And I do need one.'

'You do?'

'Oh yeah.' She waggled the glass at the barman, who immediately started pouring her another. 'I'm always better after I've 'ad a few.'

The Bacardi and Coke was plonked down in front of her. The barman eyed Don expectantly as he stated the price. There seemed nothing for it but to pay. 'Ta,' the barman said mechanically.

'Cheers.' Bren clinked her glass against Don's and downed a slug. Then she leered at him. ''Spect you're wonderin' wot it makes me better *at*, ain't you?'

'Er, not really.'

'No need to be shy. You didn't come in 'ere lookin' for a quiet drink, did you?'

'Maybe I did.' Don smiled awkwardly. 'You never know. Matter of fact, I think I'll step outside. It's a bit, er, crowded in here.'

'Yeah. I'll come with you. I could do with a fag.'

Don headed for the exit, with Bren in tow. There was no obvious way to shake her off and he supposed Blake could be in no doubt where her mother was if she actually saw her. He noticed Bren wink at her friends as she left and tried not to wonder what the wink implied.

Don glanced towards the distant MG as they emerged into the gun-grey evening. The windscreen was a reflection of the sky. He could not see Blake, which he reckoned a mercy. He stepped to one side as he left the doorway, manoeuvring Bren so she faced away from the car.

'Got any fags?'

'No. I, er . . . gave up.'

'Want one of mine?' She pulled a pack of Regals and a plastic lighter out of the pocket of her hoodie.

'No thanks. Like I say, I, er . . .'

'Givin' up can be bad for you.' Bren lit a cigarette for herself and more or less obliged him to accept one. He looked past her as he took it and saw Blake climb out of the MG, glance once in his direction, then hurry away along the street until she turned into the alley she had pointed out earlier and vanished from sight.

'Depends what you're giving up,' Don said, taking his first drag.

'Wot you got in mind?' The clearer light showed the lines and crevices on Bren's face and neck. Her skin was blotchy, her hands prematurely gnarled. Don looked for something – anything – to remind him of her daughter and saw only a ghost of similarity in her eyes. 'You can tell me.'

'There's, er, nothing to tell.' Don was aware he really should have been capable of managing the conversation better. He was out of his depth. And this woman knew it.

'Wot you do for a livin', Don?'

'I'm, er . . . an estate agent.'

'Oh yeah? Lots of nice fat commissions, I bet.'

'Sometimes.'

'You can spend it on me if you like.' She gave him a look he suspected was meant to appear coquettish. 'Wanna come back to my place?' She gestured with her cigarette. 'It's only just round the corner.'

'I'm fine here, thanks.'

'I could give you a really sexy time.'

'What?'

She smiled at him. 'For the right price, it's no 'oles barred.' Don felt suddenly sick. 'Know what I mean?'

❖

I head along the alley, telling myself not to waste my time wondering what the fuck Don's playing at – or what Mum

266

might be saying to him. I never wanted to see her again. And I never wanted Don to see her at all. But what the hell, I need that passport.

I reach the street. There's the house. It looks like all the others. But there's a difference. It's the one I grew up in. It's the one I spent years planning to escape from. I so don't want to be here.

The street's empty, bar a couple of kids on chopper bikes most of the way down towards the bend. They're too young to know who I am. And those who aren't too young probably wouldn't recognize me at a glance. This is my chance. I have to grab it.

I walk fast to the gate. Or where the gate should be. It's gone missing since I left. Up the cracked concrete path to the door. As I slide the key into the lock, I see all the pits and scratches in the paintwork around it and I know at once, just by them, that Mum hasn't changed. She was never going to. She hasn't got it in her.

I step into the hall and close the door behind me. It's twilight inside. There are shadows everywhere. But it's still and quiet. There's no one here, thank Christ. Then the smell hits me. I'd forgotten it. Maybe it's worse. I haven't been here to open the windows. Cigarettes. Booze. Drugs. Stale take-away food. That stinking perfume she wears. And something worse I can't put a name to.

I shake my head. I push the memories away. I'm here for one thing and one thing only. I take the stairs two at a time.

I reach the landing. The door to what was Daisy's bedroom is just a few steps away. It's closed. I can almost believe she's in there, listening to music on her headphones. But that's crazy. I'm not going in. No, no, no. I'm not doing that. I'll see her again if I do, slumped on the floor, with sick on her chin and her eyes rolled back. I have to concentrate. I have to focus.

*

267

I head for the door into what was my bedroom. I move fast, just fast enough to stay ahead of the past. It's behind me, dark and heavy. And it'll overtake me if I let it.

The room's a mess. My bed's still there, but it's covered with old clothes and collapsed cardboard boxes. Christ knows what they contain. There are more boxes on the floor, half buried in plastic packaging pellets. I shovel several handfuls of pellets out of the way and stoop by the ragged join in the carpet close to the door. There's a really foul smell in here. When I pull up the edge of the carpet, I see droppings of some kind and the horrible idea occurs to me that mice could actually have eaten my passport.

I've brought a screwdriver with me from Don's flat. I used to prise up the loose section of floorboard with scissors. But the screwdriver does a much better job. The smell's even worse. Christ, what a tip this place is. But here's what I'm after: a small package wrapped in a bin-liner.

I snap off the rubber bands, unravel the bin-liner and open the envelope. My passport and some old fivers I saved slide out into my hand. I open the passport and hold it up to the light from the window to check it really is mine. There I am, in a laminated photograph from eight years ago. I look nervous. I look frightened.

I'm nervous now. But frightened? No. Not any more. I'm past being frightened.

I shove the passport in the pocket of my jeans and jump up. I'm out of here.

❖

'Are ya playin' 'ard to get, darlin'?'

Bren's leer as she looked at him was almost more than Don could stomach. He thought of Blake and how badly she would have wanted him never to meet this woman who was her mother.

268

'I know what you came 'ere for, Don.'

No. Assuredly, she did not.

'You don't need to look any further.'

And, miraculously, that was true. In the distance, Blake appeared, walking fast towards the MG. She glanced in his direction as she reached the car and nodded. Then she jumped in.

'I've got to go,' Don said hoarsely, smiling awkwardly.

'You only just got 'ere.'

'It was, er . . . a mistake.' He set down his half-full glass on the edge of the nearest table.

Suddenly, he heard the MG's engine burst into life. Blake must have lost patience, slid across to the driving seat and started her up.

'Sorry,' Don said in a undertone.

'Sorry?' Bren scowled at him. 'Wot's that supposed to fuckin' mean?'

The MG sped to the junction, where Blake paused only briefly before swinging out in a wide arc and skidding to a halt about twenty yards past the pub. Bren paid no attention. The sounds of skidding car tyres meant nothing to her. But she was paying attention to Don.

''Ad your little thrill, 'ave you?'

'This has all been a . . . misunderstanding.' He moved past her. 'Sorry again.'

'Yeah,' she called after him. 'Fuck off, why don't you?'

It was all he could do not to break into a run. He marched to the car and climbed in, glancing back just once to check Bren was not following him.

Blake said nothing. She shoved the car into gear and started away, accelerating hard.

'This is a thirty limit,' said Don, noticing for the first time how dry his mouth was. He glanced in the wing mirror and saw a figure, dwarfed by distance, turning back towards the door of the pub.

'You weren't supposed to talk to her,' said Blake.

'Believe me, it wasn't my idea.'

'I don't want to know anything she said.'

'OK.'

'You didn't mention me to her, did you, Don?'

''Course not. D'you think I'm stupid?'

'Sometimes, yeah.' It did not seem to Don she was joking.

'Did you get your passport?'

'Yeah.'

'Any problems?'

'No. Unless you caused some.'

'Well, I didn't.'

'Good. In that case . . .' She braked sharply to a halt at the side of the road. The driver behind blared his horn at her and added a middle-finger salute as he pulled out round them. 'You can drive the rest of the way.'

Don tried to shape a pacifying smile. 'OK.'

Blake looked at him. She did not respond to his smile with much more than a nod, which seemed to be directed more to herself. Then she checked the rear-view mirror and nodded again. 'OK.'

Blake did not relax until they were back on the M40, heading south. It was dark now and late and Don was weary, drained by his encounter with Blake's mother but barred from talking about it. At his insistence, they stopped at Warwick Services, where he drank coffee and they shared a Danish pastry in a sea of empty tables.

'We'll fly to Zürich tomorrow, right?' said Blake, the immediate future her only concern now they had left her distant past safely behind.

270

'If you're still sure you want to go,' said Don.

'We're not going to go through that again, are we, Don?'

He held up his hands in a gesture of surrender. 'Can I see your passport?'

'Why?'

'Because I assume it'll be me who pays for our flights and hotel rooms at the other end and I'd like to be sure you actually have a valid passport before I start loading up my credit card.'

'It's valid. And I'll owe you my share of the cost.' She looked seriously put out by his remark and he realized just how grievous a thing it was to trample on her feelings. 'I'm not looking for a handout.'

'You must know I'm not bothered about the money.'

'Aren't estate agents always bothered about the money?'

'Not this one. Besides, Fran sacked me, if you remember, so technically I'm not an estate agent at the moment. I don't have any clients.'

'What about friends? Got any of those?'

'You tell me.'

She reached into her pocket for her passport and laid it on the table. 'It doesn't expire until 2020.'

'Good.'

'I don't want you to look inside.'

'Why not?'

'You'll laugh.'

'Why would I do that?'

'Because my first name always makes people laugh. It's why I never use it.'

'I promise I won't laugh.'

'I'd rather not take the risk.'

'OK. But when we get back and go online to book a flight, we'll have to enter the full name that appears on this' – he tapped the passport – 'in the system.'

'Fuck.' She grimaced. 'I hadn't thought of that.'

'Sorry.'

She sighed. 'Let's get it over with, then.' She grabbed the passport and held it open in front of him. 'Funny, right?'

Don kept a solemnly straight face. 'Not at all. Rather lovely, actually.'

'*Lovely?*'

'I like it.'

'Yeah? Well, don't get any ideas about using it. We're going to stick with Blake.' She snapped the passport shut. 'OK?'

He risked a smile. 'That's fine by me, Primrose.'

Don was exhausted by the time they reached Islington. When Blake asked him if he thought he was too old for so much gadding around, he said she was welcome to call in a young, fitter replacement if she had one available. She volunteered to make him some cocoa if he would just get on with booking their flights to Zürich. He opted for whisky instead.

✢

I would've woken early anyway, just not this early. The doorbell's ringing and, though it's already light out, it's still a thin dawn light. The clock says 5.20. No one rings doorbells at 5.20.

Except the police maybe. I don't know why I think it actually could be the police, but I jump out of bed, throw on jeans and a top in case Don gets up too – underwear will have to wait – and run to the entryphone by the front door of the flat.

I pick up the phone and say, 'Hello?'

The voice at the other end is male, hoarse and either anxious or angry, or maybe both. 'Is Don there?'

272

'Yeah, but . . . Who wants him?'

'Peter Revell.'

Peter Revell? I guess he must be Fran's husband. What the fuck is he doing here? 'Maybe you could—'

'Who is it?' Don calls. Looking round, I see him come stumbling out of his room in his pyjamas, rubbing his eyes, hair sticking out at angles. He looks at me like he's having trouble focusing.

'Peter Revell,' I tell him.

'Peter? What the hell . . . Why is he here . . . at whatever ungodly hour this is?'

'I don't know, Don.'

'Let me speak to him.' He takes the phone from me. 'Peter?' He's already frowning and the frown only gets deeper as he listens. 'I don't—' he says at one point, before being interrupted. Then he says, 'Come up,' prods the door release and hangs up the phone.

'What's going on?'

'No idea.' Don rubs his eyes again and shakes his head. 'The bloke's close to hysterical. Apparently . . .' He shrugs. 'Apparently, Fran's disappeared.'

I don't get much time to ask Don what 'disappeared' means exactly. Peter Revell must have run up the stairs judging by how quickly he's through the door Don's holding open for him. He's tall, about Don's age, with centre-parted grey hair, round horn-rimmed glasses and a prominent chin. He looks all over the place, hair and clothes a mess, eyes skittering, hands twitching.

Don closes the door behind him. 'What's going on, Peter?' he asks, speaking slowly, in an attempt to get through to the guy.

'I don't—' Peter begins. Then he looks at me. 'Who's this?'

'I'm Blake,' I say. 'A friend.'

Peter glares at Don. 'You know what's happened to Fran, don't you?' He stabs with his finger. 'Is your tart in on it too?'

'Hey, fuck you,' I say, glaring at him.

'You're way out of line, Peter,' says Don.

'*Out of line?* It's you who—' Peter breaks off. He kind of crumples in front of us. He bends over and lets out a terrible sort of despairing moan. He puts a hand to his face. 'I don't know what to do,' he whimpers. 'The police won't take me seriously. I haven't told the girls. You're the only one I can turn to. What in God's name is going on, Don?'

'I don't know,' says Don. 'You haven't told me.'

'Let's go into the lounge,' I suggest.

Don nods. We help the guy up and kind of lead him through to the lounge, where he slumps on the sofa.

'You want something?' Don asks.

Peter rubs his eyes. 'Coffee, maybe.'

I signal I'll go and make it. I walk into the kitchen, fill the kettle and set it to boil, then move closer to the doorway to hear what Peter says next.

Fran went down to Cornwall on the Sunday-night sleeper, apparently, to sort out the sale of Wortalleth West after sacking Don. She saw the house and met Robin Pawley. She told Peter everything was going smoothly. She spent Monday night at the Polurrian Bay Hotel and in a breakfast-time conversation with Peter on Tuesday morning said she'd be catching the 4.40 train from Truro back to London after returning her hire car. That would have got her into Paddington at 9.30.

'She never kept her appointment with Pawley yesterday morning,' Peter goes on as I make the coffee. 'He couldn't get her on her mobile, so eventually he phoned her office to see if they'd heard from her. They hadn't and they couldn't get hold of her either. It was only when the hire car agency phoned them to say she hadn't returned the car on time that they contacted me. I called her. I texted. Nothing. And she wasn't on that train. Or the one after.'

I bring in the coffee and sit down. Peter looks exhausted as well as worried sick. I'd feel sorrier for him if he hadn't been such a prick when he first walked in. But I suppose I can overlook it.

'This is all about Harkness, isn't it? It's my fault he's got his claws into Fran. That's what makes it so . . .' Peter's voice tails off. He waves his hand, then presses it to his face. 'What am I going to do?'

'How's it your fault, Peter?' Don asks.

'Does it really matter? I got in over my head. Harkness paid off some debts for me. But he expected Fran to do his bidding in return. She doesn't know I know that. But I do.'

'What kind of debts?'

'Er . . .' Peter rubs his unshaven chin. It makes a rasping sound. 'Gambling.'

Don looks at him like his low opinion of the man Fran preferred to him has finally been vindicated. 'I always knew you—' I catch his eye and he breaks off. There's no point going in hard. 'Never mind.'

'I don't feel good about myself, Don,' says Peter. 'Does it satisfy you to hear that?'

'I can't say it does. But laying into you won't help Fran. Just as long as you know I *could* lay into you.'

'What sort of trouble has she got into, Don? You must have some idea.'

'There are people looking for the money Harkness supposedly stole from his American partners. It's possible she ran into some of them.' I glance at Don. It's obvious who he means. But it won't do anything for Peter's anxiety levels to hear about French and Zlenko. I can see Don decide to back off a touch. 'I guess it's also possible she just reckoned she . . . needed a break.'

275

It's a wounding remark in its way. But Peter's already wounded. 'That's what the police said. Bastards.'

'Maybe you should wait a bit longer before doing anything,' I suggest. 'She's only been out of touch for twenty-four hours.'

He stares at me like I'm crazy. Then he sucks in a deep breath and stands up. 'I'm obviously wasting my time here. It's what Fran always says about you, Don. Bugger all use in an emergency.'

'Hold on,' Don protests. 'I never—'

'Forget it,' Peter shouts. 'Just forget it.' He heads for the door, throwing a parting remark back over his shoulder. 'I'll sort this out with no help from you.'

A second later, the door slams behind him. He's gone.

'Bloody hell,' says Don quietly. He reaches for his coffee and takes a sip. 'If Fran's somehow got entangled with French and Zlenko . . .'

'It doesn't have to be that bad,' I reason. But I know I want to believe it doesn't have to be because, if Don thinks it is, he may convince himself he has to go down to Cornwall and try to rescue Fran from whatever trouble she's in rather than fly to Switzerland with me.

'Peter might've got it all out of proportion,' Don muses. 'He's not the most level-headed of blokes.'

'Exactly.'

'Maybe I should phone her myself. See if she picks up.'

'It's not even six o'clock yet, Don. You can't call her now.'

'OK. I'll leave it for an hour.'

There's the sound from the street below of a car accelerating away. Don hurries to the window and looks out. 'There he goes. Daft sod. What Fran ever saw in him . . .'

'She's not your responsibility,' I say. It's true. But it's self-serving as well. I wonder if he knows that. 'She divorced you, right? Doesn't that mean you don't have to worry about her?'

276

'It ought to,' Don replies. But I can see just by the set of his shoulders it doesn't.

'We are flying to Switzerland this morning, aren't we, Don?'

He turns towards me and forces out a reassuring smile. 'Of course we are.'

⁜

Don had a shower and a shave and some breakfast while he did his best to convince himself Fran was in no danger. Somehow, though, his best was not good enough. Peter was a wash-out. If anyone could help Fran, it was Don – an enduring truth, to his mind, which she had blinded herself to.

It was just after seven when he called her. There was no answer, which he told Blake did not worry him. He left a call-me-back-as-soon-as-you-can message. Gareth had texted him at some point overnight with the name of his hotel in Zürich: the Marriott. Don texted back that they would contact him there later that day, then went to pack a bag.

He had done no more than plonk a case on his bed and open it when his phone burbled. To his considerable relief, the caller was Fran.

Except that it was not. The caller was using Fran's phone. But the caller was Amos French.

'Hi, Don. You're quite the early riser.'

'What the hell's going on? Where's Fran?'

'Taking some time out. At a location I specially selected for her. I'm there now.'

'If you've harmed her in any way . . .'

'You're mighty solicitous for an ex-husband, I must say. If someone called me to say they were holding my ex-wife captive, I'd tell 'em to go on holding her until hell froze over.'

Don instructed himself to stay calm. He turned, phone in hand, and saw Blake standing wide-eyed in the doorway. 'What do you want, French?'

'Same as when we first met. Information. About where Harkness has stashed the money.'

'I don't know. Fran doesn't know either.'

'No? Well, maybe that's true. Maybe it's not. But she's going nowhere till I'm sure on the point, and because I sense you're still carrying a torch for her, that should be a good incentive for you to dig something up.'

'How d'you expect me to do that?'

'Dunno. If I did, I'd do it myself. But you and the fragrant Fran are tied into Harkness's affairs pretty damn tight, so I give you a fair chance. There's this panic room at Wortalleth West tickling my curiosity, but breaking into it won't be easy, so I'm giving you the chance to spare Fran a more . . . shall we say intensive level of questioning by coming up with what I need. How does twenty-four hours sound for a deadline?'

'I can't—'

'Yes you can, Don. I'm backing you to do it. Call me on this number when you've got something to report.'

'I want to speak to Fran.'

'You do? See, that's another thing I'd never say about my ex-wife. You're a softy, Don, that's your problem. OK. Here she is.'

There was a pause and a rustling in the background. Then Fran's voice was in Don's ear, hoarse and strained. 'Don? Is that you?'

'Yes.'

'If there's anything you know . . .'

'Are you all right?'

'Yes. But—'

Suddenly, French was back on. 'That's enough pillow talk for now. Twenty-four hours, Don. You got that?'

'I—'

The call was over.

✥

Don's shocked. He doesn't know what to do. This is worse than anything he was expecting. Looking for clues about what happened to Jane Glasson was one thing. The risks we were taking were all kind of theoretical. But kidnapping is on a whole other level.

He sits down on the bed, the phone cradled uselessly in his hand. His brain's whirling. I can sense – I can share – the mess his head's in. 'They must've grabbed Fran somewhere between her hotel and her appointment with Pawley in Helston. And they're holding her till she or I or someone else gives them what they want.'

'The whereabouts of Harkness's money?'

'Exactly. And I've no more clue where he's hidden it than I'm sure Fran has.'

'She might've gone back to Wortalleth West. They could've been waiting for her there. Or she could've walked in on them while they were trying to get into the panic room.'

Don nods glumly. 'Could well be.'

An idea comes to me. 'Gimme your phone. I'll call Glenys. She's an early riser. She won't have been to the house yesterday, but she might know something.'

Don hands the phone over. His expression doesn't convey a whole lot of confidence that Glenys is going to be able to tell us anything valuable. I punch in the number.

It rings a long time. It's a landline with no answering service, so I guess she'll wait a while to see if the caller gives up. I don't. Eventually, she picks up. She doesn't actually speak.

279

But that's how it's been whenever I've called her, so I'm not surprised.

'Glenys? It's Blake.'

'Blake? You're up with the lark and no mistake. Where are you?'

'Don's place in London.'

'Homely, is it?'

'Not so you'd notice. Listen, have you seen anything of a solicitor called Fran Revell at Wortalleth West?'

'Yeah. She was there Monday. With Pawley, the estate agent.'

'Everything all right?'

'Far as I could tell. I've not been since.'

'You're going over there this morning?'

'No. Funny you should ask that. I had Harkness on late last night.'

'*Harkness?*'

'He told me not to go in. Stay away till further notice. That was the gist.'

'Why doesn't he want you there?'

'Didn't say. He's not someone you can cross-question. You know that. But he laid it on the line. *Don't go in.*'

'And you won't?'

'He's paid me till the end of the month. I guess he has the right to pay me *not* to work if he wants to. Though that'll only make more work for me eventually, specially if we get any rain.' Glenys pauses. I can almost hear her thinking. 'What's up, Blake?'

'Nothing.'

'You sure about that?'

'Do as Harkness says. Stay away.'

'OK,' she responds hesitantly.

'Got to go, Glenys. Take it easy.'

She chuckles. 'Wouldn't know how.'

"Bye for now. I'll be in touch.'

I end the call and hand the phone back to Don. 'Did you get that?' I ask.

He nods. 'Harkness has told Glenys to stay away from the house.'

'Yeah. Weird, right?'

'He knows something's wrong. Maybe French has spoken to him as well.'

'If French has spoken to him, what's he planning to do?'

Don shakes his head. 'God knows.' Then his expression hardens. 'But he can't leave London, can he? He can't even leave his house without the police knowing. Not while he's ankle-tagged.' He stands up. 'I'm fed up pussy-footing around. Let's go and see him.'

'Now?'

'Yeah.' Don heads for the door. 'Right now.'

⁘

The scene outside 53 Belgrave Square that soft June morning was not what Don had expected. Jack Harkness's house should have presented a mute and motionless frontage to the world, like its big, high-porched neighbours. Instead, there were two marked police cars and a third unmarked car parked out front with radios crackling. A uniformed policeman was slumped in one of them and another was standing by the half-open front door. Several bystanders were watching what was going on.

As Don and Blake approached slowly from where they had left the MG, another car sped into view, with a flashing blue light clamped to its roof. It surged to a halt outside number 53 and two burly, grim-faced detectives jumped out, hurried up the steps and vanished indoors.

'Something's happened,' Don muttered.

'You think so?' said Blake, with a hint of sarcasm.

281

'If you're so smart, find out what.'

'OK. Guy with the schnauzer looks like he might be chatty.'

Schnauzer Man was stationed by the gate into the gardens in the centre of the square. He was sixtyish, sallow-skinned, with curly grey hair and a moustache, dressed in smartly creased trousers and a light, expensive-looking zipped jacket.

They crossed to his side of the road and Blake made a beeline for the dog, who seemed delighted to be ear-ruffled and generally cooed over. Its owner was hardly less delighted. He enthused about the animal and made a lot of beaming eye contact with Blake. He spoke with an accent – Spanish, maybe – and his manner was mildly flirtatious.

Schnauzer Man – Miguel by name – lived in the square. During his regular morning stroll with Luisa – the dog – he had been surprised to see a man hammering on Harkness's door. 'You know of Jack Harkness? Maybe you have read about him in the newspaper. Except, of course, someone of your age, *señorita*, does not read a newspaper.'

'We've heard of Jack Harkness,' Blake smilingly assured him.

'*Bueno*. So, there is a strange man at Harkness's door, shouting and banging. What is he shouting? "Come out here. Come out and talk to me, you bastard." That is what he is shouting.'

'What did he look like?' asked Don.

'Ah, tall, grey hair, but straight, not like mine. Glasses. Big chin. You know him?'

'No,' Don replied. But he did know him, of course. The description fitted Peter Revell to a tee.

'Don meant did he look dangerous?' Blake cut in, covering his tracks and shooting him a reproving glance.

'Dangerous?' Miguel considered the point. '*Quizá*. It is possible. Certainly loud. It was very not Belgrave Square. I think the policeman at the Turkish Embassy called the station. A car was here soon. Then another. The man, he went on shouting. They took him away. But then they started knocking on the door too. The police, I mean. The housekeeper came up from the basement to let them in. They said to her a lot, "Where is Harkness?" She said he was not there. That worried them, it seemed. I was not surprised. He should have been there. Or they should have known where he was.'

'Because of his electronic ankle tag,' said Don. 'I read about that.'

'The tag. Yes. *Exactamente*. Harkness cannot be . . . unlocated.'

'But he is.'

'*Sí.*' Miguel nodded and grinned, enjoying his story-telling role. '*Ausente*. Gone. Disappeared. *Pfff.*' He waved his hands. 'Lots of police then. Lots of in and out and round and about. These other people' – he gestured to the other onlookers with a superior curl to his lip – 'come then. They want to see the show. No reporters yet. But soon they will be here also. Where is Harkness? Where has he gone? And how? Big mystery. Big story.'

'For sure,' said Blake.

Miguel suddenly frowned. 'Are you reporters?'

'Absolutely no—' Don broke off when he saw movement at the top of the steps leading up from the basement of number 53. A thin, dark-haired young man in a T-shirt, combat shorts and bright white trainers appeared, his arms handcuffed behind his back, a policeman in close attendance. He was pretty clearly under arrest. A door in one of the patrol cars was being held open for him.

'Look at his left ankle,' Blake said quietly, nudging Don.

283

Don saw it as she pointed: an electronic ankle tag.

'That'll be the housekeeper's nephew,' Blake murmured.

Don and Miguel both gaped at her. How she knew he was the housekeeper's nephew was a mystery to them. But it was evidently not all she knew.

'And that'll be Harkness's tag on him. Somehow they've switched. Harkness has given the police the slip. Probably just like he was always planning to.'

'Bloody hell,' said Don.

'*Extraordinario*,' said Miguel.

As the young man was loaded into the car, Blake shook her head slowly. 'No one will have any idea where Harkness is now. Or what he's doing.'

They left Miguel then and walked back quickly towards the MG. With Harkness gone, there was nothing to be gained by lingering in Belgrave Square.

'How'd you know about the nephew?' Don asked.

'Harkness mentioned him to me. It was only a guess. But it makes sense. Harkness always finds someone to do what he needs doing. He'll have paid him well.'

'He always does, doesn't he?' Don sighed. 'As to what we're going to do . . .'

'I figure he's headed for Switzerland . . . or Cornwall.'

'Then we can't both go to Switzerland.' Don glanced at his watch. 'We ought to be starting for Heathrow soon.'

'But only one of us is getting on the plane?'

'I can't just abandon Fran, Blake. I have to do whatever I can to help her.'

'Maybe Harkness has gone to help her.'

'Maybe. There's no way to know.'

They reached the car and climbed in. The moment of decision had come.

'I could tell the police about the phone call from

284

French,' Don said slowly. 'But it'll take them for ever to get their heads round what's going on. Peter will tell them most of what they need to know anyway, little good though it'll do him, at least in the short term. And the short term is what we have to contend with where Fran's concerned.'

'You're going to Cornwall, then?'

Don nodded. 'I think I have to.'

'Then I'll go to Switzerland. Don't worry. I'll have Gareth to help me. And I might learn something that'll help Fran. This is *all* connected, y'know. Everything. It all comes back to whatever the fuck it is Harkness is planning.'

Don looked round at her. 'You know I talked you into leaving Wortalleth West because I thought it'd be safer for you in London, don't you?'

"Course I know. But I had my own reasons for letting you.'

'The truth can be overvalued, Blake. Life teaches you that.'

'I don't reckon this truth can be.'

'You can't rely on Gareth. You don't know enough about him.'

'I'll rely on myself. Always have. As for you . . .' She leant over to her bag on the back seat, unzipped it and pulled out a small brown paper bag which she handed to Don.

He frowned. 'What's this?'

'If you're going back to Cornwall, you're likely to run into Wynsum Fry again. That's insurance . . . against any trouble she gives you.'

'Insurance?'

'Or protection. The dewitcher Maris went to for help after Fry started messing with her head said the best way

285

to break a witch's hold was to burn something she's worn next to her skin at the place of her birth.'

'*What?*'

'Wynsum Fry was born at Tredarvas Farm. The ruins of the house are still there, in a field off Ghost Hill.'

'And this parcel contains . . .'

'You don't want to know. All that matters is it's what the dewitcher said Maris needed. Maris never actually did anything about it.'

'But you did?'

'I took it from the old bitch's airing cupboard while you were having your doorstep chat with her Saturday evening.'

Don nodded. 'You came and went via the bathroom, didn't you?'

Blake looked surprised. 'How'd you know?'

'Never mind. But come off it, Blake.' Don stared at the parcel in a mixture of bafflement and disbelief – and just a sliver of horror. 'You can't be serious about this.'

'Doesn't matter. It's the kind of stuff Wynsum Fry deals in. The kind of stuff she *believes* in.'

'And if I'm desperate enough to try it . . .'

Blake shrugged. 'Then I guess you'll be glad I gave it to you.' A moment passed. Then she added: 'And I guess I'll be glad too.'

❖

Don and I are standing in the Terminal 5 departures hall at Heathrow Airport. I'm about to fly for the first time in my life. Loads of people who've flown loads of times are milling around us, lugging bags, pushing trolleys, shepherding children. Don's holding the plastic packaging of a phone he's just bought for me. He couldn't believe it when I told him I didn't have one, even though he's spent most of the past week with me. Like I explained to him, you don't stay off the grid by making yourself easily contactable.

But he and I have got to stay in touch now we're going our separate ways. We're a team, I guess, though I can't exactly get used to the idea. Neither of us has a clue what we'll be walking into at the end of our journeys. It's leap-in-the-dark time.

'This is for you as well,' says Don, handing me a credit card. 'I've got three, so don't worry. I won't be strapped for cash. The pin is four five double two.'

I smile as I pocket it. 'I could max you out, Don.'

'Buy some Swiss francs, a decent hotel room and a few square meals with it. Basically, whatever you need.'

'You're a trusting guy, aren't you?'

'Just be careful, Blake. That's all I ask.'

'I'll be as careful as you.'

He smiles weakly. 'I guess you will.'

I glance up at the departures board. There's my flight. *Wait in lounge*, it says. I feel nervous. More nervous about flying, actually, than whatever's waiting for me in Zürich. 'I better go,' I say.

'Yeah.' Don nods. 'Good luck.'

'You too.' I lean forward and kiss his cheek. I wonder if he knows how big a deal that is for me. ''Cos we'll both need luck, right?'

'Call when you land. And when you've spoken to Gareth.'

'Will do.'

It's time to go. I pull my rucksack on to one shoulder and head for the security gate. I don't look back. When you've said goodbye you've said goodbye. That's just the way it has to be.

287

I suddenly regret not looking back when I'm shuffling forward in the queue to have my rucksack X-rayed. It's a surprising feeling. I realize then how much I'm going to miss Don. And I know he's going to miss me.

We're on our own now.

FOUR

DON TOOK THE SAME ROUTE TO CORNWALL HE'D USED THE week before. Just a week, a fragment of a life. But it felt to him his life had changed – had moved – in that short space of days. If he'd turned down Fran's offer of a job, he'd have missed it all. But it would have happened – some version of it, anyway. Harkness's secret would still be the same secret.

Blake would also still be in danger. Somehow, he felt certain of that. Nothing could have stopped her going after the truth. He was not sure he really understood her, but he knew she was honest, direct and single-minded – bloody-minded sometimes.

He wished he could have gone to Switzerland with her and shielded her from danger. But he could not abandon Fran. Which was ironic, as he fully intended to remind her some happy day, since she had abandoned him seventeen years ago in preference for the hapless Peter. So far as he could tell, she had never regretted ditching him.

But maybe – just maybe – she did now.

❖

There are newspapers in bins at the bottom of the ramp leading to the plane. I glance towards the pile of *FT*s as I pass. Force of habit, I guess. And there's Harkness's name in the headline. *Bribery allegations against Harkness Pharmaceuticals spread to encompass addictive painkiller prescriptions.* I grab a copy and step on to the plane.

The paragraph on the front page leads me to a full-page article inside. I sit down in my aisle seat and have to stand up more or less straight away to let people into the seats beside me. I check my new phone for messages, which is crazy, since only Don knows the number and what's he going to tell me? I switch the phone off and follow the preparations for take-off. Everyone else has probably done it hundreds of times. It's all new to me. But I try to look as if it isn't.

After the spiel about oxygen masks, escape chutes and lifejackets, which half convince me we're actually going to have to use them, I open the *FT* and read the article about Harkness while we taxi out to the runway.

Seems the US Justice Department has opened up a new line of attack. Thirty-nine doctors in the States – yeah, *thirty-fucking-nine* – have been charged with taking bribes from Harkness Pharmaceuticals to prescribe some painkiller called Fenextris to patients suffering from back, neck and shoulder pain when it should be reserved for cancer and really serious stuff because of its addictiveness. Medicare spending on Fenextris soared 75 per cent last year and cost the system more than $280 million. Two hundred and eighty million. Jesus. Harkness really doesn't do things by halves. Some neurologist in Indianapolis racked up $6.7 million in Fenextris prescriptions all on his own. He's pleaded guilty and is 'cooperating with the authorities'. Sounds to me like more big trouble for Harkness, though a company spokesman's naturally denied bribing anyone to do anything.

I've asked myself before and now I'm asking myself again. Why has Harkness resorted to jacking up his profits illegally and siphoning money out of his own company? He's been rich for years – richer than anyone needs to be. Why run the risk of spending the rest of his life in a US jail when he's never going to be able to spend more than a fraction of his wealth? It just doesn't make any sense.

I suddenly realize we've taken off. The plane's climbing into the sky. I look past the people beside me and see the sunlight gleaming on the reservoirs near the airport as the pilot banks and turns.

I've never been so far off the ground. There are houses below me, strung around looping avenues and cul-de-sacs. They look so small from up here, so delicate, so fragile. It reminds me, just a little, of what Harkness said about the Earth seen from space. All our vulnerability is so obvious from up here.

My ears pop as the plane goes on climbing. I glance down at Harkness's photograph in the paper. It's a picture they've used before. He's hurrying into the court in London, gazing past the camera and smiling slightly, as if he can see something no one else can, behind everyone's backs, very nearly out of sight.

He's got plenty to worry about. But he never looks worried. He looks like a man with a plan. A plan that's working, just exactly as he intended.

There's an answer waiting for me in Switzerland. I know there is. I just do. And I'm going to find it. I just know that too.

⚜

Don stopped at Exeter Services, as he had before. He needed petrol, the loo and something to eat and drink. He calculated Blake would be landing in Zürich soon and hoped she would remember to text him from the airport.

Meanwhile, as he sat in the MG in the farthest corner of the car park after filling her up, he phoned Pawley, but only got his secretary, who knew nothing. He tried

Pawley's mobile, but there was no answer, so he left a message and headed for the shops.

He only checked the *Financial Times* in WHSmith because he wondered if Harkness had done a bunk on account of some turn in the case against him. He reckoned he might be right when he saw the headline. *Bribery allegations against Harkness Pharmaceuticals spread to encompass addictive painkiller prescriptions*. He bought a copy – the only copy, as it happened – and went off to the café to read it.

✣

A hundred minutes in the air and we're there: touching down at Zürich Airport. I can't quite believe I'm actually in Switzerland. But there are adverts for expensive watches and Swiss cheese to remind me and the immigration officer who checks my passport looks like he operates by clockwork.

Don's credit card takes its first hit when I buy some Swiss francs. Then I go to the tourist office and ask about cheap but decent hotels. They recommend the Marta – five minutes from the main railway station – and phone the place for me before I catch the train into the city. Two nights for two hundred francs. They say it like it's a bargain and I suppose it is. They give me a street map and helpfully mark the Marta – and the Marriott – on it with red crosses. Then I'm on the train.

It's a short ride. Zürich looks big and grey and clean. I call Gareth, but his phone's on voicemail. I leave a message telling him my number and saying I'll call again soon. Then I text Don to say I've arrived. We cross a river and I see trim blue and white trams moving along orderly, rain-smeared streets. I guess Zürich is how I imagined it: cool, calm, contained.

The train reaches Zürich Hauptbahnhof. Everyone gets off in a jumble of suitcases and rucksacks. I walk along the platform and on to the crowded concourse. According to the map, the Marriott's almost as close as the Marta, but I head for the Marta first to check in and drop my bag.

Outside the station, there are more trams and lots of people on a busy riverfront. I follow the mobs across the bridge to the other side of the river and trace my route by the map to the Marta.

It takes me all of about ten minutes to check into my small, spotless, functional room. I call Gareth again. Still no answer. I look at the map again. The Marriott's just a short walk away. I may as well go and see if he's there. I head out, free of my bag now, moving fast. We need to talk, Gareth and me.

✣

Don got Blake's text message when he was most of the way through the *FT* article, read over two cups of coffee and a toasted sandwich. Well, she was all right so far, which relieved him to a ludicrous degree. But what happened next? That was the question.

As for Harkness, his lawyers would presumably go on denying everything. But that would not spare him eventual extradition. And once in the coils of the US legal system, God help him. So, maybe he had done a runner.

That, at any rate, was Don's working assumption as he swallowed the last of the coffee and made for the exit.

✣

The Marriott's just what I expected: a smart muzak-and-marble chain hotel. Gareth probably chose it because of the superior WiFi connections. He's a wired kind of guy.

The woman on the desk, like everyone else I've met in Zürich so far, speaks perfect English. She's cool but friendly. I ask if Gareth Lawler's in. She asks me to repeat his name, which is the first off note, because she looks like she knows exactly who I mean.

295

'Gareth Philip Lawler?' she says, eyebrows arched. Her voice has tightened. What's with the middle name? I wonder. That's the second off note.

'He's a friend of mine,' I explain. 'From England. He arrived yesterday.'

'Ah.' Deep frown. 'Yes.'

'You have got a record of him, right?'

'*Jawohl.*' The switch to German is strange. And it continues. '*Herr Lawler.*' She closes her eyes for a second.

'What's the problem?'

She licks her lips nervously and looks straight at me. 'I am sorry. There has been . . . an accident.'

'What kind of accident?'

'Traffic.' She points past me. 'Out there. But . . . I was not here. Hold on, please.' She picks up the phone and speaks to someone in German while my mind races. An *accident*?

A door opens behind the desk and a middle-aged man in a suit comes out. He's fingering his moustache like he's thinking hard.

'Ah,' he says, rounding the desk to speak to me. 'Miss . . . ?'

'What's happened to Gareth?' I ask, cutting off any idea of introducing myself. Which I reckon is kind of unwise at the moment.

'There was a traffic accident this morning. I regret Mr Lawler was hit by a truck. Right outside the hotel. A terrible thing. Yes. Terrible.'

He's not exaggerating. I'm speechless. My mind can't seem to compute what this might mean. In the end I say, lamely, 'How did it happen?'

'We, er, think he forgot traffic drives on the right here. Just, er, an awful mistake.'

'You say this was right outside?'

'Yes. Let me show you.'

Moritz – well, that's the name on his lapel badge – escorts

me over to the revolving door, where there's a view of the street. It's a busy riverside highway, with fast-moving traffic. I walked here along a quieter street on the other side of the hotel.

'Mr Lawler took a telephone call during breakfast and left right away, by this door, still using his phone. When he tried to cross the road, it seems he looked the wrong way. Right, not left.' Moritz sighs. 'Tragic. And unnecessary. There is an underpass nearby. It leads direct to a bridge into Platzspitz Park. Maybe that was where he was going.'

'But he was hit by a truck?'

Moritz nods dolefully. 'Yes.'

'How badly is he hurt?'

'It was serious. He was not conscious and . . . it looked . . . not good.'

'But he's alive?'

'Yes. He was taken to the University Hospital. I called the hospital later to ask about his condition.'

'What did they say?'

'They said he was in surgery. They could not tell me anything.' Moritz strokes his moustache. 'I do not know any more. I am sorry. Very sorry.'

✢

Don was most of the way across the car park when he realized a man was leaning against the MG's tailgate, gazing into the middle distance. He was wearing a baseball cap, tracksuit and trainers. His arms were folded. A bulging leather bag was on the ground beside him. He looked relaxed and idle, like someone contentedly killing time in the middle of a journey.

A few more strides brought a sudden realization to Don. He knew the man. He had never met him before. But he knew him – from his photograph in the newspaper.

Harkness seemed to register Don's arrival only when

they were a few yards apart. He pushed himself upright and smiled, but said nothing.

'You're Jack Harkness,' Don said, not bothering to disguise his surprise.

'Yes.' Harkness went on smiling. 'And you're Don Challenor.'

'What are you doing here?'

'Looking for a lift, actually. To Cornwall. Going my way?'

✤

I walk out into Platzspitz Park. There are rivers on both sides. They meet at the sharp end of the park. I look around at the trees and the benches and the swings. I can hear children's voices and adults' footsteps on the gravel paths. I think about Gareth and the phone call that got him hurrying out of the Marriott. He should've used the underpass and the bridge, like I did. Instead he headed straight across the road, looking right instead of left. It must've been an accident. Surely. Unless the phone call was a trap. But how would that work? No one could know – no one could *plan* – the route he took.

Was he coming here, like Moritz suggested? *'Meet me in the park, just across the road from your hotel.'* Was that the message? *'Meet me there right now.'*

I have to find out how he is. Maybe he's conscious. Maybe he can tell me exactly what happened. The University Hospital – *Universtätspital* – is marked on my map. It's not far.

I start walking towards the Hauptbahnhof at the other end of the park.

✤

Don eyed Harkness warily. He should have been pleased to see him. He had badly wanted to speak to him earlier that day after all. But as Blake had said more than once, Harkness was serving no one's agenda except his own. He

298

was where he was because he wanted to be. He knew – he always knew – exactly what he was aiming to achieve.

'Aren't you supposed to be banned from leaving London?' Don said at last.

Harkness looked breezy and happy and confident. The idea of anyone banning him from doing anything was patently absurd. 'You mean the electronic tag?' He hitched up his trouser-legs to reveal unfettered ankles.

'How did you manage that?'

'With a little help from an expert quarter. But listen, Don, shouldn't we get started? We're going to Cornwall for the same reason. And it won't wait.'

'What reason's that?'

'Come on. Fran. I'm guessing French phoned you as well. We've got to get down there and do something. That's why you're here, isn't it?'

'Did you follow me?'

'No, no. This is what they call a chance meeting. I left my car in the long-stay at Heathrow Airport, where I took good care to parade myself in front of the CCTV cameras inside Terminal Five. I'm hoping that'll convince the authorities I've left the country. I've been reliant on lifts since then. Rather fun, actually. It's like reliving my student days. I saw this car and knew it had to be you.' Harkness patted the roof of the MG. 'Recaptured youth or what?'

'How'd you know what car I drive?'

'I think Fran mentioned it.'

'Really?' Don found that hard to believe.

'How else would I know?'

How indeed? But Don sensed pursuing the point would be futile. 'You expect me to drive you to Cornwall?'

Harkness nodded. 'I do. And if Fran's welfare is your primary concern at the moment, as it is mine, you will.'

'French wants to know where the money is.'

'I know.'

'Will you tell him?'

'I think I can get Fran out of this in one piece, OK? That's all you need to know for now. Except that I have to be in Cornwall to do it and I'm technically a fugitive from justice at present, so I could use a little help to get there without attracting too much attention. Are you going to give me that help, Don? Or shall I try my luck in the lorry park?'

'All right.' There was no point arguing any further. Don did not trust Harkness one inch. He was unsure if the man really cared about Fran at all. But for Fran's sake he had to assume they were in this together. He moved to the passenger door and unlocked it. 'Get in.'

'Thanks.'

By the time Don had circled the car and climbed in, Harkness was settled in his seat, turning the handle to wind the window up and down.

'Lovely,' he said. 'Just lovely.'

Don started the engine. It growled into life.

'Wonderful,' purred Harkness.

They pulled away, following the signs for the exit.

'Where's Blake, Don?' Harkness asked suddenly.

'I don't know.'

He drove down on to the roundabout beneath the motorway and stopped at a red light.

'Where is she, Don?' Harkness asked again.

'No idea. She said someone was going to pay her a lot of money to steer clear of your affairs and that's what she intended to do.'

'So, boarding a flight to Bangkok even as we speak?'

'Could be.'

The lights changed. Don accelerated away and joined the slip-road up on to the southbound M5.

'I hope she really has taken the money and run,' said

300

Harkness. 'It's just a pity I can't quite bring myself to believe you.'

'That's your problem.'

'Where's she gone?'

'I wouldn't know.'

'You're not a great liar. You know that? It's kind of surprising. For an estate agent, I mean.'

'Here's one for you,' Don countered as he slipped out into the traffic. 'What's in the panic room at Wortalleth West?'

'There's no panic room.'

'But there's a secret room of some kind.'

'Is there?'

'What's in there, Jack? French thinks you may have used it to store some of the stolen money, but that doesn't make any sense.'

'True. Even if there were any stolen money, which there isn't.'

'It's all yours, to do with as you please. Right?'

'Exactly right.'

'Quintagler Industries don't seem to agree with you. Nor does the US Justice Department.'

'I see you have today's *FT*.' Harkness glanced over his shoulder at the paper, which Don had tossed on to the back seat next to Harkness's bag. 'Something about me in it, is there?'

'You and Fenextris and thirty-nine bribed American doctors.'

'These sawbones, eh? What can you do with them?'

'You tell me.'

'There's no hidden pile of cash, Don. At Wortalleth West or anywhere else.'

'Spent it all, have you?'

'What if I have?'

'You're not going to get away with it, y'know.'

'Am I not?' Harkness's confidence was undented. He looked and sounded like a man without a care in the world. 'We'll see.' He peered suspiciously at the speedometer. 'This is a V8, isn't it, Don? For God's sake put your foot down, will you? The clock's ticking.'

And so it was. Don could not deny it. He flicked the indicator and moved smartly into the outside lane.

❖

I take a funicular most of the way up the hill to the University Hospital. I've never actually been on one before. Another new experience for me. The hospital's a sprawl of buildings, some old, some modern. I go in the main entrance, where there's an *I* for Information sign. But the guy on the desk redirects me to another entrance round the corner. He draws the route on a map for me and writes the name of the department I want in capitals. *NOTFALLSTATION. Emergencies.*

The guy at *Emergencies* is a bit less helpful, but looks up Gareth's name on his computer and says he's in the Intensive Care Unit. That means no visitors. But maybe I can go there and find something out from the nursing staff. He draws a second route on my map and adds another word in capitals. *INTENSIVSTATION.* Off I go.

I pop into the loo halfway to splash some water on my face. I'm sweating and I'm nervous. I don't want them to tell me Gareth's a mental vegetable or paralysed or whatever. I hardly know him, but the accident – if it really was an accident – seems totally crazy. Besides, with him out of the game, what exactly the fuck am I going to do? Everything's on a knife-edge now.

I step out into the corridor. I see the sign *INTENSIVSTATION.* I follow the arrow.

The corridor's long and straight. There are echoes of voices and footsteps from either end. The afternoon light falls in brilliant splashes across the floor, spaced by the distance between each window. There's one person walking towards me. No one else, behind me or ahead.

She's a slim, middle-aged woman in jeans, white shirt and light tweedy jacket. The footwear's serious and thick-soled. It hits the floor solidly. She's not carrying a handbag, or any bag at all, which makes me think, subconsciously, that she works here. And that makes me consider, just for a moment, asking her to help me.

Then I see it. Her face. Her hair. Her eyes. Like one of those *Can-you-see-what-it-is?* puzzles. The image swirls for a second in my mind, then, as she draws a few more strides closer, it locks.

Jane Glasson.

Older than the woman in Holly's photograph. But, like Gareth said, not very different really. There's no doubt in my mind. It's her.

She's past me before I've properly registered the reality of the situation. I saw the expression on her face as we crossed – grim, preoccupied – and realized she was barely aware of my presence. Why should she be? We've never met before. We don't know each other. I'm no one who should be looking for her.

I have to make a choice. I guess she's just been told as much as Intensive Care are willing to reveal about Gareth's condition. It doesn't look like it's good news. But what *is* good news about Gareth for this woman? Does she want him dead or alive?

I turn round and start following her. No choice really. This is my only chance.

*

She moves fast. But she doesn't look back. Not once. She moves like someone who wants to be somewhere else – badly.

Before I know it, we're back at the entrance. She marches out into the air and pauses to take a few steadying gulps of it. Then she does something really odd. She presses her thumb to her wrist for several seconds, as if measuring her pulse.

I can't tell if she's worried or not by the result. She heads down the road and I follow. She pulls her phone out of her jacket pocket and checks something on it. The time, maybe? She picks up her pace. So do I.

It really is her, isn't it? I'm so caught up with not losing her that I can't get a fix on the answer to that question. I think it's her. I feel it's her. I believe it's her. It can't be, but it is. One moment it's all theory and what-ifs. The next she's a living and breathing stranger walking fast ahead of me – a real part of the real present.

We reach the corner. The main entrance is left. Opposite is some big high-domed university building. Jane stops and looks right, squinting slightly. What can she see? What's she thinking?

A tram appears round the corner from the direction of the funicular. Jane darts across the road, heading for the tram stop. I go after her. A car driver blares his horn at me. Fuck. I looked right instead of left. But Jane doesn't glance round. She's in her own controlled, concentrated world.

I see the number and destination of the tram. 6. The Zoo. But we're not going to the Zoo, I guess, as Jane hops aboard and I follow. Some stop short of the terminus? Her home, maybe?

She takes a single seat by the window. I manage to get the seat behind her. The doors clunk shut and the tram starts off. I've got no ticket, of course. Better hope no one checks.

As we trundle past the main entrance of the hospital, Jane presses a key on her phone and holds it to her ear. I lean forward, straining to hear. There are a couple of schoolboys nearby, talking loudly. And the tram's a rackety thing, with lots of clinks and clatters.

But still I manage to catch most of her words.

'It's me . . . It's bad . . . I just don't know . . . He should've used the underpass . . . . I heard it from the park . . . Such a thump, Filippo, such an awful sound. And when I went over there . . . I walked away. I had to. I couldn't involve myself.' No more doubts, then. Filippo has to be Filippo Crosetti, creator of Elixtris. Which means this woman has to be Jane Glasson.

The tram takes a sharp left. There's a lot of creaking and squealing from the wheels. I can't hear Jane over it. I see her press a finger against her other ear to blot out the sound.

The next words I catch are, 'I know. She has to be our priority . . . I agree . . . Where are they putting her up? . . . Right. Well. I know why they've gone for the Dolder. Keep her isolated. That'll be their plan . . . What time's the meeting? . . . OK . . . Where? . . . Christ, that'll be soulless.'

The tram pulls up at a stop. More noise. Doors opening and closing. Passengers leaving and boarding. The two schoolboys have a fit of the giggles over something on their phones. We set off again. I try to screen everything out except Jane's voice.

'Yeah . . . OK . . . No, we have . . . Agreed. My place, nine o'clock . . . We'll talk it all through then . . . Yeah . . . See you. 'Bye.'

The call ends. Jane cradles the phone in her hand and stares out of the window. We're going uphill now, round a long bend. She slips the phone into her pocket and goes on staring. I hear her sigh. She shakes her head, regretting something, Gareth's accident maybe.

I guess now it really was an accident. She was waiting for him in the park. It must've been a call from her that sent him hurrying out of the hotel – straight into the path of a truck.

What else have I learnt from her phone call? She does work for Harkness. Or *with* Harkness, somehow or other. And with Filippo Crosetti, who's been summoned from Locarno to meet Ingrid. So, Ingrid must be the woman the company's putting up at the Dolder, wherever that is. She and Crosetti are due to get together tomorrow in Zug to discuss '*contra-indications*' as well as specialist contractor 55. I know that from the *Jane Glasson?* file.

Now I know something else. Specialist contractor 55 is surely sitting right in front of me. Specialist contractor 55 is Jane Glasson.

The tram trundles on, steadily uphill through the suburbs. People get on and people get off. But Jane stays where she is. And so do I. At some point, I guess we really are going to the Zoo.

Everyone gets off at the terminus. We're high above the city. I can see the tops of all the buildings and the shimmering water of the Zürichsee.

Jane heads along the road signposted to the Zoo and I follow. There are more people leaving than arriving at this time of the afternoon. Lots of children, some of them clutching fluffy toy animals. They mostly look tired but happy. Zoos do that to some people. Not me. I hate seeing animals in cages.

Jane's got some kind of pass. She goes straight through the electronic turnstile. I have to buy a ticket. But there's no queue, so I'm inside before she's gone far.

She obviously knows where she's going. She strides off uphill, by various winding paths, moving a lot faster than other visitors. There are signposts pointing the way to different animals – elephants, flamingos, orang-utans. Far as I can tell, we're heading for the lions and tigers.

306

Just the tigers, as it turns out. There's a kind of viewing structure where you look out on them. Well, on one of them, anyway. A big, sombre, loose-limbed, sad-eyed tiger who lifts its head and stares morosely towards us. Jane stands gazing towards it and I'm just a few metres away from her when she raises her right hand and speaks, too softly for me to hear.

The strange thing is I get the feeling the tiger knows her. It looks at her with its cold green eyes and you could, like, almost believe it understands what Jane is saying. Then some kids scamper up, screeching delightedly at their sight of a stuffed tiger come to life and the mood's broken.

Jane's off, walking more slowly now, but still quickly enough. We're going downhill by more winding paths, under a bridge and past enclosures of goats and donkeys, then along an underpass leading into a huge glass-roofed building housing a tropical rainforest. The air's thick and hot and humid. According to a sign this is a recreated chunk of Madagascar. Jane wanders a little way in and just looks, mostly up, at the high branches of the trees. I try to look engrossed in some lizard I've spotted on a leaf. I pull out my phone and pretend to take a picture of it. I actually take a picture of Jane, though I've only got her half-face and it doesn't come out very well.

Jane doesn't stay in the Madagascar building long either. She walks on through and out the other end, past some aquariums into a souvenir shop, then . . .

She leaves. We're out of the Zoo on the other side of the road from the entrance, walking back towards the tram. Jane doesn't pay anyone – me included – the slightest attention. She's in her own world.

At the tram stop, she checks her phone, but only briefly. She doesn't make any more calls or send any messages. There's quite a crowd by the time the tram shows up and I have to sit a couple of seats behind her.

307

Down we go, back into the city, while I wonder what the visit to the Zoo was really all about. It meant something, inside Jane's head. But I can't get there. All I can do is stick with her and see what happens.

The tram reaches the Hauptbahnhof, where a lot of passengers get off. And a lot more on, but Jane doesn't budge until we get to somewhere called Paradeplatz. I follow her from there down to the river and over a bridge into a network of narrow, pedestrian-only streets winding between buildings maybe old enough to be medieval.

We come out near the river, where it's widening to join the lake. Jane dives into a small convenience store, and, rather than trail round after her pretending to shop and maybe getting noticed, I sit at a table outside a café opposite.

I order and pay for a tea and wonder if it'll get to me before Jane leaves the shop. It does, but only just. She comes out with a well-filled plastic carrier bag in each hand and I'm about to get up when I realize she's walking straight towards me. I kind of freeze. I actually think for a moment she's going to stop and say, 'You were at the hospital. You were at the Zoo. What the fuck d'you want with me?'

None of that happens. There's a side-door into the building housing the café, a few metres to my right. Jane pushes it open and goes in. I wait a couple of seconds, then jump up and move to the door. It's glazed. Inside, I can see a rack of post-boxes, a flight of stairs and a lift. The lift door's just sliding shut.

I go in through the door and watch the clock-style floor indicator track Jane's progress. 2, 3, 4, 5, 6. It stops at the top. I look at the post-boxes. Company names, far as I can tell. Except for number 7. A surname only. And not Swiss. Not Glasson either, as if it would be. Townsend. That's all. No initial.

The lift comes back down automatically. But I don't get in.

Instead, I take the stairs. Quieter. And you can see what's waiting for you before you get there.

Landing windows give an ever wider view of Zürich as I climb. Roof gardens and clock towers and skylights and aerials. I reach the top, moving oh so cautiously from the last half-landing up.

But it's not the top. I'm on floor six, with the entrance to *Kommerziele Übersetzung AG* in front of me. The lift stops here. So do the stairs. Except there's a door marked *7* where the stairs should continue.

I push open the landing window. There are railings outside and a sort of balconette holding boxed geraniums. I lean out over the railing and look up. There are dormer windows in the tiled roof above me and, as I lean out still further, more railings above that. A rooftop terrace, maybe. It must have quite a view.

I look across at one of the clock towers. It's 6.20. I know Jane's expecting Filippo at nine. Maybe she'll stay put till then. Maybe not. Either way, I don't want to push my luck.

I close the window and head down the stairs.

No one's taken my tea away. I sit down and drink it. The early evening crowd flows past along what the map says is Limmatquai. I think of phoning Don to tell him what's happened, but I decide to leave it till I'm somewhere more private. I check to see if he's replied to my earlier text. No. That's a bit unlike him. But he'll be in touch. I can count on that. I think of phoning the University Hospital too, to ask about Gareth's condition. But that'll have to wait as well. I crane my neck and look up the face of the building. I can't see the dormer windows on the seventh floor from here. But I know they're there. I know Jane's there too.

I've found her. And I'm not going to lose her.

✥

If Don had hoped to learn any more from Harkness during the drive to Cornwall, he was to be disappointed. His passenger withdrew some of his earlier enthusiasm for the MG when told the rake of his seat could not be altered while the car was in motion. But still he managed to fall asleep, eyes shaded by the baseball cap, before they even reached Okehampton. He did not wake until they were approaching the outskirts of Mullion.

Don had checked his phone while Harkness was asleep and read a brief text from Blake reporting her safe arrival in Zürich. He had not risked replying. He would contact her later.

'Ah, Mullion,' said Harkness, yawning and stretching as Don negotiated the one-way system in the centre of the village. 'Not that much has changed since I grew up here.'

'You want to go straight to Wortalleth West?'

'Yes. I think we should see whether French has left his mark there.'

Don's first impression, as they drew up in front of the house, was that nothing had changed. 'Aren't you worried about someone round here recognizing you, Jack?' he asked before they got out. 'One word to the police and they'll realize you've done a runner.'

'They probably already know that,' said Harkness, in a tone that verged on complacency. 'I imagine Peter Revell has been in touch with them by now. They'll take a lot of convincing Fran hasn't simply left him – the standard assumption when a husband reports a wife missing – but they're bound to follow up any mention of me.'

Don had decided to tell Harkness nothing about Peter and the scene he had witnessed at 53 Belgrave Square. But it seemed Harkness had deduced for himself what the

310

sequence of events was likely to have been. 'You think they're already looking for you?'

Harkness nodded. 'Probably.'

'Then surely—'

'Believe it or not, Don, I came down here to help Fran. My original exit route was a small airfield in Kent and a fast car across France to the Swiss border. I have dual British and Swiss citizenship and the Swiss don't tend to give up their own, whatever they're accused of. As it is, though, here I am. Ready to do as much as I can.' Harkness turned and looked at Don. 'Does the same go for you?'

'You know it does.'

'Let's move, then. As you've just pointed out, I don't have an unlimited amount of time at my disposal.'

The house was locked, but the alarm was off. It was fair to assume Fran had been there, probably with Pawley, but Don would have expected her to set the alarm on leaving. He knew she had the code. He had got it from her in the first place.

Inside everything seemed entirely normal. The stillness and emptiness of the place were exactly as Don remembered. He followed Harkness into the lounge and on through to the study. Harkness looked around, nodding to himself as if working his way through a mental checklist.

'What are you looking for?' Don asked.

'Some sign that French has been here.'

'And so far?'

'Nothing. Let's try upstairs.'

They went up and glanced into several bedrooms, before arriving at the master. 'Are you going to look in the dressing-room closet?' Don asked provocatively.

'Why don't you do the honours, Don?' Harkness appeared unabashed. He was clearly going to continue

311

admitting and denying nothing where the panic room was concerned.

Don headed past him into the dressing room and opened the closet. His reflection gazed back at him from the mirror at the end. He walked up to it and pressed his hand against the frame. The mirror swung open. And there was the steel door – as firm and solid as ever.

But something else was not.

'You should see this, Don,' Harkness called from the bathroom.

Don hurried to join him. 'What?'

Harkness was standing in front of a jagged hole in the plaster covering the wall backing on to the rear of the closet. Beneath the plaster was a steel surface.

'Are you going to tell me that isn't the reinforced wall of a panic room, Jack?'

'All I'm going to tell you, Don,' Harkness replied, stooping and running his fingers over the surface of the steel, 'is that someone's tried to smash their way through here, probably with a sledgehammer, only to realize it wasn't quite man enough for the job.'

'French.'

'He's the obvious candidate.'

'Maybe he's planning to come back with something more powerful.'

'Maybe. Or maybe he hopes he won't have to. I suspect he did this before he ran into Fran.'

'Here?'

'It could well be. Let's go back downstairs.'

They descended to the hall. Harkness went into the study again and looked around more carefully. Then he headed for the kitchen, with Don right behind him.

Nothing looked out of place to Don at first glance. The

312

work surfaces were clear and clean. He saw only what he had expected to see. Then Harkness switched on the light, unnecessarily, it seemed.

But what the glare of the light revealed, as Harkness prowled around, with Don in tow, was a set of scuff-marks on the floor tiles, deep, dark scuff-marks radiating from an area near the telephone.

'What would you say caused those, Don?' Harkness asked, in a tone that suggested he already knew.

'No idea.'

'Probably because you haven't seen anything like them before. There I have the advantage of you. The kitchen of a Moscow apartment owned by a deceased business associate of mine. Recently deceased, at the time. It happened in the kitchen. The flooring was cheap lino, not this ridiculously expensive Tuscan ceramic Mona chose. But the marks are strikingly similar. And there's another common element. Zlenko. He'd paid the Moscow apartment a visit. And I think we can be sure he was here too.'

'How did your business associate die?'

'Strangled. With his own tie, actually. Poor old Igor was particularly fond of that tie. Old Harrovian. Which naturally he wasn't. The marks were caused by the heels of his shoes as he kicked in his death throes.'

Don stared in horror at the marks on the floor. 'You don't think—'

'Killing Fran would have made no sense, Don. Besides, I insisted on speaking to her when French phoned. And he was using his mobile. Which doesn't work here.'

Of course. All that was true. Don had spoken to her as well. They would hardly have brought her back to Wortalleth West just to — 'Who did Zlenko strangle, then?'

'I don't know. Let's just . . .'

The door leading to the utility room stood half open. Harkness marched through it, switching the light on in that room as well as he went.

'Ah.'

'What is it?'

'In the corner.' Harkness pointed to a stack of white reinforced plastic trays and containers. 'They're from the freezer.' Harkness stepped across to the sink. Over his shoulder Don saw several packs of frozen food piled up, no longer frozen. 'These are from the freezer too.'

He moved towards the freezer. As he reached for the handle, Don braced himself for what – for who – they would find.

Harkness pulled at the handle and opened the door a few inches. He held it there, straining against a weight inside, then peered in and nodded for Don to take a look too.

All Don could see when he got there was the top of a blond-haired head and a pair of shoulders in a pale suit, dusted with ice. 'Jesus, it's—'

'Mike Coleman,' said Harkness with an effort. He tried to close the door again, but Coleman's head had fallen forward against the frame, blocking it.

'Get him out of the way, Don, for God's sake.'

Don laid a hand gingerly on the crown of Coleman's head and pushed it clear. As he did so, the dead man's face, grey-white, with staring eyes and parted, swollen lips, met his gaze.

'That's it. Mind your fingers.'

Don let go and jumped back as Harkness closed the door with a thump. 'Bloody hell.'

'No blood, actually,' said Harkness. 'But probably quite a lot of hell.'

'Why would they . . . ?'

314

'Hard to say. He had an irritating manner. And he was always trying to manipulate situations to his advantage. My guess would be that he got out of his depth without being aware of it. Zlenko tends to react violently if you rub him up the wrong way.'

'But . . .' Don was shaking like a leaf in a breeze, he suddenly realized. He felt weak. His heart was fluttering. 'They murdered him.'

'Looks like it.'

'I didn't think . . .'

'They were the murderous type? Or that there was anything at stake worth murdering *for*?'

Don stared at Harkness helplessly. 'What do we do?'

'About Coleman? Nothing for now. He'll keep. Literally, as it happens. As for Fran, I need to make a phone call. While I do that, perhaps you could bag up the no-longer-frozen food and take it down to the bin at the end of the drive. Tomorrow's collection day, as I recall. I'll find a cupboard to store the trays and containers in. We don't want anything to draw attention to the freezer, do we? Not with Mr Renewables inside.'

Don went on staring. 'How can you be so calm?'

'It's my temperament, Don. It's not always a blessing. People mistake it for arrogance. But just now . . . it's an aid to clear thinking.'

'Who are you going to phone?'

'An old friend. Amazingly, I do have a few of them. Now . . .' Harkness looked at Don encouragingly. 'Chop chop. We have work to do.'

Lumbering down to the end of the drive with a couple of bulging bin-bags a few minutes later, Don's thoughts were a swirl of shock and confusion. French had uttered a lot of threats. But now he had actually killed someone. Or

Zlenko had, probably acting on his say-so. These were the people holding Fran and they were clearly not to be trifled with. Harkness claimed he knew how to deal with them, but Don was not so sure. Maybe, at this point, they should call in the police, who would start taking Fran's disappearance seriously with Coleman's dead body to grab their attention.

Rubbish binned, Don walked on up the lane towards the Mullion road, checking his phone for a signal. As soon as he got one, he called Blake.

No answer. He left a brief voicemail message. *'I'm at the house in Cornwall. I'm OK. I'll call you again later. Call or text when you can, but remember I might not get it right away. Don't use the landline number.'* Don did not want Harkness picking up the phone with Blake on the other end. *'I'll explain why later.'* That done, he headed back to the house.

He saw Harkness closing the garage door as he went up the drive and altered route to intercept him in the colonnade.

'Find something up there?' Don asked.

'Coleman's Merc.'

'No sign of Fran's hire car?'

Harkness frowned. 'She had one, did she?'

Don hesitated. It would not be easy to explain how he knew that without recounting the details of Peter's visit to his flat. He decided to plead guesswork instead. 'I suppose she must have.'

'Pawley didn't mention it.'

'You've spoken to him?'

'Just now. He's worried about Fran, of course. Probably about his fee as well. Doesn't know what to do for the best. Seemed relieved to be told to leave everything in my hands. I made it very clear he wasn't to come back here. He thinks I'm in London, of course.'

316

'What about your friend?'

'Ray Hocking? He's the fellow who delivers my papers. I was at primary school with Ray. He uses his eyes and ears far more than his mouth. I like that. Apparently, he has some valuable information for us. He lives in Mullion, so we'll wait until dark before we go and see him. Don't want any nosy neighbours clocking us, do we?'

'What sort of information does he have?'

'The kind you don't discuss over the phone. Talking of which, you took your sweet time with the rubbish. You didn't go walkabout in search of a mobile signal, did you?'

'No.'

'We need to be careful who we talk to right now, Don. Coleman's murder makes Fran's situation even more delicate.'

'You think I don't know that?'

Harkness looked at Don soberly. 'I can work this out, Don. Truly, I can. Just let me.' Now, suddenly the smile was back. 'OK?'

❖

I go back to the Marta and call Don. Still no answer. I don't leave a message this time. I decide to try again after taking a shower.

When I come out, I find *he's* called *me*. The message says he's at Wortalleth West, he's OK and he'll call again later. But he also says I shouldn't use the landline. I don't understand why. I can't contact him any other way when he's at the house.

Seeing Jane Glasson has made me twitchy. I don't know what Don's doing and he doesn't know what I'm doing. We have to trust each other. That's it. No buts. He'll do what he thinks is right. I know that. I'll do the same. And he knows that too.

It's time to head back to Jane's flat. I want to be there when Filippo arrives. We'll see what happens then.

It's nearly dark when I get there. The café's still open. I sit at an outside table and order a beer and a *croque monsieur*. The beer goes straight to my head. When I eat the sandwich, I realize how hungry I am. I order a coffee to cut through the beer. I pay for everything up front. I may have to leave in a hurry. I can see the glow of lights on in the top-floor flat. Jane's waiting for Filippo. So am I.

He arrives about five minutes early. A small, slim guy in his mid- to late thirties, with thick brown hair, a narrow face, a neat, tailored beard and almost black eyes that dart about a lot as he approaches the door that leads to the stairs. He's wearing blue jeans, a grey jacket and striped shirt. They're all pressed and fitted with a dose of Italian chic. But there's a dose of Swiss nerd as well. He has to be Filippo Crosetti.

He goes in and takes the lift. I know where he's going. I follow him by the silent stairs route.

The sixth-floor landing's empty and quiet when I get there. The door to the seventh floor is firmly closed. I open the window and lean out. There are lights on in several windows above me, but they're not open. I can hear a low hum – air conditioning, maybe – and faintly, music – Spanish guitar, it sounds like – but no voices. There's light further up as well, on the roof terrace. Maybe that's where they are, enjoying the view of the city.

Above my head is a narrow parapet. I clamber up on the windowsill and try to figure out what my chances are of getting up there if I stand on the railings. It's a long drop. The table I was sitting at outside the café looks like doll's house furniture from up here. And I don't reckon I'd actually have the strength to pull myself up. Fuck.

Then I do hear a voice. Crosetti's. Definitely male, anyway, and the accent's Italian. I catch a drift of cigarette smoke. He's up on the terrace. I can't quite see him, but there's a shadow I sense is his. And a few words float down to me.

'*Si, si.* I know. The answer is the same always . . . It is logical, but . . . You understand. I know you do.'

He turns away. I don't hear any more. Except a door closing. Then a light comes on in another window. It's shut, like the others. I won't hear anything they say in there. I climb back down from the windowsill.

I need to find out more. But how? What *is* the answer that's always the same? What are they planning? The 'something big' Perkins reckons Harkness is using all that money for? But what? What can it be? And how is Jane tied into it?

I don't exactly know how to take the chance I've got. But I'm not going to let it slip away. I'm totally not.

In the end, I decide to go back down to the café and wait. I drink another coffee. I text Don. *Progress here. What about you?* I don't know when he'll get it, though. Or when he'll reply. I'm tightrope-walking without being sure the tightrope's actually there.

An hour's nearly up when Crosetti comes out. He looks edgy. Whatever he got from Jane, it's not peace of mind.

I'm out of my chair and after him. He lights a cigarette, which slows him down. He walks down Limmatquai to the end, where there are lots of tram stops. He eyes the information screen at one of them and waits. I hang around close by.

Just after he's finished his cigarette, a number 4 shows up and he gets on. So do I. I sit a few seats back from him, ready to edge closer if he uses his phone. He doesn't. I stay where I am.

It's not long till we reach the terminus, on the other side of the river from the Hauptbahnhof. Crosetti heads across the

319

bridge. I tag along behind. He fits in another cigarette. He's definitely nervous.

I wonder if he's going to catch a train. But no. He's going back to his hotel, the Schweizerhof, a swish-looking place opposite the side entrance to the Hauptbahnhof. Inside, he collects his room key, then heads straight into the bar.

The bar's cool and dark and quiet. Crosetti plonks himself on a stool. I sit at a table. The barman takes Crosetti's order. Tequila. He downs it in one and orders another. Yeah. Definitely edgy.

I go up to the bar and sit on a stool. The bar's right-angled and I'm looking across the corner of it at Crosetti. He doesn't seem to notice me. He fiddles with his phone, then puts it down. He sips his second tequila. He fiddles with his phone again. He puts it down again.

I order a G&T and try to look relaxed. And I try to think. Crosetti's a few feet away from me. He knows everything I want to know. What can I do, in however long I've got?

Then there's a ping from my phone. And as I look at the text that's come in from Don, an idea comes into my head.

✛

As soon as it was properly dark, Harkness told Don he was ready to leave. Their destination was close by: a nondescript semi-detached bungalow on the western side of Mullion, home of Ray Hocking and his wife Linda. Harkness had apparently failed to mention over the phone that Don would be coming with him. He needed to go in and prepare the ground. He would fetch Don as soon as he had explained everything to Ray.

Left alone in the MG, Don reached immediately for his phone. Blake had not replied to his last message, so he sent another. *Away from house. Free to speak for short period if you want.*

320

It was worth a try, Don reckoned, though he suspected Harkness would call him in before Blake responded. But he was wrong about that. She texted back more or less straight away. *Can't explain but phone Schweizerhof Hotel Zürich and ask to speak to Filippo Crosetti urgently. Tie him up long as you can if you get him.*

Crosetti was the genius who had developed Elixtris for Harkness. What the hell was Blake up to? He texted back. *Don't understand.* And he got a short answer. *Just do it.*

'OK,' Don muttered to himself. He Googled the hotel and got a number. He hesitated for a few seconds, then rang it.

'*Hotel Schweizerhof.*'

'Hello. Can I speak to Filippo Crosetti please? It's very urgent.'

'Herr Crosetti?'

'Yes. Filippo Crosetti. It's very important.'

'Who shall I say is calling?'

Good question. Don Challenor did not sound like a good answer. 'Peter Revell.'

'Hold on, please.'

Don struggled to concoct something to say to Crosetti as he held. Blake had landed him in an impossible situation. No doubt she had done it for a compelling reason. But impossible it nonetheless was.

He expected the man who had answered the phone to come back on the line and say he was putting Don through to Crosetti's room – or alternatively that Crosetti had refused to take his call. Instead, an Italian-accented voice said suddenly, 'Crosetti here. Who is this?'

'Ah. Filippo Crosetti?'

'*Sì.*'

'My name's Peter Revell.'

'*Sì.* They told me. Who are you, Mr Revell?'

'Er I'm, er, a spokesman for . . .'

'*Che?*'

'A spokesman for, er, a recruitment agency.'

'Recruitment?'

'Your achievements haven't gone unnoticed by your company's competitors in the pharmaceuticals industry, Signor Crosetti. Given your employer's current difficulties, my agency's client, who must remain anonymous for the present, wonders if, er . . .'

'If *what*?'

Good God almighty, thought Don. *Where the hell am I going with this?* 'You'll appreciate, I'm sure, that this is a very delicate subject. I'm just, er, floating a possibility. You understand?'

'I do not understand, Mr Revell. How did you know I was at this hotel?'

'Ah, well . . .'

'*Sì? Sì?* Well? Well? How did you know?'

'Bloody hell.'

'What? What did you say?'

There was a movement at the edge of Don's vision. He looked towards Hocking's house and saw Harkness standing in the doorway, waving him in.

'Who are you? Who do you work for? Answer me. Now. *Subito.*'

'Sorry.'

'What?'

Don could not continue. Crosetti was speaking to someone else now, in German. He did not sound happy. And Harkness did not look happy. His waving had become impatient.

'Hope that's achieved something, Blake,' Don murmured as he ended the call.

✤

It was just a gamble. A long shot. A very long shot. But it came off. My phone doesn't look very different from Crosetti's. Well, that's what I'll say if I need to, anyway. And it's kind of true.

I deleted all the texts I'd sent and received, which was easy, because there weren't many. That left me holding a dataless phone when Crosetti was called to reception to take an urgent call. And he was so surprised HE LEFT HIS PHONE ON THE BAR NEXT TO HIS TEQUILA.

I slide my phone round the corner of the bar as I stand up and swap it with Crosetti's as I move past his stool. I see him ahead of me, stepping round the concierge's desk to reach the landline phone. I walk straight ahead, not hurrying, but not dawdling either. I see a sign pointing to the loos and I follow it. I hear Crosetti saying, 'Crosetti here. Who is this?' I don't know how long Don will be able to stall him. But maybe it'll be long enough.

I lock myself in a cubicle in the ladies' and see what there is on Crosetti's phone. The latest stuff all seems to be in German or Italian. I can't read any of it, of course. I should've realized that. Shit. I scroll through the slabs of text. There's nothing I can make any sense of.

Hold on. At last, something in English. An email from Ingrid Denner, dated 12 June – yesterday. I fast-read through the guts of it.

The subject of the meeting with you and Ms Townsend will be her role in your ongoing management of the Elixtris project, in particular the significant budgetary allocation made for the engagement of the outside scientists listed in the attachment, whose first recorded point of contact with the company was in each case Ms Townsend. Their expertise in nanotechnology and bioelectronics does not appear directly relevant to the delivery of a classical cosmetic and will require explanation. I am asking Hertha Rietz by copy of this email to reserve a symposium room at HQ Zug for our discussion on Thursday 14. Please note all communications with me should be via my BlackBerry – this number – until further notice. She doesn't explain why. But I can guess. She found the sapper. I suppose that means Gareth never read this email.

I look at the attachment. More than twenty names, professors and the like, at universities in Europe, the US, Canada, Australia and Japan. I check for a reply from Crosetti to Ingrid. Nothing.

But I do see the name Rietz. A short email, a few hours after Ingrid's to her and Crosetti, in English. The meeting's to be in symposium room B4 at noon.

Tomorrow. Not much over twelve hours from now. I'd like to be a fly on that wall. But I can't be. Can I?

I scroll through Crosetti's list of contacts. There are mobile and landline numbers listed for Astrid Townsend. I tear off a sheet of loo paper and jot them down. I jot down the numbers recorded for Harkness and Ingrid Denner too – just in case.

I reckon I've pushed my luck – and Don's – far enough. It's time to go back to the bar and act totally innocent, maybe a bit fluffy. That should do it.

Crosetti's not in reception any more. I see him ahead of me at the bar, babbling and gesturing at the barman. He's got my phone in his hand.

I breeze in and give him one of my best smiles. 'Hi,' I say. 'That's mine, isn't it?' I hold out his phone. 'And this must be yours.'

Crosetti frowns at me. He's not sure what's going on. He's suspicious. But then he's got a lot to be suspicious about. 'Who are you?'

'A ninny, obviously.' I carry on smiling sweetly. 'I must've picked up your phone instead of mine when I was leaving. Sorry.'

I pass him his phone and he takes it. I gently tug mine out of his grasp. He looks at the pair of phones and his frown deepens. Maybe he thinks they're not similar enough for me to have got them mixed up.

The barman says hopefully, 'Everything is sorted out, yes?'

'I am sorry.' I grimace and flap my hands a bit, doing my best to look girlishly empty-headed. 'All my fault. Embarrassing or what? But no harm done, right?'

'I suppose not,' Crosetti admits, though he's still frowning.

'Good. Well, I'll, er . . .' I give him a last, cheeky little grin. 'Goodnight, then.'

A minute or so later, I'm out on the street. Crosetti hasn't followed me. I'm in the clear. He and Jane Glasson, alias Astrid Townsend, have a crunch meeting tomorrow with Ingrid Denner. I know where and when. But they don't know I know. I have to make that advantage count.

All the way to the Marta, I keep asking myself: how?

From the Marta, I text Don. But there's no response. Maybe he's gone back to Wortalleth West. And he's told me not to phone him on the landline there. He must have a good reason. He'll contact me when he can. I know that.

I phone the University Hospital and ask about Gareth. I'm put through here, put through there. The nurse I end up speaking to is cagey. She wants to know my name and relationship with the patient. I say Jane Glasson, a friend. Well, Jane's not using her own name, so why shouldn't I use it instead?

The nurse eventually describes Gareth's condition as stable. But his injuries are very serious. He can't have visitors. Bottom line: he's in a bad way and he won't be talking to anyone any time soon. He's alive. But only just.

Poor Gareth. He came here with high hopes. And he was close – so close – to the truth.

I'm going to finish what he started. I still don't know how. But I'm going to.

❖

Whether Harkness realized Don had been using his phone was unclear. He said nothing about it as he led the way into Ray Hocking's house. A mousey woman Don took to be Linda eyed him timidly from the kitchen as they walked through to a small rear sitting room, crowded with more books and maps and newspapers than even the two walls of shelving could accommodate.

Ray Hocking was a stocky, salt-and-pepper-haired man with a pockmarked face and a lugubrious gaze. He looked as tight-lipped as Harkness had said he was. His clothes were old-fashioned – trousers with braces, fleecy shirt, baggy cardigan – and the aroma in the room suggested he was a pipe-smoker. He shook Don's hand, but uttered no word of greeting.

'Don's in this with me all the way, Ray,' said Harkness as they gathered round a table on which a large-scale Ordnance Survey map of the Lizard peninsula had been spread out flat.

'Right.' It sounded as if monosyllables were Ray's standard mode of communication.

'It seems French and Zlenko have been more conspicuous than they may have supposed, Don.'

'They stick out a mile,' Ray growled.

'Indeed.' Harkness smiled. 'As a result, Ray knows where they're staying.'

'You said keep an eye out.' Ray apparently objected to the hint of nosiness.

'I did. And there's no more watchful eye than yours, Ray.'

'Where *are* they staying?' asked Don.

Ray's answer was a fat-fingered stab at the map. It landed quite a few miles east of Mullion. Don saw a quadrangle of forest, a long, straight road, a few field boundaries and lots of heath symbols. But not many dwellings. There was one, though, close to Ray's finger.

'Chybargos,' said Harkness.

Ray nodded.

'What's the history?'

'Couple of labourer's cottages knocked into one plus a barn conversion, for holiday lets. Never properly finished. Owner ran out of money. He wouldn't ask many questions if the price was right.'

'And it would be,' said Harkness.

'You think . . .' Don hesitated. He did not know whether he should mention Fran or not.

'I think they may not be alone there,' said Harkness.

'Less I know the better,' said Ray.

Harkness smiled at him. 'But you always know so much, Ray.'

'Saw Wynsum Fry yesterday.'

'How nice for you.'

'Could be trouble for you if she finds out you're back.'

'Could be trouble for me if *anyone* finds out.'

'They won't from me.'

'I know that. There'll likely be mention of me in the news, by the way.'

Ray nodded. 'Often is.'

'I hope you don't believe everything those papers you sell say about me.'

'Never 'ave. Good or bad.'

Harkness chuckled. 'Very wise.'

'Want the map?'

'It'd be useful.'

327

Ray folded the map up and passed it to Harkness.

'Thanks.'

'You be careful, Jack.'

'Always am. Let's go, Don.'

Harkness sent Don out to check the coast was clear, then followed him to the car. He told him to drive back towards Wortalleth West and they set off.

'If we know where they're holding Fran,' said Don as soon as they were clear of Hocking's house, 'maybe we should go to the police and let them handle it.'

'Or mishandle it,' Harkness countered. 'They're not called Plod for nothing.'

'You still haven't unveiled your own masterplan.'

'No. But stop at the next turning and I will. We'll be safe from snoopers and curtain-twitchers there. And you'll get a signal for your phone.'

'I'm calling someone, am I?'

'You are, Don. Amos French. And before you ask, yes, I do know what I'm doing.'

Don pulled in, as instructed, where the road to Mullion began its descent towards Poldhu Cove.

The night was soft and starless. With the MG's engine off and its lights out, they were cocooned in darkness.

'So tell me, Jack,' Don asked, 'what am I going to say to French, *if* he answers?'

'Oh, he'll answer when he sees it's you calling. And as for what you're going to say to him, well, you're going to say you have what he wants: full details of where the money is he's been paid to find.'

'But I don't.'

'No. But what you will have, when you meet him, is half of what's in that bag of mine on the back seat. Which I'm betting will persuade him to call off the search – and release Fran.'

Don glanced over his shoulder, to no purpose, since the bag was merely one dark shadow among several. 'What does it contain?'

'Five million Swiss francs.'

'*How much?*'

'Five million. Thanks to the Swiss fondness for high-denomination bank notes, that doesn't actually take up much space.'

'You mean . . .'

'A straight pay-off, Don. Easy money for French. A happy outcome for Fran. And you, of course.'

'You're serious?'

'Absolutely. Don't worry.' Don sensed rather than saw Harkness smiling. 'I can afford it.'

'I don't understand you, Jack. Why steal all that money from your partners, from your own company, if—'

'The greater good, Don.'

'What?'

'Tell French you'll meet him at Lizard Point car park at eight o'clock tomorrow morning. When he gets there, offer him the two and a half million against another two and a half when they release Fran. I'll be standing by close to Chybargos, ready to deliver the second instalment in exchange for Fran as soon as French says yes and gives Zlenko, who he's sure to have left on guard, the OK to let her go. That's on the clear understanding, mind, that they'll stop looking for the money I've supposedly stolen.'

'But . . . where will that leave them with their employers?'

'I think you'll find French is willing to trade his share of five million Swiss francs for a testimonial from Quintagler Industries. And Zlenko's share will keep him in vodka for the rest of his life. They'll take the deal.'

'Why don't you just repay Quintagler, if you're so flush with cash?'

'Because they're after me for billions, Don, not a piddling few million. And I don't have it.'

'You don't have it?'

'I spent it.'

'What the hell on?'

'Are you going to make the call, Don? We're not here to discuss my financial dispositions. We're here to get Fran out of the fix you landed her in by walking out on the job she sent you down here to do. So, why don't we just get on with it?'

'Have you got something for me, Don?'

'Yes. I have.'

'Is it what I asked for?'

'And then some.'

'How did you pull that off?'

'I'd rather not discuss it over the phone.'

'OK.'

'Lizard Point car park. Eight o'clock tomorrow morning. You can see what I've got then.'

'All right, Don. It's a deal.'

Don drove the short distance to Wortalleth West trying hard not to think too much about the stream of events he was being carried along in. Harkness's scheme had a lot going for it. He knew French – as well as Zlenko – a lot better than Don did. There was every reason to believe he could buy Fran's freedom. All Don had to do was play the part Harkness had written for him.

But he could not forget what had happened to Mike Coleman. The sensation of his hand resting on the dead man's head as he pushed him back into the freezer kept coursing through him.

There was little in the house, but Don did not feel hungry and nor, evidently, did Harkness. He did feel in the mood for a fabulously expensive bottle of Château Latour, however, which he fetched from the wine cellar and shared with Don in the lounge.

'Smooth, isn't it?' he asked after Don had taken his first sip. 'Like velvet.'

'How much did you pay for it?'

'No idea.'

'Well, it certainly tastes expensive.'

'No, Don. It tastes . . . noble.'

'Do you feel noble, Jack? Doing . . . whatever the hell it is you're doing.'

'You don't have any children, do you, Don? Neither do I. So, when we look to the future, we don't have a personal stake in it. Tell me what you see out there, from your disinterested perspective.'

'I don't think about the future much.'

'No? Perhaps that's discouraged among estate agents. Well, I do. And I have a crucial advantage over you. I can afford to pay experts in the field to give me their insights and predictions. And I can . . .' Harkness smiled and shook his head. 'Never mind. Suffice to say I worked for that advantage. I aimed for it, almost as far back as I can remember. It's never been about personal enrichment, hard though you may find that to believe as you roll my claret round your tonsils. No, no. It's never been about that at all.'

'What, then?'

'It's been about putting myself in a position to do what needs to be done.'

'And what's that?'

'A hard thing. A thing I can't trust anyone else to do. Although, in a sense, thanks to the arrangements I've made, other people will do it for me, eventually.'

'I've no idea what you're talking about.'

'I know.'

'Do you enjoy being an enigma?'

'Not particularly. Tell you what, Don. Ask me a yes or no question – a single question – and I'll answer it truthfully. No bullshit. No evasions. No enigma at all. A straight yes or no.'

Something in Harkness's eyes, as lamplight reflected in the wine washed across his face, told Don he was in earnest. He would not lie. Find the right question and Don could unlock his soul.

'Well?'

'I need time to think about it.'

'Sorry. It's now or never.'

'One question?'

'That's it.'

'And I know you'll answer truthfully because . . .'

Harkness set down his wine glass gently on the glass-topped table between them. 'You have my word, Don.'

Yes or no meant Don could not ask what was in the panic room, or what Harkness had done with all the money he was accused of stealing. Yes or no narrowed the field, as Harkness clearly intended.

'My solemn word.' Harkness picked up the bottle of Château Latour. 'But if I refill my glass before you ask me a question . . .'

'Did you kill Jory Fry?'

Harkness put the bottle back down and smiled across the table at Don. 'Yes. I did.'

The shock of the admission silenced Don for a moment. Then he said, 'You murdered him?'

'I might have pleaded provocation if it had come to court. Murder? Manslaughter? Justifiable homicide? You can take your pick.'

'Why? Why did you kill him?'

'Jory Fry was a cruel, evil-hearted boy. He enjoyed torturing animals, something I particularly detested. It's hard enough to have to share this planet with humans without having the likes of Jory Fry tearing your wings off or gouging out your eyes. When I came upon him among the rock pools down at Poldhu Cove that Saturday morning all those years ago, he was pulling the claws off a crab he'd just plucked out of the water. Only a crab, you might say. My father made a living catching them, for God's sake. Where's the difference? Well, there is one. There's a line. And Jory Fry crossed it. When I saw what he was doing, something in me snapped. I grabbed him and forced his head under the water in one of the rock pools and I held him down until he'd stopped struggling and then a bit longer just to be sure he was dead. I did it consciously and deliberately. And I've never regretted it, though I probably would have if anyone had seen me doing it. Wynsum Fry is the only one who knows. And she knows in a way the law doesn't cater for.' Harkness poured more wine into his glass and raised it to drink. 'Oh, and now there's you, of course.'

Don stared numbly at Harkness. He did not know what to say.

'Lost for words, Don?'

He was. But, eventually, he found some. 'You killed Jory Fry because he was torturing a crab?'

'You could say that.'

'What other way do you want to put it?'

'I killed him because the sort of person who wants to do such things has no right to live.'

'You can't mean that.'

'But I do.'

'What about all the other random acts of cruelty in the world? Why stop at Jory Fry?'

'You don't get clean away with something like that unless you're very lucky, Don. I realized I'd used up more than my fair share of luck that day. I didn't actually want to go to prison. Though, as you know, the threat does rather seem to be hanging over me at present.'

'Whose fault is that?'

'Start allocating fault and you'll find yourself on a long road to nowhere, Don. There are only actions and consequences, problems and solutions. There are only choices of different futures.'

'You've lost me.'

Harkness took a deep swallow of wine, set the glass down and stood up. 'I'm off to bed. I'll leave you to finish the bottle. Try to get a good night's sleep, Don. Use whichever bedroom suits. We'll be making an early start. It promises to be a busy day. Besides which, sooner or later the Met are going to give up chasing my shadow round Europe and ask the local police to check this place over, so I really ought to make myself scarce. I'll leave at the same time as you and drive over to Chybargos in Coleman's Merc. Our friends helpfully left the key in the ignition. It's blocking my Ferrari in, but that might be too noticeable anyway. And cheer up. Everything will go smoothly. I've always found money is the most effective lubricant of them all. French and Zlenko are in this for what they can get out of it. And five million Swiss francs will more than satisfy them.'

'I hope you're right.'

'I usually am. As my company's shareholders can testify.' Harkness chuckled. 'Well, until recently they would have, anyway. Goodnight.'

Don did finish the bottle, but Harkness's revelation had sobered him irretrievably. He knew he should go to bed, but he felt fretful and alert. The house was utterly silent. Harkness was presumably sleeping the sleep of the unregretful up in the master bedroom, unworried by what the panic room contained because, of course, he knew.

Don let half an hour slowly and soundlessly pass. Then he went into the study, sat at the desk and picked up the telephone.

⬥

I'd only been in that shallow kind of sleep where you're almost conscious of being asleep when the phone rang. I knew it had to be Don even before I rolled over and grabbed it. Who else could it be?

'Are you at the house?' I ask at once.

'Yeah. With Harkness.' He's speaking in an undertone, as if frightened of being overheard. I notice he doesn't use my name. I decide I'd better not use his either.

'How's that happened?'

'He has a plan to free Fran. It seems to make sense. I'm going along with it.'

'What's the timescale?'

'Tomorrow should see it done. What's going on at your end?'

'There's no danger he's listening in, is there?'

'I don't think so.'

'But are you sure?'

'I just wanted to check you were all right. If—'

'I'm fine.' I decide in that split second I'm not going to tell him about Jane until I can be totally certain the information

335

stays and stops with him. 'I'm following something up. Something that . . . may give us some answers.'

'And what's your timescale?'

'Like yours. Tomorrow should see it done.'

'You *are* being careful, aren't you?'

'You can count on that. And you?'

'Likewise.'

'Thanks for, er . . . earlier.'

'Did it help?'

'A lot.'

'I'll check in whenever I can.'

'Me too.'

'Until then . . .'

'Make good choices.'

'I'll try.'

'So will I. Night-night.'

I look at the time on the phone in the second before the screen goes black. It *is* tomorrow, already. I lie back on the pillow and gaze up into the darkness above me. I know what I'm going to do. I wasn't sure, when I was speaking to Don. But now I am. It's obvious. It's inevit-able. And maybe it's even right.

We'll see. Very soon.

THREE

THE MORNING MOCKED DON'S PROBLEMS WITH ITS CRISP EARLY summer refulgence. He drove down the main road to the foot of the peninsula, through a landscape of glowing greenery, while the deep blue sea shimmered and glistened between folds of field and heath on either side.

From Lizard village he followed the sign for the National Trust car park. The narrow lane was made narrower still by sagging swags of wild mustard. The sun was climbing in the sky. In the clear, strong light, everything looked as solid as marble. Only his confidence was insubstantial.

Lizard Lighthouse appeared ahead of him, white and glaring. He turned into the car park, saw the ticket booth was unattended and took a looping route to a patch of grass distant from any of the few other vehicles that were already there.

He stopped and looked into the bag on the passenger seat beside him. The money was there, in banded wads: 2.5 million Swiss francs. He saw the reality of it, though he could scarcely believe it. Out to sea, waves broke lazily on shelves of rock and specks that might have been seals bobbed in the swell. Through the open window, he could hear a skylark singing above the soft whisper of the surf. He was as ready as he would ever be. And he did not feel ready at all.

He climbed out of the car and stood, leaning back against it. Even the dusty bodywork of the MG looked golden in the brazen light. He felt the breeze on his face and wondered how long he would have to wait. According to his watch, he was five minutes early.

But French, as it turned out, was early too. His bulky black 4WD nosed into the car park with a couple of minutes still to go till eight o'clock.

He pulled up alongside Don, but facing in the opposite direction. When he climbed out of the driver's seat, sunglasses obscuring whatever look there was in his eyes, he was within touching distance.

'This is a surprise, Don,' French said in a neutral tone. 'I didn't expect you to come through.'

'Sorry to disappoint you.'

'You haven't. It's a *pleasant* surprise. Assuming you really do have what I asked for.'

'How's Fran?'

'She's good.' French smiled humourlessly. 'Roughing it these past couple of days won't have done her any harm. Now, show me what you've got.'

'I'll think you'll be impressed.'

'I'll be the judge of that. Where'd you get the information from, anyway?'

'Just come and see.' Don led the way round to the other side of the MG.

'This got anything to do with Harkness going on the run? According to this morning's news the police think he's flown out of the country on a fake passport.'

'I hadn't heard that.' Don opened the door and flipped

back the flap of the bag where it lay on the seat. He gestured for French to take a look inside.

French frowned and prised the bag open. Don heard his sharp intake of breath at first sight of the money. 'What the fuck is this?'

'Two and a half million Swiss francs.'

French turned and stared at him in amazement.

'That's what the fuck this is,' Don said, holding French's gaze.

'I asked for the whereabouts of the money Harkness stole from Quintagler Industries.'

'Sorry. I can't oblige with that. But the bag contains half of what Harkness is willing to pay for Fran's freedom – on condition you call off your search for Quintagler's money.'

'You're . . . working with Harkness?'

'We both have Fran's welfare at heart.'

'Where the fuck is he?'

'Do we have a deal?'

'We *had* a deal, Don. Fran's release in return for full particulars on where Harkness has stashed the cash. Which amounts to way more than a few million Swiss francs.'

'But this is all yours. To bank and spend, no questions asked. And I'm guessing it's way more, to use your own phrase, than the commission you're on with Quintagler.'

'Harkness thinks he can buy me?'

'Well, you are for sale, aren't you?'

French suddenly tensed. A hand shot out. He grabbed Don by the collar. 'What did you say?'

'We know where you're holding Fran,' Don said, forcing himself to ignore the pressure at his neck. 'You give the word and Harkness will deliver the other two and a half million to Zlenko and take Fran off his hands. It can all be done right now – done and dusted.'

The anger squirming in French's face suggested he did

not like being made a counter-offer – especially one that was too good to refuse.

'The money's gone,' Don continued, the voice of reason. 'Where or on what I don't know, but Harkness has spent it all. Quintagler will never pay you a cent, because you'll never recover a cent for them. That's how it is. It's this or nothing. And this is a hell of a lot more than nothing.'

French's grip slackened. He let go of Don and delved in the bag, pulling the band off one wad of notes and fanning them out to check the denominations. Then he dropped them back into the bag.

'You can count it if you want to,' said Don.

'You'll count it. In front of me.'

'Does that mean we have a deal?'

French's tone was regretful, but resigned. 'I'll take it.'

'We'll need Zlenko on board as well.'

'That won't be a problem.' French glared at Don. 'I don't like Harkness. I don't like how easily he solves his problems.'

'This solution is easy for you too.'

'Yeah. And I don't like that either. Wait here.'

French returned to his car, climbed in and slammed the door shut, then tried to make a call on his phone. It did not go well. A few seconds later, he was back out of the car and stalking towards high ground, muttering incredulously about how anyone could live in an area with such poor signal coverage. He was about fifty yards away before contact was established. Several minutes passed while he prowled around, phone to his ear. Then he hurried back down the slope to rejoin Don – and the bag of money. 'We're good to go,' he growled.

'Zlenko's OK with this?'

'Just call Harkness and tell him Zlenko's expecting him, Don. Then we'll go join them. You and Harkness have got yourselves a deal, OK? So, let's get it over with. The sooner the better as far as I'm concerned. And I'm guessing that goes for you too, right?'

It did. Beyond question, it did. Don nodded. 'Right.'

⁛

I get to the side entrance of the Limmatquai building just as a couple of guys are arriving early for work. I follow them in. They head up the stairs, hardly noticing me, chatting away about something – last night's football, maybe.

Then, when they've gone into their office, I press the button numbered 7 on the intercom panel.

Jane answers almost at once, like she's expecting someone. Not me, obviously. '*Hallo?*' she says. But she's wary. She doesn't say, like, '*Filippo?*'

'HI,' I respond, keeping my voice cool and calm. 'Can I come up, please?'

'Sorry? Who are you?'

'I'm Blake. You don't know me. But I know you. Like, who you really are.'

'I'm sorry. I—'

'You need to speak to me before you meet Ingrid Denner. You really do . . . Jane.'

Long pause. Heavy. She hasn't bargained for this. Then: 'There's no one here called Jane.'

'We both know there is.'

'You're mistaken. I'll have to ask—'

'Don't make me tell Ingrid what I know. What I can prove. That'd be stupid. And you aren't stupid, are you? You're actually very clever. You must be, to have . . . totally reinvented yourself. So, can I come up . . . Jane?'

Another long pause. I can almost hear her thinking. Then: 'All right.'

*

I take the lift. I want her to hear me coming. When I step out on the seventh floor, there's a difference in the light that tells me her outer door is open.

But she's not there. The door's just standing ajar. I push it open and look up a flight of steps.

She's waiting for me at the top, in the doorway. She's wearing tailored black trousers and a white blouse. Brisk and businesslike. My guess is she's already dressed for the noon meeting in Zug.

'Leave the door open,' she says. 'Who are you?'

'Blake. I used to work for your father, Andrew. At the house in Helston. They never moved. Well, I expect you know that.'

'I don't know what you're talking about.'

'Yes you do. Otherwise, you wouldn't have let me in. Can I come up?'

She doesn't say anything. But there's a kind of nod that means I can.

I go up and walk past her into a wide, wood-floored lounge. There are big dormer windows on either side. I guess we're directly below the roof terrace. The furniture's angular and modern. There aren't many personal touches. It's all clean and neat and kind of soulless.

Except there's a painting on one of the walls I recognize. Well, I recognize the style: sweeping lines, blocks of colour. The sea? The land? Or something in between, seen from above. I turn and look at Jane.

'That's a Lanyon, isn't it?'

She doesn't react. She's hard to read. Maybe she's trained herself over the years to be blank, to give nothing away. But it's not actually blankness. It's like she's just stopped smiling, or frowning, or something. But you can't tell what.

'Did Harkness give it to you? I think he likes Lanyon. There's one at Wortalleth West. I worked there too.'

344

'My name's Astrid Townsend,' she says, sounding totally sane and reasonable. 'I can prove that.'

'That's weird. I can prove you're Jane Glasson.'

Actually, what's really weird is what she says next. 'Why would you want to?'

Why? The question catches me unprepared. Why do I? *Really*. Is it because she ran away from a loving family for no reason that makes any sense? Am I just angry that she gave up on something I never had? Do I resent how easily, how irreversibly, she turned her back on them? I wouldn't have. I'd have cherished what I had – what she had.

'What brought you here?' She frowns slightly. 'Have I seen you before?'

'Why did you go to the Zoo yesterday, Jane?'

'You followed me.'

'What did you say to the tiger?'

She takes one step towards me. She looks into my eyes, trying to analyse me. 'What do you want?'

'The truth.'

'I told you. I'm Astrid Townsend.'

'You walked out of your old life twenty-two years ago. I want to know why. I want to be able to explain it to your father.'

'If there was any truth in what you say, it'd still be none of your business. People are free to lead their life as they choose.'

She's right. They are. Interrogating her is totally against what I believe in. But still I have to do it. 'Tell me there was a good reason, Jane. I want to believe there was.'

'There have been good reasons for everything I've done.'

'You talk like Harkness. You work for him, don't you? Why? Tell me how the green campaigner winds up boosting the profits of Big Pharma.'

'What did you say your name was? Blake?'

'Yeah.'

'Where do you come from, Blake?'

'It doesn't matter. This is about you, not me.' That isn't completely true. I know that. But she isn't going to.

'And what am I . . . about, Blake?'

'I don't know.'

'You should leave it that way.'

'I've found out too much already to do that.'

'And what exactly have you found out? Tell me.'

'OK. You disappeared twenty-two years ago. For most of the time since then, you've been working for Harkness Pharmaceuticals as some kind of consultant, under the name Astrid Townsend. I don't know why you want to hide what you're doing from your family. It can't just be because it goes against your environmentalist principles. Holly Walsh told me about those. You're funding her Ditrimantelline treatment, aren't you? And Ditrimantelline's a Harkness drug.'

She doesn't react to any of this. She doesn't seem to be shocked or angry. She studies me like she's trying to spot a weakness, a flaw. She studies me like I'm under a microscope and she's looking down it.

'I spoke to Gareth Lawler. He saw you at Paddington station earlier this year. He came here to find you. You arranged to meet him yesterday morning. But he wound up in hospital instead.'

'That was an accident.'

First mistake. She's admitted something now. She can't go back. 'I know it was an accident. But maybe you were relieved because it got you off the hook. Sorry. It didn't. I followed you from the hospital. To the Zoo. Then here. And then I followed Filippo Crosetti.'

'You should stop, Blake. You should drop this and go. Whatever you think you're doing, you're wrong. You're interfering in something you don't understand.'

'Make me understand, then. Tell me the truth.'

'I don't have to tell you anything.'

'You do. If you want to stop Ingrid Denner finding out what I've found out.'

'Say what you like to her.'

'You don't mean that.'

'Don't I?'

A mobile phone rings somewhere behind Jane, then stops. She glances over her shoulder, then looks back at me.

'It'd be best for you if you left now, Blake.'

'Is that Filippo? You've been expecting him, haven't you? Are you travelling to Zug together for the meeting with Ingrid?'

'Leave. Please.'

'What have you and Filippo been doing for Harkness? What's in the panic room at Wortalleth West? What is this all about?'

'Walk away, Blake.'

'I want to know the truth.'

'You don't. Not really.'

'But I do.'

'You carry on like this when Filippo arrives and I don't think we'll just be able to drop it.'

'I don't want to drop it.'

'You should.' The look in her eyes. What is it? Sincerity? Fuck. I think it just might be.

'It's too late for that. I've come too far.'

'Too far?' Jane nods. 'Yes. You have. Maybe we all have.'

There's a noise behind her. The clunk of a door closing. Then footsteps on the stairs.

'You should've left, Blake,' Jane says quietly. 'While you had the chance.'

✢

In the course of forty-eight hours, Fran's terror had congealed inside her, till she was exhausted by the weight of it. She could no longer judge her chances of survival and had stopped anticipating what the future held. She thought more about the girls and how their lives would be altered if she died. She held on grimly to as much dignity and optimism as she could find within herself as her world shrank around her.

It comprised now the bare space she was confined to. She was handcuffed to a steel frame, supporting a sink. The room was small and windowless, lacking all utilities beyond the sink itself. Through a half-open door ahead of her, she could see part of a kitchen and a window looking out on to a yard.

She knew the layout of Chybargos from her arrival there on Tuesday morning – a pair of slate-roofed stone cottages, knocked through and partially modernized, on one side of a cobbled yard; a part-converted barn on the other.

There was a camp-chair for her to sit on, along with a mattress and a sleeping bag. There was soap in the sink for her to wash herself. Since arriving she had only left the room for visits to the loo, closely supervised by Zlenko. He had a gun, which she knew he would use if the need arose. And she also knew he was capable of killing her quite easily without using the gun. She had heard, though not actually seen, his grisly despatch of Mike Coleman, who had made the fatal mistake of suggesting a rise in the price of his cooperation, in addition to displaying what Zlenko had called 'bad attitude'.

If and how either Don or Harkness would react to French's terms for her release Fran did not know. She was confident Don would try to save her, but was doubtful of his ability to do so. With Harkness it was the other way round. As for Peter, she knew he would be in a desperate state following her disappearance. He must have gone to

348

the police by now. But what they would do, if anything, she had no way of knowing.

French had barely spoken to her since leaving Wortalleth West. He had evidently concluded she could be of no help in penetrating the panic room or leading them to wherever else Harkness had hidden the money they had been hired to recover. Her value now, in his estimation, was as a hostage only. And that left her in Zlenko's charge.

Though brutal and ruthless when called upon to be so, Zlenko was also bewilderingly amiable, even considerate. He kept telling Fran to 'Not worry.' He even consulted her about what topping she wanted on her microwaved pizza.

'Could be worse' was another of his repeated reassurances, which she failed to be reassured by. On one occasion, when French, as far as Fran could tell, was absent, Zlenko opened a bottle of vodka and drank most of it. The only discernible effect was that he began reminiscing about his experiences as an eighteen year old conscript in the Soviet army clearing up in Chernobyl after the nuclear accident back in 1986. Vodka, to hear him tell it, was the sole reason he had not succumbed to radiation poisoning, as many of his comrades had.

There had been an improvement in the mood of her captors the previous evening. French had looked and sounded fractionally more cheerful, though he had said nothing to explain why. Zlenko, meanwhile, had added, 'You be OK,' to his other pet phrases, as if the chances of her being OK really had increased.

She had heard French drive away early that morning, destination unknown. Later, she had seen Zlenko out in the yard, pacing to and fro as he talked on his phone, presumably to French. When the call ended, he had walked into the room, smiling broadly, and announced,

'All good.' She had asked what he meant, but he had merely added, 'Not worry,' and left her to her own devices.

Now, as she fretted and hoped and wondered, time passed slower than ever. The sunlight in the yard strengthened. And Zlenko kept his distance. She swore to herself that, if she survived this experience, she would live by different rules. And she began to imagine what those rules would be.

Her waiting ended in the sound of a car drawing up in the yard. But the engine note was somehow different from French's 4WD. She saw Zlenko walk past the kitchen window. She heard a voice. Not his. Not French's. Whose was it? She strained her ears. She could not make out any words, but the tone of the newcomer's voice was . . .

Harkness.

Some minutes passed. Maybe five, though it felt longer. Then Zlenko came into the room, smiling as before. He unlocked the handcuffs and helped her out of the chair in some ludicrous parody of Victorian drawing-room etiquette. 'Go time,' he announced with evident pleasure.

They exited into the yard. Harkness was standing by a bright red Mercedes convertible that Fran felt sure was Coleman's. Harkness too was smiling. In one hand he held a canvas holdall.

'Hello, Fran,' he said. 'I'm sorry you've been through the mill on my account.'

'What's happening?' she said as they approached him. Zlenko was holding her by the elbow, but lightly, as if he had become more of an escort than a captor.

'We've done a deal. You're free to go.'

Zlenko's hand left her. He reached out and took the bag

from Harkness. She glimpsed wads of cash inside. 'You've paid them to release me?'

'I have. Handsomely, it must be said.'

'How did you get here? You're not allowed to leave London.'

'Yet here I am.'

He touched her back, gently encouraging her to leave. She felt suddenly close to tears, but swallowed them down and clenched her jaw. 'Am I really free to go?' she asked hoarsely.

'Yes. And you should, without delay. The key's in the ignition. Drive wherever you like. But, please, don't contact anyone just yet. French will give Don your phone when he and I are done.'

'Don?'

'He's been very helpful. He's on his way here now with French. I'll leave with him when we've wrapped everything up. I suggest you meet him at Pawley's offices in Helston at . . .' Harkness glanced at his watch. 'Noon should do it. We'll all have gone our separate ways by then.'

'Where does that mean . . . for you?'

'Not a question my wife's solicitor needs to know the answer to, Fran. Just get in the car and drive away.'

'It's Coleman's . . . isn't it?'

'That's not something you need to worry about at the moment. There'll be a lot of sorting out to be done in due course. The police will have to be notified of what's occurred. But French and Zlenko will be long gone by then. And so will I.'

'Where—'

'No more questions.' There was a look of urgency in Harkness's eyes. 'Just go.'

He opened the driver's door for her. She climbed in and

turned the key. The car burst into life. She looked up at Harkness. 'Thank you,' she said simply.

He winked at her disarmingly. 'You're welcome.'

'*Do svidaniya,*' said Zlenko.

She reversed slowly round in a half-circle, then drove out into the lane, where she stopped. Glancing over her shoulder, she saw Harkness signalling for her to turn right. She nodded, pulled out into the lane and accelerated away.

Within seconds, the place where she had spent the last two days was out of sight. She was free.

❖

Filippo Crosetti stares at me as he walks through the door. He looks shocked. He wasn't expecting this. He wasn't expecting *me*.

'*Gesù.* What is she doing here?'

'You know each other?' Jane looks surprised as well.

'She was at the Schweizerhof last night.' His stare turns into a glare. 'That wasn't an accident with the phones, was it?'

'No.' I don't flinch. I look him in the eye. Then Jane. 'I got a peek at the messages on Filippo's phone. That's how I know where and when you're meeting Ingrid Denner. Head office, Zug. Symposium room B4. Noon today.'

Jane glances reproachfully at Filippo, but she says nothing. Instead, he says, 'Why is this woman here?'

'My name's Blake,' I butt in. 'Pleased to meet you. Again.'

Filippo's getting angry now. Maybe angrier with Jane than with me. 'What the fuck is going on?'

I keep telling myself I'm not going to be intimidated by these people. Jane tried to frighten me just before Filippo arrived. Now he's turning volcanic. But they have nothing on me. Nothing at all. 'I know who Astrid really is,' I say, super cool.

Jane stays silent. Filippo's eyes bore into me. His jaw clenches and unclenches. Eventually, he gives an irritated little toss of his hand and says to Jane, 'Tell her to go away.'

'I've tried that,' Jane responds matter-of-factly.

He turns on me. 'What do you want?'

'The truth about you two and what you do for Harkness.'

'And if we tell you to just fuck off?'

'Then Ingrid Denner will learn Astrid really is Jane Glasson, just as Gareth Lawler claims. Which I guess will open you up to a lot of questions from her you won't want to answer.'

'You think we will want to answer *your* questions?'

'I think you have to choose. Hers or mine. I'm trying to help Jane's father find out what happened to his daughter. Ingrid? Well, her agenda's about pinning the blame on someone for the scandal Harkness Pharmaceuticals is caught up in. Which conversation would you rather have?'

Filippo gives Jane a dark look. 'I told Jack this would happen one day.'

Jane sighs faintly, like he's trying her patience. 'We should say as little as possible, Filippo. Don't let her get under your skin.'

'Under my skin? What is that? English fucking irony?'

There's a glass fruit bowl on the table about three strides away. Filippo covers the distance in two, grabs the bowl and hurls it towards the sleek black stove in the fireplace. It hits the marble hearth in an explosion of fragments. Apples and oranges roll around the wooden floor.

I start back from the scattering fragments. But Jane, I notice, doesn't react at all, apart from shaking her head ever so slightly.

Filippo's breathing heavily now. He wipes a hand across his mouth and looks at me. 'How much to go away, little girl?'

I think he's trying to bribe me, which is really pitiful. I get the vibe Jane knows just how pitiful. 'I'm not looking for a pay-off,' I tell him – and her.

'Make her see some sense, Astrid,' he snaps, almost pleadingly.

'If only I could,' she responds.

'It just gets worse,' he continues, sounding now as if he's talking more to himself than either of us. 'This is supposed to be about the big picture. Insurance against . . . disaster.' He runs his fingers through his hair. 'There's not meant to be any way we can be . . .'

'We've done the right thing, Filippo,' Jane says softly, reassuringly.

'It won't sound like the right thing if anyone ever . . .' He moves to one of the windows and glares out at the city. 'I keep wondering what Jack is doing,' he mumbles. Then he says in a louder voice, as if posing a question, 'What is he doing *now*?'

'I have no idea,' says Jane.

'Why has he gone on the run?'

'I don't know.'

'Where is he? Where—'

'Cornwall,' I cut in.

Filippo turns round and stares at me. 'What did you say?'

'Harkness is in Cornwall.'

'How do you know?' He's not sure whether to believe me, but the idea that Harkness could be in Cornwall seems to have frightened him for some reason. There's sweat on his forehead.

'I spoke to a friend of mine in Cornwall last night. He mentioned Harkness.'

'Mentioned him?'

'They're working on something together.'

This sounds evasive, even to me, and it totally freaks out Filippo. 'What the fuck does that mean?'

354

'You don't want to answer my questions. Why should I answer yours?'

'Is it to do with the house – Wortalleth West?'

'Could be. But I'm—'

'For Christ's sake, Astrid.' Filippo's shouting now. Something's snapped inside him. 'Don't you see? Jack's not willing to wait any longer. In case we decide it shouldn't go ahead – ever. He knows I'm away from the lab because of fucking Ingrid Denner. And he's made his move.'

'You don't know any of that for certain, Filippo,' says Jane, trying to reason with him.

'You tell me what other explanation makes any sense.'

'Tell us what Jack and your friend are doing, Blake.' Jane urges me with her eyes to help her defuse whatever crisis it is Filippo is convinced they're facing. 'Please.'

'Not till you've told me what Jack and *you two* are doing. What it is you might decide shouldn't go ahead – ever.'

'*Merda*,' snaps Filippo. 'What are we going to do, Astrid?'

'We're going to keep calm,' she replies, keeping calm herself. 'And we're going to get through this.'

'We should leave. Now.'

'There's plenty of time.'

'No. There isn't.'

'We're not due to meet Ingrid Denner until—'

'I'm not talking about her. I'm talking about Jack.' Filippo strides across the room and grasps Jane by the arm. 'He's going to do it. I know he is. *He's going to do it.*'

'He won't go back on our agreement, Filippo. He's a man of his word.'

'He's a twister of words. That's what he is. He'll get someone else to do it. Someone who doesn't understand. Then technically he won't be breaking our agreement.' Filippo gestures towards me. 'It could be this friend of hers.

You know what he calls people like that. Useful idiots. He probably thinks we're useful idiots too.'

Jane closes her eyes. She takes in a breath and lets it out. Then she looks at Filippo like really sombrely. 'What do you want to do? Go back to Locarno?'

Filippo's still holding her arm. I see his grip tighten. 'I don't think there's time. But there's a relay in his office at HQ.'

'Is there?'

'It was on a schematic I wasn't supposed to see. An override for my override would be my guess. He's never trusted us, Astrid. Not totally.'

'And now you'll be proving he was right not to.'

'You and I, we've argued this through again and again. Look at what's happening. It's late, but it's not too late. We don't have to do this. I told Jack right at the start. *Come ultimo ricorso, sì.* Yes. If it was the only way. But I don't believe it is. Not any more. And neither do you.'

'Don't I?'

'We can't let him make the decision on his own. It's too big.'

'Phone him.'

'He doesn't answer.'

'Phone him *again*.'

Filippo pulls out his phone and punches in a number. He shows Jane the screen. 'Voicemail. Every time.'

Jane looks sharply at me. 'What is your friend doing with Jack, Blake?'

'I told you just now. If—'

'We're running out of time, Astrid,' wails Filippo. 'We have to move.'

'At least phone your friend and ask him where they are.' Jane shakes Filippo off and steps closer to me. 'Will you do that for me?' For *me*, I notice. Not us.

There doesn't seem to be any really good reason to refuse.

If I do this, maybe Jane will tell me a bit more than she has so far, which is nothing. It's probably less than fifty-fifty that Don will answer anyway. I pull out the phone and make the call.

No answer. I don't leave a message. He'll know I called. That's good enough. If he could've answered, he would've. I slide the phone back into my pocket. 'Sorry,' I say with a shrug.

'*Per l'amor di Dio*, Astrid,' says Filippo, sounding just a fraction less hyper. 'Do you agree there's a chance I'm right about why Jack's gone to Cornwall?'

Jane frowns, as if thinking it through. Then she says, 'Yes. It's possible.'

'And do you agree, if I'm right, we have to stop him?'

A long time seems to pass before she answers that one. And it's almost a whisper. 'Yes.'

'Then we have to get to his office at HQ. As soon as we can.'

She looks at him in a way I can't decipher. And I bet he doesn't even notice the little drift of something behind her eyes. She nods. 'OK.'

'A taxi's the quickest way. We can pick one up at Bürkliplatz.'

'Take me with you,' I cut in.

'No,' says Filippo, almost without thinking.

'I'm your best chance of finding out what Harkness is doing.'

'We don't need her, Astrid,' Filippo insists.

'Sounds to me like you need all the help you can get,' I counter.

'You don't understand. You know nothing.'

'She should come with us,' says Jane, calmly but firmly. Why she wants me along I'm not sure. Maybe she thinks I really can help. Or maybe she thinks I'll do less harm if she keeps me close. As for the possibility that I'll find out what's going on, she's obviously willing to risk that.

'No, no,' Filippo protests.

'Yes.' In Jane's voice, the word sounds final.

And Filippo seems to accept that. 'Crazy,' he growls. But he doesn't argue any more. 'We have to go. Now.'

'Then stop talking,' says Jane, glancing at me. 'And move.'

✤

Don had stuck doggedly to French's tail from Lizard Point. Harkness and Zlenko were waiting for them in the yard at Chybargos, leaning against a wall and chatting amiably, or so it appeared. Certainly Harkness was smiling. But that, as Don well knew, meant little. What concerned him far more was that there was no sign of Fran.

Harkness seemed to read his mind, however. 'Don't worry,' he called, waving cheerily as he walked over to where Don had pulled up alongside French's 4WD. 'Everything's OK.'

'Where's Fran?' Don asked at once through the open window of the MG.

'En route to Helston in Coleman's Merc. I've said you'll meet her at Pawley's office at noon. She's going to keep the lid on this till then.'

'So all we have to do is . . .'

'Put the two halves of the money together for this pair and take our leave.'

As Don climbed out, he saw French talking animatedly to Zlenko, who by contrast looked half asleep. Zlenko opened the holdall Harkness had delivered for French to examine the contents. He gave a curt nod of approval.

'You have my bag, Don?' Harkness asked.

'Here.' Don leant back into the car to retrieve the money-filled bag and handed it over.

358

'French is happy?'

'I wouldn't exactly say that. But you were right. He couldn't say no.'

'Money's the universal pass-key, Don. It opens all doors.'

At that moment French shouted across the yard to them, 'We have somewhere better to be even if you don't.'

'I won't hold you up long,' Harkness shouted back as he ambled round to the rear of the 4WD, carrying the bag. As he went, he glanced into the storage compartment of the car, where a tarpaulin was draped over something bulky. 'What have you got there, Amos? Oxyacetylene cutting gear by any chance?'

'Nothing you need to worry about now.'

'Who said I was worried?'

'I guess you must be sometimes. The laid-back couldn't-give-a-shit act doesn't fool me.'

'Nothing fools you, does it, Amos?'

'Not much.'

'Sorry our latest run-in is ending so anti-climactically.' Harkness handed the bag to French. 'Two and a half plus two and a half makes five,' he went on. 'That'll buy you all the fun there is to be had in the land of cowbells and cuckoo clocks.'

French gave him a stiff look. 'You want to laugh about making Gennady and me rich, go right ahead. We'll be the ones laughing when they measure you up for a prison jumpsuit.'

'I don't see that ever happening.'

'You can run from Uncle Sam, but you can't hide from him. You'll learn that the hard way.'

'Will I? Well, thanks for—'

Harkness broke off at the sound of a vehicle approaching along the lane. They all looked towards it. An interruption was the last thing any of them needed. Don found himself fervently hoping the vehicle would drive on by. He noticed Zlenko reaching behind his back and lifting his jacket clear of something in his waistband that Don greatly feared was a gun.

The vehicle did not drive on by. Worse still, as it turned into the yard, Don saw that it was a police car. It stopped and a fresh-faced young uniformed constable got out. He had a passenger, who also got out. To Don's utter astonishment, it was Wynsum Fry.

'Can we help you, officer?' Harkness asked casually. Then, and only then, he saw Fry. 'Well, well, well,' he added, as if merely mildly surprised.

'Are you Jack Harkness, sir?' the constable asked.

'That's 'im right enough,' said Fry. 'The King o' Spades.'

The constable glanced down at a piece of paper in his hand. A print-out of Harkness's photograph was Don's guess. 'Well, sir?'

'I have the feeling there's no point denying it,' said Harkness.

''E murdered my brother,' said Fry, her face flushed with satisfaction.

'Perhaps you should get back in the car, Miss Fry,' said the constable, though it was obvious he had little expectation that would happen.

'I take it you're not here to pursue the outlandish allegation Miss Fry's just made against me, officer,' said Harkness.

'I'm here concerning a breach of your bail conditions in London, sir. I'm going to have to ask you to come with me.'

'If I refuse?'

'I'll have to arrest you.'

'You've come rather light-handed, haven't you? You obviously didn't expect any problem.'

The constable glanced at Don and French and Zlenko.

He did not look reassured by what he saw. 'Is there going to be a problem, sir?'

'Perhaps you didn't expect to find me here. I could well understand if you doubted Miss Fry's word.'

''E don't doubt me now,' said Fry.

'How did you know I'd be here, Wynsum?'

'Linda 'Ocking trusts me more'n 'er brainless 'usband. That's 'ow.'

'Ah, I see.'

'Are you going to be reasonable, Mr Harkness?' the constable asked plaintively.

'Certainly. Mind if I bring my luggage along?' Harkness pointed to the bags standing on the ground next to him.

'The bags stay,' said French suddenly, his voice a shard of ice in the warmth of the morning.

'They belong to me,' said Harkness, stooping to gather them up.

'Leave them where they are,' said French, grabbing Harkness by the arm.

It was not clear to Don how what happened next actually happened, but one of the bags fell open in Harkness's grasp and the contents spilt out on to the cobbles.

Nobody spoke for several seconds. Then the constable said, 'That looks like a lot of money.'

Harkness smiled at him. 'A tidy sum, officer, yes. And all mine.'

'Or 'is creditors,' Fry cut in.

The constable looked round at her, then back at Harkness – and French. 'Bring the bags along, Mr Harkness. If these gentlemen have any—'

'The bags aren't leaving here,' said French, his tone implacable.

'In the circumstances,' the constable said slowly, 'I think they're going to have to.'

361

'No.'

'I'm afraid—'

Maybe it was a step – or half-step – the constable took towards the bags that set Zlenko off. The gun, an automatic pistol of some kind, was in his hand – in both hands – before Don was properly aware of it. He fired three times in quick succession. And the constable toppled backwards.

He hit the cobbles with a gasp that was probably just breath being expelled from his body. He did not move. Neither did anyone else. Blood, thick and dark, began to ooze from beneath him, filling and soon overtopping the crevices between the cobbles.

Then someone did move. Wynsum Fry began to run towards the lane. Don turned towards her. Three more shots – then a fourth – boomed out.

The bullets took her in the back. She stumbled and fell, face down beside the police car. A sound came from her mouth – a groan, an inaudible word. Her legs moved, as if she was trying to crawl forward. Zlenko walked unhurriedly over to where she lay and fired two more bullets into her. She was still then, quite still. Soon there was more blood spreading across the cobbles.

'You shouldn't have done that, Gennady,' said Harkness, with no hint of alarm in his voice. 'This isn't Russia. Killing a police officer has serious consequences. And you can't buy yourself out of them.'

Don was too frightened to move. He clung to the precarious notion that they had forgotten he was there – and somehow might go on forgetting.

'Don't think I'm ungrateful where Wynsum Fry's concerned. The woman was a thorn in my flesh. But the policeman? Nice young fellow, wearing a wedding ring, I notice. You might find a snap of his wife and children behind the sun visor in his patrol car, if you care to look.'

'It was your fault,' said French. 'If you'd agreed to leave the money behind, he'd still be alive.'

'True. But fault and responsibility aren't quite the same thing, are they?'

'Now you've landed us in this shit, give me one good reason why I shouldn't let Gennady shoot you here and now and give me the pleasure of never hearing your sanctimoniously superior voice again.'

'There are actually several good reasons, Amos. We can start with a subject close to your heart. The money.'

'What about the money?'

'You can't spend it.'

'Why the fuck not?'

'I'm afraid it's all in withdrawn notes. The Swiss National Bank has been busily issuing new notes over the past couple of years. And those in the bag are old stock. Redeemable at the bank, of course. But nowhere else. I'm not sure you'll want to jump through the bureaucratic hoops necessary to realize their face value. There could be a lot of awkward questions for you to answer.'

French looked as if he could not decide whether to believe Harkness or not. 'Why would you tell me that now?'

'Because, if you take me to Wortalleth West, I can open the panic room and give you what Quintagler want. Then you'll still come out of this with a healthy profit. Whatever cutting gear you've got hold of, it'll take you longer to get through the door than you want to spend in the area after what's happened here. Fortunately, there's an emergency opening mechanism. And I can show you where it is.'

'What's in the room?'

'A computer system that operates a continuous rolling sweep of my assets, moving them from account to account, from jurisdiction to jurisdiction, faster than anyone can keep track of. But you'll have the access codes to pass on to Quintagler, so it'll be job done as far as they're concerned.'

French paused and thought for a second. Then, to Don's horror, the phone in his pocket started ringing. He pulled it out and switched it off. But French was looking at him now. And so was Zlenko.

'I'll cooperate only if you agree to let both of us go after you've got what you need,' said Harkness. 'There's to be no more killing.'

It occurred to Don, as he felt sure it must have occurred to Harkness, that French could easily give such an under-taking, only to break it later. All Don could do was hope Harkness had taken that possibility into account.

French was still looking at Don. 'Toss the phone over here,' he said flatly. Don obeyed. French pocketed it, then turned to Harkness. 'Yours too.' Harkness handed his over. 'And the keys for Wortalleth West.' Harkness sur-rendered those as well.

'OK,' French continued after a pause. 'Get us into the room. Get us the codes. Then you and Don walk. Agreed. But if you pull any more tricks . . .'

'No tricks, Amos. I just want this over.'

'Amen to that.'

Don realized he was trembling uncontrollably. The morning was still and bright, the sunlight strong on his back. The sight of the two dead bodies lying in the yard seemed to have no place in the silence and serenity by which they were surrounded. But they were there. And so was he.

Suddenly, the silence was split by the buzz of a Royal Naval helicopter, moving low across the sky away to the south-west. French watched anxiously as it flew on, then said to Harkness, 'We need to get these bodies out of sight. You and your friend can move them into the garage. We'll stow the patrol car there as well.'

'You're the boss,' said Harkness.

'Yeah, I am. So, get to it.'

The garage was the only part of the barn conversion that had been completed. Zlenko opened the doors and stood by while Don helped Harkness carry the policeman and Wynsum Fry into the building. It was a gruesome and arduous task. They ended up dragging the policeman on his heels. Blood trailed across the cobbles behind him. Carrying Wynsum Fry face down left Don grasping her ankles, with her skirt riding up around her mottled legs as they went. He tried to pretend the horror he was caught up in was not actually happening, but his senses told him otherwise. The touch of her flesh against his hands made his stomach heave. He had to stop at one point when a wave of nausea swept over him. He wondered if the spell Fry had cast on him the week before could still be affecting him.

Harkness seemed to guess what he was thinking. 'None of the special powers she claimed to have were any use to her, were they, Don?' He spoke in an undertone, as Don leant forward, breathing heavily and resting his hands on his knees. They were just out of Zlenko's earshot and French had gone into the cottage. 'Life and death are realities even she couldn't deny.'

'Why . . . did you . . . refuse to leave the money?'

'I couldn't think of any other way to stop myself getting arrested. I had no idea how Gennady was going to react.'

'So, what he did . . . wasn't your fault. But you *were* responsible.'

Harkness smiled grimly. 'I can't argue with my own words, can I?'

'Are you . . . planning something?'

'What's hold-up?' Zlenko called before Harkness could reply.

'No hold-up,' Harkness shouted back over his shoulder. 'We're coming.'

They heaved Fry off the ground and staggered on towards the garage. Harkness caught Don's eye and winked. *Trust me*, he might almost have said. *We'll be all right*.

But how could they be all right? Zlenko had killed three people already. Why should he hesitate to kill two more? There was no way out of this horror as far as Don could see. None at all.

As they lumbered past him, Zlenko said something to Harkness in Russian. And Harkness smiled.

'What was that?' Don whispered as they reached the rear of the garage and lowered Fry to the floor beside the policeman.

'I'll tell you later,' Harkness replied.

Later. In that moment, it sounded to Don more like a place than a time. It sounded like the promised land – which he might never reach.

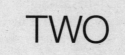

TWO

WE'RE ON THE MOTORWAY, HEADING TOP SPEED FOR ZUG. FILIPPO'S TRIED to talk the taxi driver into going even faster, as far as I can tell from their exchanges in German, but he isn't having any. There's not much traffic, though. We're eating up the miles. There was a long tunnelled section after we left Zürich. Now we're in the open, surging along in silence.

I'm in the back with Jane. No one's saying anything. Filippo's squirming and twitching and eyeing the satnav like it's hiding something from him. But Jane's still as a statue. Occasionally, she pushes back a strand of hair from her forehead. Otherwise, she's just super-chilled. I tried to ask her some questions right after we set off, but she shook her head and whispered, 'Not here.' Then I tried telling her a few things, about her father and sister. She soon cut that off. 'Don't talk to me about them.' That was what she said, with a kind of hollowness, a distance in her voice.

I don't understand her. Maybe I never will. Or maybe, when we get to Harkness HQ—

My phone rings. I pull it out of my pocket, relieved Don's called back.

But he hasn't. The caller's withheld his number. It's someone else. And no one else should have *my* number.

I feel sick looking at the pulsing call symbol on the screen. Do I answer?

Shit, yes. I have to. 'Hello?'

No voice at the other end, just a faint crackle.

'Hello? Who's that?'

They cut the call. They've heard enough. Shit, shit, shit.

'Your friend?' murmurs Jane.

'No.'

'You look worried.'

I am. But I'm not going to admit that to her. I turn the phone off. 'I thought you didn't want to talk.'

She gives me a cool, calm, superior glance. 'I don't.'

I return the glance with knobs on. She gets the message. But she probably sees through it too. There's something in Jane that reminds me of Harkness. It's like he's moulded her in his image.

'You could phone the hospital,' I suggest, partly to get under her defences, partly because I'd like to know how Gareth is and she'll be able to find out much more easily than me. 'Check on Gareth.'

She looks like she's actually considering it, then says, 'Not now.'

'No calls,' Filippo cuts in, leaning back over the seat. 'No *chiacchierata*.' He flaps his thumb and fingers together, then slashes his hand through the air. The driver glances at him warily, but Filippo doesn't notice. He's looking straight at me. 'No nothing till we're there. OK?'

I shrug. 'OK.'

The driver flexes his shoulders, like they're aching. Maybe the tension's getting to him too. There's plenty of it about. How far *is* it to Harkness HQ now? I peer past Filippo for a view of the satnav. 5.27 kilometres. That's all. We're nearly there.

✥

Don's brain refused to obey him. It continued to replay, over and over, the deaths of the police officer and Wynsum Fry. It dwelt on the blood and the seeping bullet wounds and the clammy touch of Fry's flesh and the staring blankness of the young man's eyes. What it would not do, bludgeon it however Don liked, was devise any way out of the nightmare he was living through.

They were in French's land-cruiser, driving west from Chybargos towards the main road. Harkness was at the wheel, with French alongside him, holding a gun, a smaller, stubbier-barrelled weapon than Zlenko had used. Don was in the back, next to Zlenko. From the main road it would probably take less than twenty minutes to reach Wortalleth West, though they might as well already be there for any difference thinking about it was likely to make.

'Bloody hell,' he muttered under his breath as another wave of recollection hit him, bearing the exact sound of the policeman's body hitting the cobbles at Chybargos.

'What's that, Don?' French glanced back at him.

Don swallowed hard. 'Nothing.'

'Where's your friend Blake?'

'I don't know.'

'Sure about that?'

'Leave the poor chap alone,' Harkness cut in.

French gave him a theatrically wide-eyed stare. 'Well, pardon me all to hell. I guess you don't like my idea of light conversation, Jack.'

'Not much.'

'Let's change the subject, then. The Fry bitch. Tell me what made her think you offed her brother. And did you, by the way?'

'What does it matter? He's dead. Now she's dead. End of story.'

'You said she was a thorn in your flesh. What kind of thorn?'

'She caused me as much trouble as she could. But it was never anything I couldn't handle.'

'Why'd she call you the King of Spades?'

'Oh, she fancied herself as some kind of fortune-teller. Card readings, that kind of thing.'

'She looked quite a handful to me. In the short time we were acquainted.'

'She was a witch,' Don said, his voice dull and almost, to his own ears, disembodied. In the second after he had spoken, he did not know why he had spoken at all.

French frowned at him. 'The real thing, you mean? Spells? Cures? Curses?'

Don nodded feebly. 'The real thing.'

'Well, I declare. Hear that, Gennady?' French grinned at Zlenko. 'You killed a witch. Is that a first for you?'

Zlenko responded initially with silence, then: 'Witch?'

'The old woman was a witch. Y'know. Eye of newt and tongue of frog.'

'*Toe* of frog,' Harkness corrected him.

French scowled. 'Is that right? Well, happen to know the Russian for witch, Jack?'

'*Vedima*,' Harkness fired back.

'Great. There you go, Gennady. The old woman was a . . . *vedima.*'

More silence from Zlenko. Then a sudden burst of Russian. He did not sound happy, a point he emphasized by leaning forward and grasping Harkness's shoulder so tightly he had to correct a sudden swerve.

'Watch what you're goddam doing,' French complained.

But Zlenko took no notice. 'Is true?' he rasped. '*Vedima?*'

'A lot of people thought so.'

Zlenko released Harkness and rounded on Don. 'You. You said it. Is true? She was . . . witch?'

Don shrugged. 'Yeah.'

'How you know?'

'She put a curse on me when I wouldn't do what she wanted.' Zlenko looked worried now and Don saw no reason not to worry him some more. 'Maybe you should watch out.'

Zlenko's mouth flapped open. His face suddenly lost a lot of colour. His eyes revolved helplessly. '*Nyet*,' he murmured. '*Nyet*.' Then he crossed himself and mumbled something in Russian. And then he grabbed Harkness again and shouted, 'Stop car.'

'We're not stopping till we get to Wortalleth West,' snapped French.

'*Stop car.*'

Harkness was being pulled so far out of his driving seat by now he had little choice but to brake sharply to a halt. The car bumped up on to the verge, the roadside hedge scraping against its metalwork and the gas cylinders clunking together in the luggage compartment.

They were all pitched around and French dropped his gun, which he retrieved with an oath.

'What the fuck are you playing at, Gennady?' he demanded, whirling round to confront his partner.

'She was witch,' Zlenko replied, as if that was an explanation in itself.

'So?'

'So . . . we have to . . . do something.'

'We are doing something. Our job. Now shut the fuck up and let's get on with it.'

'No.' Zlenko pressed at his throat, as if he felt sick. 'You cannot . . . look away from eye that never blinks.'

373

'*What?*'

Zlenko slumped back in his seat, almost visibly deflating. 'I am dead,' he muttered.

French offered no sympathy. 'For fuck's sake pull yourself together.'

'Fuck you,' growled Zlenko. '*I* shot her. Not you.'

'Well, we'll sacrifice a goat later if it makes you feel better. Meanwhile—'

Zlenko let out a wild cry and tugged at his collar. 'I am burning.' His face was bathed in sweat. His hands were shaking.

'You're imagining it.'

'That's what I told myself when I couldn't use my right hand properly,' said Don. 'But I still couldn't use it.'

Suddenly, Zlenko flung the door open and half climbed, half fell out into the road. He blundered across to the opposite verge and threw up.

'Both of you stay where you are,' said French. 'I'll shoot either of you if you get out of the car.'

'We're going nowhere,' said Harkness, soothingly. 'Isn't that right, Don?'

'Sure,' said Don.

Zlenko staggered back to the car and clambered in, though he left the door open, even when a van blared its horn as it pulled out round them.

'Close the fucking door, Gennady,' growled French.

Zlenko made no move. Don stretched cautiously past him and pulled the door to. He caught Zlenko's eye as he did so and saw in it all the fear ancient superstition could inspire. An idea came suddenly to him and he knew at once he was going to act on it.

'There's a way to neutralize her power over you,' he said, looking at Zlenko.

'*Shto?*' the Russian mumbled.

374

'Another witch told me about it. You need a piece of clothing she wore next to her skin.'

'Shut the fuck up, Don,' French cut in. 'We don't need your ten cents' worth.'

'*You* shut up,' Zlenko growled. He prodded Don. 'Finish what you say.'

'Well, you have to take a piece of clothing she wore next to her skin to the place where she was born and—'

'Hold on, Don,' said Harkness, twisting round in the driving seat. 'Where—'

'Close your mouth,' Zlenko shouted, pushing the barrel of the gun against the back of Harkness's neck. 'Now finish what you say, Don. What you do at place where she born?'

'You burn the piece of clothing.'

'And then?'

'Then you're free of her.'

'We're not—' French began. But his words were swallowed by Zlenko's.

'You know where she born?'

'Yes. Tredarvas Farm. It's a ruin near Mullion. Jack knows where it is. He can take us there.'

'Is true?' Zlenko demanded, still pressing the gun into Harkness's neck.

'I could take you there, yes. But—'

'We're not going anywhere except Wortalleth West,' said French, with fractionally less confidence than before.

'We go Wortalleth West *after*,' said Zlenko with flat finality.

'For fuck's sake—'

'We go back for piece of clothing now.'

'That's crazy. It's only a matter of time before the cops show up there looking for their buddy.'

'We go back. We get what we need.'

'What *you* need – or are stupid enough to believe you need.'

'Then we go to . . .'

'Tredarvas Farm,' said Don.

'You think you're being clever, don't you, Don?' rasped French. 'You'll change your mind about that before we're done. You've got my personal guarantee on that.'

'Turn round car,' said Zlenko.

'We shouldn't go back to Chybargos,' Harkness said, glancing cautiously towards French.

'You don't need to tell me that.'

'Who was the other witch you spoke to, Don?'

'She never gave me her name. Maris Hemsley put me in touch with her.'

'Is that really true?'

'Why would I lie?'

There was an obvious answer to that question, but Harkness never got the chance to supply it. 'Turn round car now, Harkness,' shouted Zlenko. 'Or I blow off your fucking head.'

French pressed his hand to his forehead. 'You better do as he says.'

And Harkness nodded glumly. 'OK. We go back.'

❖

The taxi dumps us in the forecourt of some massive corporate complex on the outskirts of Zug. It's Harkness Pharmaceuticals HQ, a little city of its own built of blue steel and grey glass, with lots of water to reflect its towered roofline and lots of trees to soften its image.

There's a fountain out front. The water's playing on a statue of a pair of serpents wrapped round a staff with wings on it. I recognize the thing as some kind of medical symbol. It should mean the company's dedicated to keeping

376

people well, I guess. But it could mean they're only joking about that.

'What's that?' I ask Jane as we hurry past the statue towards the building's main entrance.

'The Caduceus,' she says quietly. 'The wand carried by Mercury, messenger of the Gods.'

'And what's the message?'

'The message for you is that you can still turn and walk away and we won't try to stop you.'

'I'm not going to do that.'

'I know. But you should.'

Two sets of doors slide open to admit us. Filippo speeds to the reception desk – a long slab of dark blue guarded over by a poker-faced guy in a matching suit. He recognizes Filippo, but he's not quite sure about Jane and he's definitely not sure about me. There's some chit-chat in German. Filippo and Jane press their palms against some kind of reader and get issued with passes to hang round their necks. I catch myself wondering if Jane ever had her fingerprints taken when she was still Jane Glasson.

There's no palm-printing for me, just a picture. I dodge eye contact with the camera lens and get a pass stamped *GAST*. We're in.

We go up several floors in a virtually silent lift. I can hear Filippo breathing like a guy who's just been jogging. Jane, on the other hand, doesn't seem to be breathing at all.

'What are you planning to do in Harkness's office, Filippo?' I ask.

He glares at me. 'Talk to Astrid, not me. I don't want you here.'

'We're not going to tell you what we're doing until we've done it,' says Jane.

'That's not good enough.'

'It's all you're getting.'

The lift doors swish open, which is the only sign we've reached the floor Filippo pressed the button for. I never noticed any deceleration at all. We step out and move along a wide, gleaming corridor. The floor's . . . sprung, I guess. It gives slightly, or seems to. Sound is faintly muffled. Light is bright, but mellow – golden, you could say. It feels more like a top-class sanatorium than a corporate office.

'I can tell Ingrid Denner a load of stuff you don't want her knowing, Jane,' I say, quietly, but with a lot of emphasis.

'She won't be here yet.'

'But she'll be arriving soon.'

'Not soon enough.'

We cross a bridge between two blocks of the building. Down below, a car is moving slowly in the vast, L-shaped car park, while a guy on a mower cuts dead-straight stripes on a lawn big enough to graze a herd of cattle on.

Then we're back inside the steel and glass body of Harkness HQ. One turn of the corridor. Two sets of double doors. By the third, there's a security man, built like an Alp, with a face like a cliff that Filippo's twitchy little smile slides straight off. They talk in German, the volume dialling up steadily as the Alp doesn't do what Filippo wants. I guess Harkness's personal office is on the other side of the door. And I guess Filippo isn't getting the instantaneous access he reckons he's entitled to.

Jane says something. She speaks slowly and softly. She sounds . . . in control. The Alp blinks and talks into a microphone on his lapel.

A second later, the door opens. A short, slim, grey-brown-haired woman looks out at us. She's wearing a dark blue (naturally) trouser suit. She has a face like a no longer young pixie – round, lined, eager.

'*Hertha,*' says Filippo, making her Hertha Rietz, mentioned in Ingrid's last email. He goes on in German.

'Why are you here?' Hertha responds in English. 'You also, Astrid.'

'We have a meeting later,' says Jane, oh-so-smoothly.

'In symposium room B4, *ja*.' Hertha's voice is brittle and polished, like expensive glass. The message is clear. Symposium room B4 isn't here. It's probably not even close.

'We need to check a few things before we sit down with Ms Denner,' says Filippo. 'We're cleared for access to the Chairman's suite.'

'By the Chairman, *ja*. Not by the Board.'

'Chairman's clearance is good enough,' says Jane.

'That's, ah . . .'

'Arguable.' The door is pulled wider open. Ingrid Denner steps into view. She's kitted up for battle, sleek-tailored, hair just so, eyes piercing, even before they land on me. 'What in hell is *she* doing here?'

'Hi, Ingrid,' I greet her casually.

'Signor Crosetti, Ms Townsend.' The politeness is choking Ingrid, but she gets the words out. 'This young woman participated in placing an illegal spying device on my laptop while I was in London. She's a serious threat to the security of Harkness Pharmaceuticals and certainly shouldn't have been brought on to the premises.'

'We don't know anything about that,' says Jane.

'Well, you do now. You—' Ingrid flaps a hand at the Alp. I get the feeling she's about to have me escorted somewhere I don't want to go.

'I've got evidence about these two you need to hear, Ingrid.' I fire out the words and get her to meet my gaze. 'You came here for answers, didn't you? Well, I've got some for you.'

'Don't listen to her,' says Filippo. He launches a volley of German at Hertha, maybe aimed at undermining Ingrid. Harkness's personal computer is through this door somewhere.

And that's where he wants to be. Without Ingrid *or me* hanging on his shoulder.

Hertha replies in German at first. Then she switches to English. 'We are required to give Ingrid full cooperation. It is a Board decision.'

'That includes giving her the run of Jack's private office, does it?' asks Jane, accusingly.

'*Ja.* I am sorry. I personally regret, Astrid . . . where we have come to.'

'I'm authorized to do whatever I need to do to get to the truth concerning your duties for the company, Signor Crosetti, Ms Townsend,' Ingrid says in her crispest won't-take-any-nonsense style. 'That's why we'll be meeting later.'

'Why wait?' Jane looks at Ingrid with a cool, open expression. 'Why don't we just go in there, sit down and talk it through – all of us?'

'No, no,' says Filippo. 'That's not—'

Jane cuts him off with 'We have nothing to hide.' That's obviously untrue. It's so untrue it goes beyond a lie. It's more a kind of . . . dare. 'Well, Ms Denner? Will that suit you?'

Ingrid frowns at her. 'I guess you know Harkness has his private system locked up tight, don't you? That's why you feel you can get away with a show of confidence like this.'

'I – we – don't aim to *get away* with anything. Do you want to talk – here, now – or not?'

'What about her?' Ingrid points at me.

'She seems to think she has something to contribute.' You bet I do.

Ingrid's face is a picture of confusion. She doesn't know who or what to believe. Filippo mutters something to Jane in Italian. She doesn't respond. He mutters some more, runs his fingers through his hair and adds one other Italian word I do understand. '*Merda.*'

'Well?' prompts Jane.

Ingrid gives way. You can see it before she says it. Logically, she has nothing to lose. But she's not sure. She's stopped trusting logic. Even so . . . 'All right,' she says. 'You'd better all come in here.'

※

Don had hoped the police would be waiting for them at Chybargos, spelling the end of the whole horrific episode. But there were no police, except the dead officer in the garage. French kept saying how crazy it was to have returned there. 'Fucking superstitious bullshit,' he complained. But Zlenko paid no attention. He was acting within a belief system in which French counted for less than nothing.

'Give me key,' he told Harkness when they had come to a halt in the yard. Harkness pulled it out of the ignition and handed it over. 'You stay here.' He meant Harkness and French. And he obviously did not trust French to wait for him. 'We do this.' By *we* he meant himself and Don.

They got out of the car and headed for the garage. Don had not thought till now about the ghastly practicality of the idea he had planted in Zlenko's mind. He already had an item of Wynsum Fry's underclothing, but he had left it at Wortalleth West and he was doing everything he could to delay their arrival at the house. Besides, Zlenko might not believe it was genuine. As to that, there was only one way he could be certain.

Zlenko flung the garage door open and gestured with the gun for Don to go in. He made his way along the side of the police car, with Zlenko breathing like a bellows behind him. Rounding the bonnet, they reached the spot where Don and Harkness had dumped the bodies. Don tried not to look at them directly. There was a smell rising from them, of blood and death and the brink of decay. He felt sick to his stomach.

381

'Do it,' said Zlenko.

Don dropped to his knees beside Fry. He fumblingly undid the laces of her grubby grey trainers and pulled them off, then tugged the brown socks off her feet. They were damp with her sweat. He swallowed hard and looked up at Zlenko to check he was content they had what they needed.

But Zlenko shook his head. The feet were evidently not close enough to the essence of a witch's being for his purposes. He pointed towards Fry's waist. '*Trusiki*,' he growled.

Don had a queasy feeling he knew what *trusiki* meant. He could only hope he was wrong. The hope did not last long. Zlenko hitched up the hem of Fry's skirt with the toe of his shoe. '*Trusiki*,' he repeated.

'Bloody hell,' Don murmured.

'Do it.'

'OK.' Don took a deep breath and held it. He pulled Fry's coat out of the way and yanked her skirt up above her thighs. She was wearing large white knickers. There was a tide of dampness on them and he felt sure he would smell urine as soon as he took another breath.

'Do it quick,' said Zlenko.

Don reached up under the skirt and grasped the waistband of the knickers. He tried to pull them straight off, but they caught between her legs. He had to roll her first one way, then the other, to get them down over her knees. By then, he had to refill his lungs. The smell was just as bad as he had feared. He thought for a second he would throw up, but as he held his breath again and pulled the skirt down over her knees the sensation passed.

Part of a plastic bag was protruding from Fry's coat pocket. Don pulled it out, thinking to store the socks and knickers inside it. A pack of cards, bound in a pair of rubber bands, one black, one red, came with it and fell to the floor. It was surely the pack she had tempted Don with at the Blue Anchor.

'Put back cards,' said Zlenko.

Don picked up the pack and stuffed it back into Fry's pocket, exposing a card on the bottom of the pack as he did so. The nine of spades. He heard Zlenko suck in his breath. It evidently meant something to him, though not to Don. He looked up questioningly.

It was immediately obvious Zlenko was a frightened man. The gun was shaking slightly in his hand. 'We go now,' he said.

Don stuffed the socks and knickers into the bag and tied a loose knot in it. Then he stood up. Zlenko had retreated to the door and was gesturing for Don to follow. '*We go.*'

There was no arguing with that. Don hurried out into the yard. Zlenko closed the door and gestured for him to head back to the car.

French's greeting was predictably sour. 'Can we get the fuck out of here now?'

Zlenko nodded. '*Da.*' He turned to Don and signalled for him to hand over the bag. Now he had what he had come for, he did not want to be separated from it. 'We go.'

✤

As we walk into Harkness's office, I realize we're in a slender block isolated from the rest of the complex. We're looking across and down at a lot of windows, but not up at any. Above is just the grey sky.

There's a conference table and beyond that a desk set in an island of space, with a couple of PCs on a side-table. There are tall metal-doored cupboards with ventilation panels through which I can see lights blinking, on back-up hard

drives, maybe, to power whatever Filippo meant by a relay –
an override for his override in Locarno, as he called it.

There's something else I notice as well. Another Lanyon,
hanging on the wall nearest the desk, where it catches the
morning light: red and green and blue, with narrow strips of
black plastic laid across the canvas.

No one else gives the art a second glance. Ingrid sits
herself at the head of the table, with her back to the desk.
Hertha sits to her left, Jane to her right. I plant myself next to
Jane. Filippo hovers on the other side of the table, a tor-
mented look on his face, hands locked together. His eyes
keep darting towards Harkness's PC, about four metres
away.

'Are you going to join us, Signor Crosetti?' Ingrid asks.

Filippo doesn't answer. But he does sit down.

'Mind if I call you Filippo?'

He doesn't respond to that either.

'Astrid?'

Jane smiles faintly. 'First names are fine.' Maybe she's
amused by the irony that Astrid isn't her real name anyway.

'Like Hertha says, the Board requires you both to give me
all and any information I require.'

'I could argue my contract imposes no such obligation on
me,' says Jane.

'And are you going to argue that?'

'Maybe.'

'Well, your consultancy is under Filippo's direct supervi-
sion, correct?'

'Yes.'

'And you, Filippo, are an employee of Harkness Pharmaceuticals, not a consultant, also correct?'

Filippo nods dumbly.

'So, you'll be able to tell me why you've resourced so

much apparently irrelevant work in nanotechnology and bio-electronics, as detailed in my email of the twelfth.'

'It's not irrelevant,' Filippo says in a voice not much above a whisper.

'I spoke to some of these people, Filippo. High-powered in their fields. The best, in fact, charging accordingly. This company's been funding – that is, Astrid here, representing this company with your full authority – has been funding a whole range of research projects in fields which have no obvious bearing on the development of new pharmaceutical products or the improvement of existing ones.'

'How would you know?'

'I also have reason to believe you've been the conduit for a vast package of additional funding that doesn't appear to have any booked source, which I can only assume Jack Harkness put in place for the purpose.'

'I'm not an accountant.'

'No. You're a chemist. So, what is the chemical application of the work you've paid for so generously and abundantly?'

'Bioelectronics are the future, Ingrid,' says Jane suddenly. 'Implants to fight pain by targeting electrical signals in damaged nerves are a therapeutic game-changer.'

'Exactly,' says Filippo.

'Could well be,' agrees Ingrid. 'But then I have three questions. One, why is it being funded in such a surreptitious manner? Two, why is it being funded to what appears such a ruinous cost level? And three, why has the Board never been told about this . . . game-changer?'

Filippo shrugs. 'They don't want to know anything, as long as the profits keep rolling in.'

'I have checked all Board documentation for the past five years,' says Hertha. 'There is not even a single background briefing paper on this.'

'I did what Jack asked me to,' Filippo responds. It sounds like he thinks that's an answer for everything. But it doesn't sound like an answer to Ingrid. Or to me. What did Harkness *really* ask him to do?

'Doctor Alan Tau, Cambridge University. Nanotechnology pioneer. You're familiar with his work? Well, I should hope so, considering you're paying for most of it. But what are you getting for all that money, Filippo? What is Harkness Pharmaceuticals getting for it?'

'Deliverability.'

'Pardon me?'

'Can I explain?' offers Jane.

'Please do.'

'Doctor Tau's specialism is nanobot mobility and communication. Nanobots – that is, microscopic medical robots, about one-thousandth the diameter of a human hair – can be introduced into the human bloodstream and nervous system via any or all of Harkness Pharmaceuticals' existing products.'

'Hold on,' says Ingrid. 'I thought nanobots were purely theoretical devices.'

'Not as such. They can be made using current technologies and delivered via drugs and cosmetics. The problem is moving them around the body and determining where and when they perform their design function.'

'What function would that be?' I ask. Maybe we're close to an answer now.

Jane smiles at me. Anyone would think she was enjoying herself. 'It could be biochemical or bioelectronic, or some combination of the two.'

'Is this what you've been working on with Harkness for the past twenty-two years?'

Jane turns her smile on Ingrid. 'I get the feeling Blake wants to present her theory to you that I'm actually someone called Jane Glasson.'

386

Ingrid doesn't miss a beat. 'And are you?'

'You may as well hear what she has to say. Then you'll be able to make your mind up. Whatever you conclude won't make any difference, though.'

'No difference?'

'To the future.'

'Of the company, you mean?'

Jane doesn't answer. She just looks at me. 'Go on, Blake,' she says. 'Tell her who you think I once was. I'm really looking forward to hearing all about me.'

✣

Delay and diversion had so far achieved nothing. Don's last, lingering hope was that the local police might have been sent to Wortalleth West looking for Harkness on instructions from the Met. If so, he had to hope they would be there when he, Harkness, French and Zlenko eventually showed up.

French lapsed into a grouchy silence and no one else found anything to say as they drove west to the main road, then north to Mullion.

Considering French and Zlenko were both carrying guns, any idea of jumping out and making a run for it was suicidal. Don looked at the shoppers and holidaymakers wandering along the main shopping street and felt he was looking at a world he was no longer part of.

The air was clear, the light bright. It was the sort of day that should have made the spirit soar. But a black cloud of foreboding had enveloped Don's thoughts. They had not left death behind at Chybargos. It had travelled with them. He seemed to feel its cold breath on the back of his neck. French and Zlenko were killers. When they had what they had come for, what were the chances they would leave alive any witnesses to what they had done?

*

Harkness took the road to Mullion Cove, then turned off down a lane signposted to Predannack. It descended into a valley, then climbed between low-hedged, patchwork fields towards a crest. Halfway to the top, he slowed and swung the car into a rough track that led off to the left.

Ahead was a five-bar gate, beyond which the track continued to some destination out of sight round the hillside. Harkness pulled up. 'Someone needs to open the gate,' he said neutrally.

French turned and nodded meaningfully at Zlenko, who nodded back, then said to Don, 'Get out.'

By the time Don had climbed from the car, Zlenko was out too, the gun visible now in his hand. He stayed a few yards away as Don walked to the gate, pushed it open and wedged it behind a rock.

They got back in the car and Harkness drove on. As they rounded the next bend, the ruined farm appeared ahead: a weed-pocked yard, a house with the roof and most of the front wall gone, but the gable ends still standing; a half-collapsed barn, almost entirely overgrown; another, corrugated-iron structure, fallen in on itself, with the rusting carcass of an old tractor just visible beneath a drift of ivy.

'Welcome to Tredarvas,' said Harkness surprisingly. 'Ancestral home of the Frys.'

'Witch born here?' Zlenko asked anxiously.

'Yes,' Harkness replied. 'Year of our Lord nineteen hundred and fifty-three. It would have looked very different then. As it did in my childhood.'

'I don't want to know the first fucking thing about your childhood,' growled French as the car drew to a halt at the edge of the yard. 'Let's just get this done.'

'Get out,' Zlenko motioned to Don.

'You too, Jack,' French added.

They all climbed slowly from the car. There was bird-song in the air and a freshness in the breeze. But it could not dispel the heaviness of the dread that clung to Don.

'There's a jerrycan of gasoline in the back of the car, Don,' said French. 'Get it.'

Don moved to the rear of the car, raised the tailgate and grabbed the jerrycan. By its weight, it felt full. He noticed a stubby-headed screwdriver lying just clear of the tarpaulin that had been slung over the cutting gear. On some frail impulse of self-preservation, he picked up the screwdriver and slipped it into his pocket as he lifted out the jerrycan.

'It's your show now, Gennady,' said French.

'You know this place good, Harkness?' Zlenko asked.

Harkness smiled grimly. 'I used to.'

'Show me.'

Harkness nodded and led the way to the ruined farm-house. Zlenko tagged along behind him. French brought up the rear with Don.

Harkness stepped through what must once have been the front door. They followed him as he crossed the skel-etal remains of several internal walls until he was standing in the lee of one of the gable ends, next to a weed-choked fireplace.

'This was the kitchen,' he announced. 'As close to the spiritual centre of the house as you'll get. Calensa Fry, Wynsum's grandmother, used to do her readings here. Wynsum learnt most of the witchcraft she knew from Calensa. And this, I'd guess, is where she did most of that learning.'

'Good enough, Gennady?' French asked with an edge of impatience.

'*Da.*' Zlenko gazed around at the little there was to see. He looked almost awestruck. '*Da,*' he repeated. Then he moved closer to where Harkness was standing and toed away some dust and dead leaves from one of the flagstones. He bent down, opened the bag he was carrying and let the contents flop out on to the floor.

'You took those off her?' French asked Don.

All Don could do was nod.

'Rather you than me is all I can say. Get over there with the gasoline.'

Don moved forward and offered the jerrycan to Zlenko.

'No,' said Zlenko. 'You.'

Don opened the can, then started pouring petrol on to the socks and knickers. He did not stop until Zlenko raised his hand.

'Enough.' Zlenko crossed himself, then took out a box of matches, struck one and dropped it on to the clothes. They started burning with a woomph and a dragon's-tongue of blue and yellow flame.

'Can we go now?' asked French, who was standing at Don's shoulder.

'When all burnt,' Zlenko replied, staring at the flames. 'Then we go. Not long.'

Looking at the fire, Don had to agree. It would not be long.

❖

I get the feeling Ingrid's only really interested in the possibility that Astrid Townsend is actually Jane Glasson because it's another example of Harkness's double-dealing. The company's hired her to fight fires and this is another curl of flame she has to stamp on. She doesn't look as if she either believes or disbelieves me. All she seems to be doing, while I speak, is weighing up the potential damage of what I'm claiming.

Jane's playing it cool, like she has the whole time since we left Zürich. Filippo, on the other hand, is het up, squirming and twitching and muttering things in Italian I can't understand but I guess mean he wants this over and Ingrid and Hertha out of his way so he can do whatever it is he came here to do.

He's getting no help from Jane in that direction, though. And Hertha wants to ask him about company funds I say have been diverted through the Nightingale account to pay for Holly Walsh's Ditrimantelline treatment. Filippo tries to brush her off with a line he's already used – 'I'm not an accountant' – but that doesn't work. Hertha pretty obviously smells a rat. 'The Board will require a full report on all this . . . unorthodox and . . . unapproved . . . use of funds that were not allocated for such purposes.'

Ingrid probes Hertha a bit about why a mere consultant – Jane, alias Astrid – has been given so much access to company funds and the authority to spend them pretty much as she pleases. Hertha throws that back on Harkness. 'Chairman's discretion.' Ingrid looks unimpressed. Black mark for Hertha in her final report to the Board, maybe.

A lot worse for Filippo, surely. And for Jane. But she's doing a good impression of not giving a flying fuck. When I've finished, she just says, 'Total nonsense, I'm afraid.'

'So,' says Ingrid, 'you categorically deny being Jane Glasson?'

'Certainly. I'm Astrid Townsend.' She gives a little this-is-all-madness laugh. 'And I always have been.'

Her phone rings at that moment. She takes it out, looks at the screen, then presses a button and puts it away. The whole move only takes a few seconds. But there's a change in her face as those seconds flash by. I see it, though I'm not sure anyone else does.

Except maybe Filippo. He looks at her enquiringly. He seems to want to speak, but he swallows the words. Jane shakes her head so slightly you'd have to be staring hard at her – like I am – to notice. And she smiles, faintly, reassuringly. It's all right, she's telling him. There's nothing to worry about.

But I bet there is.

❖

Zlenko stared at the clothes as they burnt and so did Don. He hardly noticed Harkness turning his back on the scene and reaching into his pocket. Nor did he register the muffled ping of a mobile phone.

But French did. 'What the fuck was that?' he shouted.

Harkness looked over his shoulder at him and smiled. 'Nothing.'

'You've got a second phone, haven't you? Who've you just called?'

'No one.'

'Give it to me.' French pushed past Don and strode through a thick patch of weeds to reach Harkness. He grabbed him by the arm and pulled him round. In his other hand he held his gun. He was angry, as much with the situation as with Harkness's concealment of a second phone. 'I said—'

Then something gave way beneath him. There was a crack of splintering wood. The floor vanished beneath French's feet. He plunged downwards, pulling Harkness with him. Harkness lost his balance and both men tumbled into the hole that had suddenly opened. Don glimpsed the rotten frame of a wooden hatch and the treads of a steep, narrow stairway – the entrance to a cellar, he guessed.

There were several loud thumps as the two men landed at the foot of the stairs. French's gun went off, the noise of the shot echoing like a thunderclap. Someone moaned. Then . . . nothing.

Don rushed to the edge of the hole. Below him he saw

French lying on his back, apparently unconscious. The gun was a foot or so from his right hand. Harkness was slumped in a foetal position against the lowest stair. Blood was spreading from the region of his stomach, a pool of black, as it appeared in the limited light, expanding in a sea of grey.

Don started down the stairs on instinct. They creaked beneath his weight and one tread broke away altogether, but he made it to the bottom and stepped gingerly over Harkness, clear of the blood.

Harkness grimaced up at him. It seemed to Don he was trying to smile. 'Looks like the bitch got me in the end, eh, Don?' He forced the words out through gritted teeth. 'Never should . . . never should have come here. That's . . . down to you.'

Don leant over him. 'Where's the blood coming from?'

'Somewhere in my gut. That damned idiot French didn't actually mean to shoot me. His gun . . . went off when we hit the floor. It doesn't . . . hurt much . . . but I'm a goner. I can feel the life . . . oozing out of me.'

'We'll call an ambulance.'

'Zlenko'll never let you do that.' Harkness craned his eyes upwards. 'Will you, Gennady?'

Zlenko loomed above them in the splintered, cob-webbed hatchway. 'No calls,' he said bluntly. 'If you go for gun,' he added for Don's benefit, 'I shoot you.' The gun in his hand was pointing down at Don, to prove the point.

'They'd be too late . . . anyway,' gasped Harkness. 'Listen, Don. Your only chance . . . of getting out of this alive . . . is to open the panic room.' A groan came from French in that instant. His legs twitched. He began to stir. 'These two . . . will be so busy . . . with what they find . . . you'll probably be able to get away.'

'I don't know how to open it.'

393

Harkness grabbed Don's shirt and pulled him closer. Don knelt down on the cold, hard floor and leant forward until he could feel the weak fanning of the dying man's breath against his face. 'There's a painting . . . on the drawing-room wall. Abstract by . . . Peter Lanyon. *Far West*. Behind it . . . there's a safe. Inside the safe . . . there's a switch. Throw it . . . and the panic-room door opens. Simple.'

'What's the combination?'

'Three numbers. It's an old-fashioned . . . mechanical safe. You know what I mean?'

Don nodded. At the first estate agency he had worked in, there had been an old Chubb in the boss's office. Don still remembered the combination, wheedled out of the boss's secretary over several gin and tonics.

'It's the date . . . I killed Jory Fry. One. Eight. Seventy. Got it?'

Don nodded again. 'Got it.'

'I have a couple of Lanyons. The other's . . . in Zug. And I gave a third . . . to a friend. They're all . . . from his Cornish period. Ever done any gliding . . . Don?'

'No.'

'Clarity. Perspective. Freedom. That's what you find . . . in the sky . . . with no power but the wind to keep you up there. If you can't . . . make it back to the aerodrome . . . you have to put down . . . wherever you can. We call that . . . a field landing . . . Can be bumpy . . . Can be fatal if you get it wrong. I guess . . . this is my field landing . . . Not where I expected . . . but then again . . . Be sure . . . you open that door . . . Don. It's *got* to be opened.'

❖

'I guess I should thank you, Blake,' says Ingrid with a sickly smile. 'You've demonstrated there's no case for making any kind of settlement with you. Your claim that a company consultant may have changed her identity twenty-two years ago doesn't represent any kind of reputational threat to Harkness Pharmaceuticals. The amount of money that may have passed through the Nightingale account is in budgetary terms insignificant. And you've offered nothing in the way of proof that Anna Marchant was planted in Holly Walsh's life by Harkness. To speak frankly, there's no good reason why we should care whether Astrid is actually Jane Glasson or not.'

'Hear that, Jane?' I've got nowhere else to go now. 'You may as well admit it.'

'I'm admitting nothing,' Jane replies, with not a single flicker of a facial reaction.

'How did Harkness talk you into it? What persuaded you to join his team? It went against all your principles, for Christ's sake.'

'I haven't betrayed my principles, Blake. Not then. Not now. Not ever.'

'So, there was a *then*, was there?'

'It doesn't matter,' Filippo cut in. 'Didn't you hear what Ingrid said? This is all . . . bullshit. We should end this meeting.'

'I think you should certainly leave us, Blake,' said Ingrid. 'You have nothing else to contribute, I assume?'

'What about Gareth Lawler?' I'm getting desperate now. 'He wound up in hospital for daring to ask Astrid about her past.'

'That was an accident,' says Jane coolly.

'You know about this?' Ingrid glances at Hertha.

Hertha shakes her head. 'No.'

'*Per l'amor di Dio.*' Filippo thumps his forehead with the heel of his hand. 'Who cares about Gareth Lawler?'

'What happened to him was nothing to do with me,' says Jane. 'He was hit by a truck crossing the road outside his hotel. He probably looked the wrong way. A common mistake by people just arrived from the UK.'

'Still,' says Ingrid, 'I'd like to know more about his activities. I believe he may have put Blake up to planting a bug on my laptop.'

'Ask Blake, then.' Jane suddenly stands up and takes out her phone. 'Ask her all about it.'

She glances at the screen of her phone and thumbs a button, then turns and starts hurrying towards Harkness's desk.

We're all too surprised to react.

There's a whirring noise and I see a steel-shuttered screen descending from the ceiling. It's coming down fast, like a fucking guillotine. It's between us and the desk. And Jane is already the other side of it.

I jump up. So does Filippo. We both move towards Jane. But it's too late. The screen thwacks down into a metal groove in the floor. I hear bolts clicking into place. Jane's out of sight now. The office has been cut in half. She's in one half. We're in the other.

Filippo crashes into the screen and literally bounces off it. He slides down on his knees and rests his head against the steel. He mutters something under his breath.

'What just happened?' Ingrid asks.

I'm not sure if she's expecting an answer.

But she doesn't get one.

❖

French groaned and sat up. He raised one hand to his head and squeezed his eyes tightly shut, as if to ward off a pulse of pain. Then he opened them and looked blearily at Don through the shadows of the cellar. Belatedly, he seemed to focus on Harkness, who lay motionless in a pool of blood at the foot of the stairs.

'What happened?' French asked in a slurred voice.

'You killed him,' said Don. 'You fired your gun as you dragged him down with you.'

'Fuck.'

'Is true,' Zlenko called from the hatchway.

French squinted up at the Russian. 'Fuck,' he repeated.

'But he told Don how to get into panic room before he died, I think.'

French turned his gaze back to Don. 'Is that right?'

Don nodded. 'Yeah. He did.'

French scrabbled around, found his gun and pointed it at Don. 'Tell *me*.'

'Put gun down, Amos,' Zlenko called. 'Or maybe you shoot him also.'

French appeared to register the point, albeit reluctantly. He lowered the gun. 'How do we get into that room, Don?'

'I'm not completely stupid. Take me to the house and I'll open the door for you. Then we're done. That's my offer.'

It was an offer French considered for several long moments. Then he said, 'OK. Let's go.' He turned on to his side and raised himself unsteadily to his feet.

'D'you need help to get up the stairs?' Don asked.

French scowled at him. 'I'll manage. Move.'

Don had to step over Harkness's body to reach the stairs. He climbed gingerly up them and emerged into the daylight to see Zlenko stirring the ashes of Wynsum Fry's burnt clothes with the toe of his boot.

Zlenko looked at Don and gave him a one-sided smile as he clambered out of the hatchway. 'You saw card in witch's pocket? *Devytih pik.*'

Don shrugged helplessly. 'The card showing on the bottom of the pack? It was the nine of spades.'

'*Da*. Nine of spades. Card of death.'

'If you say so.'

'But is Harkness's death. Not mine.' Zlenko chuckled. The irony evidently amused him. 'Now everything OK.'

French appeared behind Don, hauling himself to the top of the stairs. He paused to suck in some breath and looked up. 'Everything isn't OK for you, Don,' he panted. 'Remember that.'

✣

Filippo slithers round and slumps back against the steel screen. He shakes his head slowly and mutters something I can't make out.

'Talk to us, Filippo,' I say, dropping to my haunches beside him. 'What's Astrid done?'

He doesn't look at me. But he does reply. 'The call must have been a message from Jack. She sealed herself in there with his computer to stop me operating the override.'

'The override for what?'

'Cascade.'

'What does that mean?'

'You'll find out soon. Everyone will.'

'How soon?'

'I don't know. It hasn't happened yet. That's why she's locked me out. To make sure I don't stop it. She only pretended to agree with me. It will happen for certain now.'

'What will make it happen?'

'Opening the panic room at Wortalleth West.'

'That's the trigger?'

He nods dolefully. '*Sì*. Cascade cannot be stopped now. Better you don't know what's coming.'

'Maybe it can be stopped. My friend Don. He's in Cornwall. He might be at Wortalleth West. Or close by.'

'Ah. Your friend. The useful idiot.'

398

'That's not what he is.'

'If he's at the house, you can't contact him. Mobile signals are blocked to protect the integrity of the system. If he's not at the house, it's too late.'

'There's a landline, though. I can get through on that.'

Filippo frowns at me, like he's considering whether to pin any hope on what I've just said or not. 'Landline?'

'Isn't it worth a try?'

He's still frowning. But he nods faintly. '*Sì*. It is worth a try.'

'But you're going to have to tell me first what it is we're trying to stop.'

He jumps up, pulling me to my feet with him. 'No time. Make the call.'

'No.' I shake him off. 'Tell me what this is all about, Filippo. Or I do nothing.'

He grimaces, like he's in pain. 'You're crazy. There's too much at stake for a long explanation.'

'Then make it a short one.'

'*Make the call.*'

'*Tell me.*'

For a second, he stares at me dumbly. And I stare back. One of us is going to have to give way. It's not going to be me.

✢

The four-by-four lurched and juddered along the rough track and the farmhouse passed from sight round the swell of the hill. Zlenko was driving, relaxed and self-assured now his brush with black magic had been resolved to his satisfaction. French was sitting up front beside him. Don was in the rear. There was nothing he could do to escape his fate, whatever it was. The lassitude of hopelessness had overcome him.

'Got it,' said French as they rumbled through the open gateway into the last stretch of track before the lane. He had been fiddling with something since leaving the farm and now Don saw what it was: a bloodstained mobile phone. 'The message Jack sent back there. To someone called Astrid Townsend.' French looked over his shoulder. 'Heard of her, Don?'

Don shook his head. 'No.'

'"Cascade imminent." That was the message. What the fuck does it mean?'

'Nothing to me.'

'Me neither.' French switched the phone off. As they swung out into the lane, he lowered the window and tossed it into the hedge. 'We don't need Jack any more. We've got you, Don. Our very own Ali Baba.'

⁘

Filippo looks at me hard. He must be able to tell I'm not going to blink first. '*Merda*,' he mutters. Then he says to Hertha, 'Get Ingrid out of here. Wait for me in your office.'

Hertha responds with a question in German. She sounds clipped and panicky.

'I don't know,' says Filippo. 'But Ingrid shouldn't hear this.'

'That makes me think I *should* hear it,' says Ingrid.

'Get out, Hertha,' Filippo shouts. '*Gehen Sie weg.*'

He looks kind of wild-eyed now. And he sounds close to the end of his tether. Hertha gets that even if Ingrid doesn't. 'OK. We'll go to my office. But I'll, er, need a full report, Filippo.'

'Just go.'

Ingrid looks as if she's going to object. But Hertha's tugging at her elbow. 'I'm sorry, Ingrid. I really think it's best if we leave. I need to consult Head of Security about this screen. I was unaware it existed.'

'It seems there's quite a lot you're unaware of,' says Ingrid acidly. But it doesn't matter. They're halfway through the door by now. I glimpse the Alp outside, looking confused by their hustled exit.

Filippo pushes the door shut and turns the handle as far as it'll go, locking us in. He turns to look at me and runs his fingers through his hair. His eyes are bloodshot. His hands are trembling.

'*Please*,' he says. 'Make the call. It's our only chance.'

'Explain first.'

'It will take too long.'

'That's your problem.'

'No. It's everyone's problem.'

'You're the one wasting time, Filippo.'

'OK, OK.' He holds up his hands. 'I'll tell you. You want to know. So, I'll tell you.'

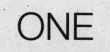

ONE

ZLENKO CUT THROUGH THE LAFLOUDER FIELDS HOUSING estate on his way to Wortalleth West, bypassing the centre of Mullion. The rear doors of the car were on childproof locks. Don had no way out and he was only too well aware French would turn his gun on him if he had to. They travelled as if in a bubble, insulated from the carefree summer's day around them.

Shortly after turning out of Laflouder Fields on to the Poldhu road, they passed Ray Hocking's house. Linda was coming out of the front door at that moment, shopping bag in hand, unaware of the consequences of her betrayal of Harkness to Wynsum Fry. And that, no doubt, was how she preferred it.

It occurred to Don that French and Zlenko were in denial too. Without Harkness, it was unlikely they would be able to make any sense of whatever they found on the panic-room computer system. But they did not want to think about that. They needed a conclusion of some kind. And they meant to have it.

✜

Filippo moves to the foot of the conference table. He leans forward, pressing his hands down against the flat wooden surface. He lets out a long, composing breath. Then he begins.

'Jack and Astrid took me onboard twelve years ago. They convinced me. I believed what they planned to do was right. I still kind of believe it. I just can't—' He pushes his hair back. 'To hold global temperature increase to two degrees above pre-industrial we have to cut carbon emissions to fifty per cent current level by 2050 and then go on cutting down to zero. That won't reduce the temperature rise, but it will hold it at two degrees, where it will stay for a very long time because of the amount of carbon dioxide already in the atmosphere. That means we can't – absolutely can't – go above eight hundred gigatons total carbon emissions. We are over five hundred already. That leaves less than three hundred to go. At current rate, ten gigatons a year, we have less than thirty years to go. Then emissions will have to drop to zero straight away. If not, climate change becomes dangerous. Floods. Storms. Droughts. Famine. Like we've never seen before. You understand? For the human race . . . total disaster.' He stares at me. '*Sì?* You *do* understand?'

''Course.' And I do, kind of, though I can't remember anyone actually spelling it out to me like he has.

'Meantime we're destroying hundreds of thousands of other species on the planet. Plants *and* animals. Current estimate is at least twenty per cent of all species extinct or near extinct by 2050. There have been five mass extinctions on Earth in the last half-billion years. This will be number six. The worst since the dinosaurs were wiped out by the dust from a massive asteroid strike sixty-six million years ago. But *we* will have caused it. Us. *L'umanità.* The human race. You understand?'

'Yes,' I reply. 'I understand. But what's this got to do with—'

'Jack wants to stop it happening. So does Astrid. So do I. So does anyone with a brain. But Jack decided to actually do something about it. That's why he got into pharmaceuticals. He calculated they would be the answer. He recruited Astrid to help him. Then me. We developed a programme to get the result we agreed the world needs: the nanobot programme. Everyone who's used a Harkness Pharmaceuticals drug or cosmetic over the past five years has nanobots in their bloodstream. Also everyone who's eaten food grown using Harkness Pharmaceuticals pesticides or meat from animals treated with Harkness Pharmaceuticals antibiotics. Beauty treatments. Headache cures. Anti-malarials. Pain relief. Elixtris. Fenextris. And the rest. Nanobots are in all of them. Millions of people have swallowed them and injected them and absorbed them through their skin. They're everywhere. They flush out of the system eventually, but they get replaced by more, all the time, rolling out of our factories around the world. Click, click, click, click goes the production line, feeding them out. More and more and more and more. They're a plague without symptoms. Until . . .'

'Until what?'

'Until they're switched on. Doctor Tau has cracked the problem that's held back nanotechnology for the past decade. How to control nanobots from outside the host. How to trigger their pre-designed function. His technique is basically a chain reaction. Trigger one and it triggers another, then another, then another, as long as they're within ultrasonic range. He calls it – we call it – Cascade. The Wortalleth West system is powerful enough to initialize the process. There are overrides here and in Locarno that only Harkness and I know how to operate. Otherwise, no control. No way of stopping it once it starts.'

407

'And what will start it?'

'Breach of the panic room. Jack tried to make it easy for me. Someone will break into the room eventually. They'll trigger Cascade. We won't actually have done it. But they won't realize what they've done. Only we will. Soon, though, very soon, the effect will be clear.'

'What is the effect?'

'Doctor Tau believes we're planning to use his technology to phase nerve-stimulation therapy powered by nano-transducers. But I redesigned the components so the nanobots will discharge an electrical signal modulated to interfere with the bioelectronic system of the host.'

'Interfere with? What does that mean?'

Filippo looks at me for a long moment before he answers. Then he says, his voice so soft I only just catch the words: '*Un arresto cardiaco.*'

'What?'

'Heart failure.'

'You're serious?'

'Completely serious.'

'How many?'

He shrugs. 'More than anyone will be able to count. But more than enough also . . . to keep temperature rise below two degrees.' He shrugs again. 'It's crazy and it's totally sane all at once. Humans are the biggest threat to the human race and all the other species on Earth. You cut the number of humans – you cut it enough – and the threat, it does not go quite away, but . . . it reduces. It reduces massively. You understand?'

I understand. I look at him and I believe him. This is what Harkness designed Wortalleth West for. This is why he took all those steps to protect the power supply to the panic room. This is why he doesn't care about prosecution or imprisonment in the US. This is his masterplan. And all I can say is, 'Fuck.'

✥

Don saw the battered pick-up truck parked up by the garage block as they drove up to the front of the house. French saw it too. 'Whose is that?' he snapped.

'*Sadovot*,' Zlenko replied. 'Woman who digs.'

'The gardener? Shit.' French looked round at Don. 'Why didn't *you* tell me that?'

'I don't recognize the truck,' Don lied – unconvincingly, he suspected. In fact, he recognized the truck very well. What he could not understand, since Glenys had told Blake Harkness had instructed her to stay away from Wortalleth West until further notice, was what she was doing there.

'Can you see her anywhere?' French asked, peering up towards the garden.

'*Nyet*,' said Zlenko.

'Does she have a key to the house, Don?'

'Not as far as I know.' That at least was not a lie.

'OK.' French thought for a moment. Then he said, 'If she doesn't bother us, we won't bother her. Let's get this done.'

French got out of the car. His face was grey and drained of blood and he looked unsteady on his feet. Don reckoned he had to be suffering from concussion after what had happened at Tredarvas. He waggled the gun at Don, signalling for him to get out too.

Zlenko brought up the rear as they climbed the shallow steps to the front door. French unlocked it and in they went. After he had closed the door behind them, he stood listening for a moment. No sound reached Don's ears. He

409

had no reason to think Glenys was in the house, though she was unlikely to have gone far without her pick-up. 'Check the terrace door and the back door, Gennady,' said French when he had listened long enough.

Zlenko crossed the hall and went out into the passage running along the rear of the house. Don heard a rattling of a handle. Zlenko came back and announced, '*Nichivo.*' Then he headed for the kitchen and the utility room.

A few seconds later, he called out, 'Come here. *Bihstri.*'

'Move,' said French. He gestured for Don to lead the way.

They went through the dining room into the kitchen. He was not there. They pressed on into the utility room.

Don flinched in shock when he saw the reason Zlenko had called them. The door of the freezer had opened, probably because of the weight of Coleman's body inside. But he was not inside any longer. His swollen, half-frozen, half-thawed corpse lay on the floor in a pool of water like some massive deep-sea fish discarded on a wharf.

'He fell out,' said Zlenko.

'Yeah,' said French. 'So I see.'

'What you want do?'

'Nothing. We don't have time for you and/or Don to bust a gut heaving him back in the freezer. Leave him where he is and let's get on with what we came here to do. Is the back door locked?'

'*Da.* Locked.'

'Then it's over to you, Don.' French smiled grimly. 'Time to open the panic room.'

✣

I look at Filippo. I scan his face for any sign – any hint – that he doesn't really mean what he's said. I don't see any. 'This is true?' I ask numbly.

410

'*Sì. La verità*. The truth absolute. Cascade will happen once the panic room is breached.'

'And you've been pumping these . . . these nanobots . . . into the world for, like, years?'

'Years, yes. Not so many years when they have been properly designed for the job they will do. But enough years. They will work. Cascade will work.'

'Why did you go along with it?'

'Like I told you. It is madness. But it is sanity also. There is no right answer. Only a wrong answer now and a worse answer later. A choice of catastrophes. Jack would say – Astrid would say – I have lost my nerve. I guess they would be right. But it does not matter now. They have taken it from my hands.'

'But . . . Jane – Astrid – paid for Holly Walsh to get hold of Ditrimantelline. And you're saying . . . it'll kill her.'

'I guess Astrid wants her friend to be comfortable before the end. Her mind cuts through everything. That is why she put her family out of her life. So she would see clearly – without conscience. It is simple to her. Like it is to Jack. Problem. Solution. No turning back. No doubts. No compromises. I thought I could persuade her to wait at least. There is a chance, with a switch to renewables in the next decade, that we can get where we need to be without . . . this. But I was kidding myself. She believes like Jack believes. They have always been partners in this. They won't stop. No more waiting. No more hesitation. This is it for them. The moment.'

'As soon as the panic room's opened . . .'

'It begins.' Filippo marches over to the screen behind me and bangs helplessly on it with the flat of his hand. 'And it cannot be stopped.'

✜

They walked back out into the hall. Don did not know what to do. As soon as the panic room was open, he would no longer be useful to French. But there were no rescues on hand. And he had run out of diversions and delays. 'Why did you kill Coleman?' he asked, in a last, futile attempt to postpone the reckoning.

'He was greedy,' French replied. 'And he asked too many questions. You're in danger of doing that yourself, Don.' He pointed his gun at him. 'I want the panic room open. And I want it open now.'

'OK. This way.'

Don led them into the lounge. He moved to where *Far West* was hanging. He gazed into the painting's blue and green blocks of colour and imagined, for a second, that he was gliding peacefully above the Cornish coast on some gentle thermal, as, according to Harkness, the artist had – and Harkness too, in his turn. But there was no flight path to carry Don away from the fix he was in.

He lifted the painting off its hook and propped it against the wall. There, in front of him, was the safe, about two feet square, grey steel, with a countersunk handle and dial. There were numbers inscribed round the dial, running from zero to a hundred.

French rounded on Zlenko. 'How come you didn't find this?'

Zlenko's answer was a shrug.

'Fuck me,' said French. He turned back to Don. 'What's in there?'

'A switch. Throw it and the panic-room door opens.'

'And Harkness told you the combination?'

'Yes.'

'So, open the safe, Don. Now.'

'No.'

'What?'

Don swallowed hard. He was about to attempt the most outrageous bluff of his life – or his death. 'Here's the deal. You two go upstairs and wait by the panic-room door. I open the safe and throw the switch. The door opens for you. I leave. We never meet again.'

'No, Don.' French raised his gun and aimed it straight at Don's head. *'Here's* the deal. Gennady goes upstairs. I watch you open the safe and throw the switch. Then, when he calls down to say the door's open, I join him up there. And you leave. And we never meet again.'

'No.'

'You open that safe or I'll blow your brains out.'

'Then you'll never get into the panic room. The police will find their way here before you can cut through the wall. After the carnage you've strewn around the neighbourhood, it really won't be long before they show up. I think you realize that.'

'Open it.'

'I will. On my terms.'

'You don't get to dictate terms, Don. Not with a gun to your head.'

'But I do. Take the deal or fire away. Your choice.'

✣

I punch in Don's number on my phone. The call goes straight to voicemail. He's not answering. Maybe – just maybe – because he's at Wortalleth West.

Filippo guesses what I'm thinking and grabs the landline phone that's standing on a side-table. He plonks it on the conference table in front of me, the cable stretched taut from the wall. 'Landline to landline will give you the best connection. Nine for an outside line. Then double zero double four for the UK and drop the zero from the local code. You understand?' His voice cracks with the tension of the moment. His face is tight. His eyes are staring at me intently.

I nod, pick up the receiver and press nine. A second passes. Then there's a dialling tone. I start stabbing in the numbers.

✣

The bluff had worked, as far as it went. Don intended to make a run for the front door as soon as he threw the switch. He was gambling French and Zlenko would be so glad to be inside the panic room at last that they would forget about him long enough for him to make his escape. It was quite some gamble. But it was the only card he had to play.

Three loud thumps on the bathroom floor above his head were the signal that French and Zlenko were in place. There was nothing for it now but to go ahead.

Don dialled one four times anti-clockwise, eight three times clockwise, seventy twice anti-clockwise. Then he eased the dial back in a clockwise direction. That would release the lock if the safe worked as he expected.

A click told him it did. He lowered the handle and pulled the door open.

There were a few documents lying inside the safe. But what he was looking for was also there: a red fuse-switch, housed in a plastic frame embedded in the rear wall of the safe. The switch was down, in the off position.

At that moment, the telephone started ringing. Leaning back slightly, Don could see it through the open doorway that led to the library-cum-study. It was there, on Harkness's desk. The main phone in the kitchen would be ringing as well. Don could not actually remember if there

414

was a second extension in the master bedroom. But, if there was, that too would be ringing.

He could not seem to think clearly in that moment. He wanted the phone to stop ringing. That one thought at least formed in his mind.

What he did next hardly involved a decision. He walked into the study, moving fast, intent on picking up the phone and cutting the call.

✤

I'm not sure what goes through my mind while I'm waiting for the call to connect and start ringing at the other end. There's no way to contain what Filippo has said. I'm floundering. I'm sweating – a cold, fearful sweat. Cascade is real. But it's also unreal. And I wonder, like really truly actually wonder, what are *my* chances? Vegetarian. Fresh food, mostly. Quite a lot of organic. No pills. No cosmetics. No nothing. Do I get to survive? And if I do . . . what will survival be like in a world reshaped by Jack Harkness?

✤

'Hello?'

Why Don raised the phone to his ear and spoke he could not have explained in any way that was rational. But, picking up the handset, he had sensed somehow that he wanted, oh how he wanted, to speak to the person on the other end of the line.

'Don.' It was Blake. It was her, by some crazy miracle. And he was so glad to hear her voice he could hardly speak.

✤

I'm so glad to hear his voice I can hardly speak. But I have to. Fast.

'Tell me quick. You're at Wortalleth West. Has the panic room been opened?'

'Not yet. But—'

'It mustn't be. You understand me, Don? Nothing you've ever done in your entire life matters as much as this. All our futures depend on that room staying shut.'

'You sound like—'

'Harkness rigged the panic room to trigger something if it's opened, too big – too awful – to describe.'

'That's not what he told French.'

'But it's what *I'm* telling *you*, Don. For all our sakes – the sakes of millions of people you've never met – do whatever you need to do to stop that door being opened.'

'That's—'

Then the line goes dead.

⁜

The line went dead, as abruptly as if it had been physically cut – as perhaps it had. Don dropped the handset back into the cradle and moved towards the door into the lounge, his reactions slowed by the unfathomable magnitude of what Blake had said. *'The sakes of millions of people you've never met.'* What did that mean? What could it mean?

Then he saw French ahead of him, framed in the doorway between the lounge and the hall. 'What the fuck d'you think you're doing?' French demanded. 'Why haven't—'

At that moment, he noticed the safe was open. Don realized the switch must be visible from where he was standing. Which explained why French suddenly lost interest in anything except crossing the room, reaching into the safe and flicking the switch to the on position.

Don had to stop him. He charged forward, preparing to rugby-tackle French.

French did not seem to see him coming. He bent forwards as Don approached, but not in self-defence. He raised a hand weakly to his temple.

Then Don collided with him. And they went down in a heap. But French did not move after hitting the floor. He lay where he was, slack-mouthed and blank-eyed, his arms and legs limp. It was clear he would never have made it to the safe, with or without Don's intervention. His fall at Tredarvas had just caught up with him.

As Don scrambled to his feet, time squeezed itself into a suspended moment of hesitation. He heard Blake's words, as if she was repeating them inside his head. *'All our futures depend on that room staying shut.'*

He moved quickly to the safe, closed the door, raised the handle and turned the dial until he heard the click of the lock engaging. He pulled once on the handle to be sure, then swung round and headed for the hall.

As he reached the doorway, a bulky figure loomed suddenly in front of him. Zlenko pulled back his arm and elbowed Don hard in the chest. And Don went down.

From the floor, Zlenko looked taller than he really was. He towered above Don. But, for the moment, he was not looking at Don. His glance moved to French and then to the safe.

Then Don heard in the distance the wow-wow-wow of a police siren. Zlenko heard it too. His face twisted in annoyance more than anger, as if the arrival of the police was a predictable setback, one he could readily accommodate in his generally phlegmatic view of the world he moved in.

He pointed his gun at Don and raised his other hand, as if ordering Don to remain still and silent. He was listening to the siren, Don realized, judging whether it was drawing closer and whether there was more than one. It sounded to Don like yes on both counts. Which, in that moment, sounded like bad news for him.

Zlenko lowered his hand, as if he had decided what to do. But he never got to do it.

Don saw a blurred movement behind Zlenko, then heard a dull, heavy thwack. Zlenko made no sound, but he fell like a demolished smoke-stack, crumpling vertically before sprawling out across the floor, finishing on his side, staring at Don through sightless eyes.

Glenys Probert was standing where Zlenko had been standing an instant before. She was dressed, as on every previous occasion Don had met her, in boots, denim shorts and a T-shirt, this one adorned with a large, tattered black disc and the faded words beneath it *TOTAL ECLIPSE OF THE SUN CORNWALL 11 AUGUST 1999*. In her right hand she was clutching a large steel exercise weight, one end of which was smeared with blood.

'Think I've done for him?' she asked, almost matter-of-factly.

Don propped himself up on one elbow and looked at Zlenko, then at Glenys. All he could say was, 'Maybe.'

'Are you all right?'

'I think so.' There was a sharp pain in Don's left thigh. He reached down, wondering what kind of injury it was, only to discover the screwdriver he had taken from French's car was sticking into his leg. He pulled it out of his pocket. 'Where . . . where did you come from, Glenys?'

'The basement. I hid down there when you lot pulled in. Didn't like the look of this pair. I'd just that minute come off the phone to the police after finding Coleman's body. There was nowhere else I could rightly go. I took this' – she nodded to the weight in her

418

hand – 'from the gym. Just in case. Came up when I heard the sirens.' She looked round. 'Sounds like they'll be here any minute.'

'But why are *you* here, Glenys? Harkness told you to stay away.'

'It was the way he told me, I s'pose. Not sure, really. But I've always been one to do what I'm told not to do. Know what I mean?'

'I think I do.'

'Is Harkness around somewhere? I got the feeling he told me to stay away because he was planning a visit.'

'Harkness is dead, Glenys. So's Wynsum Fry. And a policeman. These two killed them. Along with Coleman, of course.'

'My Lord.' Glenys set the weight down carefully on the floor. 'You'll have a lot to tell the police.'

'I will. But there's something I have to do before they get here.'

Don hauled himself to his feet and moved to where he had propped *Far West* against the wall. He hoisted the painting back on to its hook, obscuring the safe, then looked round at Glenys.

'You never saw what's behind this, OK?'

Glenys nodded. 'OK.'

'Blake will explain everything when she gets back.'

'Should be interesting.'

'Yeah. It should.'

'One thing, though.'

'What?'

'The picture's hanging crooked. You're up at the right.'

'Bloody hell.'

Don nudged the left-hand side of the frame up slightly. 'That'll do it,' said Glenys.

The sirens were louder than ever now. Then one of

them cut out. Through the window, Don saw a police car brake sharply to a halt in front of the house.

'I'd best go and let them in,' said Glenys. 'You sure you're all right? You look kind of shaky.'

Don managed a weak smile. 'I'll live.' And in that moment he realized he was going to. He really was.

Nothing moves in the room behind the mirror, but there is movement nonetheless: numbers changing on the wall-mounted digital clocks, figures in motion on the flickering video screens.

Most of the screens show empty rooms and vacant passages. But others show bustle and urgency: police officers, some in uniform, some in plain clothes, hurrying to and fro in the hall, while others move carefully around the corpse in the utility room, stooping and peering and examining as best they can.

Soon there will be forensic specialists in masks and gloves and overalls, photographing, measuring, sampling. Everything will be logged, everything recorded. Nothing will be missed. Not even – eventually – what happens inside this room, the invisible centre of the house, the secret heart of what Jack Harkness built. Its secret will be uncovered, its heart exposed.

That is not yet, though. That is for the future. In the present, unobserved and unsuspected, the provisions Jack Harkness made bide their measured time and await their moment.

But those provisions will fail, defeated by chance and circumstance, enemies against which there is no defence.

Harkness's moment will never come.

✤

I'm standing in a cobbled square in Zug. One side of the square looks out over the Zugersee. I'm watching the sun go down behind the mountains on the other side of the lake. The centre of the town's like something off a music box: lots of winding lanes and timbered clock towers. You'd never know there are dozens of corporate HQs like Harkness Pharmaceuticals just up the road. The lake's calm and flat and quiet. And the mountains are calm and steep and quiet. I wonder if Switzerland's like this all over.

I spoke to Don a couple of hours ago. He sounded good. Better than when I spoke to him earlier. He was at Treliske Hospital then. Apparently, the police thought he was having a heart attack. But the doctors said it was just a stress reaction. I guess seeing three people murdered in front of you has to be ever so slightly stressful. French and Zlenko are at Treliske too. They're in comas, with serious head injuries. Don's all right. But they're not. Which is totally fine by me.

Compared with what Don – and Fran and Glenys – went through, all I had to deal with here was the truth, which they don't know yet, and a bucketload of uncertainty, which is over now. Harkness Pharmaceuticals' security team eventually figured out a way to override the lock on the steel screen in Harkness's office. By then Jane must have realized Cascade was never going to happen. She didn't actually say a single word when she came out. She just walked past us all, poker-faced.

I don't know where she went. Or what she plans to do. She can't start something as big as Cascade all over again on her own. Harkness is dead. But she has to live with the failure of what they spent twenty years planning. I just can't imagine how she's going to do that.

It won't involve seeing her father again, though. I'm sure of that. Which means I have to figure out what I'm going to tell him about her. Thanks, Jane, that'll be really easy.

I guess Harkness Pharmaceuticals will try to hush everything up. They may even get away with it. Filippo's made sure Harkness's plan can't work now, even if – which I suppose is when, really – the panic room is opened. With Harkness dead, the company he founded can do a deal with Quintagler Industries. And Astrid Townsend was just a consultant anyway. Here yesterday, gone today, forgotten tomorrow – they hope. Big fine in due course. Then move on. I guess that's how they see it panning out.

Now it's all over, I can't really believe it might actually have happened, even though I know it easily could have. And what if it had? Thinking about it just blows my mind.

I suppose Harkness was insane. You'd have to be, wouldn't you, to plan and prepare what he spent so many years planning and preparing? I look around at the people drifting across the square. None of them has any idea – not a single clue – that today, here and elsewhere and everywhere, it could have begun.

But it didn't. It's OK. We dodged the bullet. We survived. Life goes on.

A thought keeps bobbing up in my head, though. I can't seem to stop it. Twenty per cent of all species on Earth extinct by 2050. That's what Filippo said. Twenty fucking per cent. By 2050. And floods and storms and droughts and famines like we've never seen before. If we don't get our act together. Which, as I stand here and seriously ask myself the question, I don't see us doing. Who's really insane, then? Jack Harkness? Jane Glasson? Or the rest of us?

I stand here and breathe the clean Swiss air and look at the beauty of this corner of the world. But in this country of clocks and watches I can easily imagine I hear the tick-tock tick-tock of time running out. There's a countdown going on.

Harkness knew that and tried, in his own ruthless, logical, inhuman way, to do something about it. He failed. And I'm relieved he failed. At least, I think I am.

But the countdown's still going on. And the fear I can't quite get out of my head is that it'll end where countdowns always end – if they're not stopped.

ZERO